LOVING SARAJEVO

CL Mustafic

Gage has problems saying I love you. After five years, he still hasn't said it to his live in boyfriend, Lucas, and it should come as no surprise to him when Lucas calls it quits, but it couldn't have come at a more inconvenient time—the eve of Gage's first business trip to Sarajevo.

It's just Gage's luck that Nikola, who's been tasked with chaperoning him during his stay, is the walking epitome of sex on a stick. Gage quickly develops an attraction to Nikola even before he's certain it could ever be reciprocated. When the feeling turns out to be mutual, Gage is surprised by Nikola's domineering bedroom persona but finds he likes being manhandled by the sexy Bosnian.

After a misunderstanding, it's up to Nikola to convince Gage that, even though they've only known each other a short time, what they feel for each other is worth fighting for. With only his cell phone and a plan, Nikola goes about getting the man who has stolen his heart to give them a chance at happiness.

This is a work of fiction. All characters, places and events are from the author's imagination and should not be confused with fact. Any resemblance to persons, living or dead, events or places is purely coincidental.

Copyright 2017 by CL Mustafic

All rights reserved, including the right of reproduction in whole or in part in any form.

Published by
NineStar Press
PO Box 91792
Albuquerque, New Mexico, 87199
www.ninestarpress.com

Warning: This book contains sexually explicit content, which is only suitable for mature readers, and scenes with D/s and spanking.

Print ISBN # 978-1-947139-99-2
Cover by Natasha Snow
Edited by BJ Toth

No part of this publication may be reproduced in any material form, whether by printing, photocopying, scanning or otherwise without the written permission of the publisher, NineStar Press, LLC

Dedication

To my mom and dad because let's face it, without you I wouldn't be here to write this.

Acknowledgements:

I'd like to thank the people who helped me along the way.

To Tonna Saunders, for being there for me every step of the way with this story. You are my rock.

To Christina Quinn and Jamila Lindsey, for being there when I need someone to complain to about editing.

And finally, to BJ Toth, my editor, who put up with me through this whole thing again. You are a paragon of patience.

Chapter One

"I SWEAR TO god, if you get on that plane tomorrow, I'm going to pack my shit and go home," Lucas shouted.

Gage sat on the couch looking up at the slight blond man who was in the middle of having yet another tantrum brought on by Gage having to leave on a business trip. "I thought this was your home," Gage replied blithely.

It wasn't the first time Lucas threatened to leave, and it probably wouldn't be the last since they'd had this same argument each time Gage left on a business trip. Still, he knew he'd get on the plane, and when he got back in a month, Lucas would be there—apologetic and looking to make up. That's the way it had gone for the last two years—ever since Gage took over the emerging markets accounts at his dad's company.

"You know that I only came here to be with you. There's no other reason anyone would come to this Podunk town." Lucas gave Gage his best scowl. "But you're never here. This isn't what I signed up for."

"I told you I'd be gone quite a bit. I never lied to you. You were the one who decided to move here. I was fine with driving down to see you on the weekends."

Okay, so he knew Lucas wasn't exactly happy in a smaller city, but it was Lucas's decision—after a year and a half of only seeing each other on weekends—to move. Lucas had been happy in Minneapolis, when they both had their own places and could see each other whenever they'd wanted but had grown weary of the weekend-only visits that were primarily spent in bed. Gage had been just as happy with seeing Lucas only on the weekends when he'd moved back north to his hometown, and with all of Lucas's drama of late, he'd been thinking he'd be happy to go back to that arrangement. He'd thought his feelings for Lucas would deepen over time but, though he cared for Lucas, he'd never fallen in love with him—or at least he didn't think this was what love felt like.

"Sure you were fine with that, but I want more. I'm not just some booty call here for your pleasure when you need to get off," Lucas spat out. And there it was. It was like there was a script for their lives, and this scene was repeated often.

Lucas wanted more, and at the age of thirty-seven Gage probably should too, but he'd come to realize more wasn't always better, and even though he tried, it was impossible to convince Lucas what they had was good enough. He'd only let Lucas move in with him because he'd been lonely, although now he was thinking he should have gotten a dog.

Pushing himself up off the couch, he went to Lucas. This was the part where he always took Lucas in his arms and let him cry it out until he decided to stay. Then Gage would take him to the bedroom, fuck him through the mattress, and Lucas would fall into a contented sleep in Gage's arms. In the morning, Lucas would wake up just enough to tell Gage to have a safe trip and that he loved him when Gage kissed him before he left for the airport. Of course, Gage would reply with a "Me too" because he'd never said the actual words to anyone before, and he wasn't about to start with Lucas—Gage had never lied to Lucas.

"Don't even, Gage," Lucas said holding up his hand to ward Gage off. "I'm not going to let you sweet-talk me into bed this time." Oops, Lucas had gone off script. He looked up at Gage with his big blue eyes on the brink of tears. "I'm really going this time. You know I love you more than anything, but I can't do this. I'm sick of being alone so much, and there's nothing here for me. All of my friends and family are back home. You're all I have here, and you're never here." His voice cracked with emotion, and he ended his speech with a sniffle Gage knew always preceded the tears that were inevitably going to come.

"Babe, come on; we do this every time. You know how this is going to play out. Can't we just skip this?" Gage grabbed his hand, giving it a tug, and Lucas let himself be pulled to Gage's chest, even wrapping his arms around Gage's waist like he wanted to be there. Lucas's chest hitched, and Gage knew he was crying before the wetness seeped through his shirt. Gage stood there holding him for a couple of minutes, hoping Lucas would come to his senses like he normally did.

"I have to leave, Gage. Maybe you were right. Maybe we're just in different places in our lives—our timing is off. I just can't do this anymore. I'm going to be gone when you come home. I hope you understand. I don't want you to hate me because I still love you. Maybe someday you'll be ready, but I can't take the chance that you may never be," Lucas said into Gage's chest after he'd calmed enough to talk.

Gage couldn't help thinking how sad it was that Lucas was the one saying it to him instead of the other way around. He should be the one ready to settle down and start a family, not Lucas, who was only twenty-six—just a cute little twink. Someone like Lucas should be out clubbing and fucking everything that moved and not tied down to a guy like Gage.

It wasn't that Gage didn't want to be with just one guy for the rest of his life and maybe adopt a couple of dogs or kids or whatever. It was hard for him to explain it to Lucas because he didn't really understand it himself. He could tell Lucas that his shrink diagnosed him with "commitment issues" that stemmed from his not "fully accepting his homosexuality," but Gage was sure Lucas wouldn't buy it for a minute—hell, Gage didn't buy it for more than the time it took him to walk from the guy's office to his truck.

"You have to do what's best for you, Luke. I just wish you wouldn't have waited until the night before I leave to tell me." Gage was more than a little annoyed at the timing.

"If I would have told you sooner, you'd have had time to talk me out of leaving. I thought about just letting you leave, thinking I was happy, and moving while you were gone, but I couldn't do this over the phone. I've loved you too long to end it that way," Lucas said softly. He tilted his head up to look at Gage, who leaned down for a kiss, which Lucas accepted, letting Gage kiss him tenderly but pulling away before it could become anything more. "I can't do one last goodbye fuck with you, Gage, I know how it will end. I'm going to go stay at Jen's tonight. I'll move my stuff out before you get back."

"You don't have to go. You can stay here. We'll just sleep. Just let me hold you while we sleep one more time." It was finally sinking in—Lucas was serious this time and was going to leave. That fact hit Gage harder than he figured it would. He wasn't sure he wanted Lucas to stay, but he was almost certain he didn't want him to go either. *Yeah, I can't even figure things out in my own head, some great catch I am.*

"No, you know that is not what will happen. I need to go now while I still have some control over my emotions." Lucas put on his coat, grabbed his car keys off the hook by the front door, and then turned his tear-stained face to look at Gage. "I'm so sorry, Gage. Have a safe trip. I love you." Opening the door, Lucas walked out on Gage without giving him the chance to say "Me too."

GAGE AWOKE TO his alarm blaring and his head pounding as he rolled over to smack the shit out of it to make it stop. He should have known better than to drink himself to sleep the night before he had to travel for seventeen hours straight. He rolled out of bed with a groan, and by the time he made it to the bathroom, he'd almost convinced his stomach to quit lurching. He grabbed pain pills out of the medicine cabinet and washed them down with a handful of water from the tap, which caused another lurch of his gut. Gage looked up to meet his own bloodshot green eyes in the mirror and cursed his reflection for being such a dumbass.

Stepping into the shower, he hoped the water might wash away the memory of the previous night as well as the smell of alcohol oozing from his pores—it didn't help. He kept seeing the hurt and sadness on Lucas's face when he'd turned to leave. To his chagrin, he also remembered how upset he'd made Lucas when he'd drunk dialed him at half past midnight to beg him to come back and spend the rest of the night in their bed, only to have Jen take the phone and tell him to go fuck himself.

Gage washed quickly, got out, shaved, and brushed his furry-feeling teeth. He ran his fingers through his hair, thankful he'd just gotten it trimmed so it wouldn't need blow-drying to keep it from freezing in the outside air. He dressed in a comfortable pair of jeans and a long sleeved T-shirt for the flight. He was no stranger to transatlantic crossings and wasn't going to endure one in a suit. He'd have a little over an hour layover in Munich to change into more appropriate attire before his final flight to Sarajevo.

He grabbed his bags and dragged them down the stairs from the loft bedroom into the living room. The condo had an open floor plan, so the main floor living area was one big room with just an island counter to divide the kitchen from the sitting room and a half bath and bedroom off the hall from the entryway.

He frowned as he caught sight of the Christmas tree in the corner, looking like a cast-off from one of those cheesy lifetime holiday movies Lucas insisted on watching every night for the week leading up to Christmas. He hoped Lucas would take the artificial monstrosity down before he left—it was, after all, his tradition that had it still standing there two days past Christmas. Knowing Lucas, he'd probably leave it up to get back at Gage for leaving just before New Year's, the idea sending a small pang of sadness through him. It would be the first one they'd spent apart in five years. Gage sighed. He didn't have time to deal with it at that moment. He needed to get to the office and then the airport, and as it was, he was running late and would have to hit a drive-through for his morning coffee.

Checking to make sure he had everything he needed for his trip, he loaded it all into his truck in the attached garage, pushing the button to open the garage door on his way so he could let the truck warm up while he got into his coat, gloves, and scarf. The mercury was hovering around zero, so not too bad, but still a bit on the nippy side. He locked the door leading to the garage, got into his truck and headed to the coffee shop to grab a cup so he could face his coworkers—many of which were also family.

Coffee in one hand and briefcase in the other, Gage walked into the office of H&S Equipment. His father and uncle owned the company, and Gage had come back to work for them just over three years earlier. He'd gotten his MBA at the U of M down in the cities and took a job there after graduating. He'd intentionally stayed away from the family business for years, but when his uncle called and offered a job setting up offices in eastern Europe at twice what he'd been making, he couldn't find a good enough reason to say no.

Though his family had been grudgingly accepting of the fact that he was gay, it had taken awhile for them to adjust. They understood why he hadn't come straight home to work for the company when he got his degree. He'd needed time and a place where he could be anonymous to sort himself out. While his hometown had grown to be pretty good-sized for this part of the country, when you came from a family with money like Gage's, people tended to know who you were, and he hadn't wanted that notoriety at a time in his life when he was still figuring things out.

Gage was barely seated at his desk when Connor stepped into his office. Connor was one of those who was both family—Gage's cousin—and coworker. He was dressed as always in an expensive suit with an obnoxious printed tie. He wasn't a bad-looking man, but the way he slicked his hair back made him look like a slimeball, and his attitude did nothing to contradict that.

"Hey, cuz, you look like shit," he said as he plopped in one of the chairs opposite Gage's desk. "Worried about meeting the Bosnian mafia tomorrow?"

"They're not the mafia," Gage countered. "You know how it is in these countries. You can't get anything done unless you know someone and are prepared to grease a few palms. I'm not worried. Everything went fine in Serbia last year, and my guy there helped me get an in with a guy in Sarajevo. He vouches for him, so I'm not worried."

"Yeah, sure, you'll probably end up held for ransom one of these days, and then I can tell ya I told ya so." Connor smirked.

Gage knew Connor was just jealous. He'd wanted Gage's job, but he still wanted to wipe the smirk off the asshole's face by telling him the old men knew Connor couldn't handle it because he was a mouthy, arrogant prick. He held his tongue for the sake of family harmony, besides he didn't feel like getting into a pissing match with Connor after the night he'd had. His pulse was still thudding a little too hard in his temples, the ibuprofen barely doing its job.

"Where's JJ? He's supposed to take me to the airport. You seen him this morning?" Gage asked, changing the topic. JJ, his uncle's other son, was someone he actually liked. JJ was only a year younger than Gage so they'd grown up together, spending many summers on their grandpa's farm, throwing hay bales and picking rocks.

"He's around here somewhere. What time's your flight leave?"

"Not till two twenty, but I thought we'd get some lunch before I have to leave the land of American fast food behind." Gage had no intention of eating fast food for his last meal before heading out. He was getting Chinese—couldn't get it easily over there, and it was something he missed when he was gone.

"My ears were ringing," JJ said as he walked through the door to Gage's office.

Eyeing Gage suspiciously, JJ could probably see there was something going on, and it had nothing to do with Gage's dislike of Connor. Gage would eventually have to tell everyone Lucas left him so decided he may as well start by telling JJ over lunch about his breakup. Maybe even see if JJ would be so kind as to spread the news around but not make it seem like a huge deal.

"Yeah right, you just knew that I'd want to go grab lunch before I head out, and you'd get to take a long break since you're driving me," Gage said. It wasn't like it was a big secret why JJ volunteered to take him to the airport every time.

"Damn straight—a free lunch and getting outta here for a few hours are worth the trip to the airport. What time are we heading out?"

"Probably around eleven. I have to meet with the old men quick."

"Cool, I'll be waiting."

JJ left, followed by Connor, who gave Gage a halfhearted wave as he walked out the door.

Gage's meeting with his dad and uncle went as planned. They knew Gage knew what he was doing, and they let him do it, but they liked to make it seem like they had a say in how things got done over there. He met JJ in the parking lot at a little after eleven. They drove Gage's truck so JJ could take it home and park it in the garage. If it was left in long-term parking at the airport, Gage would come home to a pickup that wouldn't start from sitting in the frigid temperatures for a month—a lesson learned the hard way.

They went to Gage's favorite place on Forty-Fifth Street where there was a buffet and no health code violations. Gage paid for the meal, and they piled their plates high before looking for somewhere to sit off to the side. He took a few bites of his food, stalling because he knew JJ was waiting for him to spill since he was sitting there, not eating, as he waited.

"Lucas left me," Gage blurted, figuring it was best just to get it out. Staring down at his plate, he took another bite, filling his mouth so he wouldn't have to say anything more.

"What did you do? You cheat on him?"

"What do you mean, what did *I* do? And why would you automatically go to me cheating on him?"

JJ sat there for a minute before he took a bite of food and chewed it slowly. "Well he wouldn't have left you if you hadn't done something. Everyone could see how much he loved you. Well, except maybe you, and it's sort of common knowledge you didn't feel the same about him." Gage detected a little bit of color rising on JJ's cheeks. It probably wasn't every day JJ sat around talking about one guy loving another guy.

Gage sighed and took another bite to give himself a moment to get his thoughts together on how he wanted to present his and Lucas's breakup to his family. "He was mad that I was gone so much. He wanted to start a family—you know—start the process to either adopt or find a surrogate. I told him I wasn't ready." Gage mumbled the last part in hopes JJ wouldn't pick that area of his life to grasp on to.

"Fuck, Gage, you're going be thirty-eight in what, less than a month, and you're still not ready? You should have just told him you were never going to be because you didn't love him." JJ jabbed his fork at Gage to put emphasis on his statement. "I'd have left your sorry ass too." JJ shook his head at the sad state of Gage's life. How could JJ possibly understand? He'd fallen in love and gotten married in college and had two kids with another on the way.

"He also said it was the traveling, and you know I can't stop if I want to keep my job. It will be less once everything is set up, but I'll still have to go a few times a year to check up on everything." Gage made the excuse to hide that there had been a way to make Lucas stay if he'd wanted him to. "But maybe it's better this way. I never wanted to hurt him and I probably should have told him straight out that I wasn't in love with him instead of letting him think I might someday."

"You think? But you know damn well if you'd have agreed to the kid thing he wouldn't have minded the traveling so much, and he's lived with you this long without you telling him you loved him, so he'd probably have been willing to overlook that you didn't because he loved you. He wanted a commitment, and you didn't give him one," JJ said like he knew every goddamn thing about Gage and Lucas's relationship.

"Jesus Christ, JJ, I'm going to stop going to my shrink and just start talking to you. It would save me a bundle." Gage wanted to argue with JJ but knew his cousin was right, so he joked instead.

"I'd charge you double if I had to listen to all the gory details of your life." JJ snorted and resumed eating.

The rest of the meal was eaten in an easy silence of two men who were comfortable in each other's company. Gage didn't want to talk about Lucas anymore, but he couldn't stop thinking about him. Why couldn't he have just given Lucas the one thing that would have made him happy—made him want to stay instead of pushing him away? Was loving someone really that important to a relationship if everything else worked well?

After lunch, JJ parked in front of the airport, and Gage grabbed his bags from the back. "You can tell everyone about me and Lucas. Maybe, just make it seem like it was mutual. I don't need people feeling sorry for me or thinking I'm an asshole."

"Sorry to tell you this, cuz, but everyone already thinks you're an asshole." JJ's lopsided grin took some of the sting out of his words. "But don't worry. I'll make sure that everyone knows you're not to blame for running off the only thing that made you likable for the last couple of years. Have a good flight and let us know when you land." He got back in the truck and took off before Gage could tell him to fuck off.

Gage made it through security quickly—one of the reasons he loved flying out of Fargo—and sat for over an hour waiting to board the plane to Chicago.

The flight was quick and uneventful. He boarded his flight to Munich at seven p.m. and settled into his business-class seat with a sigh. After a couple of travel-sized vodkas, he fell into a pretty good doze, and when he woke up, the plane was descending into Munich. Gage grabbed his carry-on and headed to the nearest bathroom to change into his suit. Boarding the plane to Sarajevo, he almost looked like he'd gotten a full night's sleep but was feeling like shit all the same.

Gage's stomach felt as if it was in his throat when the plane descended into the Sarajevo airport. The woman sitting next to him smiled and asked, "Your first landing in Sarajevo?" Gage nodded. "Well if you think the landing's bad, you're not going to like the takeoff when you leave. The climb will make your ears pop so hard that you'll want to scream."

"Is it really that bad?" Gage asked, for lack of anything better to say.

She was leaning over his lap so she could see out the window. "You see that mountain over there?" Gage nodded again. "They have to pull up sharp to avoid hitting it."

Gage was already dreading it. Maybe he'd just never leave. *I have nothing to go back for anyway,* he thought morosely as the plane landed smoothly.

The passengers disembarked on the tarmac and walked to the airport so Gage got his first taste of Sarajevo weather. He realized his heavy winter coat was going to be way too warm. Though there was some snow on the ground, he'd have bet his left nut the temperature was hovering right around freezing. He looked around at the snowcapped mountains looming in the distance, making him think CL at least the websites where he'd read about the decent skiing probably weren't totally false. The mountains were a pretty sight and different from the flat plains back home.

Gage followed the line of weary passengers into the airport and through passport control where he stated his reason for being there as business and got a "Have a nice stay" in return. He pulled his checked bags off the carousel and made his way to customs, which he cleared easily with nothing to declare. The airport was about the same size as the one back home, which surprised him. He'd figured an international airport in a city the size of Sarajevo would be bigger and busier.

Walking out the sliding doors to the main airport, he saw the crowd gathered to greet incoming passengers and watched tearful reunions between family members and handshakes between what were obviously other business people like him. It was as Gage looked around for the sign with his name on it that his gaze landed on *him*.

He was standing next to one of the bar tables in the little coffee shop area just to the right of the crowd and was quite possibly the most attractive man Gage ever laid eyes on. He was maybe a couple of inches shorter than Gage and not as broad but well built. His rich, chocolate-brown hair curled wildly around his head, and his eyes, surrounded by the lushest eyelashes Gage had ever seen, were so dark he could barely make out the pupils. His lips were full, and his carefully cultivated stubble shaded his jaw and added to his dark good looks.

When his eyes met Gage's, Gage dropped his gaze, but in doing so, he only managed to get a good look at the man's body. His muscular legs were encased in a pair of tight, faded jeans cinched with a belt at his narrow waist. He was wearing a skintight shirt under an open leather jacket. If Gage hadn't been in Europe, he'd have pegged him as a friend of Dorothy right off the bat, but men's fashion was quite a bit different from that in America, so there was no telling which way he swung. When Gage's eyes made their way back to his face, the man was smirking.

Gage scowled and quickly looked away to find his sign.

Chapter Two

NIKOLA AND AMEL waited at the airport for almost a half an hour before the announcement for the flight from Munich came over the PA, right on time. "We should go stand in front so he sees us when he comes out. Don't you think Nikola?" Amel asked.

"You take the sign and go stand there. I'm going to finish my coffee. Remember to speak English to him if he finds you before I get there," Nikola reminded. With a nod, Amel went to stand with all the others waiting for people to come out the doors from customs.

Nikola hated this particular aspect of his job. Shepherding around overweight old men for his uncle, Nedim—since he'd made Nikola his unofficial ambassador to the English-speaking business people who came to Bosnia looking to make a deal. His uncle took advantage of Nikola's perfect English, the product of having lived and gone to school in America for fourteen years. Nikola shouldn't complain. There wasn't much in the way of jobs anywhere in the country, and he was lucky to have one. His uncle offered him something that was at least legal, and Nikola hadn't been too proud to take what he could get. At least Nedim always had something for him to do.

His Uncle Nedim was a bit shady as most of the businessmen in Bosnia tended to be since the end of the war. Nedim walked the very fine line between what was legal and what wasn't, sometimes toeing it but never stepping completely over it. He was a decent enough guy in Nikola's opinion, and he hoped to get in on the ground floor of this new equipment business represented by the guy Nikola and Amel were waiting for. If a deal was made, it meant construction jobs to build them a building and a few more jobs for mechanics and office staff.

All in all not a huge amount of jobs, but Bosnia would take what it could get. Every foreign company that saw the country as stable enough to invest in brought even more in on their heels, which was good for the economy, and Nikola was doing his part for his homeland. Nikola the patriot—he snorted at the notion.

Nikola was still standing at the table, finishing his coffee, when his eyes met a pair of intense green ones. The man they belonged to was a giant with sandy-blond hair and a ruggedly handsome face. When the man realized he'd been looking into Nikola's eyes a bit too long, he dropped his gaze. Nikola could feel those eyes traveling over his body from his feet up and found it interesting that the look on the other man's face seemed to be one of admiration—the way a guy looks at a steak after he's fasted for a week.

Nikola couldn't help but smile a bit at the guy, but when his eyes found Nikola's face again, the man turned quickly away in search of something. That something turned out to be Amel, holding the sign that said Mr. Gage Hoffman. *Oh, holy hell, he's my charge for the next month.*

Nikola waited until the man walked up to Amel, shook his hand, and exchanged greetings. After swallowing the last dregs of his coffee, he sauntered over to them. When the blond man turned to look at who had come up behind him, his face flushed, and wasn't that just about the hottest thing Nikola had ever seen?

Nikola stuck out his hand to his new charge. "Hi there, I'm Nikola. You must be Mr. Hoffman. Welcome to Sarajevo."

Mr. Hoffman's flush deepened as he shook Nikola's hand. "You can call me Gage. It's nice to meet you, Nikola."

Gage's handshake was firm but not too hard. Nikola was already sizing Gage up for his uncle, and his first opinion was a good one. He realized—just from the man's handshake—Gage was a man who knew his strength and held it back instead of showing it off. Nikola liked him immediately.

Nikola's hand brushed Gage's as he took the strap of his carry-on from him, sending a strange, almost electric, sensation through Nikola's arm. Nikola watched the other man's face, but it didn't seem as though he had the same reaction to Nikola's touch, so he chalked it up to the dry air and static electricity even though he knew it wasn't the same thing. Amel took his suitcases, leaving him to carry only his laptop messenger bag, and Gage didn't put up any resistance to the assistance. Nikola knew Gage had set up branches for his company in Serbia, Croatia, and Hungary, so he was probably already used to the culture and had given up trying to refuse the offered help.

"You go get the car and pull it up front. We'll wait here inside, out of the cold," Nikola instructed Amel, who started out the door, and Gage followed. "We can wait in here where it's warm. He'll bring the car." Without thinking, Nikola reached out and grabbed Gage's arm to stop him, once again getting that unexplained tickle running up his arm.

Gage looked down at the point of contact, and Nikola released his grip when Gage's eyes flicked back up to his face. "We can just go to the car. I'm no stranger to the cold," Gage said with a reassuring smile.

Nikola looked him over, noticing that he was in just a suit coat with his winter jacket tucked under his arm. "Maybe you should put your coat on. It's below freezing out there."

This got a chuckle from Gage, and he seemed to relax, the strain of embarrassment from his earlier perusal of Nikola's body seemingly forgotten. "Where I come from, this is shirtsleeve weather. I'll be fine. Let's go."

Shrugging, Nikola led him out to the black BMW SUV Nedim provided him during jobs. Nikola popped the back open to stow Gage's bags and motioned for him to sit in the front—he was just too damn big to sit anywhere else—as Amel climbed into the back seat.

"I'll drop you at the hotel so you can freshen up. I'm sure you know that you should try not to sleep too much or you'll never adjust to the time difference. I'll pick you up at six to take you out for dinner." Nikola took in Gage's profile out of the side of his eye as he spoke.

"You don't have to do that. I can just order room service. I'm sure I won't be very good company tonight." Gage stifled a yawn that Nikola was sure was only for his benefit.

"It's no problem. It's my job, and if I shirk my duties, my uncle will string me up and let Amel use me as a punching bag," Nikola joked. Amel chuckled from the backseat, probably amused at the idea of punching Nikola and watching him swing. But Nikola was distracted by his own thoughts—he wasn't sure why he was unwilling to let Gage spend his first night alone in his hotel room. Nikola would usually be relieved he didn't have to babysit a jet-lagged stranger, and it wouldn't have been the first time he'd left one of his charges alone on their first night in the country.

Gage looked unsure and then lifted his arm to glance at his watch. He let out a slow sigh. "Okay, I guess it is probably a bad idea to stay in. The temptation to crawl into bed would probably get the better of me. I'll just take a thirty-minute power nap and then try to stay up until at least ten."

Nikola pulled into a parking lot in front of a big glass hotel off the main road that led into the city proper. He escorted Gage to the reception desk and gave the receptionist the reservation number before stepping away to wait while the desk clerk told Gage of the hotel's amenities. She was flirting with him shamelessly, and Nikola almost felt sorry for her when Gage's lack of interest seemed so apparent. She smiled as he thanked her. She handed over his key card and watched him with a dreamy look on her face as he walked back to where Nikola was waiting. Gage had a small grin on his face, obviously knowing what effect he had on people and enjoying it.

Nikola could feel the blood rushing below his belt as the handsome man approached him. Shifting his hip to stop what was happening from being too evident to the man causing the reaction, Nikola told his body to get a grip; the man was probably married with kids even if he wasn't wearing a ring. A lot of married guys didn't wear a ring but that didn't make them any less married. In Nikola's experience, most men who traveled didn't wear their wedding rings on their business trips for one reason, and unfortunately, he knew Nedim would be willing to provide any service to get the deal done. A small lick of jealousy toward whatever lucky woman got to service his new charge surprised Nikola. He tried to bring his attention back to the business at hand, deciding he'd deal with the situation if and when it arose.

"I can manage on my own. You don't need to hang around," Gage said, and with another of his easy smiles, he reached for his suitcases.

Nikola didn't surrender them, and Gage didn't press it. Instead, he shrugged and headed to the elevator. The car was there waiting for them, so they stepped into the little box, keeping as much distance between them as they could manage in such a small space. Gage pressed the button for his floor after looking at the key card in his hand. He was silent on the ride up, but Nikola caught Gage stealing looks at him in the mirrored door.

Stepping out into the hallway, they walked halfway down the hall to Gage's room. He opened the door, and Nikola could tell he was impressed by the look on his face. "Nedim knows the guy who owns this hotel. He gave us a good deal to upgrade you to this suite from the original room you booked. He figured you'd be more comfortable here since you're staying so long," Nikola explained.

The room included a fully furnished sitting room with a couch, two chairs, a coffee table, and a large flat-screen TV. There was a little nook with an office desk and a chair. "There's a bedroom and bathroom through there." Nikola pointed out even though it was obvious there would be.

"Wow, this is nice. I didn't expect it to be this big. All the other rooms I've stayed in have been closets compared to this." Gage moved around the room as he took it in, setting his laptop bag down on the desk when he passed it.

Gage seemed to be pleased and that sent a strange little shiver through Nikola, the reason for which he didn't want to try to analyze. He stepped past Gage to put his suitcase in the bedroom, and when he turned around to go back out, he ran straight into Gage. Nikola hadn't even heard him come up behind him. Nikola stumbled back, and when Gage's huge hands grabbed his waist to steady him, Nikola swore the room sizzled with electricity.

"Whoa there, didn't mean to startle you." Gage quirked the corner of his lips making Nikola wonder if he was lying.

"You...um...move pretty quick for a big guy..." The blush crept up Nikola's neck to his cheeks.

Gage stood there with his massive paws gripping Nikola's waist. He leaned toward Nikola, and for a brief second, Nikola actually thought Gage was going to kiss him. "You have no idea how quickly I can move when I want to." Nikola swore Gage took a deep breath, like he wanted to get a good whiff of Nikola's scent before dropping his hands and stepping back to put some space between them. Nikola shook his head to try to clear the strange musings from his mind. "You should go. I need a shower and a quick nap. I'll see you at six if you still want to get some dinner," Gage said.

Gage turned, took off his suit jacket, and then started pulling on his tie. Nikola wanted to stay to see what Gage would reveal as he peeled off his clothes, but instead, he tore his eyes away. "Yeah I'll be here at six. We'll just go upstairs and grab a bite. The restaurant is great, and it revolves, so you get a good three hundred and sixty degree view of the city. It's rather pretty at night." *Oh god*, Nikola bit his lip, could he sound any stupider? He turned and headed for the door before he could say anything else.

"Hey, Nikola," Gage called. Nikola turned around just in time to see him strip off his undershirt in the doorway of the bedroom. Nikola couldn't respond because the blood left his head to migrate south—probably for the foreseeable future around the guy. "Thanks for everything."

Nikola nodded, not daring to use his voice, and let himself out into the hallway to try to get it together before seeing Amel in the car. The last thing he needed was word getting back to Nedim that he was acting strange around the new potential business partner.

Nikola chided himself all the way down to the car. He needed to be professional, and perving on a guy he didn't even know was surely not the way he should go about doing it. It didn't matter that Gage was the first man in years who'd gotten to him so quickly and had him reacting like a horny teenager. And what was with those strange feelings he got whenever he touched Gage? Nothing good could come out of Nikola's instant attraction. Even if Gage was interested in a little something more than business, a short fling with a hot guy wouldn't put food in his mouth. His mind was totally on board with his plan—it was his body he needed to convince that Gage Hoffman was off-limits for anything other than a polite business relationship.

Chapter Three

GAGE WATCHED NIKOLA leave his room and then stripped out of the rest of his clothes on the way to the bathroom where he climbed into the shower as quickly as he could. His hard-on was throbbing and demanding attention right that instant. Nikola inspired the kind of lust Gage hadn't known since college. He couldn't figure out why he was so drawn to the man. Nikola was nothing like any of the men Gage was usually attracted to. In fact, he was exactly the opposite. He was almost the same height as Gage, and he'd always preferred men who were on the slighter side, but there was just something about Nikola that drew him in from the moment Gage laid eyes on him.

Gage stood under the spray, soaping his cock, before starting to stroke slow and easy, closing his eyes and replaying his perusal of Nikola when he first saw him. He wondered what it would feel like to have Nikola rub his stubbled chin over his nuts and nearly lost it at the image his mind conjured of those full lips wrapped around his cock—Nikola's pretty chocolate-brown eyes meeting Gage's as he looked up, silently begging him to use his mouth. Gage stroked faster as he imagined Nikola's strong legs wrapped around his waist while he fucked that amazing ass. His fantasy Nikola pleaded for Gage to give him more—his accent getting thicker as he grew more aroused, but what pushed Gage over the edge was remembering the feel of Nikola's firm waist under his hands and his rich, masculine scent.

Gage came with a whimper—one not of pleasure—as Nikola's face was replaced by the sadness in Lucas's eyes when he'd left. Gage sank to the floor and shook—not from the release—but from the bottled-up emotions of the last two days. When he finally got a hold of himself, he climbed out of the shower and dried off.

Gage slipped on a pair of boxers and called home to leave a voicemail for JJ, letting him know he'd made it and was at the hotel. Another pang of sadness hit him as he realized he wouldn't have to call Lucas to let him know the plane hadn't crashed. It was always Lucas's biggest fear when Gage traveled. He wondered if Lucas was at home packing his things. Then, remembering the time difference, he wondered if Lucas slept in their bed and if he might still be there. Gage wanted to call home. He had a feeling if he could catch Lucas just waking up in their bed, he could convince him to stay without having to commit to having a kid. Realizing it was for the best to let Lucas go, instead of calling, he lay down on the big bed and let sleep take him.

Gage woke up to darkness and someone knocking on his door. He cursed himself for not setting an alarm as it was obvious he'd slept a lot longer than just thirty minutes. Without thinking about it, he got out of bed and walked through the sitting room to open the door. Nikola stood there expectantly, holding a plastic grocery bag, his eyes widening as he took in Gage's sleep-disheveled appearance.

"Oh hey, sorry, I forgot to set my alarm, and I was out cold. Come on in; just give me a couple of minutes to get dressed." He turned to go back to the bedroom, leaving the door open so Nikola could come in. Gage didn't close the bedroom door, so he heard when Nikola set the bag on the coffee table and sat on the couch. "Is the restaurant casual, or do I need a tie?" Gage called out to ask.

"No tie. Wear whatever's comfortable."

Gage dug through his bag to pull out the only other pair of jeans he'd packed and a long-sleeved V-neck sweater that Lucas always said clung in all the right places and was more on the dressy side than a long-sleeved T-shirt. He went into the bathroom to check his hair and tried to tame a couple of wild strands, which stuck up in odd angles from going to bed with it wet. He remembered Nikola's wide-eyed look when Gage opened the door. He could imagine the picture he'd made when he'd answered with bedhead and in boxer shorts. He snorted to himself and thanked god he didn't embarrass easily.

Nikola stood a little too quickly when Gage walked back into the sitting area, making a few useless gestures with his hands before finally shoving them in his pockets. The idea tickled Gage's brain that for some reason he made Nikola nervous. Gage wondered if the other man picked up on his attraction to him. If so, he'd have to be more careful. His experience in other places he'd traveled to in Eastern Europe had shown him the tolerance for homosexual individuals seen in Western Europe did not extend east. He didn't need to alienate the one man who could be crucial to him in his business dealings.

"Ready to go?" Nikola asked. Gage followed him out of the hotel room and up to the restaurant on the top floor. They were seated at a table right by the window so they could watch the city as the view changed slowly with the rotation of the restaurant. Nikola was right. Sarajevo was pretty at night.

"So, you speak English like a native. Did you spend some time in the states?" Gage asked after they'd gotten comfortable. He wanted to get to know Nikola better and a little background was always a good thing, not just for personal reasons either; it helped with the business part too.

Before Nikola could answer, the waiter showed up and asked if they'd like something to drink. Gage hesitated. He wanted a beer but his research turned up the fact that Bosnia was a country with a diverse mix of religions, with the city of Sarajevo being predominately Muslim, so he wasn't sure if it would offend Nikola. He didn't want to get off on the wrong foot.

"I'll have a *Sarajevsko pivo*," Nikola told the waiter. Gage knew the word *pivo* meant beer, so when Nikola turned to him, he told him he'd have the same. Nikola chuckled. "So, you spent enough time in this part of the world to know the word for beer."

"Ha, I knew that after my second day in Belgrade. It was the first word I learned. *Jos pivo*." Gage smiled at Nikola's delighted laughter. "So are you going tell me how it is you speak English so well?" Gage asked, getting back to his earlier question.

Nikola's laughter died down but his posture remained relaxed. "I lived in America for fourteen years. I'm just as American as you are, got the papers to prove it and everything." He watched Gage closely as if interested in seeing his reaction.

"Really? How did you end up in the states?" Gage asked, but at the shadow that crossed Nikola's eyes, he wished he could take the words back.

"It's kind of a long story." The waiter dropped off their beer and asked if they'd like to order, interrupting what was probably going to be an uncomfortable conversation if Gage chose to pursue it. "You know what you want?" Nikola asked.

Gage realized he hadn't even looked at the menu. "What do you recommend?"

"Everything here is good. Do you like meat?" Nikola asked. Gage almost spewed beer out of his nose at the double meaning his brain attached to the question. Nikola raised an eyebrow at Gage's reaction but didn't comment on it. "I meant do you eat meat? You're not a vegetarian are you?" Unable to answer when the second question made him think of dropping to his knees to show Nikola just how much he liked to *eat* meat, Gage just nodded. He needed to get his mind out of the gutter and remember he was there to do business. "We'll have the mixed meat for two," Nikola ordered for them, giving Gage a sideways look that had him trying to come up with an explanation for his odd behavior. Nikola turned back to Gage with a raised eyebrow when the waiter left.

"Sorry, swallowed wrong." Gage watched as Nikola's eyes were drawn first to his lips and then to his neck, which made him swallow so he could watch Nikola's reaction to the movement of his throat. Gage wondered if Nikola was thinking what he was thinking—there was no wrong way to swallow, as long as you did was all that mattered. Nikola's tongue darted out to wet his lips before he grabbed his beer, and Gage watched his neck while he emptied half his glass in one long pull. Gage shifted in his seat to take the pressure off his swelling dick.

"My mom and I went to America as refugees at the end of 1995 when the war was over," Nikola said after he set his glass back on the table. "I finished high school and college there, and I got my citizenship as soon as I could apply for it."

"Oh, it must have been quite a challenge to be in a strange country so far from everything you knew." It was all Gage could think to say as his swelling member softened again. He noticed Nikola's hand clenched in a fist on the table, and he wasn't sure he wanted to hear why Nikola ended up a refugee.

"It was. My mom didn't do too well with the change. She went a bit crazy during the war and never adjusted to life in America. She did the best she could, but the minute I graduated from high school and was accepted to college, she came back here. I stayed with a cousin while I went to school."

"Is that why you came back? Because your mom is here?"

The look on Nikola's face softened, the light came back to his eyes, and a small smile pulled at his plump lips—the change breathtaking. Gage wanted to know what made him look like that until Nikola said, "I came back because of Hana."

Gage's heart skipped a little in his chest—ah a girl—he should have known a man who looked like Nikola wouldn't be single. Gage smiled the best he could after having any hope of Nikola being available to him vanished. "She must be something really special."

The waiter brought the food before Nikola could tell Gage about— what Gage assumed was—the love of his life. The waiter put a large platter in the center of the table. It was basically a plate full of different kinds of grilled meat, a meal Gage had eaten in every country in the region he'd been in so far. Bosnia's version was pretty much the same with the exception of there not being any pork on the plate. There was also a big basket of bread and a salad that was cabbage, which sort of reminded Gage of cold sauerkraut. The waiter also brought them fresh beers and Gage wondered if Nikola told the waiter to just keep them coming as neither of them ordered another. Gage picked a couple of pieces of meat and put them on his plate along with some of the cabbage.

"You'll probably meet Hana at some point during your stay. I've been appointed your official tour guide for the duration, so it's almost inevitable." Nikola continued their conversation while filling his own plate.

"I'd like that. So, what time am I meeting Nedim tomorrow?" Gage decided to get back to business. It was better to know Nikola was not an option if Gage wanted to scratch an itch as he was now free to do as a single man. Nikola wouldn't be the distraction Gage started to fear he might turn into. Really though, Gage didn't think he should even be able to think of another man in that way after having just broken up with Lucas. It probably said something about what kind of man he was, but he didn't want to analyze his character flaws while sitting across from Nikola.

Nikola looked at Gage a little sheepishly. "Actually, you don't have a scheduled meeting with him until after the first, but we will be attending his New Year's party and you'll meet him there."

The realization dawned on Gage that he could have spent another week with Lucas. They could have spent one last New Year's together and maybe coming off the high of the holiday, Lucas wouldn't have been so eager to leave him. His whole life may have been different if he'd just stayed home for one more week. Shaking the thought out of his head, he reminded himself Lucas's leaving was a good thing. It hadn't been fair for him to use Lucas as a cure for his loneliness and as an excuse to not find someone he could love. Nikola must have seen a hint of anger on Gage's face and he took a breath to say something, but Gage cut him off with a raised hand before he could get it out. Gage finished chewing, giving himself time to think of how to say what he wanted to without coming off as a huge jerk.

"So what am I doing here now? I'm just supposed to hang around and wait?" His irritation was clear in his tone, and Gage knew he should have schooled his emotions more to appear more professional. He took a deep breath and tried to smooth things over. "I'm sorry, that was uncalled for."

"That's okay. I understand why you're upset, but you have to understand, my uncle is very cautious about who he does business with. I'll be honest with you; he uses me to kind of feel people out for him. He wanted you here a week early so that I could take you around, show you the sights, get to know you, so I can tell him what I think." Nikola paused for a breath, one corner of his lips quirking slightly. "Would that really be so bad—to have to spend a week with me? Having me at your beck and call twenty-four hours a day?"

His little lopsided grin made Gage think he could come up with about a million things that could be worse than seeing Nikola every day for a week. Then, of course, Gage remembered Nikola had a girl at home, who made him melt, which made Gage feel spiteful. "What does Hana think about you having to play tour guide and be on call twenty-four hours a day for some stranger?" Nikola got that look again at the mention of Hana's name. Gage could see that the man was really in love, and it made him feel bad about being petty and throwing out her name to bait him.

"She knows that I have to work. She understands that's part of the job. So, what do you think? Will you get over Nedim's little power play and let me show you a good time?"

Gage contemplated it for a few moments. He had nothing better to do, and he was already there, so he may as well make the best of it. He nodded, and Nikola's wide smile made Gage smile in return. Gage knew he was fucked. He could see himself getting attached to that smile and the man behind it way too easily.

"You better be ready though. I just got out of a long-term relationship. I'm going to need a lot of alcohol to get me through the next few days if I don't have work to keep me busy." Gage couldn't quite figure out why he needed to point out to Nicola that he was single. It wasn't like it made any difference to him. At least Gage knew why he'd mentioned the alcohol, because Nikola did need to know that he planned on drowning his sorrows until there was work to be done.

Nikola raised his glass of beer. "That I can handle. You shall never want for a drink as long as I'm near." Gage raised his glass to touch Nikola's, and they drank. They were quiet for a while as they ate, and the waiter never let the beer run low.

"So what are you going to show me?" Gage asked after he'd pretty much polished off the plate of meat and what seemed like two loaves of bread. He noticed Nikola watching him intently. "What?"

"You eat like a Bosnian."

"Huh?"

"Most businessmen who come here are all polite when they eat but not you. You just dig in and eat like you're at home and no one's watching you," Nikola explained and then laughed at what Gage imagined was a slightly horrified look on his face. He'd grown comfortable with Nikola and let his guard down, forgetting Nikola was appraising him for his uncle.

"Sorry..." Gage started but petered out. He didn't know exactly what he was apologizing for.

"No, that's not a bad thing. I like it. You're not trying to put on an act. That will go a long way with Nedim," Nikola assured Gage. "Do you want cakes and coffee?"

"Ah no, I think I could use something stronger than beer though." It was nice that Nikola tried to put Gage at ease with his words, but he still felt the need to down a few strong drinks all the same.

Nikola's grin stretched from ear to ear. "You've had rakia, no?" Gage nodded in confirmation. "Then we should go back to your room. I brought you a present." He motioned to the waiter. They held a short conversation in Bosnian, shook hands, and the waiter wished them a good night. Nikola didn't pay for the meal, and Gage wondered if he should wait for the bill, but Nikola got up and went straight to the elevator, so he followed.

Gage used the key card to let them into his room, where Nikola surprised him by toeing off his shoes before walking to the couch. Gage followed suit, sighing at the relief being out of his shoes granted him. He sat at one end of the couch while Nikola pulled out a bottle of the clear alcohol they made out of plums in homemade stills—kind of like legal moonshine. The two glasses he set on the table were about twice the size of shot glasses. Gage sighed and got ready to get his drink on.

Chapter Four

NIKOLA WAS TRYING his damnedest to figure Gage out. He studied the man as he sat on the couch in Gage's room and pulled out the bottle of homemade Rakia and a couple of glasses. Nikola was puzzled by the look Gage got when he'd told him he'd come back to Bosnia because of Hana. The look was something like sad disappointment, and it threw Nikola off a bit.

He'd thought he'd been picking up signals from Gage and had been pretty sure—even after only a very short time—that Gage was interested in him. The look he'd given Nikola at the airport was more than just a casual glance, and the strange encounter earlier in the very room they were sitting in piqued Nikola's interest in the other man. He decided to see if a little liquid lube would loosen Gage up enough to let something slip so he could figure out what he was thinking. He poured a shot of the alcohol into each glass, raising his to Gage before putting it to his lips and throwing the drink back.

Gage did the same. He grimaced at the burn of the strong alcohol and gave his body a little shake before glancing at his watch. "I probably shouldn't have too much. It's late and I'm jet-lagged."

Nikola poured another shot for each of them. "You've got nowhere to be early tomorrow. I'll let you sleep until ten. Then I'm going to roll your ass out of bed and take you downtown to see the sights." They both knocked back the second shot. Rakia was strong stuff. There was no way to tell the exact alcohol content to it since it was homemade, but it was stronger than anything sold in a store. Nikola could feel the effects after only two shots.

"Fair warning, I'm grumpy when I'm hungover and jet-lagged at the same time. Don't be surprised if I take a swing at you when you try to 'roll my ass outta bed,'" Gage said with a bit of challenge in his voice and a sexy smirk on his lips.

Nikola poured again. Gage looked at Nikola with a "Remember, you asked for it" written on his face before swallowing his shot, licking his lips, and putting the glass on the table for another. Nikola poured for him but didn't drink the one he'd poured for himself. Gage grabbed the glass and settled back into the couch, visibly relaxing as the alcohol started to take effect. The slow lazy way he was looking at Nikola, with half-lidded eyes, made Nikola think the big man only needed a couple more shots before he'd become as pliable as putty in Nikola's hands.

"Do you ski?" Nikola asked to get some sort of conversation going. Gage went from gulping his drinks to sipping the one in his hand.

"Yeah, I'm not great at it, but I enjoy it. Is there good skiing around here?"

"Sure there is. We had the Winter Olympics here in 1984. There's good snow up on the mountains this year. I thought maybe we could go on New Year's Day, spend the night in my uncle's cabin, and get a couple of days in on the slopes." Nikola poured Gage another glass when he held out the empty one. Nikola took a small drink out of his still-full glass.

"That would be great. I like the outdoors. I bet with all the mountains around here there's some excellent hunting and fishing too." Gage's words were coming a bit more slowly, like he had to think before speaking. Nikola realized his glass was empty again and refilled it.

"I don't hunt, but there are some good rivers where people fish for trout. We could check it out later." Nikola set the bottle on the table, picked up his glass, and settled back on the sofa next to Gage. "So were you married?"

Gage drained his glass again and looked at it like he couldn't figure out how it was empty. He shook his head, and when he looked up at Nikola, holding the glass out so he could refill it, there was a sadness in his eyes that pulled at Nikola's gut. Nikola filled his glass once again. "Nope, not married, just together for five years."

"That's a long time. Got any kids?"

Gage snorted and laughed an ugly laugh that held no humor. "No, that was the problem actually. Well, that and the fact that I wasn't in love." He downed his drink again. Leaning forward to put his glass on the table, he sat there with his elbows on his knees and his head in his hands.

Nikola quirked an eyebrow, thinking it was a strange way to say they'd grown apart. "She wanted kids or you?" Nikola was being as nosy as he pleased. He figured if Gage had a couple more he probably wouldn't remember much of the conversation anyway.

Gage slumped back and listed toward Nikola, showing his lack of balance in the process. He was so close Nikola could smell him. He smelled good—some sort of spicy aftershave mixed with a scent Nikola knew was purely Gage. Nikola wanted to shove his face into Gage's neck and breathe him in deeply because his body was telling him to just reach out to Gage. He wanted desperately to run his hands over the soft sweater clinging to Gage's body, showing off all the hard muscles of his torso, but Nikola's brain, thankfully, stopped his body from actually doing it.

"I'm not ready for kids, couldn't commit, couldn't give him what he wanted, couldn't love him." Gage's voice was soft, the words slightly slurred and running together. Closing his eyes, he let his head fall on Nikola's shoulder.

Nikola sat there letting Gage rest against him while he tried to figure out if he'd heard him right. Had Gage really said 'he' when talking about the person he'd just broken up with? It could have just been a slip, since he was obviously drunk, or possibly Nikola just misheard the slurred words, hearing what he wanted so badly to hear.

Nikola slowly lifted his hand and brought it up to Gage's prickly cheek. Gage didn't move at the touch, but he hummed softly, and when Nikola moved to stroke his hair, Gage let out a little sigh. Nikola followed his gut instincts based on the other man's reaction to his tentative caresses and lifted Gage's head from his shoulder. Gage didn't open his eyes, and his breath was coming in soft alcohol-scented pants. Nikola decided right then that one kiss with this beautiful man would be worth it even if he punched him for it.

Taking a chance and following his instincts, Nikola leaned in and brushed his lips against Gage's. His stomach fluttered, and he couldn't believe he was actually doing what he'd imagined doing since he'd first laid eyes on this handsome stranger in the airport. Nikola had known the man for a matter of hours, and there he was outing himself for a kiss. He was also taking advantage of Gage's drunken state, but he couldn't help himself. Something about Gage drew him in and made it hard for Nikola to think straight. He wasn't a believer in love at first sight or just knowing when that one person was your soul mate, but something about Gage threatened to turn him into one. The pull on him toward Gage was stronger than anything he'd ever felt with anyone else in his life—it was inexplicable. He took a moment to send up a silent prayer that he wasn't making the biggest mistake of his life.

Nikola's fear eased when Gage's lips came to life under his own. Gage was suddenly in control of the kiss, pushing with his tongue for Nikola to let him in. Nikola opened for him, and Gage gasped into his mouth before he dove deep with his tongue. He pressed Nikola back into the arm of the couch and ended with Gage lying half on top of a startled but pleased Nikola.

Nikola took the opening Gage presented to him, by sprawling his big body across Nikola's, to run his hands down Gage's sides to feel the hardness beneath his clothes. He felt so good against Nikola, and it had been so long since he'd kissed anyone that he couldn't stop the moan that passed his lips. "Oh god, Gage."

Gage stilled at the sound of Nikola's voice, before jerking back. "Oh, fuck," he groaned. His eyes were wide as he stood up, shook his head, and his mouth worked to try to form words that never passed his lips. He gave up and turned away from Nikola to go to the bedroom.

Nikola grabbed his wrist. "Wait, Gage…"

Gage shook him off. "I can't do this. It's not right." Gage didn't look back as he stumbled into the bedroom and slammed the door behind him.

Nikola got off the couch and walked over to the door to lean against it so he could listen to Gage moving around the room. Nikola raised his hand to knock but stopped before his knuckles hit the wood. He had no idea what he was going to say to Gage if he opened the door. He'd said kissing Nikola wasn't right, but what did he mean by that? Was it not right because they'd just met, because they were supposed to be doing business, not kissing, or was it not right because they were both men?

Moving away from the door, he cleaned up the coffee table and grabbed his coat. He was sober enough to drive home, but it was snowing so he drove slowly and carefully through the empty streets. He spent the whole drive home praying that his impulsive act hadn't totally fucked the whole deal up for his uncle, and maybe in the morning, Gage wouldn't remember what he'd done. Nikola would try to act normal when he picked up Gage the next day. If the other man wanted to discuss what happened—perhaps with his fists—well, then Nikola would deal with that mess when it happened.

NIKOLA LIVED IN a two-story house that was split into two separate apartments, one on each floor. As was customary in Bosnia, his mother lived on the top, and he lived with Hana on the ground floor. When he got home, he went up to his mom's place to check on Hana. She was sound asleep, so instead of disturbing her, he left her with his mother for the night. He went down to his place and stripped out of his clothes to only his underwear and lay in bed, but he was restless and couldn't sleep. His mind insisted on replaying the way Gage kissed him back. Nikola got up and paced for a while before deciding he needed to talk to someone or go crazy.

Nikola sat at his laptop, clicked the Skype icon, and then clicked to call Garrett. His screen came to life when Garrett answered. His gut clinched with an all too familiar pang of regret as he looked into the face of his ex-boyfriend. Even after five years apart, Garrett was still one of the most striking men Nikola ever laid eyes on. His mixed heritage gave him the most beautiful, creamy, mocha-toned skin and startling bright-green eyes.

Garrett and Nikola lived together for three years, and even when Nikola made the mistake that brought Hana into their lives, Garrett forgave him. They were happy until Nikola found out Hana's mom was pregnant and going to give her up for adoption. He knew he didn't have any other choice but to take the baby, but Garrett hadn't been ready to settle down with a kid. Nikola didn't have a good enough support system to stay in America with a baby, and he was forced to make the difficult choice to move back to Bosnia so his mom could help raise his precious little girl.

Nikola still regretted leaving Garrett and still loved him, in a way. Not having a boyfriend since Garrett, just the occasional hook-up here and there was all he could manage, he missed having someone in his life to come home to everyday and in his bed every night.

"Hey there, sugar. Kinda late for you isn't it?" Garrett asked in his slow southern drawl, which always made Nikola's skin tingle. Then Garrett's eyes took in Nikola's shirtless chest, and a slow smile spread over his face. "Oh, honey, is this one of those kinds of calls? You feeling lonely again?" Garrett leaned forward and rested his chin on his hand.

"Hey, it's been a long time since I called you for that," Nikola joked, going along with the teasing.

Garrett made a face that conveyed his thoughts as sure as if he'd said "You have to be kidding me" out loud. "You call two weeks a long time ago?" Fine, he was right. It had only been a couple of weeks ago when Nikola called, and their chat turned into something more X-rated than had been intended. It had been a few months since he'd called with the intention of doing it, though.

"You know that last time it just happened, and it was your fault. That's not why I'm calling tonight. I just needed someone to talk to, and you're the only one who will understand." Nikola explained the reason for his unexpected call.

"Lay it on me, babe." Garrett relaxed back in his chair.

So Nikola did. He told him everything that happened and what he'd felt and wanted since he'd first laid eyes on one Mr. Gage Hoffman. Garrett listened to Nikola spill everything.

"So, let me get this straight—no pun intended—you don't know if he's gay or straight. You think he's been giving off a vibe that he may be into you. You got him drunk, and he kissed the shit outta you and then had a mini-freak-out, and you're not sure what caused it. So now *you're* freaking out because you may have screwed up your uncle's chances with this guy's company. But more importantly, you're freaking out because you've only known the guy for a few hours, but you think you could have something with him if he was into you, and you can't figure out why he's gotten to you so fast. That about sum it up?" Garrett asked.

"Yep, that's about it. So what do I do now?"

Garrett looked thoughtful for a minute, and Nikola could see when he came to a decision. "I know that you don't believe people can just tell they're meant to be with someone and that sometimes it doesn't take a lot of time to come to that realization. Nik, when I met you, I just knew. I knew that you were the one. I was willing to wait, even if it took you forever to realize that you loved me too. So maybe sometimes it just doesn't work out. You were the one for me, but I wasn't the one for you because I needed to make you fall in love with me, and I loved you from the minute I first heard you say my name. I felt you somewhere deep inside, and it pulled me to you like you were the center of my universe."

Garrett stopped and looked away from the screen for a moment. Nikola watched silently as Garrett tried to get himself back under control. "They say everything happens for a reason. Maybe you weren't meant to be with me, and that's why you were given Hana to lead you back where you needed to be to meet the person who was meant for you. I can't say if Gage is that guy, but I think you need to follow your heart. I, on the other hand, need to listen to my brain instead and let you go," he admitted.

"Garrett, you know I still love you too." He'd had no idea Garrett still held out hope that Nikola would come back to him. Garrett had lots of boyfriends since Nikola left; even one he lived with for two years. Of course, looking back, Nikola could see it was a little suspicious that they always broke up right before he went for a visit. Come to think of it, Garrett was always single anytime Nikola had gone over to see him. He cursed himself for being such an idiot. "Hey, sweetheart, I'm so sorry. I honestly didn't know." Nikola now realized Garrett was still in love with him, and he'd been treating him like a booty call.

Garrett looked out from the screen at Nikola with tears on his cheeks and a small sad smile on his lips. "It's okay. It was my fault anyway. If I'd just thought about what you leaving with Hana had really meant at the time, I would have done everything so differently. I was selfish and wasn't ready to grow up. I didn't want to deal with your mistake for the rest of my life. But now, I get to deal with my biggest mistake for the rest of my life instead. I always thought you'd see that I loved you so much, and you'd come home to me, but I can see now that's not going to happen."

"Garrett, please. Why didn't you tell me? Why didn't you ask me to come home? I've been so lonely, maybe we can—"

"No." Garrett shook his head. "No, Nik, I don't want you to come to me because you're lonely. I want you to come home to me because you love me, but I don't think you can love me the way I need you to because you just don't."

God, the conversation had gone seriously off the rails, and Nikola was feeling more and more confused. Garrett was safe and now Nikola knew Garrett still loved him. Garrett was good with Hana when they'd visited, but now it sounded like he was giving up on Nikola just when he was seeing they might have a chance. If he was honest about it, though, Garrett was not what he really wanted either. Suddenly it was clear and he could feel it with every nerve ending in his body. He wanted Gage. The realization threw him for a loop when it entered his head, and he instantly knew it was true. Nikola knew what he needed to do even without Garrett spelling it out for him.

"I should go. It's late and I have sightseeing to supervise in the morning," Nikola said.

Garrett did his best to flash his sexy smile, but it didn't work out as well as usual when his cheeks were tear-stained. "Go get him, tiger. Don't let him slip through your fingers. Remember somebody out there loves you. Good luck." He clicked off before Nikola could say anything more to him.

Nikola took a quick shower and got into bed, but he still couldn't fall asleep, just too much to think about. What if Gage wasn't gay? What about Gage telling him he broke up with his girlfriend or maybe it was a boyfriend because he wasn't ready to have kids, and there was Nikola with one of his own? Should he just forget the whole thing since having a kid would be a deal breaker anyway? Why couldn't Garrett have told Nikola he still wanted him before he'd met Gage? *Oh god, please let him not remember what happened tonight.* Nikola finally drifted off.

"BABO, WAKE UP. Babo, Babo, Babo." Hana's chant woke Nikola out of his slumber. He opened one eye, and her face was so close to his that she was blurry. "Nana said she'd take me to sled by the river today if you said I could. Please, Babo, please."

"Did you eat breakfast yet?"

"Nana's in the kitchen making eggs for me and you. She told me to come wake you up. Can I go sledding?"

"Let me wake up first. We'll talk about it while you eat. Go tell Nana I'll be there in a minute," Nikola said. She made a face, and he knew she was going to ask again if she could go. He pointed to the door, and Hana kissed his cheek, hopped off the bed, and left the room.

Nikola could hear her talking to his mom in the kitchen. His mom spoke in Bosnian, but Hana would answer her in English. It was kind of funny to listen to them have a conversation. Nikola always spoke to Hana in English when they were at home because some part of him saw them moving back to America someday, and if that happened, he wanted her to speak English without having to think about it.

Nikola crawled out of bed, used the bathroom, and got dressed. Trying not to think about how he was to dressing to show off his best assets in an attempt to get Gage's attention, he pulled on the tightest jeans he owned. He went to the kitchen and kissed his mom on the cheek as she stood at the stove making scrambled eggs before sitting next to Hana at the table. She smiled up at him. His girl was beautiful and every time he looked at her, it made everything he'd given up for her worth it.

"Babo, can I go sledding today?" she asked. "And can Uma and Sara spend the night for my birthday?"

It took Nikola a second to think about her questions since his mind wasn't firing on all its cylinders before his first cup of coffee. Her birthday was on the eleventh, which meant he'd most likely still be busy with Gage, but he just couldn't deny her on her birthday. "You have to ask Nana. I may still be working late hours then, so I can't promise I'll be home. You can go sledding today, but you have to be careful and stay far away from the river. Can you promise me you will?"

"Don't worry, Babo. I never go near the river. I promise to be careful and to not knock Nana over again," she said with a smile so big Nikola noticed she'd lost her second baby tooth, leaving a larger gap in her bottom row.

"Hey, you been kissing boys again, baby girl?"

She giggled and covered her mouth. "Yuck, Babo, kissing boys is gross. My loose tooth fell out last night, but the tooth fairy didn't come because I wasn't at home so she couldn't find me. I want to sleep here tonight so she knows where I am."

"Okay, I'll try my hardest to be home in time for bed. I can't promise anything though and you know how my job is. Remember we talked about this? Now eat your breakfast so you can go sledding." He ruffled her hair.

She sighed and took a bite of her eggs. Nikola ate his breakfast and talked over their plans for the day with his mom. He grabbed a packet of Caffetin to give Gage for the headache he'd likely have before he kissed them both goodbye and went out to clean the snow off his car.

Nikola went through the drive-through at the McDonalds, which shared a parking lot with the hotel Gage was staying in, and got two coffees and a couple of donuts. He stopped at the reception desk to talk to the woman behind the counter and after a few seconds of flirting, he walked away with a key card for Gage's room. *You had to love Bosnia.*

Nikola knocked softly on the door, figuring Gage would hear it if he was awake, but if he was sleeping, he wouldn't be woken up by it. When there was no answer, Nikola used his card and let himself in. He set the coffee and food on the table and took off his coat after grabbing the pills out of his pocket. He took a bottle of water out of the mini-fridge and quietly opened the bedroom door, stopping in his tracks when he caught sight of Gage on the bed.

Walking up to the side of the bed, Nikola let his gaze travel over Gage's body. He was wearing only his boxers, his massive body was sprawled across the bed, and his face looked so peaceful in sleep as he snored softly on each inhale. His chest was broad and lightly furred with small pink nipples nestled in the hair. His torso narrowed at his waist, but it was in no way what you'd call slim, and his hips were just as wide. Nikola tried to imagine what it would feel like to straddle someone that broad, and a shiver ran up his spine, knowing he'd be spread wide. Nikola was startled out of his erotic trance when Gage cleared his throat.

Chapter Five

NIKOLA WAS STANDING over him, holding a bottle of water, when Gage opened his eyes. He cleared his throat to get Nikola's attention because he was just standing there looking spaced out. Nikola jumped as Gage startled him out of his reverie, and he turned to look out the window. How easy it would have been to reach out and pull Nikola down on top of him.

He shifted from foot to foot before his gaze traveled back to Gage. "Hey there, I brought you some pills and a bottle of water. I thought you might need them after last night." Nikola chuckled nervously as he handed Gage a couple of pills and the water after he sat up. "I got you a coffee and a couple of donuts if you're hungry."

Gage opened the bottle and downed half of it with the pills. His head didn't feel as bad as he figured it would have after drinking enough to pass out. Rakia usually left Gage with a splitting headache, but to his surprise, there was just a dull throbbing. "Thanks for the pills."

Nikola nodded. His eyes darted around the room, looking everywhere but at Gage. "I'll let you get dressed; casual is fine. We're going to Bascarsija—that's the old town. You can't come to Sarajevo and not see it," he said before turning and quickly leaving the bedroom.

Gage could smell the coffee in the sitting area, and he wanted it before anything else, so he got out of bed. He almost laughed when he saw Nikola stopped to get them coffee from McDonalds. Nikola's gaze swept up and down Gage's body as he walked toward him to grab his cup off the table, and he squirmed a bit before once again staring out the window. Gage just raised an eyebrow—that Nikola didn't see—in a silent question. Shrugging off Nikola's odd behavior, he walked back toward the bedroom.

"Thanks, for the coffee. Is it okay if I take a quick shower before we go?"

"Um...yeah, we don't have a schedule to keep, so go ahead. Make sure you dress warm though. It's colder today, and it snowed last night."

"Will do." Gage went through the bedroom and on into the bathroom, locking the door behind him. His coffee was just the right temperature to drink so he gulped half of it as he got the water in the shower started. Setting his coffee on the counter, he looked at himself in the mirror and tried to remember exactly what happened the previous night. Nikola was back to acting skittish around him, and he wondered if he'd said something to tip Nikola off that he was gay and if it was what was making the man avoid eye contact. He remembered talking about skiing, hunting, and rivers with trout, but then his memory got a bit fuzzy. Gage snorted. They'd had a lot to drink, so fuzzy didn't quite cut it. After the fourth drink, Gage couldn't remember shit.

He stepped into the shower, trying to remember what exactly had been said but was still drawing a blank when he stepped back out minutes later. He dried off and wrapped the towel around his waist before he picked up his cup and downed the rest of his cold coffee. He decided he'd see how the day went, and if Nikola didn't loosen up, Gage would figure out a way to ditch him. He sure as hell didn't want to spend time with someone who was obviously quite bothered by being in his presence.

Gage dug through his suitcase for something to wear. He went with cargos, deciding suit pants would be weird with a casual shirt. He dropped the towel and just as he bent to pull on his boxers, Gage looked up and met Nikola's eyes in the mirror. Nikola jerked his head to look in the other direction as Gage pulled on his cargos and a long sleeved T-shirt. He opened his garment bag and got out his peacoat, which was lighter than his winter coat.

When Gage rejoined Nikola in the sitting room, he bit his tongue to keep from asking if he'd enjoyed the show. He didn't need to make things even more awkward between them since Nikola was obviously embarrassed at being caught watching. He wouldn't meet Gage's eyes even briefly to acknowledge him. Yeah, joking about it probably wasn't the best way to go. Gage draped his coat over the back of one of the chairs and sat down on the couch, leaving a cushion between them. He tried to think of something to say to put Nikola at ease. Gage wanted the man he'd shared dinner with and then drinks afterward back.

"You said there were donuts?" Wow, his brain worked overtime to come up with that one.

Nikola pushed the bag toward Gage. He took one and offered them back to Nikola, who shook his head. "I ate at home before I came." Nikola took a drink from his coffee cup and finally looked at Gage. "You sleep okay?"

"Sleep's not exactly the word for it. I passed out hard." Gage's honest answer earned him a grin.

"You said you needed a lot of alcohol. I was just doing my job." Nikola winked but Gage cocked his head in confusion. "I'm supposed to keep you happy, get you anything you ask for. Well, within reason."

"You did a good job then because I barely remember anything after we left the restaurant," Gage said only half-jokingly. What he was wondering, though, was what Nikola would think if he knew just what Gage wanted to ask for. After catching Nikola checking him out twice that morning, he wondered if Nikola would accept the offer or run from him screaming. The thought made Gage laugh. "Don't worry. I'm pretty easy. Doesn't take much to keep me happy." He finished his donut and wiped his hands on one of the napkins from the bag. "You ready to head out?"

"Yeah, let's go." Nikola got up and waited for Gage to put on his coat and scarf and shove his gloves into his coat pocket. Nikola slipped his shoes on and opened the door while Gage put his on. Gage made sure he had his key card before shutting the door. "I think you'll like the old town. There're some really cool things to see there, and there's a lot of little shops if you want to get any souvenirs."

Once in the SUV, Nikola started the engine but didn't take off right away. He pulled his phone out of his pocket and checked it. Gage waited patiently while Nikola sent a text before backing out of his parking spot. The traffic was quite heavy on the six-lane road that took them into the heart of Sarajevo. Gage sat silently as he watched the city go by, taking note of the many buildings still pock-marked with bullet holes but also of the ones that looked new. The amount of construction going on was a good sign as it helped to assure him investing in the city would be a good idea.

Everything was going just fine until Nikola turned off the main road onto a narrow side street. Gage gaped at the amount of people walking everywhere with no regard to the cars that tried to navigate through them. The road was barely wide enough for two cars to go down at the same time, but to add to the chaos, there were also cars parked on the sides of the road. Gage couldn't believe his eyes at the way people parked with half of their car sitting on the sidewalk the other half blocking the lanes, essentially reducing it to a one lane road with oncoming traffic swerving to avoid them.

He white-knuckled the oh-shit bar the entire time while clenching his jaw to stop from saying Nikola's name in alarm every time they seemed destined for a head-on collision. Gage hadn't had a harrowing experience like it in any of the other cities he'd been in—narrow roads and crazy drivers were everywhere in Europe, it seemed, but nothing compared to what he was currently going through. He let out a loud breath when Nikola pulled into, and finally parked in, a jam-packed, tiny parking lot.

Nikola looked at Gage with that grin. "You going to be ok there, *Šef?*"

"Yeah, why?" Gage asked, perplexed by his question.

"I've never seen anyone hold on that tight just driving down a normal city street. Makes me wonder how you're going to handle driving up in the mountains. I may have to give you a sedative for that." The grin stayed firmly in place on his handsome face as he teased Gage.

"I've driven through mountains before. I don't have a problem with them. But that—that was not a normal city street." Gage pointed at the carnival ride they'd just gotten off.

Nikola reached over and patted Gage's shoulder. "It wasn't that bad. You just have to trust me. I'm a great driver." Nikola chuckled as he opened his door to get out.

Gage got out, and looking around him, there didn't seem to be much of interest near where they'd parked. Nikola talked to the parking lot attendant, shook his hand, and motioned for Gage to follow him. They walked down a small path between a couple of buildings and came out into a public square. It was like stepping into another world as he took in the old town. The ground beneath his feet wasn't paved—the stones weren't what you'd call cobblestone—and it was uneven and hard to walk on. In the center of the square, there was what looked like a small tower surrounded by tons of pigeons and people who were taking or posing for pictures and some—mostly children—who were feeding the birds. Ringing the square were restaurants and small stands where proprietors called out to people as they passed, while others sat having coffee near the big, outdoor propane heaters.

"That's a *Sebilj*, a fountain. Some people call this the pigeon square. They sell bread crumbs so you can feed the pigeons if you want," Nikola told Gage as he pointed out an old woman selling bags of bread crumbs.

"Yuck, why would you want to do that?" Gage hated pigeons—rats with wings was an accurate description in his opinion. "It's very pretty though." He pointed at the fountain and ducked when the entire flock of birds decided to take wing around them and then just as quickly settled back down.

"You must have offended them." Nikola tsked while Gage tried to evade the stinky birds. "Come on. Let's go this way. There's a mosque down here you have to see." He grabbed Gage's arm, pulling him in the direction he wanted to go. A small tingle went through Gage's body at Nikola's casual touch, but he let go as soon as he was confident Gage was with him.

He followed Nikola but kept stopping to look in the shops. Nikola showed a good amount of patience, which Gage was sure he'd cultivated during other such trips as a tour guide. Nikola would give explanations about the souvenirs when Gage asked what they meant or why, for example, a wolf was their mascot. Nikola told him the story of Vučko, the Olympic mascot, as Gage browsed through the rest of the shop.

"You know you're worse than a woman," Nikola said after they'd been going in and out of shops for an hour and were finally standing in front of the old mosque that Nikola wanted him to see.

"How's that?" Gage asked. "How old is this mosque?"

"It was built in 1532 by the Turks. You can't pass up a shop without going inside to see what they have. It took us over an hour to walk a few blocks." His words were delivered with a smile to soften the insult.

"I like to see things. I like new things. Stuff I've never seen before. It makes me realize just how much is still out there to see, touch, taste. Gives me a reason to live, knowing that I will never see it all, but I can die trying," Gage explained, looking up into the dome of the building.

Nikola looked at Gage with a thoughtful expression on his face. He was probably thinking Gage was crazy, but he didn't care. Nikola watched Gage walk around the courtyard of the mosque and waited patiently while he read all the plaques. When Gage was done, he walked back outside the fence to meet Nikola, where he stood watching an old man talk to everyone who passed by, trying to get people into his shop.

"Want to get something to eat?" Nikola asked. His eyes never leaving the scene in front of him.

"Sure, do they have a good pita place here?"

"You want to eat at a *buregdžinica*?"

"Yeah that's a pita place, right?" Gage knew the word for the type of restaurant he wanted to eat in, but he'd be damned if he was going to watch as Nikola laughed at him trying to pronounce the tongue twister of a word.

Nikola nodded and started walking. He walked so close to Gage that their hands brushed a couple of times, but Gage didn't move away. He'd noticed before in the other countries he'd been to and even in that moment—the other men walking down the street right now in front of them—there wasn't the stigma attached to men touching or walking close that there was in America. The innate need Gage always felt to distance himself from another man to keep up appearances wasn't necessary here. Just because one man walked or sat close to another didn't automatically brand him as gay in Europe like it did back in the states. Gage witnessed many young men walking with arms casually thrown over the shoulder of their male companions and no one gave them a second glance.

Nikola found the place he'd been looking for and held the door open for Gage. Gage walked past him, only to be greeted by an older man who ushered him to a table. "*Dobar dan*," he greeted them with a huge smile.

Nikola talked to the man for a minute before he sat at the table across from Gage. "He says they just pulled new pita out of the *sač*. Do you know what you want to drink? They have colas and Kefir or water, either plain or mineral."

"I'll just have a cola, cold if they have one." Gage didn't drink Kefir. It was thick and reminded him of the buttermilk his grandma forced him and his cousins to drink on the farm. He'd also learned his lesson on ordering pop in the region. You needed to specify you wanted it cold, otherwise if it wasn't the middle of summer, you'd get a room temperature drink—Europeans and their lack of ice. Go figure.

"And what kind of pita do you like?" Nikola asked.

"I'd like cheese if they have it." He knew from previous trips that pita was basically dough stretched really thin and then filled with something: meat, potatoes, or a cheese that was like cottage cheese, before it was rolled up and baked. It spoke to Gage's German roots and reminded him of the cheese buttons his mom made, so that was what he usually ordered.

Nikola ordered a half kilo of *sirnica* for Gage and a half kilo of meat or *burek* for himself. It only took a couple of minutes until the waiter brought their drinks. Gage's cola was in one of those tiny glass bottles, which he touched and was happy to note was cold. The waiter set a plate with silverware in the middle of the table and left, only to return right away with the food. Gage reached for his silverware at the same time as Nikola, their fingers brushing. Nikola grabbed Gage's hand, instead of his napkin-wrapped utensils.

"Your hand is freezing. You need to wear your gloves when we go back out." Nikola used the same tone Gage's mother used when she scolded him as a child.

Gage pulled his cold hand away from Nikola's warm one. "Yes, Mom." Gage started eating so he could avoid having to meet Nikola's menacing glare.

"If I were your mother, I would spank you for being insolent." Nikola smirk turned to a laugh when Gage choked on his food.

Gage took a drink and coughed some more before he got himself under control enough to respond. "Guess I'm lucky you're not, then, 'cause my ass would always be red."

"Just wear your gloves, and we won't have to worry about it."

Was Nikola flirting with him? The heat rose from Gage's neck to his face as his cheeks turned pink. Dropping his gaze, he started to eat like it was his last meal.

Nikola ordered coffee after they were done with the food, and while they drank it, he told Gage more about Sarajevo and what was being done in the way of rebuilding and infrastructure. Gage was having trouble concentrating on what Nikola was saying because his eyes were constantly drawn to Nikola's full lips. He did nothing to help stop Gage's distraction with the way he kept licking his bottom lip every time he finished a sentence. Was it an unconscious habit or a deliberate bid to keep Gage entranced? Gage couldn't tell which.

He pulled his wallet out in an attempt to pay when they got up to leave, but Nikola gave him a look that made him put it back into his pocket quickly, thinking, *maybe if I insist on paying, he'll threaten to spank me again.* The images in his mind made him warm in a way gloves never would, until he realized how strange it was for him to be thinking about being spanked.

At the door, Nikola gave Gage's hands a pointed look and waited until Gage put his gloves on to go out. "Good boy," Nikola said quietly as they walked side by side down the narrow path back to the main square. Nikola was walking even closer to Gage, so much so their shoulders brushed together most of the way down to the bridge where the shot that started WWI was fired. Nikola again waited patiently while Gage wandered around the area, until his phone rang.

Nikola answered and then spoke in rapid-fire Bosnian, only giving a brief pause for the person on the other end of the call to respond. Gage could tell Nikola was upset, just by the set of his jaw. "I need to run home quick. Hana's had a small accident, and I need to make sure she doesn't need me," he said, looking worried. "I can drop you off at the hotel on the way, if you want, and come back to get you when I'm done."

"If you don't mind me tagging along, you could skip dropping me off and get to her sooner," Gage offered. As much as he hated to admit it, he was curious about Hana and wasn't above taking the opportunity to meet her. He wasn't sure if Nikola would want him at his home or not, but at the look of relief on his face, Gage knew that wasn't a problem. Nikola's curt nod confirmed it.

"Let's go then," Nikola said.

They made their way back to the parking lot at a pretty good clip, Gage thankful for his long legs, as Nikola strode purposefully through the crowd in the square. Gage strapped in, and in no time, they were speeding down the road. They actually passed his hotel on their way out to what could only be called a suburb of a suburb of Sarajevo. Gage thought the ride on that side road in the city was bad, but the roads out in the area where Nikola lived were terrifying, and Nikola drove fast. Gage caught Nikola glancing at him a couple of times, and it seemed no matter how worried Nikola was about Hana, he still got a kick out of Gage's reactions to his driving. Thankfully, they pulled up in front of a two-story house soon after entering the neighborhood.

"Here we are and in one piece," Nikola announced. "My mom lives on the upper floor, and Hana and I live on the bottom." He motioned to the house through the windshield of the car.

"I think you're trying to kill me," Gage grumbled, ignoring that Nikola just told him he lived with his girlfriend.

"Oh, I am not that's how everyone drives here."

Gage shook his head, not bothering to argue as he followed Nikola to the front door. He took Gage's coat and hung it in the closet before offering him a pair of slippers when he took off his shoes. He opened the door at the end of the hall and called, "Hey, Mom, where's my baby?"

Gage walked into what was the living room and kitchen where there was an older woman standing by the stove, Nikola's mother, Gage assumed. Nikola walked over to the couch and picked up a dark-haired little girl. Hugging her to his chest, he kissed her cheeks, and sat down on the couch with her in his lap. He was examining her little hand, which had two fingers in splints.

"Who's that?" The little girl asked when she spotted Gage standing by the door.

Nikola looked up at Gage and smiled. He motioned Gage over to the couch and pointed to indicate he should sit. "This is Mr. Hoffman. He's my job this month," Nikola said to Hana before he introduced her to Gage. "Gage, this is Hana, my daughter."

Chapter Six

NIKOLA WATCHED THE surprised look take over Gage's face when he introduced him to Hana, but he recovered quickly enough and smiled. "Hi there, Hana. It's nice to meet you."

Hana cocked her head and took a long look at Gage. "My babo needs to be home on my birthday so Uma and Sara can spend the night. You can come too since he's babysitting you. There's gonna be cake," Hana said with a self-satisfied nod at her compromise. That was Nikola's girl; think of the most important thing first and just blurt it out.

"Hana, that's not the proper way to greet someone when you first meet them. And it's not babysitting. He's not a baby." Nikola chided her, but with some humor in his voice, as the man beside him tried to hide his own laughter behind a cough and a hand.

"Sorry, Babo." Hana turned her attention back to Gage. "It's nice to meet you too. I'm sorry I said you were being babysitted, but you can still come to my birthday party since my babo is old-man-sitting you—"

Nikola put his hand over her mouth to shut her up as Gage exploded into laughter. Hana watched his fit with wide eyes, and her body shook as she giggled behind Nikola's hand. The horrified look on Nikola's face just fueled Gage's fit, and he snorted a few times until he got himself under control enough to speak.

"I would love to come to your party if it's okay with your dad. He has to give me permission since he's my old-man sitter." His statement set Gage off again, and Hana was laughing along with him just as hard. Gage winked at Nikola as he rolled his eyes back at Gage.

The idea of the two of them spending any time together made Nikola's head ache. Who knew what she'd say, and it seemed Gage was perfectly happy to egg her on. When they finally calmed down, Nikola asked Hana about her accident.

"I was being careful, just like I promised. I just put my hand down when I fell off the sled, and it hurt. I told Nana, and she took me to the doctor, and he said that I breaked these two fingers," she said calmly as she held up her hand for Nikola to look at again. Then she showed them to Gage, who held out his hand to her. Nikola's baby put her damaged little hand in Gage's massive one, and he leaned down and kissed her broken fingers.

"My mom always said a kiss would do wonders for healing. She always kissed my owies." Gage told Hana, who in turn gifted him with her biggest smile.

"I think your mommy was right. They feel better already," she said earnestly. Nikola looked at him in wonder, but Gage just smiled serenely and winked at Nikola as if he was in on some sort of joke.

"I need to go talk to Nana. Will you be okay here with Gage, or do you want to come with?" Nikola asked his daughter.

Hana climbed off Nikola's lap and right into Gage's. "I can old-man-sit for you for a little bit. Don't worry. I'll take care of him." She looked up at Gage, and he started chuckling again.

"We'll be fine," Gage said as he settled Hana into his lap.

"Okay, I'll only be a second." Nikola got up to go find his mom. As he walked out the door, he could hear Hana telling Gage about her birthday party.

Nikola's mom was upstairs in her own kitchen when he walked in. She looked at him in a way that left no doubt about her feeling of him bringing his work home. "Hana's hand will be fine. The doctor said it was only a hairline fracture. It will heal quickly, and there will be no permanent damage." She filled him in before Nikola could even ask.

"That's good to know." It was a relief to know it was only a simple break, not something that would require further medical intervention. "Thanks for taking her sledding today."

"It was a nice day to be out. Kids need fresh air, and even if it is this city air, it's better than nothing." Once again, she managed to infer how unfit she believed it was to raise a child in a city instead of a small mountain village like the one where Nikola spent his early childhood.

"I know she needs fresh air, Mom." Nikola didn't want to have an argument with her, and he wanted to get back to Hana and Gage.

She narrowed her eyes at him like she wanted to continue on in the same vein, but Nikola was happy when the next words out of her mouth were more civilized. "There's *sarma* in the oven and the bread's ready to go in when you take the *sarma* out. There's enough if you want that man to stay for supper."

Nikola caught the way his mother said *that man,* and he knew what she thought was going on, even if Nikola made it clear Gage was his job. "I'll ask him if he wants to stay, and if not, I'll come and get you so I can take him back to his hotel." Nikola wasn't going to defend his decision to bring Gage home with him. It was his goddamn house!

"Fine, I'll be here." She turned back to doing whatever it was she'd been doing when he'd interrupted her. "Just be careful around that man, *sine.*" She issued the warning without turning to look at him.

Nikola didn't respond. He knew how she felt, and there was no changing her mind. She was old and set in her ways with a firm belief in what was right and wrong. He went back to his own living room to find Hana kneeling on Gage's legs. She had his face in her hands and was talking to him. Gage was listening intently to the little girl like she was telling him the secret to the universe.

"And that's how I know you haven't been kissing any boys. But Babo's got all his teeth too, so I think that maybe he's not telling the—"

"Hana," Nikola interrupted her before she could finish the sentence. "What are you doing?" She turned to look at Nikola but didn't take her hands off Gage's cheeks.

"Hana here was telling me about how you asked her if she's been kissing boys when she lost a tooth. So she was checking to see if I'd been kissing any boys." Gage's green eyes danced with amusement as he pinned Nikola down with them.

"He doesn't have any loose teeth, so I don't think he's in love with any boys," his daughter said sagely. Gage raised an eyebrow at Nikola, who fidgeted nervously as he remembered the kiss Gage gave him the previous night. They both should have at least a couple of loose teeth after that. Hana filled the silence once again. "I told Babo kissing boys was yucky, and he told me that sometimes when you grow up you fall in love and then you want to kiss boys. So, I think, if you're not kissing boys, you must not be in love."

"Hana, you know that boys also kiss girls and kissing girls doesn't give you loose teeth. Now leave Gage alone," Nikola said sternly.

She dropped her hands from Gage's face as she turned back to him. They stared into each other's eyes for a moment before Hana nodded and wrapped her arms around Gage's neck and hugged him. She whispered something into his ear that made his eyebrows rise almost to his hairline. Gage looked at Nikola with the strangest expression on his face before Hana let him go. She kissed his cheek and turned around to sit on his lap with her back against his chest—a satisfied little smile on her lips. Gage wrapped an arm around her waist and kissed the top of her head. They both looked at Nikola expectantly.

"I can see I'm going to have to keep you two separated, otherwise there'll be trouble." Nikola's stomach fluttered at the sight of them together. They looked so right sitting there on his couch. Nikola shook himself to dislodge the idea. He went to take the *sarma* out of the oven as Hana turned the TV on and found cartoons she liked to watch. He put the bread dough, which was sitting in a pan on the counter, into the oven. When he turned around, they were still sitting on the couch watching cartoons. Gage's one hand was lying palm up on Hana's lap, and her broken hand was in it—his thumb rubbing gentle circles on her wrist. Hana was completely relaxed back against him with her cheek pressed to his chest over his heart.

Nikola stopped to just take them in, to watch this gentle giant as he held Nikola's heart on his lap and let himself imagine what it would be like to come home to that very scene every night. Nikola couldn't figure out why a man who could act like this with a total stranger's child wouldn't want one of his own. Would even lose someone he loved over it. Gage looked at him and smiled in a way that made Nicola's heart melt and then motioned for Nikola to sit with them. Nikola took a seat next to Gage on the couch, and Hana lifted her legs to put them across his lap. Nikola was close enough to Gage he could feel the other man's body heat, and it was comforting to have him so near.

"Do you want to stay here for supper?" Nikola asked.

"Depends," he answered with a wicked gleam in his eyes.

"On what?"

"Are you a good cook, or will I have to deal with a nasty case of food poisoning tomorrow?"

"I'm a lousy cook," Nikola admitted. "But luckily my mom's not, and she already had supper in the oven. If you don't want to, that's fine. We can go out to eat, and I can take you back to the hotel afterwards." After the words were out of his mouth, Nikola realized he wanted Gage to stay—to watch Gage eat at his table with Hana next to him. He could be part of Nikola's pretend family for a little while longer.

"What do you think, Hana Banana, should I trust your dad that it's good?" Gage turned to the little girl in his lap and asked.

"I watched my nana make it, so it's good. You should stay. We can watch a movie after. Do you like Mary Poppins?"

"I love Mary Poppins. It's always been one of my favorites. Okay then, if you say the food's good, I guess I'll stay," Gage said to Hana while looking at Nikola.

"The bread will be done in about a half an hour, so we can eat then," Nikola said. Gage sank into the couch a little more. His shoulder pressed against Nikola, but he didn't change position to put space between them, and soon Nikola relaxed too. Hana reached for Nikola's hand, where it rested on her leg, with her free hand and held it on her lap next to the one Gage was holding. They sat in comfortable silence, watching cartoons until the timer went off on the oven. Nikola untangled himself from Hana before he got off the couch to go to set everything out on the table.

"Come eat you two. Hana, shut the TV off please." Nikola made sure Hana heard him before he finished setting the table.

Hana shut the set down with the remote and put it on the table before Gage stood up with her in his arms. He carried her to the table, sat her in a chair, and then sat down at the head of the little table. Nikola dished up food for Hana, but he let Gage dish up for himself while he cut the steaming bread and put it in the basket on the table. Nikola then sat down across from Hana.

"This looks really good. You guys over here really like your cabbage. You don't see this much of the stuff in the states." Gage popped a whole *sarma* in his mouth and mmm'd as he chewed it. "Way better than in the restaurants, I'm glad you convinced me to stay, Banana."

Hana giggled at the nickname. "I knew you'd like it. I could feel it in my tummy." Nikola couldn't help but smile fondly at her. Their easy banter seemed so natural. The way Hana just accepted Gage, and the way he let her, touched a nerve in Nikola.

"You make sure you listen to your tummy because it seems to know what's right," Gage said, and Hana nodded happily. Nikola watched the two of them eat as they made small talk about sledding, and then the talk turned to Hana's birthday plans once again.

"So how old are you going to be, and when is this party with the cake? I hope it's soon because I'll have a hard time sleeping until then, thinking about all that delicious cake." Gage rubbed his flat stomach, drawing Nikola's hungry eyes down before he caught himself and adjusted their course back to the man's face.

"It's on the eleventh, and she's going to be six. I can get you some cake to tide you over if it's going to be a problem." Nikola was only teasing, but the look on Gage's face made him wonder what he'd said wrong. "What, you don't want the cake? You don't have to have cake. I was just kidding."

"Um no, it's just that...ah it's nothing, never mind." Gage looked uncomfortable for the first time, which was saying something, considering Hana's tooth check earlier. Nikola watched Gage as he took a minute to put a smile back on his face before he looked at Hana. "So, Hana B, what do you want for your birthday?"

"I want to go to America for my birthday," she said excitedly.

Oh no, nothing good can come of this. Nikola opened his mouth to say something, only to have Gage beat him to it.

"What's in America?"

"Last time we were there, Uncle Garrett told me the next time we came to visit he'd take me to Disneyland to meet the princesses. I want to meet all of them, and then there are rides, and he said there's all kinds of good food there. So I really want to go to America." She was really working herself up over the prospect of going to Disneyland, but then she served up a curveball that had Nikola ready to send her to bed just to shut her up. "Plus, Babo is always happier after we visit Uncle Garrett because Uncle Garrett loves us, and he's really sad when we leave."

Gage's eyes were on him. He could feel the blush rising on his cheeks, and all of a sudden, he wished his kid wasn't so damn perceptive for once in her life. Nikola turned slowly to look at Gage, and the knowing smile on his face made Nikola's flush deepen. Oh god, this can't be happening. Why is this happening? Nikola wondered. He resisted the urge to bang his head on the table, knowing it wouldn't erase the embarrassment of the moment.

"Do you live near Disneyland, Uncle Gage?" Hana asked. Nikola's surprise at Hana's use of uncle in front of Gage's name had to be written all over his face. Hana didn't call anyone uncle except Garrett. She knew he and Nikola were more than just friends, and it was her way of acknowledging Garrett was more to her too.

Gage smiled gently down at her. "Nope, I live so far from Disneyland it may as well be on the other side of the world. But I do live kind of near the biggest mall in America, and when you're a teenager, that will be just as exciting, if not more."

Nikola laughed at the comical way Hana's face fell, but his mirth was cut short when she brightened back up. "Maybe next time we come to America we can visit you and go to the mall, instead." She was obviously pleased with her new plan.

"Hana, we don't invite ourselves to visit people we hardly know. Now finish eating if you want to have enough time to watch a movie before bed," Nikola scolded. He smiled apologetically at Gage, who just shrugged it off like little girls called him uncle out of the blue and invited themselves to visit every day. Wow, that sounded bad even in Nikola's own head.

"Who knows what will happen," Gage said quietly. Hana gave him an adoring look and turned to smile at Nikola to let him know she'd won.

They finished eating, and Nikola waved Gage away when he tried to help clean up. He shrugged and followed Hana into the living room. She put her movie in, and they resumed their earlier position on the couch. Nikola wanted to tell Hana to back off Gage for a bit, but he seemed content to let her cuddle in his lap so Nikola left them alone. He did the dishes and listened to Hana giggle when Gage sang along with the songs in an exaggerated funny British accent. When Nikola finished, he grabbed a couple of beers out of the fridge and went to sit with them in the living room.

Gage accepted his beer and raised it to clink against the one in Nikola's hand before taking a drink. Nikola contemplated sitting in the chair but Hana stopped him by lifting her legs for him to take his spot back. Gage's arm was up on the back of the couch behind Nikola. He wanted Gage to drop his arm down and over his shoulders so badly he could taste it. He moved a bit closer to Gage but tried to keep it casual-looking. His mind was buzzing with plans of what he'd do if Gage got the hint and—

"Babo, can Uncle Gage spend the night?" Hana asked. Nikola was startled into sitting up and pulling away from Gage. Oh god, she was going to get him in so much trouble.

Chapter Seven

GAGE REMINDED HIMSELF to breathe while he waited to hear how Nikola would answer Hana's question. Nikola looked like a deer caught in the headlights. He thought about saying something to save Nikola having to answer, but then he didn't want to say the wrong thing and accidentally make things worse.

"I'm sure he doesn't want to sleep on our lumpy couch when he's got a nice big bed back at the hotel."

Gage had to hand it to Nikola—he knew what he was doing when it came to parenting. Unfortunately, Hana also knew what she was doing, and he shouldn't have been quite so surprised when she turned her big brown eyes to him. He should have guessed the question before she even opened her mouth and had a response at the ready.

"Do you want to spend the night, Uncle Gage?" She made puppy-dog eyes at him while she waited for him to answer.

The kid was totally undoing Gage with the whole uncle thing. She was just too much sweetness all rolled into an adorable package. Nikola was looking at Gage like he was wondering what the answer would be too, but Gage needed a little time to figure out what his answer should be. He'd been totally thrown off balance after finding out Hana was Nikola's kid and not his girlfriend. Then all the little things Hana said throughout the night made Gage wonder about Nikola even more. He went over his options but knew what he wanted. Did Uncle Gage want to spend the night? Hell, yes, he did but not on the couch. So Gage said the only thing he could think of, and thankfully, it was just as noncommittal as the answer Nikola gave.

"I don't want to impose on you and your dad, Banana. He shouldn't have to old-man-sit me all night, that's going above and beyond." Gage added a teasing wink for good measure.

Hana cocked her head and studied Gage before she nodded and, amazingly, let it drop. They went back to watching her movie, and Nikola handed him a fresh beer every time he finished the one in his hand. By the time Gage realized Hana was dozing in his lap, he had a pleasant buzz going. Nikola roused her as the credits were rolling.

"Tell Gage good night. It's past your bedtime already," Nikola said.

She turned into Gage and wrapped her arms around his neck. "Good night, Uncle Gage." She kissed his cheek and pulled away with a sleepy smile. Gage kissed the top of her head and let Nikola take her from his lap.

"I'll put her to bed and be right back," Nikola said as he carried her from the room.

But Hana wasn't done imparting the wisdom of her tummy for the night. "My tummy says you could kiss Uncle Gage, Babo, and it wouldn't be too yucky," Hana whispered sleepily into her father's neck just loud enough for Gage to hear. Nikola shushed her and carried her off to her room.

Gage agreed with Hana's tummy—Nikola could kiss him, and it probably wouldn't be too yucky, at least not for Gage. Gage hoped the kid knew what she was talking about. Earlier, Hana told him her tummy liked him. It also told her it knew Gage was like her babo, and he had a pretty good idea of what she meant by that now. After the Uncle Garrett story, he felt he was pretty much up to speed. Gage wondered if Hana had come equipped with super gaydar. He listened to them talk quietly for a couple of minutes before Nikola came out of the room, went straight to the kitchen and returned with a bottle of Rakia and glasses.

He sat down heavily on the couch next to Gage, uncapped the bottle, and poured out two glasses. He handed one to Gage, without looking at him, as he slammed back the other. Nikola refilled his glass, drained it, and refilled it once more, but Gage reached out and grabbed Nikola's wrist before he could bring the glass up to his lips for the third time and finally he looked at Gage.

"So how badly did I fuck this up?" Nikola asked, clenching his jaw like he was trying to bite back any words that might dare to follow.

"Which *this* are you talking about?" Gage answered with a question.

Nikola heaved out a sigh, pushing Gage's hand off his wrist so he could drain his glass again before slumping back against the couch. "All of them, but mostly how badly did I fuck up the business end of things?"

"I haven't even talked to Nedim. There is nothing to fuck up yet." Gage didn't know what else Nikola was talking about that he could have messed up. He tipped his glass back, swallowing the fiery liquid and putting empty glass back on the table. Nikola sat forward to refill them.

"How much did Hana freak you out?" Nikola swirled the liquid in his glass and watched it intently while he waited for Gage's answer.

Gage snorted out a short, sharp laugh. Hana completely freaked him out with her oh-so-accurate tummy, but he wasn't going to tell Nikola that. "Not at all. She's the sweetest little thing I've ever had the pleasure of meeting." Gage told a partial lie since the part about Hana being sweet was totally true.

"Now *my* tummy is telling me that *you're* lying," Nikola said as he rolled his eyes.

"Well, she is really sweet—"

"Uh huh, she is that when she wants to be. But I saw a look on your face a few times tonight when she let things slip. Anything you have to say to me?"

Nikola put up his defenses as if steeling himself for whatever it was he thought Gage would have to say about the night's events. Gage had no idea what he should or even wanted to say, so it was a total surprise to him as much as it was to Nikola when he asked, "Is Uncle Garrett your boyfriend?"

Nikola hid his expression behind his glass, which he emptied once again before answering the question. "He's my ex-boyfriend. We still get together every now and then."

"Hana says he still loves you. Do you still love him?" Gage knew he didn't have any right to ask, but for some reason, it felt important for him to know if Nikola was in love with another man.

"I love him but not the way he needs me to," Nikola said, answering a totally invasive personal question asked by a complete stranger. He met Gage's gaze, and Gage was sorry he'd asked when he saw the depth of sadness in Nikola's dark eyes. Nikola didn't break eye contact, instead letting Gage sit there and soak up the feeling from him.

Nikola's answer hit close to home for Gage because it seemed he wasn't the only one who couldn't be enough, love enough, for another man. He wanted nothing more than to lean forward and kiss Nikola, but something held him back. People did the sort of thing Gage was thinking of doing all the time—having a short fling on a business trip never crossed his mind before, but now there was nothing to stop him—Lucas was no longer waiting at home. He couldn't discount how drawn to

Nikola he'd been since the minute he'd seen him. Would he regret not giving in to the attraction?

Nikola took the choice away when he slowly leaned into Gage, never breaking eye contact. Nikola watched intently as he narrowed the space between them as if waiting for him to pull away. Gage watched those chocolate-brown eyes, so full of hope, get steadily closer, until their lips brushed together—it was soft—just the barest of touches before Nikola pulled back a few inches.

"This okay?" Nikola whispered. Gage let the alcohol-infused breath from Nikola's slightly parted lips wash over his face for a couple of seconds before he nodded. The second time Nikola moved with more confidence, closing his eyes right before their lips made contact, and Gage instinctively opened for Nikola when his tongue prodded for entrance. He could taste the Rakia on Nikola's tongue as he pressed past his lips, but soon another richer flavor took over and Gage knew he was tasting the man himself.

He lost all his ability to think when Nikola pulled back and licked across and then nipped Gage's bottom lip. Gage groaned. It was just too much for him to take. He couldn't sit there passively and let Nikola kiss him like that. He clutched the back of Nikola's neck and held him in place while he pushed his tongue through Nikola's lips—thrusting deeply into the moist warmth, and he yielded to Gage, letting him take control of the kiss.

Nikola wasn't passive though—his hands found Gage's chest, and after a quick exploratory rub from Gage's collarbone to his waist, Nikola pulled at Gage's shirt. Their lips parted so Nikola could yank the shirt up between them and over Gage's head. Nikola swung his leg across Gage's lap and was straddling him before Gage could even understand what was happening. Nikola's lips were back on Gage's, and his hands seemed to be everywhere at once. Nikola was like a man possessed.

Everything was moving much too fast. Gage pushed Nikola back so he could look at him, and Nikola's hands stilled as a look of worry passed over his face. "What do you want?" Gage asked. Worry turned to relief, and Gage wondered what Nikola expected when Gage tried to slow things down.

"I want to fuck." Nikola's tone was just this side of pleading, "Please, can we just do this and not talk about it?"

Gage's eyes searched Nikola's face. "Tell me you won't freak out on me if we do this. Tell me it won't be weird in the morning, and I'll throw you down right here and fuck you until you beg me to stop." Gage didn't take his eyes off Nikola's face, needing Nikola to reassure him if they went through with what they both obviously wanted it wouldn't affect his business dealings with Nikola's uncle. Gage had to make it clear his business came first, since it was what he was there for after all was said and done. He couldn't let sex screw that up—no matter how much he wanted the man on his lap.

Instead of answering, Nikola whipped his shirt off and pressed their chests together. Nikola's lips slammed back against Gage's in a punishing kiss, and Gage took that to mean Nikola's answer was yes and let his tongue tangle with Nikola's as each man fought for dominance. Nikola thrust his hips against Gage, and he was so hard he knew if Nikola kept it up he was going to lose it and come right there in his pants.

Gage pushed forward until his ass was on the edge of the couch cushion while Nikola wiggled into position to get his legs wrapped around Gage's waist. It took all the strength in Gage's legs, but he managed to stand up with Nikola clinging to him. Nikola pulled away from Gage's insistent mouth with a startled look of panic at being manhandled and tried to unwrap his legs so he could stand on his own, but Gage held his ass and growled, "Bedroom now."

Nikola nodded eagerly. "Second door on the left."

He resumed kissing Gage's neck as he was carried to his bedroom. Gage kicked the door shut behind them, then took four steps to the bed, and dropped Nikola onto his back on the mattress. Nikola unbuttoned his jeans, and Gage reached down, grabbed them at Nikola's ankles, and with one tug, yanked them off.

Gage stopped to take in Nikola's body. It was better than he'd even imagined it could be—all long, lean muscles and tan skin. Nikola lay there and let Gage take him in for a minute before he sat up on the edge of the bed and, with an unsteady hand, managed to quickly get Gage out of his pants and boxers. With heavily lidded eyes, Nikola looked up at him and licked his lips as he reached out to stroke Gage lightly.

He shuddered at Nikola's touch, trying not to thrust his hips, but when Nikola rubbed his cheek against Gage's shaft, he couldn't help himself. "God, please Niky, suck me, please."

A small, wicked smile spread slowly across Nikola's lips before he puffed a breath on the head of Gage's cock. A shiver ran up Gage's spine as he put his hands in Nikola's hair, which was soft and long enough to get a good grip on it if he had the mind to. Gage didn't pull Nikola to him even though he wanted nothing more than to make Nikola take him into his mouth. Nikola's tongue darted out to lap at the precome pooling in the slit of Gage's cock.

Nikola hummed and ran his tongue around the crown before he nibbled at the sensitive skin right beneath. Nikola was teasing him, and Gage would let him have his way for a couple of minutes.

All too soon he'd had enough, so he used Nikola's hair to hold his head as he pushed his cock past Nikola's lips, stuffing Nikola's mouth with as much as he could cram in before Nikola put up some resistance.

Nikola grabbed Gage's cock with one hand, preventing him from choking on the full length while gripping Gage's ass with the other as he willingly sucked the cock into his warm, wet mouth. Gage admired how sexy Nikola looked with his lips wrapped around his length, but Gage's breath caught in his chest when Nikola looked up to meet his eyes. He knew he wasn't going to last long. The longing in Nikola's eyes would be Gage's undoing before the man even really started with his mouth.

Gage started slowly thrusting his hips, and Nikola let him set his own rhythm. Gage slowed as he pulled out to give Nikola time to use his tongue around the crown and shoved back in. The hand Nikola had on Gage's cock moved farther down toward his balls as Nikola took him deeper into his mouth with every thrust, and eventually, taking Gage into his throat. The first time Nikola swallowed around Gage's cock, the fluttering and spasming of the muscles pulled a moan from so deep in Gage it felt like it started in his toes. He pulled the hair fisted in his hands, and Nikola's responding moan around Gage's tightly encased cock made him come without warning. Nikola gagged but kept sucking until Gage's cock was too sensitive to have all that attention lavished on it, and he used Nikola's hair to gently pull him off.

Nikola lay back on the bed, propped on his elbows, looking Gage over. His hunger written all over his face, mingling with the same look of longing Gage had glimpsed earlier, and Gage wanted to give him whatever it was he needed to get rid of that look. He bent to pull Nikola's underwear off and motioned for him to move up the bed. Nikola pulled himself to the head of the bed as Gage crawled after him to settle between his thighs. Gage kissed and nipped at his puffy red lips, tasting his own flavor on the man's tongue as Nikola wound his arms around Gage's neck and pressed their bodies tightly together. Gage lifted his hips to line up their cocks, and when they brushed, Nikola groaned into Gage's mouth.

Nikola pulled away from Gage's lips. "Still so fucking hard. God, I want you so much," Nikola panted out. He planted his feet on the bed so he could push his hips up to thrust his cock against Gage, and they rocked together until Nikola's breath came in harsh pants. Nikola moved his hands to Gage's ass and dug his fingers in so hard Gage knew he'd have bruises in the morning, but he relished Nikola's strength. He'd never been with anyone who was nearly as strong as he was—this could get interesting.

"Do you have lube?" Gage panted into Nikola's neck.

"In the top drawer with the condoms."

Gage reached out and pulled the drawer so hard it almost came all the way out. He found the lube and popped the top, before pushing to his knees between Nikola's thighs. Nikola watched Gage warily as he poured lube into his palm. Gage once again covered Nikola with his body, supporting himself on one arm next to Nikola's head. Gage lined up their cocks and grasped them in his slicked-up hand.

"Oh, oh, that's good, so good," Nikola gasped as Gage began firmly stroking their cocks together. Nikola wrapped his legs around Gage's thighs to get leverage to help him rock against Gage, pushing his cock through the hand tightly wrapped around it. Nikola was moaning and babbling in Bosnian, and Gage was so turned on—so much better than his fantasy—he could feel his own orgasm building again. Gage pumped faster and squeezed tighter. Nikola came with an inhuman growl that seemed as though it was ripped from his chest. Gage kept stroking him as he spurted between their bodies.

Gage bent to lick at the milky puddles and then kissed Nikola with his own spunk on his tongue. Nikola grabbed ahold of his head to kiss him deeper, and Gage moaned into Nikola as he came again. He pulled his hand out from between their bodies, dropping down on Nikola, and rested against him until he came down from the high.

Nikola kissed Gage, but Gage needed to catch his breath, so he pulled back. Nikola trailed kisses across Gage's jaw to his neck, keeping his mouth busy kissing, licking, and nibbling as Gage struggled to get ahold of himself. Nikola's hands ran up and down Gage's back and ass as if he were trying to memorize every contour. If Nikola kept it up, Gage would get hard again eventually. It might take a while but it would happen. Gage wondered if that was what Nikola was aiming for. When Nikola started moving his hips, and Gage felt his growing erection, there was no question about what he was doing.

"You gotta give me a few minutes, Niky. I'm not as young as I used to be," Gage said as Nikola grabbed at his ass to grind Gage down on him harder. Then in one powerful move from Nikola, Gage was on his back staring up at the other man with wide eyes. Nikola smiled down from his position above Gage, taking his breath away. Gage's cock twitched—apparently it liked it when he was manhandled.

"You don't have to be hard for me to fuck you," Nikola said. His smile turned into something more like a sexy smirk before he added, "And for the record, if you call me Niky anywhere other than when we're in bed—" He leaned down close to Gage's face. "—I'll spank you."

Whoa, wait a minute here. Did Nikola just say he was going to fuck him? He hadn't bottomed since college, and then it was only with his first boyfriend. Gage was not a bottom, and he wasn't prepared to make himself one for Nikola—or for any man for that matter—right then. His cock was starting to wake up, even with Nikola mentioning spanking, which contrary to what Gage would have thought, was actually speeding that process along. Could it be Nikola found a kink Gage didn't know he had? Nikola was sitting on Gage's crotch, so he'd no doubt registered Gage's reaction to his threat. Nikola's eye held a wicked gleam Gage didn't much care for.

"Um...ah," Gage stammered. How did one explain that one didn't get fucked but only did the fucking? Gage had never been in that position before because every guy he'd been with knew where they stood on that count.

Nikola snorted down at Gage. "You don't want me to fuck you, right? Is it just me, or are you a dedicated topper?" he asked in a slightly amused tone. Nikola was still moving his hips but with no real urgency like before. Gage's dick was caught between them with the head nudging the back of Nikola's balls as he moved. Gage reached behind Nikola, finding his ass cheeks were spread wide as he straddled Gage's hips. It made it easy for Gage to run his finger down the crease, and Nikola moaned as Gage rubbed a finger against the entrance to his tight little hole.

"It's not you. I just don't bottom very well, and I haven't been with anyone who wanted me to for some time," Gage said. Gage kept up his attention to Nikola's ass—rubbing to soften the muscle. Nikola's head hung down as he moaned and pushed back against Gage's probing finger. Gage took that as a good sign. Maybe his unwillingness to bottom wouldn't be a deal breaker.

Gage took advantage of Nikola's distraction and flipped them back over, Nikola letting out a yelp of surprise. Gage kissed him hard and fast and then made his way down Nikola's body. He stopped to suck on the hollow of his throat, and Nikola purred. Gage kissed his way down and took one of Nikola's nipples into his mouth and made him hiss. Gage pinched the other one while he sucked on the one in his mouth until Nikola cursed at him in Bosnian, making Gage smile around the nub.

Gage had Nikola writhing underneath him so he released his nips and kissed down the center of his chest. He followed Nikola's sparse chest hair down to where it thickened into a dark trail, enticing him to follow it to the end where he found his prize waiting. Nikola's cock and balls were a couple of shades darker than the rest of his skin. Gage buried his nose in the nest of curls just above his shaft and inhaled him. He was musky from their earlier activities, and Gage huffed in the earthy scent of aroused male.

"Oh fuck, Gage, are you just going to tease me or are you going to do something?" Nikola groaned.

Gage groped around the bed until he came up with the lube. He slicked up his fingers as he took Nikola's leaking cockhead into his mouth. Gage sucked on him as he fingered around his hole. When Nikola bucked his hips up to get Gage to take him deeper, Gage pressed through his ring, listening to the sounds Nikola made to guide him. Gage gave him time to get used to the penetration and only started to really fuck him when he pressed back to get more.

He took Nikola as deep into his mouth as he could without gagging and sucked hard. Nikola was babbling and fighting to get more of both Gage's mouth and finger as Gage slipped in a second finger, causing Nikola to shudder. He gasped and rocked back harder for more, so Gage slammed his fingers into him, picking up the pace at the same time. It seemed the harder Gage fucked him, the more frantic Nikola got for more. He grabbed Gage's head, when his thrusts became erratic, and lost it. Gage swallowed all he gave while he put pressure on Nikola's prostate the whole time. Nikola came completely apart above Gage—heaving out huge gulping breaths that sounded like sobs.

When Nikola finally seemed as though he was calming, Gage released his dick and slowly removed his fingers. He laid his cheek on Nikola's thigh and reached down to give himself a couple of hard yanks. That's all it took to make him come over his hand, not much left in the reserves, the orgasm so intense it was almost painful. It had been a long time since he'd come three times in such a short period.

One of Nikola's hands was still buried in Gage's hair, stroking Gage's head as they came back to themselves. They lay there long enough Gage started to drift off until Nikola pulled his hair a bit to get his attention.

"I don't mean to be a douche, but you can't sleep in here."

Gage slowly sat up and was about to tell Nikola he could drive him back to the hotel for all he cared, but Nikola cut him off with an explanation that curbed Gage's anger.

"It's not that I don't want you here. I'd gladly let you sleep in my bed, but I can't let Hana see us together like this. I'll make up the couch. It's actually pretty comfortable and not lumpy. If that's okay. I'm sorry." Nikola looked as if he meant it, like he regretted having to kick Gage out of his bed.

Gage kissed him to show he understood and there were no hard feelings. "I understand, and it's not a problem. The couch will be fine." Nikola smiled in relief. He kissed Gage a little more passionately than Gage had him.

"The bathroom's across the hall if you want to get cleaned up. I'll go make up the couch for you." Nikola climbed off the bed and went to an armoire, pulled out a pair of track pants, and threw them at Gage. "They may be a little tight—you got a bigger ass than me," he noted with a playful grin.

Gage flipped him off but took the pants to the bathroom with him. After Gage washed up and put the pants on, he realized Nikola was right—they were almost obscenely tight across his ass and crotch, but he had no other option unless he wanted to sleep in his cargo pants. The track pants were snug but the fabric was more forgiving, and he'd be moderately comfortable while he slept.

Gage found Nikola sitting on the bed he'd made up in the living room. He had a small smile on his swollen lips as he used the tip of his finger to rub the bottom one. When he saw Gage, his eyes were drawn down to his crotch, and Nikola's smile turned into a sly grin.

"Fuck you, *Niky*," Gage said, unable to hide a grin of his own.

The gleam in Nikola's eyes turned wicked. "Those pants are hot on you. They're so tight I can see the head of your prick." Nikola flicked his tongue out to swipe his bottom lip and crooked a finger at Gage to get him to come closer. Nikola then made a twirling motion with his finger. Obediently, Gage turned so Nikola could see his ass in the too-tight pants.

"I told you your ass was bigger than mine." Nikola stood up and smacked Gage's ass hard. It caught Gage off guard as did the small whimper that came out of his mouth. It was something Gage thought about since Nikola threatened him with it earlier, but he hadn't imagined Nikola would actually attempt it. Nikola did it again and leaned in so Gage could feel his breath on his ear. "I told you—" *swat* "—that if you—" *swat* "—call me Niky—" *swat* "—anywhere but in—" *swat* "—the bedroom—" *swat* "—I'd spank—" *swat* "—you—" *swat*.

Gage stood there pulling harsh breaths into his lungs. His ass was stinging because Nikola didn't hold back, and Gage hadn't even tried to move out of his grasp. He didn't know what to say as he was a little embarrassed by his reaction to Nikola's little impromptu paddling session. He also wondered what it would have felt like to be bent over and naked while Nikola did it. The image it created made him blush. Gage couldn't find any words, let alone the ones to explain what he was feeling.

Nikola turned Gage to face him. "Now be a good boy, give me a kiss, and go to bed." It was like when Gage misbehaved as a child and got spanked and sent to bed early—until Nikola pulled his head down so their lips brushed. "You okay?" he asked when he pulled back a bit. Gage nodded, still at a loss for words. Nikola kissed him hard—it was a claiming kiss, like he was planting his flag and letting Gage know it. Gage kissed him back, but let Nikola have the control he clearly desired. He let Gage go. "Sleep tight, Gage. See you in the morning."

All Gage could get through his tight airway was, "Good night." Nikola left Gage in the living room as he went to use the bathroom before he went to his own bed. Even though Gage was confused by his reactions to Nikola, his body didn't let him dwell on it. Gage was out like a light seconds after his head hit the pillow.

Chapter Eight

NIKOLA WOKE UP to the smell of coffee. He stretched under his blankets, the delicious aches radiating from his body reminding him of the previous night's activities with Gage. The memories they provoked made Nikola smile. It had been a long time since he felt the way he was feeling on that particular morning. Though he did regret not getting to explore Gage's willingness to be spanked, which he'd only discovered after they'd already exhausted themselves sexually, but maybe he'd get the chance to let his dominant side out later.

The smile on Nikola's face got bigger when he heard Gage and Hana talking and laughing. He wished he could have woken up with Gage in his bed. It was hard leaving him out in the living room on the couch, but Nikola left the door to his bedroom open so he could listen to the soft snores coming from Gage as he slept.

He wanted to kick himself for being a coward. Though it was true he hadn't wanted Hana to catch them together in bed, Nikola was also afraid to let Gage in—to hold Gage or to be held by him through the night. Nikola couldn't let him in. It would most probably mean heartache for Nikola and Hana if he let her think they were more than friends. Gage would leave—of that, he was certain.

Nikola got out of bed and dressed before he went into the bathroom. Afterward, he walked into the kitchen, to find them sitting at the table next to each other with their heads bent over Gage's phone. Gage had a coffee cup, and Hana had a half-eaten bowl of cereal in front of her. They didn't look at Nikola, and after another minute of watching the tiny screen, a not very manly scream emitted from the phone. Hana giggled and Gage said, "Hey now, that wasn't that funny." But he was laughing too.

"What's so funny?" Nikola asked, then at the look on Gage's face added, "Or not so funny whatever the case may be?"

"You have to see this video. Uncle Gage is afraid of cows, and they made him run and scream, and then he falled in the mud," Hana said through her giggles.

"Oh, you be quiet and eat your breakfast, B. It wasn't a cow. It was a bull, and I wasn't afraid. I was just startled, and I didn't fall. I jumped and…" Hana was giving him a "Don't you lie; you ain't foolin' no one look," which made Gage's words trail off. "Fine, I did fall, but it was still a bull that startled me," he said with a pout, making Hana giggle again.

Nikola raised his eyebrows at Gage, but Gage just shook his head sadly, offering no explanation. "I see you found the coffee." Nikola changed the subject from Gage's humiliation caught on camera.

"Yeah, it's a good thing you have instant. I have no idea how to make that other kind. Hana was trying to tell me how, and then she offered to make it for me, but I didn't think it was a good idea to let a little kid play with the stove." Gage sipped his coffee and sent a pointed look at Nikola's daughter.

"I could do it. I watch Nana do it all the time." Hana scowled before going back to her cereal.

"Hana, you know you're not allowed to use the stove." To Nikola's surprise and Hana's delight, Gage stuck his tongue out at her. Nikola gave Gage a withering look for his childish act. "I'm not sure that you're mature enough to handle it either." Which only made Gage turn to Nikola and stick out his tongue at him.

Hana tried to hide her giggles behind her hand. "You better watch out. He may spank you for that." Gage turned bright red and sputtered something into his coffee.

Nikola went to the stove to make his own cup of coffee but also to hide the satisfied grin on his face. He had Gage's number whether or not the man knew it. "Hey, baby girl, how's your hand feeling this morning?"

"It's fine, Babo. I made Uncle Gage kiss my fingers again so they'd get better faster."

Nikola turned to look at Gage, but they were back to staring at Gage's phone. Nikola watched them and listened to Gage tell Hana about his family's farm, and every time she'd ask him who's that, he'd answer her with a name and some type of relation to him. Then after one such question Gage hesitated, and Nikola saw a look pass over his face that told him exactly who it was in the picture. Hana looked at him expectantly, and he finally answered.

"That's Lucas. He was my friend," Gage said quietly.

"Why isn't he your friend anymore? Did you guys have a fight?"

Nikola saw the pained expression on Gage's face and decided it was time to intervene. "Hana, maybe you should—" Nikola started, but Gage interrupted him.

"It wasn't a fight exactly," Gage said. "He was sad that I had to travel a lot, and he was lonely when I was gone. So he went back home to his family so that he doesn't have to be lonely any more when I'm not there."

Hana looked sad for him, and then thoughtful, before she asked, "But now when you go home, won't you be lonely because he's gone?"

Surprised by the question but not one to brush it off, Gage tried to smile. "I guess I will be kind of lonely, but it's better for him. He did what was best for him."

"I don't think he's a very good friend," Hana said.

Nikola fixed his coffee and went to take a seat at the table. When he passed behind Gage, he got a glimpse of Lucas on the screen and hated him instantly. He rubbed his hand across Gage's back before he sat down. When Gage's knee found his under the table, Nikola smiled at him and rubbed their knees together to let him know he appreciated how patient Gage was being with Hana.

"It's kind of complicated. It's adult stuff, though, so I'm not sure you'd understand," Gage said.

"Okay, do you have any more funny videos?" Nikola was surprised Hana let it drop so easily. Usually, if anyone told her she wouldn't understand, they'd just have to spend extra time explaining it to her because she wouldn't let it go. Gage poked his phone a couple of times and handed it to her.

"So, what are we doing today?" Gage turned to Nikola once Hana was busy with his phone. Their gazes locked, and Nikola couldn't help but remember the previous night. He tried to tamp down the heat rushing through his body so he could answer and not sound like he was choking on the words.

"I thought we'd go to the Vrelo Bosne. It's a park where the Bosna River starts. Then we'll drive out of town to the lake by Konjic. It's a nice drive—the lake is really long and runs quite a few kilometers along the road so it will take a while. Everything is nicer in the summer, but there's not much we can do about that." Nikola stopped babbling and looked down at his coffee cup as he found Gage's intense eye contact too much to bear.

"That sounds like fun. What's B doing today?"

"I'll leave her with my mom, why?" Nikola looked back up at Gage wondering what he was getting at, and at least with thoughts of Hana now circling his head, his body calmed down some.

"Well, if it's not a problem, if you don't mind, and maybe if she didn't have other things to do, she could come and hang out with us today." Gage sounded unsure, like he wasn't quite certain if it was okay that he was suggesting it. Maybe he figured he was overstepping the boundaries.

Nikola noticed Hana was studiously ignoring the conversation. She knew better than to get involved. When it was work, she wouldn't interfere. "Hey, Hana, do you want to go out with us today?" Nikola half hoped she'd say no—that it would be boring, but Nikola knew better as he watched the huge smile take over her face, and she started bouncing.

"Oh, thank you, Babo. I want to go." Hana was looking at Gage. He apparently knew what she wanted and bent to her to let her wrap her arms around his neck so she could kiss his cheek over and over again. Then she whispered in Gage's ear, making him laugh as she kissed him some more.

Nikola realized he'd been played. They'd most likely planned it all along. A little pang of jealousy spiked and then he chided himself for it. It was sweet that Hana had taken to Gage so instantly, but it also worried Nikola because it might mean disaster when Gage was finished with his business and was no longer in her life.

Hana finally let Gage go. He turned back to Nikola, and a shadow passed in his eyes at what he saw on Nikola's face. Gage put his hand on Nikola's knee and gave it a gentle squeeze. "You don't need to worry about everything so much."

But he didn't know. Gage couldn't really know how kids changed your life. Nikola knew every decision he made wasn't just for himself anymore. He needed to consider how it would also affect Hana, and Nikola learned even small decisions could have unexpected consequences. It wasn't just his heart he had to protect from this man who somehow managed to get past his defenses so quickly. Nikola would make sure Hana didn't come out of this experience any worse for wear.

"We should get ready to go soon, then. Did you eat anything?" Nikola asked.

"I didn't eat, but I rarely eat in the morning anyway. As long as I have my coffee, I'm usually good to go. I would like to run back to the hotel so

I can change clothes if that wouldn't be too much trouble." Gage finished his coffee and put the mug on the table.

"Yeah, we can do that. I'd offer to lend you something, but as we found out last night, you're a bit too big for my britches." Nikola laughed as Gage blushed again. Nikola noticed and was glad to see Gage already changed back into his own pants. He'd also put the couch back together and folded the blankets. He was a good houseguest.

"I'm going to go get dressed," Hana said. She handed Gage his phone and left for her room.

"Make sure you dress warm," Nikola called after her. As soon as she rounded the corner, Nikola turned to see Gage smiling after her, and the look in his eyes made Nikola want to kiss him, and then before Nikola could talk himself out of it, that's just what he did. Gage stiffened, but then he kissed Nikola back. It was soft and almost too tender, but it was also short. Gage pulled back from Nikola, breaking the kiss.

"Can't let Hana see," Gage said with a glance toward the hall. Nikola nodded and got up to clean the few dishes they'd used.

"I've got to run up to my mom's to tell her that I'm taking Hana with me. I'll be back in a minute, okay?" Gage nodded, distracted by his phone at the moment.

Nikola went to his mom's and endured the look she was giving him long enough to tell her she didn't have to watch Hana until after supper. He knew she was unhappy that Gage had obviously spent the night downstairs. Nikola told himself he was a grown man and didn't need to explain anything to her, but it still hurt to know how she felt.

When Nikola got back downstairs, they were waiting for him with their coats and shoes on, eager to get going. Grabbing his own coat, Nikola lead the way to the car. When they stopped at the hotel, Gage got out to go to his room alone leaving Hana and Nikola to wait for him.

"Babo, did you and Uncle Gage kiss last night?" Hana asked out of the blue.

"Why would you ask that?"

"I don't know. I think he likes you."

"Why do you think he likes me?"

"Because he smiles at you," she said with one of her own splitting her face.

"He smiles at you, so does that mean he likes you too?" Her smile was contagious, and Nikola's face mirrored hers.

"He does. I can tell, and I like him too. He's really funny and nice. Do you like him?"

"I like him well enough, I guess," Nikola admitted.

"That's good." She sat back in her seat and that seemed to be the end of it.

They listened to the radio and waited until Gage came out of the hotel doors. Gage was wearing the same fitted coat he'd worn the day before, and he looked good in it. Nikola's eyes were drawn downward as Gage took the steps. The faded jeans he wore clung to his powerful legs, and for some reason, Nikola imagined Gage looked like the man he should be, instead of the stuffy businessman he pretended to be. The jeans were well worn and tighter than anything Nikola had seen him in so far—excluding Nikola's own sweatpants. Nikola couldn't wait to see Gage's ass in them, or to peel them off, if he was being honest with himself.

Gage got in the car. "Sorry it took so long. I couldn't resist hopping in the shower for a quick rinse off."

"That's fine. We didn't mind waiting," Nikola assured him.

Nikola could smell the cologne Gage put on, and if Hana hadn't been in the car, he'd have leaned in to get a good lungful of Gage's scent. It was like it enhanced Gage's natural smell—one Nikola remembered fully from the previous night. If Nikola wasn't careful, he might get addicted to it. Gage hadn't shaved and his stubble was darker than his dirty-blond hair. Again, it was something that made him look edgier and sexier. Nikola was starting to think he should have left Hana at home so he and Gage could have just gone up to the hotel room and spent the day in bed. Nikola couldn't remember being so horny since he'd been a teenager.

As Nikola pulled out of the parking lot, he enjoyed listening to Gage and Hana talk about all kinds of things. It seemed they never ran out of topics of conversation. Nikola also enjoyed Gage's reaction to his driving. The way Gage gasped and grabbed the door handle kept Nikola entertained, even though he was mostly left out of their conversation. Nikola would reach over and pat Gage's knee after many of his near misses. It didn't seem to ease Gage any and his white-knuckled grip never let up, even as he kept up his end of the back and forth with Hana.

When they got to the park, Hana grabbed one of each of the men's hands. Nikola got the one with the broken fingers, so he held it gently. Hana walked between them for a bit until Gage picked her up and put her on his shoulders. Nikola was glad he did because then he could walk closer to Gage. Every once in a while, when Nikola's hand would brush Gage's, he'd give it a gentle squeeze. It was always quick and not when anyone was around, but it still made Nikola's breath catch each time. Of course, there weren't many people in the park. It was the off-season, so mostly it was local people who were heading to the restaurant for coffee or an early lunch.

After they'd watched the swans in one of the ponds and taken some pictures with Gage's phone, they went into the restaurant to have lunch. Hana was full of questions as usual. Gage didn't mention Lucas when Hana questioned him about his family and friends. She seemed to want to know everything there was to know about the man. Nikola gave Gage more than one apologetic look during the inquisition. He was being a good sport, though, and just shrugged at Nikola and answered Hana's questions. By the time they were finished with lunch, Nikola had an edited version of Gage's life history.

On the way to Konjic, Hana, thankfully, fell asleep. Nikola took a chance and put his hand on Gage's thigh, and Gage promptly covered it with his own. He gave a quick squeeze and then made lazy circles on the back of Nikola's hand with his thumb. It was comfortable, but Nikola told himself to keep his distance even as he tried to get closer to the man next to him, reminding himself it was only a hookup and destined to be a short one at that.

"So how's your idea working out for you?" Nikola asked, breaking the comfortable silence that had descended on the car with Hana's nap.

"Hmm, what?" Gage asked clearly confused.

"It was your idea to bring her with us. How's it working for you?"

"I'm actually enjoying her company," Gage said with a fond smile. "She sure is full of questions though. It reminded me of when I met Lucas's mother." Gage looked like he hadn't meant to mention his ex's name, but he realized it was too late to take it back. Nikola gave his thigh a squeeze, and Gage smiled back.

"I'm sorry if she's bugging you by wanting to know everything about you. She's just naturally curious, and even though she's been in America a couple of times that she can remember, it's still exotic to her. You know what it's like, when you meet someone who's different or from somewhere different, you want to hear about what it's like to be that person." Nikola was babbling, but he felt like Gage didn't want to talk about his ex, so he was directing the conversation away from it. Nikola didn't like to feel like he needed to make an excuse for his child's insatiable curiosity, but it seemed to be a safe course to take.

"It's fine. She's great. I love kids, and usually they love me," Gage said, to Nikola's surprise.

"I thought you didn't want kids." Nikola blurted the words out before he could stop himself.

"What makes you think that?"

"Well you ah...told me that you and your ex broke up because you didn't want kids."

"Oh, I guess I don't remember saying that. It's not that I don't want kids." Gage paused as if he needed a moment to think about what he was going to say before he elaborated. "To tell you the truth, I've never really been in love with anyone enough to consider that type of a commitment. And the more I think of it, the clearer it gets that being with Lucas and not loving him probably made my decision not to have kids with him the right choice. But now, not having the pressure Lucas put on me to start a family, I realize not wanting kids with him is not the same as not ever wanting them. With the right guy, I could see myself having a couple of kids." Gage looked away, maybe embarrassed about oversharing with someone he barely knew. Nikola wasn't sure.

"So, you weren't in love with Lucas?" Nikola could have kicked himself as soon as the words left his mouth. "I'm sorry. That's too personal, you don't have to answer. Just forget I asked." Nikola couldn't judge the expression on Gage's face as he wouldn't look at Nikola, and he didn't answer the question.

"No, I wasn't in love with him. At first, I thought I might be, but now I feel bad about leading him on for so many years, but it was easy to be with him and not have to think about being alone." Then, Gage pulled a Hana and completely changed the subject. "How often do you go to visit your ex?" He was watching the scenery go by, not looking at Nikola.

"I usually go every couple of years, but the last two years I've been back four times—twice alone and twice with Hana." Nikola answered, feeling it was only fair since Gage already shared a lot about his life, even if he'd been sort of pushed into doing it by Hana. Nikola still knew way more about Gage than Gage knew about him, and answering a couple of questions about his own life wouldn't hurt him any.

"You've been back and forth almost as much as I have, and that's got to get expensive. Your uncle must pay well." There was something in

Gage's voice Nikola couldn't place, and his thumb stopped brushing Nikola's hand.

"Well, actually, Garrett bought the tickets. He seems to know when I'm starting to get antsy and need to get out of here. He's been kind of my lifeline, you know?" Nikola wasn't exactly proud of the fact that Garrett footed the bill for him to go and get his fill of fucking him, but Nikola didn't want to lie to Gage either. It was better if Gage knew just what kind of relationship Nikola had with his ex. "I guess he thinks it's worth the price of the tickets to see me and Hana." Nikola winked to try to lighten the mood.

Gage chuckled, but it sounded forced to Nikola. "I'm picturing this Garrett as some guy even older than I am—you know, like a silver fox. A man who's got kept men all around the world. He's sitting at his big desk in a skyscraper in New York, and he's planning his schedule for when he flies in one of his boys. Telling you he loves you to keep you coming back to him." Gage said. He turned to look at Nikola. "Tell me I'm off the mark there, and you're not just some piece of ass to him."

Nikola could hear the sadness in Gage's tone when he'd said that last sentence, like it hurt Gage to think of Nikola as someone's play thing but it didn't soften the sting of the words themselves. Nikola pulled his hand out of Gage's and off his leg. Gage was way off the mark, and he'd made Nikola angry, no matter how he'd sounded. Who was Gage to judge? What was Nikola to him except a convenient piece of ass?

"You're so off the mark it would be funny if it wasn't so insulting," Nikola spat at him. It came out much harsher than Nikola intended, and immediately he wanted to take the words back or at least make them come out differently. Gage's posture went from relaxed to stiff and on guard.

"I'm sorry. I didn't mean it that way."

That just seemed to fuel the anger inside Nikola because what way had he meant it? He'd basically just called Nikola a rent boy and he was sure letting Gage into his bed last night after knowing him for a whole day spoke volumes as to Nikola's moral character to a man like Gage. When he was younger, he'd thought nothing of taking someone he'd just met into the backroom for a quickie, so why should falling into bed with Gage so quickly bother him all of a sudden? *Because you care what he thinks about you, and you don't want him to think that you're easy and just another piece of ass,* Nikola's stupid brain supplied the answer for him.

Nikola realized Gage was watching him, waiting for him to say something either to ease Gage's rigidness or maybe for Nikola to tell him to go to hell. "It's not like that. Garrett's in love with me. Like I told you, I just can't love him in the same way." Nikola didn't feel up to defending his choices to a man who seemed to have already passed judgment on the subject.

Gage didn't lose his rigidness, but he nodded, and then there was silence. Nikola didn't know what to say to smooth things over, and Gage didn't seem too eager to make amends either. Maybe it was better that they both just shut up before they could do anymore damage.

Hana woke up when they pulled over so Gage could take a few scenic pictures of the river in Konjic. She was quiet as she studied them, and then when everyone got back in the car to head back to Sarajevo, she asked, "Why are you fighting?"

Gage raised an eyebrow in Nikola's direction and then looked out the window. Nikola guessed it was his job to explain to her why they were suddenly so awkward with each other. "We're not fighting. We just had a disagreement. It's no big deal," Nikola said, the last part aimed at Gage in the hopes that Gage would understand he was willing to let it go if Gage was.

Hana looked back and forth between them before poking Gage in the shoulder. He turned to look at her and gave her a smile that probably even she could tell was forced. "We really aren't fighting, B. It was just a misunderstanding. Sometimes I can be kind of a doofus." This time when Gage grinned, it was genuine, and Hana giggled at him as he made a face as if to prove he was indeed a doofus.

They resumed their earlier banter and soon Gage was questioning Hana. When they hit the topic of boys she liked, she made a face and declared that all the boys were yucky, and she was never getting married. Gage found this funny and tried to convince her that eventually she'd like a boy enough that she'd get all swoony over him, and they'd get married and have at least five kids who would call Nikola Grandpa Niky. They laughed, but when Gage caught Nikola's eye, he gave Gage his best you're-asking-for-it look. Gage's eyes flashed with what Nikola hoped was lust because, even after all was said and done, Nikola still wanted to get Gage into another bed.

They hit the Sarajevo city limits just in time to find a restaurant for supper. As they were having their after-dinner coffees, Nikola said,

"We'll go drop Hana off with my mom, and I can take you back to the hotel." He tried to convey his message to Gage through a meaningful look, hoping Gage would see he was trying to tell him all the stuff they'd said earlier wasn't going to stop him from getting back into bed with him.

"You don't have to go out of your way to drop Hana off. You can just drop me at the hotel. I'm pretty tired and don't think I'll need anything tonight that I can't handle myself through room service." When he saw the look on Nikola's face, he quickly added, "I'm sure tomorrow's going to be a long day with the party and all. I need a good night's sleep so that I'm on my game tomorrow night."

Nikola couldn't hide his disappointment. "Okay. I guess that's probably for the best anyway." That was it. Gage had blown him off. After having his one night of fun, he didn't want Nikola anymore. He'd made himself clear, and Nikola would respect Gage's decision even if it hurt more than he wanted to admit. Nikola rolled his eyes, feeling stupid. What had he expected anyway? He guessed after all the hand holding and long looks, he hadn't expected to get kicked to the curb quite so quickly even after their little disagreement.

Hana watched silently, but Nikola could tell she felt the tension between them. He kept hoping she'd do or say something that would defuse it, but Hana just let them stew in their own mess to do whatever damage they'd do to themselves.

When they parked in front of the hotel, Gage turned to give Hana an awkward hug between the bucket seats and then clapped Nikola on the shoulder. "I have some work to do tomorrow, so what time should I be ready for the party?"

So there it was—not only did Gage not want Nikola in his bed, but he was going to distance himself even more by only seeing Nikola when business was involved. The spiteful side of Nikola wondered if Garrett would want some houseguests—like tomorrow. Then Nikola reminded the childish part of himself that he'd only known Gage for two days. They'd had a little fun, and that was all this was, and maybe if Nikola was lucky, Gage might want to do it again at some point. Maybe after a few days he'd need some companionship again.

Nikola plastered a fake smile on his face. "The party starts at eight, but we can arrive any time after that. It's just upstairs in the restaurant where we ate supper the other night. So, I'll pick you up around then if that's okay."

"That sounds good." Gage's eyes darted about Nikola's face as if he couldn't bring himself to make eye contact before he turned to Hana. "Hey, B, you be good till I see you again." He finally looked Nikola in the eyes for a moment. Gage looked he was trying to work up the courage to say something more but decided against it. "Good night, Niky." He was out of the car before Nikola could even say good night back to him. Nikola watched until Gage disappeared into the hotel.

Hana put her hand on his arm. "It's okay, Babo. He still likes you." Nikola nodded and drove home.

Chapter Nine

GAGE CLOSED HIS hotel room door before sagging back against it with a sigh. He'd fucked up, and he knew it. With no idea how to fix what he'd wrought, he shucked his shoes and coat before sitting on the couch to think about why everything with Nikola was so difficult. Finding out Nikola had a sugar daddy in the states pissed Gage off more than he had any right to let it. If Nikola was interested in more with the guy, Gage was sure he'd have gone back to stay instead of just visiting when he needed a release. Gage hung his head. He regretted making Nikola's relationship sound sleazy, but at the time, that was how he'd wanted to see it to justify his own recent behavior.

Gage thought for a moment and dug deeper into what had turned his curiosity about Nikola's life into a burning need to make Nikola feel ashamed. The answer blindsided him. He'd been jealous. Nikola didn't hide his relationship with "Uncle" Garrett from Hana, while he had taken great pains the previous night to hide the fact that Gage had been in his bed. On some level, Gage knew it was stupid of him to compare himself to Garrett. Garrett had been around for a lot longer than Gage's measly two days. Gage massaged his temples—Goddamn it to hell—he had no idea where the fucking jealousy was coming from. He'd never felt so possessive of anyone, let alone someone who was practically a stranger, and he didn't like the feeling at all.

As if the world couldn't help kicking Gage when he was down, his phone chose that moment to buzz with an email from JJ. He hit the necessary buttons to open it. JJ had sent him a quick note to let Gage know Lucas had called JJ to let him know he was driving back to the cities in the morning. Lucas had wanted to make sure someone would be able to pick up the mail and check in on the condo every once in a while until Gage returned. JJ assured Gage in the email that he would pick up the mail and water the nonexistent houseplants. JJ ended the email with an invitation to call if Gage needed someone to talk to. Great.

What a wonderful end to such a wonderful fucking day. Gage dialed JJ's number and waited for him to answer.

"Hey, Gage, how's Sarajevo?" JJ asked as soon as he picked up.

"It's good. I got your email. So, he really left, huh?" Even though he'd known Lucas hadn't been fooling around about leaving, a little part of him thought he might change his mind. Gage was relieved Lucas hadn't stayed. The more time that passed, the more he knew the breakup was for the best because it was long overdue.

"Yeah, man, he told me that he just packed up a few clothes and would be back for the rest sometime before you come home."

"Well, I guess that's for the best. We really didn't need to have a long, drawn-out fight about it anyway."

"He's kind of a prick to do this to you when you have to be halfway around the world from any kind of support system. He could have at least had the decency to wait until after your trip to do this. How are you handling it? Are you all right?"

Gage couldn't help but feel touched at the concern he heard from his cousin. "I'm fine, really. Did you tell anyone yet that he left me?"

"Well, yeah, I told Vicky, and of course, she told my mom, so then I had to tell your mom before she heard it from my dad. You know how it is. So yeah, pretty much everyone knows by now." JJ sounded a bit bemused, but it didn't surprise Gage. JJ's wife couldn't keep a secret to save her life, and it was inevitable that it would only pick up speed once the family grapevine was involved.

"So, do I even want to know what they're saying?"

JJ laughed. "No, Gage, you really don't."

Gage could just imagine. It really sucked when your family liked your boyfriend better than they liked you. "Should I just stay here and apply for residency?" Gage asked, only half-jokingly.

"It's not that bad. Most of the womenfolk hate your guts for running him off, but I think that most of the guys don't give two shits either way. Just make sure the next one you bring home is as big of an asshole as you, and then we won't have this problem again."

Gage wondered what his family would make of Nikola and knew they'd all flip a shit over Hana—who wouldn't? Gage pushed the idea out of his mind since there was no way that would ever even be a possibility. "Well, I guess as long as no one will be giving me the stink eye during sports center, I'll live."

"So, how are things going over there? What's that Nedim guy like?" JJ deftly changed the subject before things got too heavy.

"I haven't actually met him yet. I've been playing tourist with his nephew so far." The flush of warmth that ran through Gage at just the mention of Nikola surprised him.

Gage suddenly wished JJ was the kind of guy he could talk to about what happened between him and Nikola, but he knew JJ wouldn't be able to offer him any advice on the matter. He'd be more likely to tell Gage to keep it in his pants and do the job. The brief notion of calling his friend Matt crossed his mind, but he pushed it away. There'd be plenty of time to let his friends bitch him out about falling into bed with another man so quickly when he got home.

"Sounds like fun. So what do you think about Sarajevo?"

"Loving Sarajevo so far, though every time I get in a car, I feel like I'm gambling with my life. You would not believe the way they drive here. I don't think there are any traffic laws, or if there are, nobody follows them." There was no way Gage was going to give up the chance to whine about it to someone who would take him seriously, unlike Nikola, who seemed to think Gage was just overreacting.

"You should take some video. It may come in handy if you want to ask for a raise." JJ chuckled.

"Yeah right, like that would happen. As far as the business goes, I do think that there's potential here. They have the infrastructure, and there's a demand for heavy equipment rental since they're building a highway." Gage moved on since he obviously wasn't going to get any sympathy from JJ either.

"Good, glad to hear that. The old guys will be happy when you send in your progress report then."

"So anything else going on over there?" Gage didn't care, but talking to JJ was helping his frame of mind tremendously. JJ reminded Gage there were other things he needed to think about besides the weird feelings he was having for a certain Bosnian.

"Nope, nothing of note." JJ paused for a second to listen to something in the background that Gage couldn't make out. "Hey, I gotta get going. We're going shopping. Vicky volunteered us to help with the New Year's party this year. You can call me anytime though if you need to, you know that, right?"

"Yeah, sure, I know. Give everyone a hug and kiss for me, and let them know everything is going fine here. I'll talk to you later."

"Will do. Talk to you later." JJ hung up.

Gage felt a little better, but it took exactly two minutes for his thoughts to go straight back to Nikola. He tried to distract himself, first with the TV, and when that failed, he checked his emails. When that didn't hold his attention, he checked out the happenings on Facebook. When he couldn't stand one more cutesy post about crap he didn't care about, he slammed his laptop shut.

Gage realized he couldn't stand being in the hotel room for even one more minute. That's when he remembered the hotel had a full gym with a pool. He decided it might not be a bad idea to work off some of the stress of the day. He changed into his workout clothes, went down to sign into the gym with his room number, and got to work.

Gage didn't pay much attention to the other people in the gym, preferring to keep to himself for the night. After a particularly punishing run on the treadmill to get himself warmed up, he looked around while toweling the sweat from his face and neck. There were only a couple of other guys working out. Gage noticed one of the men kept trying to catch his eye, and when he did, he smiled in an all too familiar way at Gage. It was one of those smiles that was an invitation to start some small talk that would turn to flirting and eventually to more in one of their rooms if both were so inclined. Gage smiled back before he could stop himself.

The man in question was definitely Gage's type—well, he was before Gage met Nikola. He was slender and shorter than Gage by probably close to a foot. He was young, maybe twenty-five if he was lucky, blond and pretty, the kind of guy Gage usually went for. Gage sighed as he lifted the heavy weights to take his mind off what his body was trying to tell him would be a good idea.

The young man worked his way toward Gage until he was exercising his legs on the machine next to Gage's. He didn't say anything at first, just kept doing his workout. Gage was doing bench presses on one of those machines most hotels had instead of free weights. He guessed the insurance was cheaper since even an idiot couldn't get hurt using the thing. Gage was pushing one hundred and twenty kilos for the fifth time when the guy finally said something.

"You are very strong, no?" His words were heavily accented. Gage grunted as he pushed the bar up again but didn't answer, hoping maybe the guy would go away if he thought Gage didn't understand him. "I know you understand me. I saw you in the restaurant, and you were speaking English." His amused expression made Gage's brief impulse to pretend he couldn't speak English seem childish. "You and your date made quite the handsome couple. All the eyes in the restaurant were on the two of you. Is he waiting for you in your room?" He flashed Gage a flirty smile.

Gage let go of the bar and sat up to give him an appraising look. "He wasn't my date, and I'm staying here alone." Judging by the man's expression, Gage just told him what he'd wanted to hear.

The guy upped the wattage on his smile before he stopped doing leg presses and turned to face Gage. "So are you looking for some company tonight then?" he asked getting straight to the point.

Gage was tempted for all of about a minute. The problem was that every time he tried to picture how the evening would go, with this slight young man pinned underneath him, his mind would replace him with the bigger presence of Nikola. It was also out of character for Gage to have two different men in his bed on two consecutive nights. He just wasn't a player. It wasn't something Gage could do and still look at himself in the mirror in the morning. Adding to that, he was certain if he did take the young guy back to his room, he wouldn't be able to face Nikola. The last thought was what made up Gage's mind.

"Sorry, not really up for company tonight."

"Well, I'll be here for the next week. If you feel up for anything at any time, let me know." With a sly smile, he got up, and Gage watched as the guy made his way to the locker room. Instead of following him, Gage went back to his room to shower, thinking it was better to not tempt fate.

The workout hadn't done a very good job of relieving Gage's stress, so he got dressed and made his way up to the bar in the restaurant where he and Nikola had eaten, looking for something to help him sleep. His hand itched with the need to call Nikola. Maybe he'd want to join him at the bar, but then he remembered the hurt look on Nikola's face when he'd told him he didn't want him to come to the hotel. Gage ordered a double and downed it in one go before ordering another.

Gage took his time with the second drink, but still, the glass emptied quicker than he figured it should have. The bartender didn't give Gage time to order another before one was sitting there for him. He nodded in thanks and got a tip of the head in response. Gage was looking into his glass, thinking he should lighten up on the booze, when the stool beside him was filled by his gym stalker. He was dressed in skintight everything, and was looking exceptionally fuckable, which was probably the point.

"Fancy meeting you here," he said after he ordered vodka on the rocks. Gage could almost feel the press on his skin as the guy's eyes ran over his body. He sipped his drink to try to damp down the fire in his gut. He was getting the feeling he was going to get fucked one way or the other whether he wanted it or not.

"Just needed something to help me sleep. I'm still jet-lagged." Gage made an excuse for his presence in the bar without knowing why he felt the need to.

"Ah yes, coming from America is much different than the little hop from Austria, no time difference for me," he said with a shrug. "What kind of business are you in?"

"How do you know I'm not here on vacation?" Gage's lip quirked, letting the guy know he might be pulling his leg.

He laughed heartily. "Because Americans don't come to Bosnia unless they're forced. Now if we were standing in St. Peter's Square, I'd ask you if you'd been to see the Spanish Stairs yet—not what type of business you were in." He took a sip of his drink and made a show out of licking his lips when he put the glass down.

Gage let out a chuckle he couldn't contain at the guy's adept assessment of the situation. He was right. Sarajevo wasn't a vacation hotspot for most Americans. When Gage mentioned to people where he traveled for business, more often than not, they'd ask if it was safe over there.

"Heavy equipment. How about you? You here on vacation?"

"Business for me too. I'm helping to set up some computer systems for my company. I have a couple of days off for the holiday though. I thought about going home, but it wasn't worth the trouble, and now I'm glad I didn't." His eyes once again traveled over Gage. "Do you have plans for ringing in the New Year?"

"I have a business engagement tomorrow night." He tried to sound a little disappointed for the other guy's benefit, but deep down, he was glad he would be busy. Gage gratefully accepted the refill the bartender set in front of him. He raised it to his lips, but before he could take a drink, his phone chimed, letting him know he had a text message. Gage set his drink back on the bar and looked apologetically at his drinking companion before he pulled out the phone to check it.

It was from Nikola: *I'm in your room. Where are you?*

Shit, Gage hadn't expected Nikola to show up after their fight. He looked up from his phone to his new buddy to find a smirk on the guy's face. Gage forgot to hide his reaction, and the guy picked up on the fact that whatever was in the text had surprised Gage.

"Not good news, I take it?" he asked.

"No, it's just that guy from the other night showed up unexpectedly. He's downstairs wondering where I am."

"Oh, well then, it's a good surprise I suppose." He winked.

Gage smiled in return but then was perplexed as to why the guy's expression turned first to one of surprise and then to what could only be described as fear in a second as he looked over Gage's shoulder. Gage turned to see what put the expression on his face, and Nikola's chest filled his vision, so he tilted his head back to look up at him. Nikola was obviously angry—very angry if the flared nostrils were any indication.

"What are you doing here?" Gage asked.

"I was just about to ask you the same damn question." Nikola looked over Gage's company with a sneer.

The Austrian—god, Gage realized he didn't even know the guy's name—put out his hand. "Hi, I'm Henrick." Nikola gave him a withering glare but shook his hand quickly.

"Nikola," he said curtly before he turned his attention back to Gage. "We need to talk."

Gage didn't like the tone Nikola was using or the possessive vibe he was giving off. But then he reminded himself just a few hours earlier he'd been struggling with his own bit of possessiveness and decided to cut Nikola a break. He turned, grabbed his drink, and tipped it in a go-on gesture before draining it, trying to be cool in the face of Nikola's anger.

Nikola wasn't willing to play along with the act though. He took the glass out of Gage's hand and slammed it down on the bar before grabbing Gage's arm and pulling him off the barstool. Gage stood there, a little unsteady on his feet at being yanked to standing, but not trying to get out of Nikola's tight grasp, which sent a flare of warmth through him.

"It was nice to meet you." Nikola's gruff words made it clear that it was in no way nice to meet Henrick. Nikola turned them abruptly and pulled Gage to the elevator before he could even say good night. He did hear Henrick snort and say, "Have fun, boys," at their retreating backs.

Nikola pushed Gage into the elevator, jabbed the button for Gage's floor, and then stood there silently staring at the mirrored doors as though they'd offended him in some grievous way. His grip on Gage's bicep was just short of painful.

"You want to tell—" Gage started, but Nikola cut him off.

"We'll talk when we get in your room," he growled.

When the doors opened, he led Gage to his door. Nikola used a key card—one Gage hadn't given him—to let them into the room. He didn't get a chance to ask where Nikola got it because he prodded Gage toward the bedroom. Gage put up a little resistance but realized the bedroom was just where he wanted to be. He was so fucking hard, had been since Nikola pulled him off the stool in the bar.

But he was pissed too, which confused him. Why Nikola's rough treatment was making Gage angry but turning him on at the same time made him want to fight back. He managed to slow their progress a little and was about to start laying into Nikola, but the look in the other man's eyes made his words stick in his throat. Gage had never seen a look that scarily intense in his life. He'd wait to hear what Nikola would say before he told him how much he didn't appreciate the macho, he-man bullshit Nikola was pulling on him.

"Strip," Nikola ordered. That hadn't been what Gage expected to come from Nikola's mouth. He stood there frozen, for a second, before he opened his mouth to protest, but Nikola stepped into him and grabbed his right wrist. Nikola used his grip to turn Gage and pulled his arm up between their bodies. He covered Gage's mouth with his other hand and growled into his ear, "You will do as I say, and you won't question me. No more talking."

The threat in Nikola's statement was clear, but instead of dampening his arousal, it only fueled it. Nodding so that Nikola would release him, Gage took a deep breath and kicked off his shoes. Knowing he wasn't in any real danger from Nikola, he wanted to see where this was leading.

Chapter Ten

NIKOLA WATCHED GAGE as he slowly undressed before him, but his mind was wild with everything that had led them to this moment. Nikola stewed at home until he couldn't take it any longer. The entire drive to the hotel was spent with Nikola trying to tell himself he was being stupid; no one had such strong feelings as he was having after just meeting someone. Garrett and his love-at-first-sight bullshit was banging around Nikola's head. Fuck that. He was just having a bout of extreme lust brought on by his lack of available partners. Nikola decided whether it was lust or something more didn't matter. He couldn't just let Gage walk away from him without a fight.

Nikola planned out what he was going to tell Gage. He'd tell the other man he was okay fine with just fucking for as long as Gage wanted it. If it ended when Gage went home, that was fine, but he needed to give Nikola a chance to be with him while he could. Nikola knew he was pathetic, but he just wanted Gage to fuck him for a month. It would be a month of heavenly bliss, and Nikola wanted it desperately.

All Nikola's well-thought-out points on how it would benefit Gage to have someone to relieve the tension of doing business with Nedim flew from his mind when Gage didn't answer his knock. Upon using his ill-gotten key card to let himself in and finding Gage's room empty, Nikola almost lost it. His heart was slamming into his rib cage as he sent off a text to his errant charge. When Gage didn't immediately answer, Nikola wondered, *where would I go if I didn't want to sit in the room alone all night?*

The memory of Gage telling him how he needed a lot of alcohol to drown his sorrows came back to Nikola, and it suddenly hit him. Gage was bellied up to the bar in the restaurant—no surprise—but Nikola's anger bubbled to the surface when his eyes took in the man sitting next to Gage. Nikola wanted to pound the little fucker so badly that he could already feel his hand swelling from the hit, but the fear on the guy's face stopped him short. The confusion on Gage's face turned Nikola's rage back where it belonged. Nikola wasn't proud of how he manhandled Gage out of the bar and into his room, but he couldn't control his need to dominate the man. Nikola was the one in control, and Gage wouldn't forget that anytime soon.

Nikola was pulled out of his reverie when Gage let out a nervous little cough. He was standing there in only his boxers. Gage's flesh was pink. Nikola couldn't be sure what caused it—embarrassment or the alcohol— but it made him look unbearably sexy. Gage's trembling hands were poised at the waistband of his boxers, but Nikola could tell he'd need some encouragement to take them off, even though his arousal was apparent through the thin fabric straining to contain it.

"Take them off. If I have to do it for you, you'll be sorry," Nikola growled menacingly.

A flicker of an unidentifiable emotion passed over Gage's face as he obeyed the order. He pulled the elastic out and over his erection and slid them down his legs. His big cock was rigid and reaching out to Nikola, showing definite proof of his arousal. It took all of Nikola's willpower to not fall to his knees and worship the perfect specimen before him.

"Turn around and put your hands on the bed," Nikola commanded before he lost control of his baser desires.

Gage only hesitated for a couple of seconds, many emotions crossing his face before he did as Nikola instructed.

"Spread your legs a bit." Nikola was calmer now that he knew Gage was going to play nice. He moved his feet out just a little. "More. Don't make me do it for you." Nikola used the threat that worked like a charm earlier, and Gage spread them a little further than shoulder-width with no hesitation. "Good, now don't move unless I tell you to." Gage nodded and held the position.

Nikola toed off his shoes and socks, and then he paced back and forth as he tried to calm himself even further. As Nikola walked up behind him, Gage's muscles all tensed at once in anticipation of the unknown. Nikola ran his hand down Gage's flank and rubbed him as if he were gentling a skittish horse. Gage relaxed a bit then, but Nikola could tell the man was apprehensive at not knowing what Nikola was going to do. Nikola wondered what Gage expected to happen—did he think Nikola would try to fuck him? Nikola hoped Gage wouldn't think he was the kind of man who would push another man to do something against his will.

Nikola wanted to tell Gage he was safe in his hands, and even though he was angry, Nikola would never do anything to hurt him. He couldn't get the reassuring words to cross his lips. Gage had hurt him in a way no stranger should have been able to. Nikola couldn't explain his feelings—didn't even want to try—but he knew Gage needed to understand that Nikola wanted him, and he didn't like to share with pretty little men.

Nikola continued caressing Gage's back and his ass all the while admiring the bulging muscles. Gage's ass clenched when Nikola teased a finger down his crease. Nikola moved down to grab Gage's balls in one hand, and then fondling Gage, he watched the precome drip onto the bedspread. However nervous Gage was, it appeared he was also as turned on as Nikola. He pressed a soft kiss to the small of Gage's back, feeling the shiver that ran through the other man at the faint touch.

"You have a great ass, and I can't wait to taste it," Nikola murmured. Gage shuddered under Nikola's hands. "But before I can do that, I think you need to take your punishment."

"Wha—?"

Nikola slapped Gage's ass, not hard, but enough to cut off anything he wanted to say. Gage's breath caught and held.

"Breathe. You need to breathe, Gage." Nikola reminded Gage when it seemed he'd forgotten breathing was a vital function.

Gage gasped in a harsh breath. "Why are you doing this?" he asked so quickly Nikola didn't have time to stop him.

"At first, I wanted to punish you for running away from me. Then I wanted to hit you for that little twink in the bar. Now—fuck—now I just want to spank you because you're so fucking beautiful all spread out like that. I can't even think straight..." Nikola stopped to take a few slow, calming breaths and to let sanity return to his jumbled mind. "Which is why I have to stop this right here. It's not right for me to do this with you when you didn't consent to have it done," Nikola said when the reality of what he'd almost done hit him full force. "Shit! Fuck! Goddamn it!" Nikola couldn't stop the sexpletives from rolling off his tongue. "Get up and get dressed so we can talk." All his anger at Gage was gone, only to be replaced by an even more intense anger directed at himself.

Gage shook his head and stayed the way Nikola told him to. "No."

"What do you mean, no?"

"No, I won't get dressed so we can talk." Gage's voice quivered with pent-up sexual tension.

"Fine. I'll leave if that's what you want," Nikola said dejectedly.

"No!" Gage turned to glare at Nikola.

"Gage, I don't understand what you want from me, and to tell you the truth I'm too emotionally drained to try to figure it out right now."

"Do what you need to do. I consent to whatever it was you were planning to do," Gage said quietly, turning to face the bed once more.

Nikola stood stock-still. He wasn't sure he'd heard Gage correctly. His lust-addled brain wasn't above twisting the other man's words to his own desires. "You don't know what you're asking for," Nikola whispered.

"You're right. I don't, but I want you to...do something, anything to make me feel something other than what I feel right now."

"How do you feel, Gage?"

"Empty," Gage said in a voice so lost Nikola's knees almost buckled at the sound.

"Okay." Nikola pulled his shirt over his head and tried to get back into the mental space he'd need to play this thing he'd started to the end.

"Nikola..."

Nikola's hand came down on Gage's ass in a sharp, stinging slap. "No more talking. That's one of the rules, and for each rule you break, you'll get a set amount of spankings." Gage groaned at Nikola's words. "I'm going to tell you two words now, and you need to remember them. Do you think you can do that?" Gage nodded again. "Okay, if you need me to slow down, you say yellow. If you need me to stop, you say red. You have permission to speak, so you can repeat what I just said so I know you understand."

"I understand. Yellow slow down, red stop," Gage repeated.

"Good, now we're going to go over all the rules you broke today and how you can avoid doing that in the future." Gage opened his mouth as if to say something, but Nikola stopped him short with another stinging blow to his backside. "The no-talking rule is in effect again until I say otherwise, or if you need to say your safe words." Gage nodded his understanding once again.

"Okay, then. You're a smart guy, so I'm assuming you've heard the phrase, ignorance of the law is no defense? Well that holds true in this case, but since I'm such a nice guy, I'm willing to show you a little leniency, but you're not going to get a full pardon," Nikola explained as he rubbed Gage's ass.

"I'll explain the rules to you as I mete out your punishment. I think you can handle ten but you have your safewords and I expect you to use them if you need to. If you have any questions, you can ask them after. If you behave, I might even answer them for you. Now be a good boy, and if you understand, nod your head for me." Gage nodded and then let his head hang between his shoulders. Nikola could feel a little of his equilibrium returning now that he knew Gage was a willing participant.

"Good," Nikola said just as he landed his first real blow across Gage's left cheek, but it was still just a small fraction of the power Nikola could have used. He intended to make a point with the spanking, but since it was their first time together, he didn't want to overdo it. Gage swayed a bit and whimpered as Nikola smacked his right cheek. "Those are for the first time you called me Niky today." Nikola gave him two more rapid slaps, alternating cheeks, and then stopped to rub Gage's ass, which was pinking up nicely. "I told you, if you called me that outside of the bedroom, I'd spank you, so the last two were for the second time you said it today."

Gage was rocking his hips, and his breathing was coming in harsh little pants. His back was almost as flushed as his ass. Nikola gave him one more. "That was for sticking your tongue out at me. I believe you were informed of the consequences after the fact for that one." Nikola stopped to unbutton his jeans with a hand that was tingling from administering the swats to Gage's perfect ass. The zipper pressed uncomfortably against his engorged prick, so he reached in and adjusted himself quickly, wanting to get back to the business at hand.

Once again, he smoothed his hand over the heated flesh of Gage's ass. "Gage, are you doing okay?" Gage nodded. "I need to know that you remember and have the ability to use your safewords before I go on, so tell me again what they are."

Gage sighed. For a moment, Nikola thought he was going to be difficult and not answer. When he did, his tone conveyed his annoyance. "Yellow slow, red stop. I'm not stupid."

"Didn't say you were." Nikola shook his head at how, even bent over the bed in a submissive position, Gage was still pushing his buttons.

It was time to get down to the real reason Nikola wanted to punish Gage, if you could still call it that. Gage was enjoying what was being done to him much more than Nikola expected he would, going by the copious amounts of precome leaking and pooling under him. Nikola didn't think Gage had ever been spanked before, but he could bet it wouldn't be the last time—at least, Nikola hoped it wouldn't be the last time.

"Now, I know we had a misunderstanding in the car. I'd be happy to tell you anything you want to know about my ex and our relationship as it stands right now. The rule you broke in the car was not talking to me and leaving me feeling like it was over between us without me getting a say in it. From here on out, you talk to me." Nikola landed two more swats on his ass. Gage moaned out. He started moving his hips until Nikola grabbed them to stop Gage from rubbing his cock on the bed.

"No, baby, you don't get any relief until I tell you that you can. We still have one more rule to discuss," Nikola purred the words into Gage's ear before he stood back up. His hand came down three more times, for a total of ten, not counting the two warning taps. Gage cried out, and only Nikola's hands grabbing quickly for his hips kept him in his stance. He did put his head down on his folded arms on the bed. Nikola allowed it since it was obviously Gage's first experience with this sort of thing. When they did it again though, he'd get extra for his disobedience, and the promise of things to come made Nikola grin.

"Those were for you being in the bar drowning your sorrows instead of just manning up and calling me to come to you. For future reference, if I ever catch you chatting up some tart on my turf again, this will feel like I just gave you a massage in comparison." Nikola's voice was gruff, barely containing his emotions.

Gage was trembling against the bed. His eyes squeezed shut, but he nodded against his arms. Nikola took the nod to mean Gage understood and agreed to his rules. Nikola gently massaged Gage's red ass. "The next time I'll make you count them off for me, and then when we're through, you'll have to thank me for keeping you in line." Gage shivered and nodded again.

Nikola stepped to Gage's side, pulled him off the bed, and then shoved Gage to his knees on the floor in front of him. Gage kept his eyes down, but Nikola grabbed Gage's hair and pulled until he lifted his head so Nikola could see his face. Gage still didn't meet Nikola's eyes. Instead, he kept them trained on the denim-clad crotch in front of him. Nikola let go of his hair and pulled his zipper down in front of Gage's slightly glazed eyes. Gage licked his lips, which was good. Nikola had been waiting for a sign from Gage that he'd gone too far, but the simple gesture egged Nikola on.

"Take out my cock," Nikola commanded. Gage pulled the zipper down and pulled Nikola's jeans until they were around his thighs before he reached in and pulled the hard cock free of the briefs holding it captive. "Now, suck me," Nikola said, trying to keep his voice steady but already fighting to keep his control in place.

Gage bent his head to take Nikola's cock into his mouth. Nikola held his gasp in—not wanting to show Gage how he'd been affected. Nikola grabbed Gage's head and pulled him closer to his pelvis—forcing Gage to take his cock in deeper. Nikola stopped before Gage gagged. "Look at me." Nikola wasn't able to keep the huskiness out of his voice. Gage lifted his eyes to meet Nikola's. "From now on, when you're here, and by here I mean anywhere I can get to you in less than a day by car, you're mine. Do you understand?" Nikola growled, not caring if Gage could hear the possessiveness that shone through in his words.

Gage's eyes widened, but he gave a slight nod before he looked down quickly, breaking their eye contact. "Don't do that. Don't hide from me, Gage." Nikola needed Gage to see how much he wanted him. How much having Gage on his knees with a cock in his mouth was pleasing him. Nikola gave Gage a second to make his decision before Nikola would make it for him. But then, Gage lifted his eyes once again to latch on to Nikola's gaze, and Nikola let out the breath he'd been unconsciously holding.

"Now, I'm going to fuck that beautiful mouth of yours until I come down your throat. You are going to take it all, and you're going to love it. When I'm done, I'm going to flip you over and eat your ass until you beg me to stop, and then I'm going to let you fuck me," Nikola said, mapping out his plans for the rest of their night. Gage moaned around Nikola's cock before he started working his tongue along the shaft in his mouth, all while staring into Nikola's eyes.

Nikola gave him no quarter, holding Gage's head as he fucked his mouth just like he'd told him he would. It was fast and bordering on brutal, but Gage knelt there obediently while Nikola used him for his pleasure. It didn't last nearly as long as Nikola wanted it to. When Nikola came, he was buried in Gage's throat. Nikola couldn't stop himself from chanting "Mine, mine, mine" as he made Gage take a part of him into his body—marking him. Gage was his. Nikola didn't know why he knew Gage somehow was meant to belong to him, but he knew now that he needed to make him see it was true.

With that realization, Nikola wanted to take Gage into his arms and hold him, but they weren't done. Nikola needed to finish what he'd started before he could give in to his tender side. He shoved Gage roughly away from him. "Get on the bed on your back. Grab your knees and hold yourself open for me," Nikola ordered.

Gage did as he was told. He got on the bed while Nikola grabbed a couple of condoms and lube out of his pocket before he pushed his jeans and underwear the rest of the way off. Gage looked like pure sin lying there spread open and waiting for him. His lips were swollen from Nikola's abuse, and his face was flushed. Nikola couldn't tell if the color in Gage's cheeks was from their earlier activities or if he was flushing from embarrassment at being in such a submissive position again.

Nikola crawled between Gage's thighs so that he could kiss his lips. The kiss started out tenderly, but then Gage dropped his legs so he could wrap his arms around Nikola's neck. Gage clutched Nikola to him while he started thrusting his hips to get some friction for his rock-hard cock. Nikola pulled away from Gage's lips and used one hand to stop his hips.

"You have to be patient. You're doing so well. You've been a very good boy. I'm happy with you right now, so don't give me a reason to punish you again," Nikola whispered softly. Gage looked up at Nikola with something akin to wonder in his eyes as he nodded. "Now spread 'em for me, baby." Gage did as he was told. He was very obedient, which Nikola loved. He made his way down Gage's body with stinging nips followed by soft kisses to ease the little pains. Nikola gave Gage's cock a quick suck but then moved lower and settled in.

Nikola started with a nice slow lick from the top of Gage's crack to his perineum. Gage gasped at the first contact of Nikola's tongue. Nikola used his hands to spread Gage open farther as he kissed the spank-reddened cheeks. "You have the nicest, little pink asshole that I've ever seen," Nikola said. Gage wriggled, uncomfortable at the attention, or maybe hearing the words surprised him. Nikola pressed his lips to Gage's pucker, and Gage shuddered. Nikola loved Gage's reaction to him—it only made Nikola want more. He laved Gage's asshole with his tongue, and soon Gage started rocking back to get more anytime Nikola pulled even the slightest bit away.

Gage was moaning and groaning above Nikola, and when he speared his tongue into Gage's tight hole, Gage screamed "Oh fuck!" Then an endless litany of "More, Niky—more, please—give me more—don't stop—please, don't stop" streamed from his mouth. Nikola tongue-fucked him until Gage was begging for Nikola to actually fuck him. Nikola pulled his tongue out and kissed Gage's pucker one more time as he whimpered at the loss.

"Please, Niky—fuck me, please." Gage begged for Nikola to give him his dick. "Fuck me. I want it hard so I'll feel you all day tomorrow."

It took all of Nikola's willpower not to give in and give Gage what he was asking for. He didn't want to do anything Gage might regret in the morning. Instead, Nikola grabbed a condom and rolled it onto Gage's leaking dick. Spreading lube on two of his fingers, he reached around to shove them into his own ass quickly, spreading the lube, but not doing much more in the way of preparation before he pulled them back out. He lubed Gage's condom-clad cock and straddled him. Nikola lined the stiff pole up to his hole and sank slowly down onto Gage, only stopping when his ass landed on Gage's balls. Nikola took a moment to adjust to the sheer size of Gage's dick. It had been a long time since Nikola had been fucked, so it was a good thing he'd always loved the burn.

Gage stared up at him as he lay still beneath Nikola. He gave Gage credit for not moving. With Gage as out of it as he was, he'd expected to have to remind him to wait. When Nikola's body relaxed around the intrusion, he leaned forward and kissed Gage sloppily. "Fuck me hard and fast, baby, give me all you got."

Gage took Nikola at his word. Planting his feet on the bed, he lifted Nikola up a couple of inches, and started pounding up into his ass with a force Nikola had never gotten from any of his previous lovers. "I'm not going to last. I'm gonna come," Gage grunted, and then he did just that.

Gage's body spasmed below Nikola. Nikola rode Gage hard through it, pulling himself up and dropping back down with as much force as he could. Gage stilled, but his breathing was uneven as he gasped to take in more oxygen. Nikola thought he saw a tear at the corner of Gage's eye but quickly convinced himself that the small drop of moisture was just sweat as he bent down to kiss him tenderly.

Gage was still hard after coming, just like the previous night, but Nikola hadn't been as quick to recover—his own cock was only at half-mast after having already come in Gage's mouth—so he pulled off Gage and stripped the condom from him. He tossed it into the can by the bed before getting up to get a wet towel from the bathroom only to find Gage lying with his arm over his eyes. Nikola cleaned him up and threw the towel back toward the bathroom.

He nudged Gage to get him off the blankets so he could crawl into bed and then cover them before pulling Gage onto his side. Nikola wrapped him up in his arms so that Gage's face was pressed into Nikola's chest. Nikola rubbed his back, kissed the top of his head, and just held him, waiting to see if Gage needed to talk about what they'd done. If he was honest with himself, Nikola half expected Gage to push him away and demand an explanation, but Gage just let Nikola hold him. Nikola's fears were put to rest when Gage's arm snaked around his waist before snuggling down further into Nikola's warmth.

Nikola knew he should probably get back up to look for some lotion to rub on Gage's raw behind, now that he knew Gage was okay, but his breathing slowed and Nikola didn't want to wake him. Nikola's mind drifted as he tried to figure out how he was going to make this thing with Gage more than just a quick and convenient business trip fling. No magic solution presented itself to him, so he closed his eyes and let Gage's warm body and steady breathing help lull him to sleep.

Chapter Eleven

GAGE WOKE UP alone. He remembered Nikola holding him as he fell asleep, but he wasn't in the bed any longer, and Gage felt a strange sense of disappointment at Nikola's absence until he heard movement in the sitting room. Gage also smelled the enticing aroma of coffee and food just before Nikola appeared at the door to the bedroom. He hesitated but then walked slowly toward the bed, smiling a shy little smile, but his steps seemed to falter as he got closer to Gage. Gage was sure he was imagining it, but it seemed like Nikola was a bit unsure of himself. After the night they'd experienced, Gage had a hard time reconciling the man tentatively walking toward him with the confident one from the previous evening.

Sitting on the edge of the bed, Nikola reached out a hand to touch Gage's cheek. "How are you this morning?" His eyes searched Gage's face.

Gage could tell that Nikola wanted a real answer and not just an "I'm fine." "I feel pretty good, not hung over, and that's good." The look on Nikola's face told him that wasn't the answer he was looking for. Nikola wanted to talk about the sex, or more specifically, the spanking before the sex, but Gage didn't want to discuss last night before he'd had at least one cup of coffee and a little time to think it through. So in an attempt to change the subject, Gage asked, "Is that coffee I smell?"

Disappointment flashed across Nikola's face, but to Gage's relief, instead of pushing it, he smiled. "Yeah, I got a whole pot for you, and I ordered some food too. It's almost eleven, come and eat." Nikola leaned down and gave Gage a quick kiss. Gage wanted to take the kiss deeper but kept his mouth closed because it tasted like a small mammal had died in there. Nikola pulled back with another soft smile for Gage before he got up and went back out into the sitting room.

Gage crawled out of bed and pulled a pair of sleep pants out of his bag. He took them into the bathroom with him and couldn't resist taking a quick shower, which gave him some time to think about Nikola before going out to face him. Nikola seemed like a changed man in the morning light. Gone was the controlling, confident person who made Gage fall apart under his firm hand, and in his place was an unsure, almost timid guy who seemed to need Gage's assurance they were still okay.

Gage toweled off and brushed his teeth before walking out into the sitting room while still pulling up his pants. Nikola was sitting at the small table with a cup of coffee and a plate of steak and eggs. There was another covered plate across from him that Gage assumed was for him, but more importantly, there was a cup of coffee.

"Feel better?" Nikola asked looking up from the paper he was reading.

"Yeah, much better." Gage sat down a little gingerly, because yeah, Nikola had done a number on his ass. Gage could definitely feel it, and he flushed as the memories flooded back. He looked down in hopes Nikola wouldn't notice his blush as he uncovered his plate and sipped his coffee. "Oh, that is definitely what I needed," Gage said, taking a bite of his food. He realized he was famished and dug in, only stopping long enough to swallow more coffee before he went back to shoving food down his gullet. After Gage devoured the entire plate of food, he sat back and found Nikola studying him from his seat across the table.

"You were hungry." Leaning forward, Nikola refilled Gage's coffee, and Gage sat back to enjoy his second cup. Nikola was quiet, watching Gage drink his coffee but appearing to be nervously trying to work his way up to saying something. He'd open his mouth like he was going to start talking, but instead, he would just sigh. Finally, he took a deep breath and looked Gage straight in the eye. "I'm sorry about coming here uninvited last night. I know I shouldn't have. You said you had things to do, and I should have just left you to do them."

Gage studied the downturn of Nikola's lips and was sure Nikola finding him in the bar with the Austrian—Henry or something—was the cause of the expression. Gage set down his coffee cup while he tried to think of what Nikola wanted to hear. He still wasn't ready to talk about what happened between them after they'd gotten back to his room. He needed time to process what he was feeling, so Gage decided to take a different tack to distract Nikola.

"So tell me about Garrett."

Nikola looked startled at the direction Gage took the conversation. Gage watched his face as he made a decision, and then Nikola finally sighed. "Can we go sit on the couch?"

"Sure." Gage got up and went to sit on the couch, Nikola following.

Sitting at the end of the couch, Nikola turned to pull one leg up so he was facing Gage. "So what do you want to know?"

Having no plan when he'd switched the topic of discussion to take the heat off himself, Gage had to think awhile before he responded, "I don't know. I guess I really don't even know why I want to know anything about him, but it feels important that I do." He shifted nervously on the couch not knowing why it felt so important for him to know about Nikola's past, but a nagging need to reassure himself Nikola wasn't still in love, and therefore unavailable, was there all the same.

"Well, to set the record straight, he isn't some old guy that keeps boys for his personal pleasure. He's a year younger than I am. We met when I got my first job after college. We moved in together, and I was with him when I got Hana's mom pregnant. When I decided to keep her, he couldn't deal with it, thinking I was throwing my life away. I came back here so my mom could help with the baby. I was just a stupid, young guy who didn't know shit about kids. We broke up, of course, but he was there for me—is there for me still. I turned to him when things got rough here, and I wanted to give up." The words rushed out of Nikola like he knew if he didn't get it out quickly, he wouldn't be able to. He stopped and rubbed the back of his neck.

"He makes pretty good money. He's an architect with a big firm in Atlanta. The first time he offered to buy me a ticket to go see him, I didn't want to accept it, but he was pretty insistent. I went for two weeks, and I had a hard time coming back here, but I knew I had to for Hana. It took me a long time to go back again because I was afraid that I *wouldn't* come back." His eyes pleaded with Gage to understand how hard everything had been for him. "I've gone a few more times over the years, but these last two, I went once by myself, and then he invited Hana to come with me. So I was back there in less than a year with her in tow. He's pretty good with her, but there's still something there that's not right, almost like maybe he resents her for taking me away from him. I think he spoils her to make up for that, though—maybe he feels guilty about it but can't help it. He admitted to me that he still loves me, but he doesn't want me to come back to him because I'm lonely. He wants me to be in love with him like he is with me, and I'm not. So I guess that's all there is to that."

He stopped and put his hands over his face. "I can't believe I just told you all of that. I've never told anyone how I'd considered not coming back, just leaving Hana here with my mom. Fuck, I feel like such a selfish prick." Dropping his hands, he stood up and walked across the room and then back to stop in front of Gage. He looked down at him, his eyes once again pleading for understanding.

Gage grabbed Nikola's thighs and pulled him closer so that Nikola straddled his legs and then Gage wrapped him in his arms before saying, "I'm sorry that I got upset about you and him yesterday. I had no right to question how you live your life, and I admire you for making the decision to raise Hana. It must have been tough to give up everything in your life for her. Though I have to say after meeting her that I think you made the right choice and are doing a damn fine job."

Nikola smiled that smile Gage begun to think of as his Hana smile. "Thanks for saying that, but I know I'm not the best father in the world. It's just that I got an amazing kid."

Nikola kissed Gage then, and there was something different about the way he did it. There was something indefinable behind it, not lust, more like Nikola was trying to convey some deeper emotion through the connection of their lips. But Gage wouldn't let his thoughts go down that road too far—he was being a sap, trying to read something into it that wasn't there. Pulling back, Nikola gazed into Gage's eyes, making him think Nikola might confess to feeling the same strange feelings he was having, but instead, he ruined the illusion.

"So, are you okay with what we did last night?"

Gage looked down to hide his face because when he remembered what he'd let Nikola do to him and how much he'd enjoyed it, he was embarrassed. Gage hadn't ever imagined he would be into that sort of thing since he was about as vanilla as could be when the bedroom door closed. But there was something about being with someone who was pretty much his match in strength that was a total turn-on. Having Nikola manhandle him and take control in the bedroom got him as hard as a rock. He had no clue why the commanding tone Nikola used made him want to obey anything Nikola told him. Gage had been apprehensive at first, but once he'd let himself go, it was the single hottest thing he'd ever experienced. After Nikola fucked his mouth in the nastiest way ever, he actually hoped Nikola would flip him over and fuck his ass too.

What should he tell Nikola? That he liked it so much he wanted nothing more than for Nikola to drag him to the bedroom again? Not only that he wanted Nikola to do it again, but this time, he wanted Nikola to hold him down and fuck him until he screamed? Gage snorted. As much as the idea turned him on, he knew he didn't trust Nikola enough to let him do that yet—no matter how much he'd begged for it in a moment of lust-induced want.

Nikola put his hands on Gage's bare chest. He wriggled in Gage's lap, making him aware of how hard he'd gotten thinking about doing it again. "You liked it," Nikola purred. He wiggled his ass against Gage's hard-on again to emphasize his point. "I think you liked it a lot, and you're thinking about what I'm going to do to you the next time I have you bent over in front of me. Tell me, Gage, was I your first?"

He wondered which first Nikola was asking about. The first guy who'd spanked him, who'd made Gage beg to be fucked or who made him feel the strange way he was at that moment? The answer was yes to all, so Gage simply said, "Yes."

Taking a chance, he looked up to meet Nikola's eyes. He thought he'd find a smirk on Nikola's face or an expression that would make him sorry he'd admitted anything to him, but he was surprised to see Nikola's expression was one of tenderness. Gage wanted to look away from what he saw there because he wasn't sure he could handle it. Everything felt so unreal, like he wasn't in his own body anymore. In that tender look, Gage saw everything that could be between them if he'd just let things unfold as they would.

He could see himself falling in love with Nikola and everything that would follow if he did. They'd be a family—Nikola, Hana, and him, and for once, the fear that usually gripped him at the idea of a commitment didn't take hold and make his chest ache. All of a sudden, a new fear took hold because Gage knew it was too soon. He hardly knew the man sitting in his lap and looking down at him with such tenderness in his eyes.

Nikola's phone rang and broke the spell he had cast, slamming Gage back to himself with a different, clearer picture in his mind. One where he was what he knew himself to be—a commitment phobe—a guy who didn't fall in love, a guy who couldn't make somebody like Nikola happy no matter how much he would try—he'd disappoint Nikola. Gage would break his heart, and in turn, Hana's heart, and that would be just too much for him to bear.

He was glad when Nikola got off his lap to fish his ringing phone out of his pocket, had a brief conversation, and then gave Gage a regretful look. "I have to run upstairs and check on a few things for the party. We'll finish this later." Bending down, Nikola brushed his lips lightly over Gage's before he turned and left with a wave, leaving Gage to stew about his new conundrum.

After staring at the door for some time, Gage got up and pulled out his laptop thinking he needed a distraction to keep him from examining his mixed up feelings about Nikola. He turned the computer on and cleared out his email, having already read the important ones on his phone. He looked over some of the files for the business, but it was a half-hearted attempt since he figured there wouldn't be a lot of business talk at the party. Gage knew how it worked; he was supposed to show up and let them observe him. He wouldn't actually be doing any real work, but he knew if they didn't like what they saw, his job would be that much harder. He needed to be on his best behavior at the party, which meant not drinking too much, and he'd have to make sure to be totally appropriate around Nikola—no easy task there.

Fuck, Nikola. What was Gage going to do about him? He couldn't believe he'd gotten himself into this kind of mess. Maybe if he put some distance between the two of them, Nikola would back off and give him some space to figure things out. But that felt wrong because for the first time in his life he wanted to get closer, and he didn't know what to do about that. He'd never been so confused about anything before. He was used to being in control, and that right there was the real problem. Gage felt like patting himself on the back for figuring it out all on his own.

He wasn't in control where Nikola was concerned. He had no control over the way Nikola was making him feel, no control over his own body when Nikola was near, and Nikola made it very clear who was in control in the bedroom. All of those things were bad, but the worst part of it all was he wanted to give the control over to Nikola, to just let go and let someone else make the decisions for once, even if it was just in the bedroom.

Thinking of doing only what Nikola told him to do thrilled Gage in a way that scared him. It was like something deep inside him cracked open under Nikola's hand the previous night and freed him from whatever had been holding him back all those years. He was free to not be in control because he'd finally found someone who was strong enough to take it from him. Nikola showed him he could take care of him when he held him last night as Gage felt like his world was crumbling around him. It brought a smile to Gage's lips and right then and there he decided he was going to go with the flow for once in his life and just let what would be, be.

With that decision made, the weight lifted from his shoulders, but immediately, a different pressure settled in his chest. What if he was just a fun distraction for Nikola? He suddenly couldn't wait for Nikola to come back to his room, so he could find out where they stood. What did Nikola want from him and was it what Gage was starting to hope it would be? His thoughts turned to the bedroom and the way Nikola chanted "mine" over and over as he'd used Gage's mouth to get off. He was starting to realize how much he wanted those words to be true. He knew it was too early to feel the way he did, but he couldn't deny the attraction of what it would mean to belong to Nikola. It felt right in a way nothing else ever had.

Chapter Twelve

HENRICK, THE LITTLE twink who had been chatting up Gage the night before, was the last person Nikola wanted to see when he made his way upstairs to check on the party preparations. Yet there he was in all his flamboyant glory. He must have been primping in the mirrored elevator doors as he was making a strange face when they opened, but his expression went from weird to surprised when Henrick saw Nikola. He recovered quickly, and his eyes lit up as he flashed Nikola a flirty little smile when Nikola stepped into the elevator with him.

Though it was stupid, Nikola couldn't help but hate the man standing next to him. It was irrational, but then nothing about how Nikola felt for Gage was the least bit sane—that included the overwhelming possessiveness. He had caught a glimpse of the picture of Lucas on Gage's phone, and if Gage had a type, then Henrick obviously fit the bill—short, thin, young, blond, and blue-eyed—Henrick was everything Nikola wasn't, and it galled him that there was nothing he could do to change it.

"Hi there, how are you on this fine morning?" Henrick's annoying, knowing smirk made Nikola want to punch him, but he clenched his hands to his sides instead of giving in to his urges.

"I'm doing fine. How are you?" Nikola decided to go with polite instead of just wringing Henrick's neck. Thank god, it was only a couple of floors, so the ride was blessedly short, but Henrick followed Nikola out when the doors opened. Of course, he'd have to, considering it was the top floor. Nikola wondered if Henrick knew the restaurant was closed to the public as they set up for the private party Nedim was holding there that evening, but before he could say anything to Henrick, Nikola's cousin, Sinad, came toward them and greeted Henrick in German. Nikola heard his name mentioned, and then they turned to look at him.

"So you are *the* Nikola?" Henrick asked with a raised eyebrow and the smirk which Nikola found increasingly irritating.

"I am a Nikola," Nikola admitted having no idea what was with the way Henrick asked his question.

Henrick studied Nikola for a moment. Then he chortled. "You have no idea of your reputation, do you?" Nikola had a reputation? That was news to him, and he wondered just who Henrick would have talked to who would know anything about him anyway? "Oh how fun, you really don't know, do you?" Henrick asked when he realized Nikola was genuinely confused by the news.

Nikola turned a suspicious eye to Sinad and spoke to him in Bosnian. "What is my reputation exactly?"

Sinad paled. "What did he say? You know I don't understand that jibber-jabber." Sinad didn't speak English. He worked for Nedim in the same capacity Nikola did, but he worked with German-speaking businessmen since he'd spent time in Germany.

They were being rude by holding a conversation in a language all parties didn't understand, but no matter what language they used, someone would be left out. At the moment, Nikola didn't give a shit if Henrick thought he and Sinad were discussing the merits of killing him and hiding his body where no one would find it—and in Bosnia that wouldn't be a problem.

"He asked about my reputation and since I have no idea what he's talking about, maybe you want to enlighten me," Nikola said.

"Nikola, this is not the time or place to discuss this. Nedim would be pissed if he knew how rude you're being right now. Henrick is here with a big software company that Nedim worked very hard to woo here. I was told to make sure he is well taken care of, and it's hard enough to deal with the fact that he's so obviously gay. He likes to hit on the most inappropriate people. He'll be after you if you're not careful." Sinad nudged Nikola in the ribs with an elbow before turning away to find his charge and saying something to Henrick, part of which Nikola recognized as an apology, probably for their earlier rudeness.

Putting his hand on Sinad's arm, Henrick smiled sweetly up at him while saying something that made him pale even further, undoubtedly something inappropriate. Henrick looked at Nikola and winked, further cementing Nikola's ideas about what the man was saying to his poor cousin. After speaking to Sinad for another minute, he turned his attention to Nikola. "I'll tell you everything I know at the party tonight. I can't wait to see your friend again." On that note, Henrick left, walking with an exaggerated swishy hip movement, which made Nikola grimace.

"I told you, Nikola, he will hit on anyone. I have to try to keep him from getting his ass kicked when he eventually hits on the wrong guy. The bartender told me what happened last night, with your guy and him. It was a good thing you got up here when you did. Alan said it was like watching a mouse bait a bear. He was afraid the way he was drinking, and the way Henrick was flirting, it would end badly," Sinad said.

Nikola heard everything Sinad said, but only the phrase *your guy* kept repeating in his head, making his heart jump to his throat. If Sinad only he knew how much Nikola wanted those words to mean more than they did, but he tried to put the idea out of his head. He was glad Alan hadn't picked up on what was really going on last night.

Only Nedim knew Nikola was gay. He wasn't about to tell any of his other family. They'd lose any respect they had for him as a man. Nikola's older relatives still believed there were no gay men in Bosnia since Bosnians weren't raised that way. Nikola gave up trying to explain there were gay men in Bosnia. They were just better at hiding it because they knew what was likely to happen if anyone found out.

"Tell me what he was talking about? What do people say about me?" Nikola asked.

"It's nothing bad, Nikola. People just make up stories. You keep to yourself, and you make mysterious trips out of the country for Nedim. You know he never tells anyone what you're up to. Most people think you're a hired gun, that you are Nedim's muscle. You, Nikola, are the man everyone thinks makes people who cross Nedim disappear. People are afraid of you," Sinad said quietly.

"Are you afraid of me, Sinad?" Nikola was curious now about this new information.

"I've seen you angry, cousin. Who wouldn't have some fear of that?" he asked with a small, nervous smile. "But I do think Nedim plays it up. He uses the fact that you are close-lipped to his advantage and lets the rumors spread instead of putting a stop to them. Now we have some work to do." Sinad was obviously uncomfortable with the conversation enough to bring it to an end. He patted Nikola on the shoulder and turned to go back to doing whatever it was he had been pulled away from with the appearance of Henrick.

After a few minutes of consideration, Nikola decided he couldn't fault Nedim for propagating the rumors of his reputation. His uncle probably had his reasons, and it was, most likely, partially for Nikola's benefit.

What Nikola wondered was how his family and coworkers could think that he could be a cold hearted, murderous bastard? It was true Nikola kept to himself and was tight-lipped, but did he give off vibes saying he could put you down if you so much as looked at him funny? Nikola shuddered, just the thought of taking another's life making his stomach hurt.

Nikola didn't have time to ponder the newfound knowledge about his sinister reputation, but one last thing popped into his head uninvited. Henrick had obviously been talking to someone, and Nikola wondered who. He hoped the little shit had enough brains not to out him at least because it would be bad for Nikola if people found out. He had a friend whose family not only disowned him when they found out, but some of his male relatives took it upon themselves to try to beat the gay out of him. That guy now walked with a limp and was blind in one eye. Nikola would have to think about having a little talk with Henrick, but it would have to wait. There were things to do, and as thoughts of Gage waiting in his room danced through his head, he wanted to get them done quickly.

Nikola ran through the checklist Nedim's wife sent him to make sure everything was getting done to her standards, but right when Nikola predicted he could get back to Gage, his phone chirped with a text. The company that was supposed to deliver the extra alcohol for the night's event had a miscommunication with its driver, and he was currently somewhere near Bihać. Nikola was tapped to go pick up the shipment himself, which meant going to get the van before he could accomplish his errand. He wasn't going to get back to Gage before he needed to go home to change for the party so Nikola pulled out his phone and called Gage.

"Hey," he answered. Nikola could picture the soft smile he knew was on Gage's face just from the way he said that one word and a warm feeling spread through his chest.

"Hey, I have to make a run to pick something up, and it's going to take me a while. I'm sorry, but I'm probably not going to make it back to your room until it's time to go to the party."

"Oh, well, I guess if you have to work, you have to work," Gage said, disappointment clear in his voice.

"I do have to work, and I'm sorry we got interrupted, but we'll have two days in the mountains to talk. Don't forget to pack an overnight bag for tomorrow. We'll leave as soon as we get up." Though he hoped they wouldn't just be talking for the whole two days, he had plans for Gage in that isolated cabin. Which reminded Nikola, he needed to pack his own bag when he went home to shower and change.

"I didn't bring any ski gear with me. Are the stores going to be open tomorrow so I can pick something up?"

"Don't worry about it. Nedim has enough stuff at the cabin to trick anyone out, and we'll rent the rest. I have to go, or I'll never get everything done in time." Nikola looked at his watch and cursed softly.

"Okay, see you later."

"Yeah, later." Nikola hung up the phone, slipped it back in his pocket, and headed off to Nedim's business complex to pick up the van.

He didn't have time to mull over any of the things on his mind after that, and it was one good thing about having something else to occupy his time. Once his errands were finished, he dropped off the van and went home to find Hana and his mom finishing dinner.

"Hey there, how are my girls?" he asked as he dropped a kiss on the top of Hana's head.

"We're good, Babo. Guess what?"

"What?"

"Nana said I could stay up until midnight! She even got us some bubbly drink for the toaster," Hana said excitedly.

"It's a toast," Nikola corrected. "And do you think you'll be able to make it to midnight without falling asleep?"

"I can do it. Are you going to come home tonight?"

Nikola shook his head. "Probably not, and I'm going to be gone for a couple of days so Nana will be the one taking care of you. You promise to be good, and I'll bring you something."

Hana's lips turned down in a frown. "You're not going to be home for the party?"

"I'm not going to make it, but Nana will take you. She already has your gift from me to take along too." New Year's Day at Nedim's house was a big thing, but Nikola would miss it while he was away with Gage. "You promise to be good?"

Hana thought it over for a bit before she got a glint in her eye. "I'll be extra special good if you promise to bring Uncle Gage to visit me when you get back."

"You're a devious little thing, aren't you?" Nikola asked with a chuckle. "I promise I'll ask him if he wants to visit, and if he says yes, I'll bring him."

"Okay, it's a deal." Hana held her hand out to shake on it.

Nikola shook her small hand but couldn't help noticing the frown on his mom's face at their topic of conversation. He tried to ignore it as he bent and picked Hana up so he could give her a hug and kisses. "Okay, I have to go get ready now." He sat her back down on her chair while his mom watched silently. Her disapproving look spoke volumes without her having to say a word.

In his excitement to get back to Gage, Nikola hurried through his shower and threw on his clothes. All they had to do was get through the party, and then they would be alone for two days with no distractions and no worries about having anyone finding out what they were doing. Nikola couldn't help but feel like, for the first time in a long time, things were finally going his way.

Chapter Thirteen

GAGE SHOWERED AGAIN and shaved the three-day growth off his chin. He wasn't sure what he should wear to the party but decided to go with a suit since he was meeting Nedim for the first time. He was dressed and ready to go when Nikola let himself into the room. Nikola looked absolutely edible. He was wearing dress pants and a suit jacket with a button-up shirt in a pale-cream color, which made his skin look a shade darker. Nikola's skin was a nice creamy-caramel tone, and Gage wanted nothing more than to slowly unbutton the shirt and lick him—treat him like the candy his skin reminded him of.

Nikola made a sound, a cross between a cough and a laugh that brought Gage's gaze back to his face. He raised an eyebrow and smirked, making Gage blush when he'd been caught in the act of ogling. Nikola crooked his finger, and Gage didn't hesitate to go to him, but that didn't stop Nikola from grabbing his tie when he was within reach and pulling Gage to him. He kissed Gage hard before he said, "You look hot, but lose the tie. We're going to a party, not a meeting."

Gage took off the tie, and Nikola unbuttoned the top couple of buttons on his shirt, before nodding as if the look was just right. "I wasn't sure what to wear." Gage was unsure of his choice even with the modifications.

"You did well enough, but I don't want you to look all stiff and uncomfortable. You need to let go a bit and have some fun. Nedim will be impressed that you can have a good time with business still your number one priority."

"I considered that, but I need to be careful. I need to watch myself tonight and try not to drink too much." Gage smoothed down his shirt, making sure it was tucked in. "I don't want to do anything that may embarrass my company, and when I get too drunk, I tend to over share."

"It's a good idea to not get drunk, but I'll warn you now that you shouldn't turn down a drink if it's offered to you by Nedim or one of his people. They may take offense. The best is to have a drink in your hand at all times, and drink it slowly, but that's not going to stop all of them from giving you more. I'll stay sober enough to watch out for you and make sure you don't do anything stupid." Nikola leaned in for one more deep kiss and then released him, turning Gage to the door before patting his ass. "Don't worry. I'll watch your ass for you."

"Another reason why I shouldn't drink too much," Gage threw back at Nikola over his shoulder.

Nikola followed Gage to the elevator. "Don't worry. I wouldn't do anything to your ass that you didn't beg me to do." The innuendo dripped from his words, making Gage's mouth gape in surprise.

Nikola winked and grinned crookedly as they stepped into the elevator with an older couple. Nikola nodded to them in greeting, and they smiled back. They all got out at the restaurant where there were already a lot of people milling around and seated at the tables. There was a live band in one corner playing softly at the moment. Each of the long tables held large quantities of food laid out buffet-style with bottles of alcoholic and nonalcoholic beverages mixed in among the platters.

Grabbing Gage's elbow, Nikola led him to a table front and center and closest to the dance floor. They paused in front of a man and a woman who were elegantly dressed and seemed to be holding court with the few people seated at the table with them. Nikola waited until the man looked up at the newcomers and then stood to offer his hand to Nikola.

Nikola shook his hand, leaned in, and kissed his cheeks before turning to Gage. "Uncle Nedim, this is Gage Hoffman of H&S Equipment. Gage, Nedim Mehanovic," Nikola introduced the two men.

Gage shook Nedim's hand. "Nice to finally meet you, sir." Nedim was much younger than Gage had pictured him. He was maybe a few years older than himself, but Gage guessed not older than forty-five. His resemblance to Nikola was striking—if genetics worked the way they should, Nikola would only get more handsome as he aged.

"Ah yes, Mr. Hoffman, I have heard quite a bit about you. It is good to meet you also." Gage was surprised that Nedim spoke English. He'd assumed Nikola would have to translate for them to hold a conversation, but Nedim's English, though a little stilted and heavily accented, wasn't too bad. Nedim let go of Gage's hand and gestured to the chairs across from him as he introduced his wife. "This is my wife, Amina."

Amina's shrewd gaze took in first Nikola and then Gage and then went back to Nikola. "Sabina is coming tonight. I told her you would be happy to see her, Nikola," she said, not acknowledging the introduction, which Gage found strange. Gage wondered who Sabina was, of course, but didn't want to seem overly interested in Nikola's personal life, so he bit his tongue.

"That's nice, Teta. I haven't seen Sabina for a couple of weeks. Hana was just asking after her a couple of days ago," Nikola said smoothly as he smiled at his aunt. Nedim watched the exchange with as much interest as Gage, and he wondered if Nedim knew what was going on since it seemed Gage was missing something lurking below the surface of their polite exchange.

Amina turned to Gage, finally acknowledging his presence. "So Mr. Hoffman, how do you like our city so far?"

"It's very nice. I see there has been a lot of rebuilding done. Of course I've only seen pictures of the devastation left behind after the war, but the city has done a remarkable job coming back from it. And please call me Gage. When people say Mr. Hoffman I always look over my shoulder to see if my father is standing behind me," Gage said, putting his best fake businessman smile on his face. Amina was one of those people who instantly hit a nerve with Gage. He couldn't explain why, but he surmised her earlier comment to Nikola about someone named Sabina was a jab aimed at him.

The smile on her face was just as fake as the one on Gage's as she nodded. "I'm glad you are liking what you are seeing." Turning to her husband, she said something in Bosnian before she got up and excused herself. Gage wasn't sure if he'd just been snubbed or if the woman was just leaving the men alone to do what men do when left to their own company, but he forgot all about Amina when Nikola nudged his knee with his under the table.

"So, has Nikola been doing his job and taking you to see the city?" The little twinkle in Nedim's eye didn't escape Gage's attention.

"He has been a very attentive tour guide," Gage said with a chuckle. "He doesn't even mind that I take an hour to walk a couple of blocks."

Gage was going to make a joke about Nikola calling him a woman but stopped when Nikola tensed next to him and his expression turned icy. Gage wondered if he'd said something wrong, but then a hand landed on his shoulder, and he turned his head to find Henrick standing there behind him. He patted Gage's shoulder and then took a couple of steps to put himself between Nikola and Gage so he could shake Nedim's hand over the table while he settled his other on Gage's shoulder again. It was an overly familiar gesture that Gage didn't appreciate much and the murderous look on Nikola's face told Gage he felt even more strongly about the contact.

"Henrick, it's nice to see you again." Nedim eyed the hand on Gage's shoulder before he added, "I see that all of you have met before."

Henrick's laugh was high, almost a twitter, that sent a shudder through Gage's body. "Yes, we ran into each other last night in the gym and then again in the bar." He turned his attention to Gage. "It's so nice to see you again, Gage."

"Um, yeah, nice to see you again too," Gage replied with a tight smile.

Nedim gestured to the chair on Gage's left. "Why don't you join us for the evening, Henrick?" So that is, of course, just what he did, settling in next to Gage with a fluid ease. Nikola pressed Gage's knee with his as soon as Henrick moved, and to Gage's surprise, on the other side Henrick did the same as soon as he'd taken his seat. Gage jerked away from the contact making Henrick chuckle quietly.

They made small talk while Nikola poured drinks and tried to ignore Henrick's obvious attempts at getting Gage's attention. When Amina came back to take her place, everyone started eating. Gage noticed the way Amina's eyes seemed to miss nothing, and the way her lips pursed in obvious displeasure whenever Nikola leaned in just a little too close when he talked to Gage. He chose to ignore her in favor of the food because there was spitted lamb, plates of smoked meat and cheeses, all types of pita, and of course breads and salads. Gage made sure to eat enough to absorb the alcohol that was poured freely, and he enjoyed himself in the process, licking his fingers when he noticed it wasn't considered bad manners to do so.

Other people came to the table, some just to say hello, while others sat in the empty chairs, so Gage barely noticed when a tall, beautiful woman approached the table. Only the sparkle in Amina's eyes tipped Gage off the woman he was looking at must be Sabina. Everyone stood and hugged and kissed cheeks before Henrick and Gage were introduced to her. She sat down on the other side of Nikola and Nikola's smile seemed genuine as he leaned into her as they chatted.

Nedim was busy with other people, which left Gage with only Henrick for company. When Gage turned to him, Henrick asked. "So, is that his girlfriend?"

"I don't know," Gage answered honestly.

Gage hadn't asked Nikola if he had a girlfriend, only if Garrett was his boyfriend, but considering Nikola had gotten a woman pregnant, it wasn't totally out of the question for him to have one. Gage looked back at them, and the easy way they were together made him start to wonder. The way Nikola leaned into her to whisper something that made her blush and giggle, and the way she touched his hand and didn't move it made Gage's stomach lurch and pissed him off at the same time. It made sense that what Nikola had done with Gage would have to be on the down low and if Gage thought about it, Sabina was the one who should be pissed, not him, but that did nothing to calm him.

He couldn't stand to watch them together any longer so he turned back to Henrick, who must have read Gage's mind. He gave Gage a sympathetic look. "So is he just a closet case, or does he swing both ways?" Henrick leaned in close to ask.

"I don't know what you're talking about." There was no way Gage was going to admit anything to anyone and unintentionally out Nikola, but Henrick smiled at Gage like he knew what a big fat lie he'd just told. Gage stared at the table in front of him and decided if he had to watch Nikola flirt with Sabina all night, he'd probably need to drink a little more than he'd intended, so he downed his drink and let Henrick refill it.

Henrick moved his chair closer to Gage so their legs brushed together. "Did you know he's a hired gun for Nedim? I've heard stories from some of the people at the company I'm working with about how ruthless he is. Also Nedim uses him to carry out contracts in other countries, because he has an American passport, so he can travel freely." Henrick's eyes were wide with obvious glee at imparting his knowledge of Nikola to Gage, and he watched closely for his reaction.

Gage didn't give him the satisfaction of having one, schooling his expression to one of indifference. "I haven't heard anything about him. I only know what he's told me. I guess I think of him as just sort of a glorified tour guide." Gage snuck a look at Nikola who was still talking to Sabina and his aunt. Gage wished he could speak the language so he would know what was being said.

"You should probably be careful with him. From what I've heard, he wouldn't hesitate to put you in your place if you crossed him," Henrick said gravely. "They say that one of his cousins tried to spread rumors about his time in America—that he was living with a man—the cousin disappeared, never to be heard from again. They also say that he has a daughter, but he got rid of the mother because she also knew about his indiscretions. They talk about him, but no one would dare say anything to his face for fear of their lives. Sinad was freaked out when he saw that I'd met Nikola this morning. He gave me stern warnings to keep well away from him."

Gage didn't believe anything Henrick was saying was true. The Nikola he'd seen in the last two days didn't fit with a ruthless killer. Nikola was so tender with his daughter, and though he had shown Gage he could be forceful, he didn't strike Gage as mean or heartless. He saw just that morning how eager Nikola was to make sure he was okay with everything they'd done the previous night and Nikola had been so unsure of himself. No, Nikola was not a cold-blooded murderer. Gage was sure of that.

"Those are probably just rumors. Anyway, I'm sure I have nothing to fear from him. It's strictly business between us."

"Yes, it looked like business last night. I wish he'd come do some business with me. Maybe we could all do some business together sometime."

Gage glanced at Nikola to see if he heard any of his and Henrick's conversation, but he was still engrossed in his own with Sabina and Amina. "I hope you know enough to keep your assumptions to yourself. If what you say is true, I'd hate for you to get on Nikola's bad side."

Gage couldn't be sure with the lighting the way it was, but it seemed that Henrick's already fair complexion might have paled even further. He recovered quickly and poured each of them another drink. "Don't worry about me, *liebchen*. I know when to keep my mouth closed. Now, since it looks like you and I have been left to our own devices, why don't we have some fun?" Henrick tipped his head toward where Nikola was leading Sabina out to the dance floor and raised his glass to clink it against Gage's.

The music grew louder and people started dancing and having a good time but Gage wasn't one of them. The table where he and Henrick sat was now empty and Gage sighed while he watched Nikola and Sabina as they moved together on the dance floor. Henrick's hand landed on Gage's thigh and then his breath on his ear as the other man leaned in. "If you want, we could get out of here. I doubt anyone would notice."

Gage weighed the offer as he watched Nikola kiss Sabina. It was a pretty chaste kiss but, still, a kiss none the less. Gage looked at Henrick, and the way he was looking back at Gage—all heat and hunger—decided it for him. Why should he just sit there and be ignored with the possibility that later, after he went back to his room alone, Nikola would show up smelling like perfume and wanting to fuck? That was, of course, assuming he didn't go home with Sabina. Gage checked his watch, seeing that it was already a quarter to eleven. People might notice if they left together, but maybe if they waited until midnight, they could sneak away.

"We can't leave yet. We'll wait until everyone is distracted by the countdown, and then we can go to your room." The smile that lit up Henrick's face was amazing, showing him to be a very pretty man. Obviously, Nikola's presence in Gage's head blocked that fact out, but now Gage couldn't figure out why he'd been trying to fight what otherwise would have been a natural attraction to the younger man.

Henrick took advantage of the loud music and leaned in close to talk to Gage, placing a sneaky kiss just below his ear. "I knew you'd come around eventually. I'll make sure you can't even remember his name after tonight," he said into Gage's ear before he licked it. Gage's eyes went straight to Nikola, but the other man wasn't paying any attention to what was going on back at his table.

Gage stayed in his seat, preferring not to dance since he was sure his choice of partner for such an activity wouldn't go over too well. Instead, he drank and let Henrick steal little touches whenever he thought he could get away with it unnoticed. Thankfully, no one who drifted back to the table stayed long, only stopping to refresh their drink or grab a cigarette before wandering off into the crowd. Gage knew he should get up and mingle, but his morose mood made it impossible for him to do it.

Gage sat there and listened to Henrick chatter while he watched Nikola and Sabina mingle in between dances. They looked good together, and Nikola's arm around her waist looked natural, like it was right where it belonged. Nikola did glance in Gage's direction a time or two, and though he seemed irritated, he never made his way back to the table. Every time it looked like he wanted to head in Gage's direction, his attention was always stolen by Sabina, a hand on his cheek to draw his eyes back to hers.

When the waiters started circulating with trays of champagne, Gage glanced at his watch and saw it was five minutes until midnight. Henrick grabbed two glasses off one of the passing trays and handed one to Gage. "I'll meet you by the elevators in a couple of minutes. Don't keep me waiting." He got up and sashayed off.

Once again Gage checked the time, and after three minutes ticked by, he got up and headed to the elevators to meet up with Henrick. He briefly caught a glimpse of Nikola, and when their eyes met, Gage raised his glass to him but kept on walking. It took Gage a while to make his way through the crowd and out into the hallway to the elevators where Henrick was leaning against the wall holding his glass, waiting for him. He stood up straight when he saw Gage approaching as the sound of the crowd ramping up to start the countdown floated out into the hall, only twenty seconds left.

Henrick's smile faltered just as Gage reached him, and before Gage even had time to wonder what caused Henrick to start frowning, an iron grip on his elbow propelled him into the restrooms across from the elevators. Gage dropped his glass, causing it to shatter on the tiled floor. Taking no notice of the glass, the force behind the grip kept Gage moving until he was pushed roughly into the last stall. Nikola's lips crashed down on Gage's as he heard the large swell of voices shouting in celebration of the new year just as Gage's phone began ringing.

Chapter Fourteen

NIKOLA HATED HAVING to ignore Gage in favor of Sabina, but she was his public cover, and he couldn't blow the carefully cultivated façade they put on for everyone for the remote chance Gage might want more than just a fling while he was in Sarajevo. Nikola tried to catch Gage's eye to give him a reassuring look, but it seemed Gage decided to ignore him in favor of Henrick. It made Nikola's blood boil as Gage let the twink take liberties that Nikola was going to have to kill him for.

Nikola tried a few times to go to Gage, but Sabina knew better than to let him. She knew the tension in Nikola's shoulders wasn't from putting on a show with her as she was an expert at interpreting the vibes that were coming off Nikola in waves. A big public scene with his new gay lover and the little fucker who was all over him was the last thing Nikola needed in the middle of a big party, and she knew it. Sabina pulled Nikola to the dance floor more than once and told him he needed to calm down, assuring him that Gage wasn't going anywhere and that everybody flirted, it didn't mean anything.

But nothing could stop Nikola when he watched first Henrick go out the door, and then a couple of minutes later, Gage. He tipped his glass to Nikola, and the hurt in his eyes clued Nikola into what was about to happen if he didn't get there in time to stop it. Nikola pushed past people who tried to get his attention and entered the hallway after Gage, just in time to see Henrick give Gage his best come-hither look and smile, but when he saw Nikola, he knew his night was about to take a detour.

Nikola grabbed Gage just as he reached Henrick and then did the only thing he could think of—he pushed Gage into the toilets and kissed him as hard as he could. *I'm the only one he should be kissing in the new year with.* Nikola plundered the unwilling mouth beneath his. As the party erupted into applause and shouts of Happy New Year, Nikola's tongue found its home as Gage opened to him. Gage shuddered against Nikola, but then his damn phone started ringing and the spell was broken. Gage pushed Nikola violently away from him, sending him into the other side of the stall with enough force to shake the metal partition.

Gage pulled his phone out of his pocket, saw the caller ID, and said, "Fuck, this is the last fucking thing I need right now." He looked at Nikola. "You just fucking leave me alone." Gage stepped out of the stall as he answered his phone. Nikola's heart dropped when he heard Gage say, "Hey, Luke, I didn't expect you to call. How are you?" Nikola's rage simmered when he heard the name of Gage's ex-boyfriend.

Following Gage out into the hallway, Nikola listened to his side of the conversation, which was blessedly short. After Gage thanked Lucas for calling, he hung up and pocketed his phone before he got on the elevator, glaring at Nikola as he stepped in. When they got to Gage's room, he tried to shut the door in Nikola's face, but Nikola stuck his hand out to stop it. Gage growled at him, but he wouldn't be detoured.

"I have a key card. If you shut the door I'll just use it and come in anyway," Nikola said as he walked into the room.

"I don't want you here. Just go the fuck away. Go back to your girlfriend. I don't want to be your fucking dirty little secret. I'm not going to—"

Nikola grabbed Gage and kissed him. Gage pushed him off again with a look of indignation at Nikola's actions. He knew he was pissing Gage off, and Gage was drunk enough that sooner or later, he was going to get punched, but Nikola had never been one to back down from a fight. Gage was really angry, breathing hard as he backed away from Nikola, his face flushed, and his eyes flashing with a new light. Gage's lips turned up in a sneer as Nikola rushed him. Even though Nikola knew he had already pushed it too far, he couldn't stop himself.

Gage didn't try to dodge or even make it hard for Nikola when he wrapped his arms around Gage's waist; instead, Gage circled an arm around Nikola's neck. He twisted to break Nikola's hold on him before punching him in the gut, knocking the wind out of him. Gage let him go and turned to walk away, but Nikola jumped him, landing squarely on Gage's back and throwing him off balance. When he stumbled, Nikola threw his weight into it, driving them both to the floor so Gage ended up facedown on the carpet with Nikola sitting on his back. Then Nikola wrenched one of Gage's arms up behind his back and put his knee on the other one to keep him down. And though Gage bucked up, trying to dislodge him, Nikola was heavy enough that Gage couldn't get him off.

"Get the fuck off me, you fucking psycho. I'll fucking kill you for this," Gage growled into the carpet.

Nikola yanked Gage's arm as he leaned down to put his mouth by Gage's ear. "You are going to listen to me so I can explain to you why you are a secret but that there's nothing dirty about what is going on between us. Now are you going to be a good boy so that I can let you up, or do I have to explain things while I restrain you here on the floor?" he asked in the most menacing tone he could muster. Gage struggled enough that Nikola had to put more force on his arm to keep him from breaking free. Nikola's anger was mounting to match Gage's drunken fury, and he took a deep breath trying to reign himself in before things got even more out of control.

"I don't want to hear your excuses, *Niky*. I don't give a shit, and you can't intimidate me. I'm not afraid of you. Now get your ass off of me, because the longer you sit there, the shorter your life's getting."

Nikola could feel the tension thrumming through Gage's body, and he knew that there was no way Gage was going to listen to him right then. Gage was too drunk and pissed off, and even if Nikola explained, it would no doubt fall on deaf ears. Nikola sighed heavily as the anger drained out of him to be replaced by resignation. "I'm sorry, Gage. Please, I'll leave right now if you promise to let me come tomorrow after you've sobered up and calmed down, so I can explain everything to you."

It took Gage a moment to answer, and Nikola figured things could go either way, but gradually, Gage relaxed his tensed muscles and nodded. Knowing he wasn't forgiven, Nikola let go of Gage's arm and jumped up and away as quickly as he could, but Gage moved fast for a drunk. He pinned Nikola up against the wall both physically and with his icy glare. Resigned to his fate, Nikola waited for the blows he was sure were coming, but Gage didn't raise a hand to him.

"I don't want to see you again. You need to tell Nedim that I want a meeting set in the next two days, so we can discuss our business plans, or I'm getting on the first plane out of here." Gage managed to snarl even as his words slurred together. He pushed away from Nikola before he added, "And make sure he knows that I will not be needing your *services* anymore, and if he wants H&S to consider investing here, it would be a good thing if you stay clear of me from here on out."

The look on Gage's face as he delivered that last part tore at Nikola's heart. He would rather have had Gage hit him because the words hurt more than any punch ever could have. Nikola took a step toward him, but Gage turned away. "You can go now. You know where the door is." Gage stumbled to the bedroom and closed the door.

Nikola couldn't believe Gage wouldn't even hear him out. He was kicking himself for not foreseeing Teta inviting Sabina to the party. If he would have known, he'd have given Gage a heads-up and avoided the entire mess. Standing there, Nikola vibrated with the need to make Gage listen to him, wanting to go into the bedroom and hold Gage down again until he could make him understand. Nikola tried to decide if he should do it now, but instead, he just left. He knew there was more at stake than just his own personal hopes for a relationship with Gage. He couldn't fuck up the deal Gage was there to make with Nedim by getting in the way. He didn't know how secure Gage was in his job, but Nikola wouldn't want to be the reason he failed in Sarajevo. Maybe it was just better to leave things as they were.

Nikola made his way back up to the party, which was still in full swing and would be until the morning. Nedim eyed Nikola as he approached his table. The set of his jaw told Nikola that Nedim knew something was wrong before he even said a word. Turning to the people he was sitting with, Nedim said something that cleared the table so when Nikola sat down next to him, they were alone.

"So, *sine*, what happened?" Nedim asked.

"I screwed up, *Amidza*. I don't know what to do and you're going to kill me." Nikola looked at his hands, instead of his uncle's worried face.

"You know that's not true. I love you like a son. Tell me what happened with your man." Nedim suspected that there was more than business going on between him and Gage. The man was one of the most perceptive Nikola had ever met, and he figured it was probably what made him such a good businessman.

"He's not my man, never was. He says he wants a meeting in the next two days or else he's leaving on the next plane out," Nikola relayed Gage's message.

"Is this because of Sabina? I told your teta not to invite her. I told her you'd be busy with business, but she never listens. Said you should have your girl here, that you shouldn't have to work, that you are young and should be allowed to have fun. You know she thinks Hana needs a mother and that Sabina hung the moon. I wish you would let me tell her the truth. I think it would make some things much easier."

"I can't have anyone else know. It's risky enough as it is, *Amidza*. You know what my life would be like if people knew. My own mother threatened to disown me, and if not for Hana, she would have." Nikola reminded him again of what the consequences would be if the truth got out.

"Fine, fine, I know it's impossible for you to live your life as you want here. I won't say anything. You know you can trust me," Nedim assured Nikola that his secret was still safe. "You can bring Gage to me tomorrow for supper, and we will discuss business afterward."

"Sorry, *Amidza*, but he doesn't want to see me ever again. He told me to tell you there will be no deal if he sees me anywhere near the proceedings. You'll have to send Amel to get him. I'm so sorry." Nikola's chest hitched as he tried to hold in his emotions. When Nedim pulled him in for a hug, Nikola wanted to break down and cry, but he didn't—Nikola didn't cry—he wouldn't let Gage make him look weak. "I'm going to go home. Let me know if you have anything for me to do." Nikola separated from his uncle before people could start to wonder what was going on.

"Nikola, maybe you need to take a vacation. Maybe you should go see your friend, clear your head a little bit." Nikola was beginning to wonder if Nedim really could read his mind since the same thought was twisting in his brain. Maybe he needed to put some space between him and Gage—four thousand miles *might* be enough to do the job.

"I'll think about it, *Amidza*. Happy New Year." Nikola hugged Nedim before he said his goodbyes to everyone.

Nikola was in a funk as he drove home. The idea of going to Garrett and drowning himself in his willing flesh was appealing, but he knew now that he'd been with Gage, it wouldn't work. As stupid as Nikola knew it was, he already had feelings for Gage that wouldn't let him go to Garrett.

He couldn't get on a plane and leave Gage because he didn't like the way things between them ended. His throat threatened to close at the realization that it was over before it had really begun—before Nikola had a chance to explore the weird and wonderful feelings the other man brought out in him so quickly and unexpectedly. He needed to think of a way to make it better, to make Gage listen to him and give him another chance. He'd wait until Gage had his meeting with Nedim, so he knew where they stood on the business end, and then Nikola would figure out a way to fix it.

The sadness was almost overwhelming when Nikola dragged his overnight bag back into his bedroom, thinking about how he was supposed to have woken up with Gage and then have two uninterrupted days with him in a secluded cabin. Now there was nothing to look forward to except a long month of sleeping alone in a cold bed. Nikola stripped and got into bed, and then he tossed and turned until he finally fell asleep just before dawn.

"Babo." Nikola woke up looking into Hana's confused face. "Why are you in bed?"

"It's where people usually go to sleep."

She tilted her head to look at him before crawling into the bed with him, to sit with her back against the headboard. "You know what I meaned," she said. Looking up at her through blurry, sleep hazed eyes, Nikola knew exactly what she meant. Why was he there when he should have been with Gage? Nikola couldn't hide his emotion for her like he usually did. The hurt was just too deep. She rubbed his cheek. "Where's Uncle Gage?"

"Baby, I don't think we're going to see much of Gage anymore. He's got work to do." Nikola didn't have the heart to tell her it was his fault Gage wouldn't be around. He also couldn't stop the single tear that slipped out of the corner of his eye—the first in almost twenty years, and Hana saw it before he could turn his head away to hide it. His baby girl held her arms out to him, and he let her hug his head into her belly.

"Can I tell you something, Babo?" Nikola nodded his head against her. "My tummy told me that Uncle Gage wouldn't be my uncle for very long." She paused long enough for Nikola to think that even Hana's tummy was smart enough to know it was doomed from the start. But then she added in a whisper, "Because I was going to get to call him Daddy."

Her statement—so sure in its conviction—startled Nikola enough to make him sit up so he could look her in the eyes. Her confidence was also reflected there, and it made Nikola's heart break a little bit more at what would never be. "When did your tummy tell you that?"

"When Uncle Gage kissed my fingers to help make them better. He would be a good daddy, Babo, because he knows things like that," she stated with the simple reasoning of a child.

"He probably would, but I'm sorry, baby, this might be one time your tummy was wrong." Nikola hated having to crush her hope. He was starting to think that the whole love-at-first-sight thing was a sort of insanity that ran in families. Hana never got attached to people that quickly. Gage obviously had some powerful mojo over the Mahanovics.

Hana pursed her lips and shook her head. "Babo, my tummy doesn't lie to me. It knows that lying is wrong. Can I still go with Nana today?" she asked, abruptly changing the subject.

Nikola had to think a second before he remembered it was New Year's Day and there was a big family thing at his uncle's—a thing he couldn't go to since Gage would be there. "Sure. Whatever plans you and Nana made, you can keep. I'm going to stay in bed all day and enjoy it," Nikola lied and even tried to smile to make her believe him.

"I'm going to go get dressed and go back to Nana's so you can sleep some more," she said, getting off the bed and heading for the door. Nikola listened as his daughter rummaged around in her room for a while before she hollered goodbye and the door closed behind her.

Some time later, Nikola rolled over and grabbed his phone when it rang. He coughed to clear the sleep from his voice before answering Amel's call. "Yeah?" He listened to Amel tell him the plans for the day which hurt since he wasn't included in them. "I'll text him."

He hung up and texted Gage to let him know that Amel would pick him up at five that afternoon for his meeting with Nedim. Nikola didn't expect Gage to respond so he wasn't disappointed when nothing came back from the other man. Still holding his phone in his hand, Nikola's mood brightened a little when a plan in the form of a text message materialized in his mind. Gage said he didn't want to see Nikola but he didn't say Nikola couldn't text him. Nikola was going to find a way to make Gage listen him, and his phone was going to be the tool he'd use to accomplish it.

Chapter Fifteen

GAGE WOKE UP with a head that felt like it was about to explode. Groaning, he bolted off the couch and made it to the bathroom in time to unload the contents of his stomach. As he stood there over the toilet, he decided to seriously evaluate his alcohol consumption and the merits of decreasing it. Searching his carry-on, he found his ibuprofen and downed four of them before he took a quick shower.

Gage called room service and ordered a pot of coffee. He'd just sat down with his first cup when his phone buzzed with a text. Looking at the screen, he noticed he'd missed quite a few messages from his family, all wishing him a Happy New Year so he responded in kind as he drank his coffee. Until he got to the most recent one, and his finger paused over the message when he saw it was from Nikola. Taking a deep breath, he tapped the screen and was relieved to find it simply stated that a meeting had been set up with Nedim for that evening and Amel would be picking him up at five. There was nothing else—no apologies, no explanation.

Remembering the rage he'd felt as Nikola sat on his back and held him on the floor, brought back the urge to punch Nikola for a second time as he'd pinned him to the wall. Thankfully, he knew it wouldn't have been good to beat Nikola to a bloody pulp, no matter how much he'd deserved it at the time. He read the text again. He guessed he shouldn't have expected anything more after he'd pretty much kicked Nikola out of his life when he'd kicked him out of the room. In the light of day and with a sober mind, Gage realized he'd overreacted, but at the time, he couldn't stop the hurt from turning to anger. Even as he sat there, he couldn't find the strength to reach out to Nikola.

GAGE WENT DOWN to the café on the first floor with the idea of having a light lunch. He wasn't too surprised to find Henrick there talking on his cell phone since the guy seemed to show up everywhere. Gage joined him when Henrick motioned him over and indicated that he should take a seat, waiting patiently while he finished his call.

"How are you this morning? Did you and your *friend* work things out?" he asked with a salacious grin.

"I'm fine. How are you?" Gage ignored the second part of Henrick's question since he didn't want to get into it.

"Oh, I was doing fine, but things just got so much better," Henrick said with the expected flirty wink—he was a walking stereotype. Gage took the wink for what he knew it meant, which was that Henrick was letting him know that despite everything he was still interested if Gage was game. He admitted, if he could keep Nikola out of his thoughts long enough to give Henrick any consideration, he was attracted to the cute young man and he'd probably have a good time with him.

"Are you here for lunch?"

"Yes, I was just about to order. Care to join me? Or will your shadow be showing up to haul you off again?" Henrick glanced over Gage's shoulder as if he expected to see Nikola.

"I'd like that, and no, I don't think we'll be interrupted this time." Gage smiled at Henrick's pleased expression and resisted the urge to look behind him to make sure they were alone. They both ordered a sandwich and a drink, and then Henrick told Gage about the first time he'd been to Bosnia, which included the restaurants he'd been to. Apparently, there were some fairly nice ones downtown.

"Are you free for dinner tonight?" Henrick asked when he'd gotten done telling Gage of one of his favorite places to eat in the city.

"Sorry, I have a meeting with Nedim this evening." Gage was surprised when he realized he meant it. After getting to know Henrick a bit more, and when the other man wasn't overtly trying to get into Gage's pants, he was actually decent company. The proposition of hanging out with Henrick was suddenly surprisingly alluring.

"Oh, well, maybe another time then." Henrick shrugged like it was no big deal. When the food came, Henrick asked the waiter if he had a small piece of paper and a pen he could borrow. When the waiter returned with the requested items, Henrick wrote down his phone and room numbers and handed them to Gage. "I'd usually have my business cards with me, but I didn't expect to need them, so I didn't bother to put them in my pocket."

Gage did happen to have a few cards in his wallet, so he pulled one out. Taking the pen from Henrick, he wrote his room number on the back before handing it to him. He raised his eyebrows and smiled prettily for Gage, showing his surprise and pleasure at getting the information he'd been denied before. "Maybe if our schedules are clear, we can have dinner tomorrow night," Gage suggested.

"I'd really like that."

All throughout lunch, Henrick regaled Gage with stories of his hometown, Salzburg, Austria, and his college years in Vienna. It felt good to laugh with him, and for a little while, Gage thought he might be able to put the mess with Nikola behind him, maybe even patch things up between them enough to stand the sight of Nikola once again. It was amazing what a good meal in good company could do to one's outlook on the world.

When their lunch was finished, and they'd each drank two cups of coffee, Henrick leaned back in his seat with a satisfied sigh. "I should probably get going. I need to make some phone calls. It was really nice chatting with you, and I hope we can find time to get together again soon." The waiter must have overheard him and showed up to drop off their checks.

"I'd really like that," Gage said. Henrick paid his bill before giving Gage a small wave as he walked off. Gage looked at his watch, only to find they'd been there for over two hours, but that still left two more hours until his ride would be there to pick him up for his meeting.

Gage went back to his room and busied himself with getting everything he could possibly need ready for his meeting. With that task finished and a half an hour left, he dressed in a suit and sat down to wait. Amel knocked on the door at exactly five. Amel's polite handshake and greeting were the only times the man interacted with Gage from the time they left the hotel until they reached an apartment building on the edge of Sarajevo.

The building was surrounded by a security fence, and Amel stopped at a small guardhouse next to the gate before being quickly let through. Then he parked in an underground garage and led Gage to an elevator that he used a key card to access. After hitting the button for the penthouse apartment, he used the key card once again to open the elevator door when it stopped, the doors opening directly into a foyer, which Gage realized was actually inside the apartment.

Amel started walking toward the noise coming from farther inside the apartment. Gage followed, taking in the lavish foyer with marble floors that gave way to dark, polished parquet as they entered what was a well-used family room filled with people. In the corner stood a huge Christmas tree surrounded by presents and children, making Gage suddenly uneasy as he'd obviously stepped into what was surely a family gathering.

Gage had just turned to Amel to ask him why he was there if there was a family function going on, when he saw Hana spot him. She ran toward Gage and then threw herself at him with the total faith that he would catch her that only a child could have. And without thinking, he did just that, scooping her into his arms against his chest.

"Uncle Gage," she squealed. Wrapping her arms around Gage's neck, she squeezed him in a tight hug. Her squeal brought all eyes in the room to them, and there were some questioning looks on quite a few faces, but Hana didn't seem to care so Gage ignored the attention.

"Hey there, B. How are you doing?" Gage asked the squirming child in his arms.

Hana pulled back so she could look at him. "Did Babo come with you?" Hana looked around, and her mouth turned down into a frown when she didn't see Nikola anywhere in the room.

Gage was relieved to know Nikola wasn't already there, so he wouldn't have to face him, but immediately on the heels of that came a guilty feeling. Nikola wasn't at the family gathering, and Gage was certain it was because of him. "No, he didn't. Amel brought me. What's going on here, B?"

Her good cheer returned in an instant. "It's New Year's so we get presents. Don't you get New Year's presents?"

"Um, no, I guess not. We just get presents for Christmas back home."

"Oh. Well, we have Christmas with Nana and New Year's with Uncle Nedim," she said, like it cleared up everything.

Nedim came up to them and put out his hand. Gage maneuvered Hana onto one arm so he could shake the offered hand. "It's good to see you again," Nedim said. "I see you have a friend here." He smiled at Hana as he shook Gage's hand. Nedim said something to Hana in Bosnian, and she answered back before she turned her attention back to Gage.

"I want you to sit by me at dinner tonight, okay?" she asked.

Gage looked at Nedim, who was smiling at Hana indulgently, to make sure he wasn't agreeing to something he shouldn't. "Sure, B, whatever you want." Hana kissed his cheek and wiggled to let Gage know that he could put her down. He set her on her feet, and she returned to the crowd of kids by the tree. Gage didn't miss the narrow-eyed glare Nikola's mom gave him when his eyes landed on her for a brief moment.

"She likes you. I do not think I have seen her like that with anyone so fast. She is reserved—a lot like her father," Nedim said as the two men watched her join back in the conversation by the tree.

Gage didn't want to discuss Nikola with Nedim, so he changed the subject quickly. "I don't want to crash your holiday party. I should probably just go back to the hotel—"

"No, you will stay. We will have dinner, and we will talk business after," Nedim interrupted in a tone that brokered no argument. "Come, the food is ready."

Gage walked with Nedim into a huge dining room, which had a table that could seat at least twenty people and another for twelve more. Nedim sat at the head of the big table and motioned for Gage to sit on his right, with Hana taking the seat next to him, and to his surprise, Sabina sat next to Hana.

Smiling, Sabina leaned across Hana to speak to Gage. "Hi. It's nice to see you again."

"Nice to see you again too, Sabina." Gage tried to be polite, but he wondered if she could hear the acid he'd tried to keep out of his tone.

"Sabina will be helping me in our meeting since Nikola is unable to be here tonight," Nedim explained after watching the exchange.

Great, just what Gage needed, to spend time with the reason he wasn't in a cabin on a mountain with Nikola doing ungodly things to each other. Gage nodded and smiled since there was nothing for him to say. The food was served, and Gage ate silently while the conversation went on around him. For once, he was glad he didn't understand what was being said. It made for a good excuse to stay aloof from it all. There were a few strange looks sent Gage's way, making him a bit uncomfortable, but eventually, Hana started telling him all sorts of things about the family and her and her babo, and the dinner went by quickly.

After coffee and dessert, Nedim turned to Gage. "Well, let us go get this done." He stood and waited for Sabina and Gage to get up and follow.

Hana grabbed Gage's hand, and he bent down to her eye level. "Uncle Gage, are you still coming to my party?"

"I'm sorry, B, but probably not. I think I'm going to be really busy with work for a while." Gage was sorry and wished he could be there for her, but he just didn't see that happening with the way things stood between him and Nikola. Hana looked really sad, and like she might cry so he pulled her in for a hug. "It's not that I don't want to come, Hana Banana, but I think it's for the best if I stay away from your daddy for a while," Gage whispered in her ear.

"But my babo is sad, and I think you can make him happy again," she whispered back. It broke Gage's heart to hear that she believed he could make anyone happy when Gage knew the truth was exactly the opposite.

Gage kissed her cheek. "You make your daddy happy, B. You're all he needs. Be good, okay?"

Hana nodded, but she didn't look convinced. She turned and went back into the living room with everyone else, throwing a sad look over her shoulder at Gage that mirrored his own. Both Nedim and Sabina were staring at Gage like he was some freak show exhibit at the circus. A blush crept up his neck when Sabina smiled brightly at him, like he'd done something she approved of.

Nedim led them to his office, and two hours later, Gage was on his way back to the hotel with a tentative business agreement, a schedule of meetings, and a promise to start looking at some of the sites they lined up for him to see. Nedim tried to convince him to stay for the rest of the evening, but Gage declined, saying he didn't want to intrude any more than he already had.

Gage was tired so he hit the sack early, but still lay there awake for a while thinking about Nikola and what Hana said. He hated that he caused the other man's sadness since it was obvious Hana was picking up on it. Though it wasn't something Gage was proud of, he knew he was stubborn, and he'd told Nikola he didn't want to see him ever again. Gage didn't know how to take it back. He wasn't good at eating his words. He would have to wait for an opportunity to come up that would let him save face without having to grovel if he wanted to see Nikola again. Oh god, how he suddenly hoped there would be such an opportunity!

GAGE HADN'T GOTTEN much sleep, but even though he was dragging ass, the day flew by in a blur of meetings. He was hopeful he'd be able to get the ball rolling on the mountain of legal paperwork that needed to get done as he knew that was always the major hurdle to setting up shop. He'd gotten a text message from Henrick telling him he had run into a problem with his software and wouldn't be free for supper, so when Gage got back to his hotel at seven thirty, he knew he was looking at a long night sitting in his room.

He was in the middle of reading through one of the more complicated Bosnian laws regarding foreign-owned businesses operating within the country when his phone buzzed with a text. He glanced at the screen and was surprised to see it was from Nikola. He hesitated before opening it, but the curiosity got the better of him.

Nikola: *My family is originally from Srebrenica. I don't know if you've heard of it, but it was one of the nastier parts of the war. I was just a kid so for the first part of the war I didn't know what was happening but that changed.*

It was not at all what Gage expected to read when he'd opened the text. He'd been expecting an explanation of who Sabina was to him, or maybe an apology for what happened in the hotel room, or something about how Hana was upset after seeing Gage at Nedim's, but not this... His phone interrupted his musings with another incoming message.

Nikola: *My mom never forgave my dad for not leaving during the war. She's Croatian. We could have gone to her family near Zagreb. We could have been safer. But my dad was stubborn and we stayed.*

Nikola: *I worried about him every time he went out to fight. I cried myself to sleep every time and my mom got crazier and crazier. But my dad said that if all the Bosniaks left then the men who died already would have died for nothing.*

Nikola: *The thing I remember most from that time was how hungry everyone was. There was never enough food. Refugees kept pouring in. I know my parents went without so I had enough to not go insane from the hunger.*

Nikola: *We left on a bus in the summer of 95. My home that had become a place of so much horror. When they took my dad, I still hoped I'd see him again. My mom cried and cried. She knew but I was only twelve and had hope.*

Nikola: *I wonder how different my life would have been if we would have gone to Zagreb. How it would have been better to not go through what I did but then I look at Hana and know everything happens for a reason.*

Nikola: *I'm glad the meetings are going well. Good night, Gage.*

Gage didn't respond. What could he say? He sat there and absorbed what Nikola just told him and wondered why he'd felt he needed Gage to know those things about him. He couldn't work with Nikola's past sitting there on his phone. Nothing could erase the image of Nikola as a scared, skinny twelve-year-old boy clinging to the hope he'd see his dad again and watching his mother fall apart as they left the only home he'd ever known. The image was so far removed from the confident man Gage knew. He quickly did the math to figure out Nikola was only thirty-two. He seemed much older than his age, but then going through the things he had would explain that.

Gage went to the gym and worked until he was exhausted, and after showering, he fell into bed. Sleep claimed him quickly, but his dreams were haunted by Nikola. Gage knew he needed to save Nikola but from what, his dreams didn't reveal.

Chapter Sixteen

NEDIM CALLED NIKOLA after Gage left his apartment to give him a detailed report on the night, including how Hana clung to Gage. He promised, against his better judgment, to keep Nikola updated on how the business meetings were going, but at the same time, Nedim also told him he needed to get himself straightened out. There wasn't any other work for Nikola—no other business people for him to shepherd around since he was supposed to have been busy with Gage for a month. That left Nikola to sit at home and stew over his mistakes. It also left his mind free to figure out how to get back into Gage's good graces, if not his bed.

Nikola's phone reminded him he could still communicate with Gage without having to risk the chance of face-to-face rejection. He sent Gage the first text without really knowing what he was going to tell him, but once he started, it just came out. He felt a little stupid pouring out parts of his life one hundred and sixty characters at a time, but he decided an email would be easier to dismiss than several texts making Gage's phone either chime or vibrate a few times a night.

At first, Nikola was disappointed when he didn't get any sort of acknowledgement that Gage even read the secrets he'd revealed. On the other hand, he considered it a check in the win column when Gage didn't tell him to fuck off and leave him alone, either. Nikola imagined Gage reading each text as he sent them and prayed he was getting through to the other man.

Nikola spent time with Hana and waited until he put her to bed at nine to send more of his texts to Gage.

Nikola: *We were in a sort of makeshift refugee camp in Tusla for four months until they decided what to do with us. We didn't get a choice. My mom and I were sent to Atlanta with about twenty others.*

Nikola: *People from a Christian group were there to help us. My mother was actually treated better than the other refugees because she was Catholic where the others were Muslims. It helped that we attended church.*

Nikola: *I was almost as afraid there in a place where I didn't know anyone and didn't speak the language, as I had been starving and listening to gunshots in the night back in Srebrenica. I started school where they taught me English.*

Nikola: *It was hard for us. We were very poor and my mom had to find a job because the welfare didn't last long. She worked cleaning at a hotel where they were patient enough to teach her through charades how to do her job.*

Nikola: *She never got better even when life seemed to smooth out for us. Some of my dad's family ended up in Atlanta also so we had some people to help us. She left one week after my high school graduation.*

Nikola: *I hope everything is still going smoothly on the business end. Good night, Gage.*

The next day, Nikola continued to tell Gage his story after he'd put Hana to bed and answered her third call for a glass of water with a stern warning to go to sleep.

Nikola: *I always knew I was different. When I got to college I found myself and like any guy who has the freedom to go out and have fun, I went a little crazy and fucked my way through most of the gay student body.*

Nikola: *I managed to graduate on the dean's list even with my partying. I got a job by the end of the summer after I graduated. I went to school for graphic design and was working for a web design company when I met Garrett.*

Nikola: *He was the most beautiful man I'd ever seen. His father is African American and his mother is a southern belle. His slow southern drawl made me tingle whenever he talked to me and he always talked to me.*

Nikola: *He finally asked me out and we dated for a couple of months before I moved in with him. We were like oil and water most of the time but we always worked it out between the sheets and that was good enough for me.*

Nikola: *He loved me and I knew it. I loved him but I wasn't sure he was the one for me. I didn't think a relationship like we had could last because sooner or later one of us would kill the other.*

Nikola: *He only wanted me but I found myself always looking for something better. Not better looking or anything physical. All that was great with him but I was looking for someone who would make me fall head over heels.*

Nikola: *I heard you met with the big man today, hope it went well. Good night, Gage.*

Nikola spent the day shopping with Hana, but he was distracted as his mind was busy preparing the next set of text messages for Gage. He suspected Hana knew something was up as she had taken to filling in the gaps his silence left in their conversations. He'd been grateful when bedtime rolled around, and he could kiss her good night. He sat on the couch and tapped away at the screen of his phone before sending out probably the hardest part of his past to tell.

Nikola: *I was out to everyone except my family and the Bosnian community. I went to a wedding in the community which meant I couldn't take Garrett with me. Someone was always trying to set me up.*

Nikola: *They all thought I needed a nice Bosnian girl to settle down with. I was a pretty good catch, good-looking and making a pretty good living. The girl was Jasmina. She was a cousin of the bride from Iowa.*

Nikola: *I got drunk and woke up in a hotel room. Jasmina was in the bed with me on one side and there was a man pressed against my back. I got out of there as fast as I could. I didn't even want to know what happened.*

Nikola: *I told Garrett what happened with Jasmina. I didn't mention the other guy. I know I probably should have but I knew he would forgive me for cheating on him with someone I could never really be attracted to.*

Nikola: *He did forgive me and everything went on as usual until five months later when Jasmina called me to say she was pregnant and it was mine. Of course I asked her how she could know it was mine. There had been another guy too.*

Nikola: *She laughed and told me I was the only one who fucked her that night because Đemo had been fucking me. I asked why we hadn't used condoms and she said they'd only had two and one broke.*

Nikola: *I had insisted that Đemo wear the one that was left and she had thought it was a safe time of month for her so she'd let me fuck her raw. Now she knew better and she was going to have the baby but give it up.*

Nikola: *She wasn't ready to have a kid and she'd never find a Bosnian man who would accept her with another man's child. I didn't think about it. I told her I wanted a paternity test and if the baby was mine, I'd take it.*

Nikola: *Things seem to be going good with the legal paperwork so far. I'm glad. Sleep tight, Gage, good night.*

As Nikola prepared to send his nightly texts to Gage, the very subject he was writing about made him realize that Hana's birthday was only five days away. Five more days to convince Gage to give him another chance.

Nikola: *I told Garrett about the baby. He was pissed that I'd made the decision to take the baby without talking to him. It was his life too. We fought more than anything for the next four months. For days he wouldn't look at me.*

Nikola: *I got on a plane when Jasmina's mom called to say she was in labor and at the hospital. I wasn't prepared for how cold it was in Des Moines in January. First time labor takes forever. I got there only an hour after she was born.*

Nikola: *They did a quickie paternity test. They told me they'd need to do another one to be 100% certain but this would pretty much tell me if I was not the father. I never prayed so hard for anything to please be a no.*

Nikola: *When they told me there was a pretty good chance I was the father I ran to the bathroom and threw up. They explained my options, you know—signing away my rights and going home alone or not and taking the baby.*

Nikola: *I went to see her. They let me hold her and they asked me if I had a name picked out. I fell in love and couldn't think of anything but how she had my eyes and if I let her go I'd never see them looking back at me again.*

Nikola: *Hana, I told them, her name is Hana Mahanovic. She's my daughter and I love her and I'm going to take her home and take care of her for the rest of my life. The nurses gave me the biggest smiles and patted me on the back.*

Nikola: *I had to wait there in Iowa for the paperwork to get done. Jasmina gave up her rights to Hana and told me that she didn't want to have any contact because it would hurt her too much to know. It was better to forget.*

Nikola: *I was in over my head. I bought what I needed to get Hana home to Atlanta. Garrett's mom actually was there at the airport with Garrett to help out until I figured out what I was going to do.*

Nikola: *Wondering if you've seen any land that you're interested in yet. Have a good night, Gage.*

Nikola was starting to get discouraged by the sixth night of texting Gage and receiving no response. He briefly considered giving it up, but he just couldn't stop trying.

Nikola: *Garrett didn't want to have to pay for my mistake for the rest of his life. He made that clear. I put in my two week notice at work, called my mom and told her I was coming home with her granddaughter.*

Nikola: *I moved everything to my cousin's house and left Garrett a broken mess. My cousin's wife watched Hana while I finished out my notice. We were on the first flight I could book to Sarajevo after that.*

Nikola: *Hana did not travel well but the flight attendants were really nice to the scared first time daddy. I never realized how many kind strangers there are in the world until I made that trip with a baby in my arms.*

Nikola: *My mom was happy we were home and my family helped me a lot. I missed Garrett and my old life so much there were days I didn't get out of bed. I was not a very good father for the first two years.*

Nikola: *I loved Hana, don't get me wrong, I was just lost here. The only people who know who I really am are Hana, my mom, uncle Nedim, and Sabina. They are the only ones I can be myself around, who love me for me.*

Nikola: *Nedim says you know your job and he's happy he has someone who doesn't blow smoke up his ass constantly. Hana says hi, good night, Gage.*

Nikola left Hana with his mom so he could go out and buy the necessary birthday party supplies. He didn't ask Sabina to go with him like he normally would, instead wandering alone through the store, throwing random things into his cart. He hoped he hadn't forgotten anything as he stood in the checkout line. He was preoccupied by the fact that Gage still hadn't even acknowledged he'd received any of Nikola's messages and what that most likely meant.

Nikola: *I finally got my head out of my ass and Nedim started giving me jobs and I had to pretend to be this big bad ass to get any respect from the guys around me. I met Sabina and we hit it off as friends and I told her I was gay.*

Nikola: *She was surprised. I'm a manly type of guy. Here they still think every gay man is like Henrick. That you can just tell. She was sick of everyone asking her when she was going to get married or fixing her up.*

Nikola: *She and I pretend there is more between us than just friendship. It works for us both and she's good with Hana. I don't have anyone here. I mean no one that's not just a trick for a night and even those are very few.*

Nikola: *I miss having someone to come home to. I miss having someone to hold in my bed at night. To tell you the truth I've been thinking about Garrett a lot lately. Maybe he can be my future if I let him be.*

Nikola: *Hana misses you. Good night, Gage.*

Gage: *Good night, Nikola.*

Just those three words from Gage made Nikola's heart race in his chest. He hoped it meant he was making some progress, but he didn't hold his breath. He knew what he needed to do, and using Hana to lure Gage to his home wasn't something he looked forward to doing, but at least it wasn't a lie, he told himself. Hana had been asking about Gage, and his name was mentioned in conversation at least once in the course of every day. Nikola checked on Hana and then went to bed letting memories of his short time with Gage drag him into dreamland.

The next night he continued.

Nikola: *I found you insanely attractive the minute I saw you. I wanted to touch you. I was afraid you'd find out I was gay and you'd want someone else to be your liaison with my uncle.*

Nikola: *The first night I got you so drunk on rakia. I kissed you and you kissed me back but then you pulled away and told me you couldn't do it and it was wrong. I still don't know if you remember the kiss, do you?*

Nikola: *I tried to forget the kiss and the look on your face after that but I wanted you still. The night at my house when I saw you with Hana, I wondered why you didn't want a kid of your own. You were a natural with her.*

Nikola: *I pretended that we were a family. I knew it wasn't true but it felt so good to have you there with me and Hana. I was afraid when Hana dropped enough clues for you to figure out that I was gay.*

Nikola: *The sex that night was amazing. That you were up and sitting at the table humoring Hana the next morning went straight to my heart. I enjoyed the day we spent together, all three of us, but my heart broke when I dropped you off alone.*

Nikola: *I was so jealous when I found you in the bar with Henrick. I saw the picture on your phone of your ex. I know he is your type and I am so not like them. I'm a possessive asshole. I'm sorry if I crossed the line.*

Nikola: *I miss you. Good night, Gage.*

Gage: *You didn't. Good night, Nikola.*

Another message from Gage and hope swelled because maybe there was a chance Gage would forgive him after all. Nikola sent his final set of texts to Gage with a renewed hope that he was getting through to him.

Nikola: *I'm sorry about the New Year's party. I shouldn't have ignored you that way but I couldn't jeopardize my life here for what may be just a fling for you. You flirting with Henrick made my blood boil and I wanted to come to you.*

Nikola: *Sabina stopped me. She knew I'd make a scene if I had to break the two of you up. When I saw you follow him out I knew I had to stop what was about to happen. I just had to.*

Nikola: *I'm sorry I kissed you in the bathroom. My only thought at the time was that you shouldn't be kissing anyone at midnight on New Year's except for me. Really I think you shouldn't kiss anyone but me ever again...*

Nikola: *I should have just left you then, instead of following you to your room. If I had been you I'd have pounded the shit out of me but you didn't because you are a better person than I am. I don't deserve someone like you.*

Nikola: *Please Gage, would you consider coming to Hana's party tomorrow? For her. She keeps asking me for you and if you would come it would be a good present for her. She hasn't asked for anything else.*

Nikola: *I promise I will keep my distance. I just want my little girl to be happy on her birthday. I miss you more and more each day but I understand why you don't want me and that's okay. Good night, Gage.*

Gage: *I'm not and you do and I do still. Good night, Niky.*

Nikola wasn't sure how to interpret Gage's last text, but he decided that was it. If Gage didn't respond in some way after all Nikola told him, then he would leave Gage alone.

NIKOLA SPENT THE next day getting ready for Hana's party, with Sabina's help, they put up decorations while Nikola's mom took Hana out to shop for her birthday present from her nana. Nikola couldn't help but wonder if Gage would show up and he shared those fears with Sabina.

"I think that if he has any feelings for you at all, he'll come," Sabina said when she caught Nikola checking his phone for the hundredth time.

"Yeah, but what if the only feeling he has for me is hatred?"

She put her arm around his shoulders. "Guys who don't have feelings for each other don't act like utter jackasses when one of them hurts the other's feelings. He wouldn't have been so pissed if he hadn't been hurt, and if he was hurt, that means he feels something for you. It's not just sex, Nikola, and I think you know it, and that's why you can't give it up."

Putting his arm around her waist, he gave her a squeeze, thankful for her friendship. "I poured my entire life story out to him through SMS. I told him things I've never told anyone. He probably thinks I'm crazy and wants nothing more to do with me. Maybe I am too crazy to love."

Sabina started laughing at him then, and it took her some time to regain control of herself. "Oh, Nikola, sometimes you say the funniest things. He would be the crazy one if he didn't love you. You are a great guy. I don't care what your mother says about you." She nudged him with her elbow and made a funny face to try to cheer him up.

His mom and Hana walked in while he and Sabina were still sitting there arm in arm, and Nikola's mom's eyes lit up with hope. Pushing him away, Sabina shook a playful fist at Nikola before she went to see what they bought Hana for her birthday. The doorbell rang and the first of the guests arrived. Every time Nikola answered the door, he hoped the person on the other side would be Gage, but as the day wore on, he started to lose hope.

Chapter Seventeen

GAGE SPENT THE week in business meetings, looking at sites and hanging out with Henrick who turned out to be pleasant company as they worked out at the hotel gym and Henrick took Gage to a few of his favorite restaurants. There was only one time Gage was pulled toward Henrick in a sexual way, but his phone started chirping as he received Nikola's nightly texts, and Gage quickly pulled Henrick off his cock just as he started to get into the blow job he was giving. Gage apologized, probably far more than needed before Henrick shushed him, finally understanding that Gage was hung up on someone else and was happy to just be friends. Gage was sorry to see Henrick go when his job was done, but Henrick made him promise to keep in touch.

Gage read and reread Nikola's texts and realized he looked forward to learning something new about Nikola every night. He couldn't work up the courage to respond until Nikola mentioned Garrett and that thing about letting some man Gage had never met, but hated with a passion, be his future. A pang of fear ran through him, and a possessive growl rose from his chest as he sent a text back to Nikola before he could even think twice about it. He wanted to let Nikola know his message was getting through even if he was unwilling to say more than good night.

Thoughts about going to Nikola haunted Gage since he couldn't see a way to make it happen without admitting he'd been partially to blame. Hana's birthday loomed large in his mind as a chance for reconciliation, but just showing up at Nikola's door empty-handed didn't seem like a good idea. Gage shopped online, looking for the perfect birthday present for Hana, and when he found it, he didn't blink at the exorbitant price of expedited shipping that would get the package to him as quickly as possible. He'd had every intention of attending the party after only a few nights of Nikola's texts, so when Nikola invited him once again, he looked at it as an olive branch, and he was going to grab it with both hands.

Gage called Amel to get Nikola's address, and without even expressing surprise at the request, Amel instead offered to drive him to the party. They stopped to pick up a few things to go along with Hana's present, and his purchase caused Amel to raise his eyebrow at the huge display of balloons to go with the massive present in the backseat. Gage didn't give him any excuses for the extravagance. What could he say? He'd always been good at getting presents for kids, as there were plenty of little ones in his family. Amel didn't get out once they pulled into Nikola's driveway, remaining in the car and grinning as he watched Gage struggle to get everything in hand to wrangle it to the front door where he then rang the doorbell and waited.

Nikola's mother answered the door, and the smile on her face disappeared when she saw it was Gage standing there. "Hi. I'm here for the party?" Gage said, but it came out sounding more like a question in the face of her disapproval. She didn't say anything but turned, leaving the door open so he could follow. Gage walked in, hoping his presence wouldn't be greeted with such frostiness by the rest of the inhabitants.

"UNCLE GAGE!" The shrill shriek of pure joy echoed through the room as Hana barreled toward Gage. He crouched and managed to set everything on the floor just in time to catch her as she hurtled into him. "You came, you came, you came! I told Babo you'd come!" she exclaimed as she hugged Gage and then bestowed a few kisses on his face.

Gage stood with her in his arms as she clung to his neck. "Of course, Hana Banana. I couldn't miss your birthday now, could I?" Looking around the room, he counted six other little girls, along with Nikola's mom, Sabina, and finally, standing there staring like he'd seen a ghost, was Nikola. Gage smiled shyly at him and raised his hand in greeting.

Nikola started toward Gage, but then he said, "Excuse me a minute, I have to do something." Nikola stepped past Gage, leaving him standing there holding his daughter as he went into the hall and moments later a door closed. Gage looked back into the room and realized everyone's attention was on him and the two women in the room didn't seem all too pleased with him. Nikola's mother was shooting daggers at him with her eyes, while Sabina was giving him a look he couldn't quite decipher, but it looked like she wasn't exactly pleased.

"Hey, B, I'm going to go talk to your dad a second, okay?" Gage put Hana down.

"Is this for me?" she asked pointing at the present and balloons.

Gage forced a smile. "Of course, B. Who else is turning six today?" Hana smiled brightly as she tried to lift the big package but failed, so Sabina stepped up to help when Gage turned and went in search of Nikola.

Knocking on Nikola's bedroom door and receiving no answer, Gage turned the knob to let himself in. Nikola was standing in front of the window with his arms hugging his chest and staring out at the hedge that ran along the property line. Gage shut the door behind him but stood just inside the room—afraid to close the distance between them. Nikola didn't turn to face him or even acknowledge his presence, making Gage wonder if he regretted inviting him. Maybe now that Nikola had seen him again, he realized Gage wasn't anything special after all.

"I really didn't think you would come," Nikola said softly in a strangled voice.

Gage sighed. Maybe attending the party was a bad idea. "I can leave if you want. I thought maybe you wanted me here, but if you're second guessing asking me to come and you want me to go, I will," Gage offered him an easy out.

"Did you see her face when you walked in?" Nikola asked in an almost whisper but didn't wait for Gage to answer. "She really thinks it's true, and I don't know what to do anymore."

"She thinks what is true, Nikola? Would you please look at me? Do you want me to leave?" Gage didn't understand what Nikola was talking about or why he wouldn't turn around. He knew on some level his voice conveyed how much he didn't want to go, pleading for Nikola to tell him to stay. He wanted so much for Nikola to tell him what was going on in his mind, but first and foremost, he wanted to know Nikola wanted him there. He wished Nikola would turn and let him see his face, maybe read in his eyes that he wanted him to stay. Gage finally walked across the room so he was only a couple of steps behind Nikola and reached out to touch his shoulder. Nikola's shoulders slumped under the touch and Gage could feel the light tremors running through his body.

Turning to face him, Nikola revealed what he'd been hiding by keeping his back to Gage, who now had to hide his surprise at the tears running down Nikola's cheeks. "I don't want you to go. I never wanted you to go, but you make me weak." Nikola took a shuddering breath, "I don't cry, Gage. I haven't cried since I left Srebrenica—not even when they told me my father was dead. If you can make me cry, I'm afraid of what else you could make me do—how much you could hurt me."

Gage looked at the man standing in front of him and contemplated what he'd just said. Nikola was right. Gage could hurt him. Odds were good that he would hurt Nikola, but God, he wanted desperately not to. He wanted the chance to prove not only to Nikola, but to himself, that he could make someone happy—two someones. "What does Hana believe, Niky?" Gage asked softly.

Nikola swallowed hard and finally made eye contact. "She told me that someday she'd be able to call you *Daddy*." Nikola's lips twisted in a wry grin.

Gage tried to hide his surprise but hoped in the process Nikola didn't think it was horror he saw there in his expression. The few times he'd imagined being with Nikola—being a family, if he let things happen on their natural course—he'd never considered what he'd be to Hana if they were. *DADDY*. The word flashed bright in Gage's mind, and he tried to find the fear that always gripped him when Lucas brought up having kids but couldn't. It simply wasn't there.

"It's a bit early for her to think something like that, isn't it?"

Nikola nodded and turned to stare out the window again. "I don't know where she got that. I never... She said her tummy told her. I don't want to get her hopes up. I didn't want to pressure you into thinking we had to have something more or we needed to move fast if we did want to have it be more, but now, after seeing her look at you that way..." Nikola shook his head. "I'm scared to even try. If it doesn't work out, I know she's going to be hurt so badly that... I can't... I don't think I can put her through that. We'd be better off leaving things as they are now—you know, just me and her and—"

"And Garrett every so often until you decide he's the best you can do, and you live out your life just kinda happy because you don't want to risk Hana's heart. What about your heart, Niky? Can you live the rest of your life knowing you didn't even try for something that might have made you happy?" Gage interrupted as the anger rose. "Haven't you given up enough? Do you think Hana would want that for you?" Gage was pissed since it sounded like Nikola wouldn't even give him a chance. He'd use that little girl in the other room as an excuse to get out of making the decision based on his own feelings. Gage understood his anger in that moment because suddenly it was clear. He wanted Nikola to give him a chance—to give them a chance.

"She's just a kid. She doesn't know what's best for her. How could she even have any idea what I need?"

"I'm not saying she knows what you need, but maybe she knows what you were doing wasn't working. Did she ever tell you that she would call Garrett Daddy?" Gage asked, pushing at Nikola's weak point. The look on Nikola's face was answer enough, and Gage almost sighed in relief. Hana never got that feeling with Garrett, even if he couldn't explain why she'd feel that way about himself, it made him happy she did.

Gage made a decision and took a chance as he pulled Nikola into his arms. Nikola stood there stiffly with his arms still hugging his chest, but at least he didn't push Gage away. "I'm not saying this has to go from just sex to marriage in days, weeks, or even months, but would it really hurt to try for something more than a quick fuck anytime I'm within driving distance of you? I can't promise you that I would never hurt you, and Hana by extension, but I can promise you if we decide to do this—to try for more—that no matter what happens between you and me, I would protect Hana from whatever I could. I would do anything to save her any heartbreak that could potentially come her way. I just need you to give me a chance. Don't let Hana getting hurt keep you from giving us a chance, please," Gage pleaded. Nikola relaxed against him and looked up into his eyes, and Gage wanted to believe he saw hope in the dark-brown depths. He opened his mouth to beg again, but a knock on the door stopped him.

"We're waiting for you two to come out so we can have cake and open presents," Sabina called through the door.

Nikola tensed but didn't pull away from Gage's embrace. "We'll be there in a minute, thanks," he called back to Sabina. He pulled his arms from his chest and wrapped them around Gage's waist and let his cheek rest against Gage's jaw for a second. "Can you stay so we can talk later?"

"I want to stay for you and for Hana. I'll go out and give you some time to get yourself together." The corners of Gage's mouth tried to lift in a small smile as he squeezed Nikola tightly once, before letting him go and leaving the room. Sabina flashed him a smile, but Nikola's mom glared at him as Hana grabbed his hand and led Gage to the table where the little girls were sitting two to a chair, patiently waiting for their cake.

"Uncle Gage, you can sit with me." Gage sat in the only empty chair and lifted Hana onto his lap as she rattled something off to the little girls that included Gage's name and the word English. They giggled, and then

Hana turned to Gage, pointing at each little girl as she said their names. "That's Uma, Sara, Malika, Nehada, Fadila, and Mari. They're my best friends from school. They don't know very much English."

"Tell them for me that it's nice to meet them, would you, B?" Hana giggled, and then he assumed she told them what he'd said when they all giggled some more.

"Uncle Gage, can we watch the video of you being scared by the cow? I told everyone how funny it is, and they want to see it."

"Sure, but after cake and presents, okay?"

"Okay. Where's Babo?" A small frown line creased her brow as she looked around.

"Right here, baby," Nikola said as he walked into the room. He looked okay, but Gage could tell he'd been crying, and by the way Hana stiffened in his lap, he could tell she sensed that something was wrong.

"He's okay, B. I made sure of it," Gage whispered reassurance into her ear. She turned and studied Gage's face for a moment, before nodding.

Nikola brought the cake over and set it in front of Hana. He lit the candles, and they sang to her before Hana blew out the candles as Nikola took pictures. He handed the camera to Sabina and stood behind Gage's chair, posing while she took some more pictures. Gage gave her his phone to take a couple for him too, and then the present opening started. Nikola took Gage's phone from Sabina and continued to take pictures with it while Gage sat there with Hana as she opened all the presents except the one he'd gotten her.

Nikola put the large gift, wrapped in Disney princesses wrapping paper, on the table in front of her. She opened the card and read it to herself before turning to give Gage a kiss on the cheek, which Nikola took a picture of. She carefully pulled at the tape on the package. "Rip it open, B. That's how you're supposed to open presents. If you like the wrapping paper, I'll get you a whole roll." She squealed and ripped into it, and Gage helped her get the tape off the box. She kneeled on his thighs to open it and peer inside.

On the top was a clothing box, which Hana opened to find an outfit with the princesses on the shirt and a matching pair of jeans. She held them up so everyone could see, and the little girls at the table all squealed along with her. Nikola and Sabina were snapping pictures like crazy. Hana put the clothes on the table and pulled out the next package and again the shrieking started. There were six Precious Moments figurines in the box—Ariel, Snow White, Belle, Cinderella, Jasmine, and Mulan. Each one was pulled from the box and squealed at until Gage was sure his eardrums would burst.

The look Nikola was giving Gage relayed just how crazy he thought the extravagant gift was and probably the giver too. Hell, maybe he was. At fifty bucks a pop, it was probably the most expensive present he'd ever gotten anyone outside of his family, but Hana's squeals of delight were all the thanks he needed to know he'd done well. He was practically glowing with the warm feeling making Hana happy gave him. Turning in his lap to thank him over and over, Hana then gave him so many kisses his cheeks were liable to fall off. She finally clambered off his lap so Sabina could help her take the figurines out of the boxes so all the little girls could very carefully hold each one before passing it on so everyone could see.

With the present opening over, Gage looked up to see what Nikola was doing and found him standing by the counter looking at the phone in his hand and frowning. He wondered what Nikola was seeing on his phone that made him look so agitated, so Gage got up and walked over to him.

Nikola handed him his phone. "We'll talk later." He went to help his mom distribute cake.

Looking down at his phone, Gage hoped it wasn't something from Lucas. Gage was relieved to see it wasn't Lucas, but instead it was a text message from his parents.

It said, *HAPPY BIRTHDAY, GAGE! Hope you have a great day. Wish you were here so we could celebrate it with you. We'll have a get-together when you get home. Love you, Mom and Dad.*

Gage raised his head to find Nikola watching him intently from where he was standing by the table. So, he'd been found out. It was Gage's birthday too. *Happy-Fucking-Birthday to me then.* Gage smiled at Nikola and shrugged. What else could he do?

Hana hand delivered Gage an extra big piece of cake while he was standing there staring at Nikola. "Thanks, B, that's awfully nice of you to bring me cake on your birthday. Go have fun with your friends." Gage accepted the plate and watched her scamper off again. He stood and ate his cake while Nikola was busy supervising the kids. He flipped through the pictures Nikola and Sabina had taken, and changed his wallpaper to the one of Hana sitting on his lap behind the cake, Nikola leaning in over his shoulder smiling at the camera. It was a great picture of the three of them—hopefully the first of many.

"That was a very generous gift that you gave her," Sabina said as she came to lean on the counter next to him.

"It made her happy."

"It did. I didn't expect that you would come up with something like that. I'm surprised."

"It's really that surprising that I can buy a good gift?" Gage wasn't sure what the hell she getting at.

"Men are usually not that thoughtful. It's nice that you are. Nikola needs someone like you." She patted Gage's arm and then went to help clean up the kitchen, leaving Gage to wonder if he'd just gotten Sabina's seal of approval.

Nikola and his mother were having a discussion that looked suspiciously like an argument, but Gage couldn't be sure since Bosnian was a language that always sounded harsh to his ears. Nikola finally smiled and hugged her, so if it had been an argument, Gage figured it mustn't have been too serious. He sat on the couch and just watched the activity around him. The girls played a few games, and after about an hour, Hana asked to see Gage's cow video, he grudgingly pulled out his phone and, the girls huddled around the little screen. They laughed and snuck glances at him and then laughed some more. They sat there talking and giggling and Gage cursed Rosetta Stone for not having a course in Serbo-Croatian. It would have been nice to join in the chatter instead of sitting there smiling like a creepy old man.

Finally, the doorbell rang and adults were there to pick up most of the girls. They each said goodbye to Gage and giggled some more as they left, making Gage think he'd surely filled his quota of giggling little girls for at least a couple of years to come. Soon only three were left: Hana and the other two, who Gage assumed were the ones spending the night. He got up and went to where Nikola was standing in the kitchen with Sabina, his mom at the sink doing dishes.

"Hey, I think maybe I should head out." He'd agreed to stay to talk with Nikola, but he wasn't sure if it was a good idea with extra kids in the house. Gage couldn't promise things wouldn't get heated between them one way or the other, and he didn't think they needed an audience.

"We have a couple of things to discuss." Nikola gave him a pointed look. When he saw Gage glance at the girls he added, "They're going to stay at my mom's tonight. We'll take them up there in an hour, so they can watch a movie before they go to sleep." Gage glanced at Nikola's mom and then Sabina and back at Nikola who smiled and winked, making his intentions clear.

"Okay, but I don't want to screw up anyone's plans."

Nikola's mom gave Gage the evil eye over her shoulder. "Too late for that," she grumbled before she turned back to the dishes, leaving no doubt about how she felt about him and his presence in her son's home.

"Mom, that wasn't very nice. Gage, would you like some coffee?"

"Um…sure if everyone else is having some, but if not, don't go to any trouble on my account."

"It's no problem," Sabina said as she filled the kettle with water. "Why don't you guys go sit down and relax a bit?" She shooed the men from the kitchen. She served coffee when it was done and sat down with her own cup, leaving one on the tray for Nikola's mom, but she didn't join them. Instead she said something to Sabina and Nikola and then left without even a glare for Gage.

"She doesn't much care for me, does she?" Gage asked no one in particular. Both Nikola and Sabina looked at their coffee for a moment, and Gage figured he wasn't going to get his suspicion confirmed.

"She's just overprotective of her little boy," Sabina finally said.

"She's still hoping that one day I'll wake up and realize I'm in love with Sabina and the whole gay thing was just a phase and the love of a good woman pulled me out of it." Nikola smirked at Sabina, who rolled her eyes at him.

"Is that what you're hoping for too?" Gage asked, turning to Sabina. She laughed so loud that the three little girls gave the adults a curious look from their spot on the floor in front of a board game. Nikola snorted and play-punched Sabina in the arm. "What am I missing?"

"Sabina's actually dating a married man." Nikola waited until Gage looked appropriately shocked and Sabina's smile grew when Nikola added, "And his wife." That information did nothing to wipe the shocked look from Gage's face. In fact, his jaw dropped so he was sitting there with his mouth hanging open.

"Why, Mr. Hoffman, I do believe he's shocked you speechless." Sabina gazed at Gage over the rim of her coffee cup as she sipped.

"So you're dating a polygamist?"

"No, we don't take turns." She cocked eyebrow. "It's more... What's the word in English, Nikola?"

"Polyamory—they're a permanent threesome." Nikola supplied the word and clarified the situation for Gage. "That's why she uses me as much as I use her." Nikola smiled at her fondly and it became clear to Gage that what they had was a close friendship born of necessity.

"I can't imagine that's a common thing here." The obvious affection between Nikola and Sabina no longer sparking jealousy in Gage.

"It's not so common anywhere. I lived in Amsterdam for a while, and while I was there, I was into the alternative lifestyles. I met a few people in these types of relationships, and it just seemed like they were so happy that I decided to try it. I've been with them for over three years now. They were married when I met them, but I don't feel any less a part of the relationship because I'm not legally bound to them. I *rent* a room from them, so we can live together. It's still hard. As a single woman, I'm expected to stay with my parents until I get married, and people talk, but I say let them. It has no effect on me. I'm my own woman," she explained. Gage noticed how happy she looked when she talked about her lovers.

"Wow, you are a surprise. I won't lie. I hated you after the party, but now that I'm getting to know you, I actually think I could really like you." Gage shifted on the sofa, bringing him closer to Nikola.

Nikola reached over and put his hand on Gage's thigh. "It was my fault at the party. I should have explained before I left you at the table." Gage covered Nikola's hand with his own, and Sabina smiled softly at the gesture.

"Why don't I take the girls upstairs and say good night to Alma so you guys can *talk*," Sabina suggested as she made the word talk sound like a sexual act.

Nodding in agreement, Nikola's eyes slid over Gage's body. "Hey, Hana, go get your things and Sara and Uma's bags so you can go to Nana's."

Hana saw the way Nikola and Gage were holding hands and perked up. She talked to her friends, and they were up quickly gathering things to go. Nikola got up and made sure everything was in order, and after having a short conversation with Sabina, he hugged her.

"Thank you so much for my presents, Uncle Gage. They are so pretty," Hana said as she hugged him.

"You're welcome. Thanks for inviting me, B. That cake was delicious. Happy Birthday." Hana left with her friends, taking the giggling with them and leaving a blessed silence behind.

Right after the girls and Sabina left, Nikola turned to Gage. "So it's your birthday, huh?"

Chapter Eighteen

GAGE LOOKED LIKE he was trying to come up with an answer that would appease Nikola and not start a fight. "Yeah, it is. Everybody's got one. It's nothing special."

"Why didn't you tell me?" The memory of how Gage reacted when Nikola told him Hana's birthday was the eleventh came back to him, and he suspected he knew the reason without Gage having to explain it.

"I've had my share of birthdays. I didn't want Hana to have to share the spotlight on her day. She's a kid, and it's important to them to feel special on their birthdays. Plus, at my age, who needs to be reminded?" Gage chuckled as he rubbed the back of his neck.

Just what Nikola assumed, and though it was considerate of him, Nikola felt like he still could have at least told him. "Really, you're not that old, Gage, or did you just not want to tell me that you're turning like fifty this year?"

Gage's eyes about bugged out of his head, making Nikola laugh. "I'll have you know that I'm not even forty yet," Gage said indignantly.

Nikola plopped down on the couch next to him, and Gage shot him a dirty look. "How old *are* you?"

"Why do you want to know?"

Leaning in close and in a voice Nikola knew would make Gage shiver, he said, "I need to know how many birthday spankings I get to give you." Nikola then sat back to watch Gage's reaction, and he wasn't disappointed because he blushed and coughed and tried to stutter something out. Gage's reaction to the mention of spanking would never get old. "Don't worry. We could always split it up into a couple of sessions if it's too much."

"Um, I think we have some things to discuss first," Gage said, trying to change the subject as he shifted on the couch to face Nikola. "I want to know where you see this thing going and what you want from me."

Nikola deliberated over his answer. It wasn't that he didn't know what he wanted, but he didn't know how to say it and not make himself seem like he was nuts. How do you tell a guy you feel like you fell in love with him the minute you saw him, and he's been on your mind nonstop? How do you tell him you want nothing less than to possess him without sounding like a crazed lunatic? Who knew what Gage would think if Nikola confessed his innermost desires? He didn't want to scare Gage off, but he needed what was between them to be more, and he knew it.

"What do *you* want?" Nikola asked instead of answering.

"Why can't you just tell me what you want? It's not that hard. Just say the words, Nikola. What's the worst that can happen?"

"You could tell me I'm crazy and storm out of here," Nikola admitted his fears.

"Okay...I promise not to do either of those things. Now tell me."

Gage looked so sincere that Nikola decided to take a chance on the man sitting next to him. "I want something more, something real. I know it's really early to think that way but a friend told me sometimes you just know, you know?" Gage didn't look like he was getting ready to flee, and that alone encouraged Nikola to carry on. "I thought about what you said today in the bedroom. You're right. Maybe I hide behind Hana, but that's because I don't think I've ever had anything I really wanted before. Not like I want you."

"So you're saying that you maybe want to try to have something more than just sex with me?"

Gage sounded almost as hopeful as Nikola knew himself to be, so he moved closer to Gage. "I really would like to try. But how's that going to work?"

They lived an ocean apart, and he couldn't work out the logistics of it.

Gage pulled Nikola into his arms. "We'll think of something. If you're serious about wanting to take this thing further, we have options."

"Yeah? What kind of options?" Nikola asked, realizing the yearning in his voice might turn Gage off but not able to help it. Nikola was practically sitting in Gage's lap, and it was oddly comforting to be held in a way that showed Gage's impressive strength. Though Nikola loved being the dominant one in bed for the most part, he didn't envision a life where he was a full-time Dom, and sometimes it was nice to be the one who was being held.

Gage shifted to get more comfortable and brushed a few kisses along Nikola's jaw. "Well, we can do the long distance thing. I'm over here probably four times a year, at least, and you could come and visit when you're able. There's also always the option of me seeing if I could set up a base over here, once I have everything situated we'll still need a regional director." He said the words, but Nikola could tell he wasn't entirely thrilled with either of those options. Of course, Nikola noticed he'd left out one option that would probably make him the happiest.

"So you wouldn't want Hana and me to go with you?" Nikola asked almost timidly. He didn't want to hear Gage reject the idea.

"I guess I wasn't sure if that was an option." Gage's arms tightened around Nikola.

"Why wouldn't it be?"

"Well, your family is here, and I didn't think it would be fair to ask you to take Hana from them or them from her. Also, you know that where I live isn't anything like Atlanta. It's a fairly small community, and it has the worst weather pretty much year round." Gage shook his head and grimaced to show Nikola he meant it. That wasn't exactly the ringing endorsement of Gage's hometown Nikola had expected, but he liked that Gage wasn't sugarcoating anything to try to get him to go pack his bags instantly.

"But if you moved here it would be just as unfair for you to leave your family, and you don't speak the language. At least both Hana and I speak English. To be honest, being here has more problems than you can know. For one, we'd never be able to openly acknowledge our relationship. We'd have to be in the closet, and that's a difficult way to live." Nikola figured, since they were being honest, he shouldn't put any polish on his hometown either. "And really, how bad can the weather be? It's not like every season can be horrible." Gage's body shook with laughter, causing Nikola to pull back and raise a questioning eyebrow at him.

"Where, oh where, do I start on that one? We'll start with forty-below winter temperatures with fifty-mile-per-hour wind that whips the however many feet of snow everywhere and creates hazardous driving conditions, even in the city, that can last anywhere from October to April. When spring comes along, it's almost a given there will be flooding that lasts until May. Then summer is hot and humid and windy too, and the mosquitoes are huge and hungry and plentiful. There really isn't a fall because it usually goes from 'Shit, it's hotter than hell out there' to 'Shit, where did I put my winter coat?' If you're lucky, you may get two weeks at the end of September where you go 'Boy, it's nice out today, maybe I'll go for a stroll.'" He stopped to contemplate what he'd just said before adding, "I think I might have just talked myself out of wanting to live there anymore."

Nikola laughed when Gage sounded so serious about it. "Wow, it's a good thing that you don't write their tourism ad slogans. 'Come visit hell on earth!' I don't think it can be as bad as you say."

"Well, you know what we say, 'It keeps the riffraff out'. It's not a bad place to live. The cost of living is low and so is the unemployment rate, and there's almost no violent crime. All in all, it's a nice place to live and raise a family. The school system is excellent too," Gage said, finally giving Nikola some hope that the place wasn't horrible. There was a quiet moment where he held Nikola close and they both seemed lost in their own thoughts. "You could always come for a visit and check it out. See what you think. We have time. It's not like I'm going to ask you to move tomorrow or something."

Nikola considered it for a whole five seconds. "Yeah, I could do that. I mean, I want to do that." He leaned in and kissed Gage because sitting that close and watching his earnest face made Nikola want to crawl inside him and take up residence. Gage let Nikola kiss him softly and slowly, and he moaned a little when Nikola teased his bottom lip with his tongue. "Enough talking. I've missed you, and I want to feel you against me." Pulling away to stand, Nikola put out a hand to Gage, willing him to take it. Without hesitation, Gage grabbed it, and let Nikola pull him to his feet.

"Nikola?"

Nikola had been pulling him toward the bedroom but stopped at Gage's unsure tone. "Gage?"

Nikola could see there was a question Gage wanted to ask, but he didn't seem to want to voice it. Nikola waited, while Gage worried his bottom lip between his teeth, making Nikola want to reach out and stop him. "The whole domination thing... Is that like your thing or..."

Gage's uneasiness when talking about something he enjoyed but was obviously conflicted about was sweet. Nikola finished leading him to the bedroom before pulling him into a kiss, loving the way Gage melted against him. It didn't matter that Gage was physically bigger; when he was in Nikola's arms, Nikola felt like he was sheltering him from the world and that Gage wanted to let him do it.

He pulled back, putting some space between them but gripping Gage's face to hold him while he gazed into his eyes. "It's not something I have to do, but something in you calls to that part of me. It's like you need someone to just take control for a while so that you can relax. If you let me, I can take care of you in a way you may not even know you need or want me too."

He slowly unbuttoned Gage's shirt as he stood there contemplating Nikola's words. Gage let Nikola slide his shirt over his shoulders to drop to the floor before Nikola kissed his neck and shoulders while pulling at the buttons of those well-worn jeans he'd been fantasizing about since the first time he'd seen Gage wear them. Nikola pushed them down, following their progress with his lips as Gage stood there immobile, only moving when Nikola tapped his leg to get him to lift his feet one at a time so he could pull the jeans and socks off his feet.

Standing, Nikola took a step back to look at Gage and to his credit, Gage didn't blanch at Nikola's frank appraisal of him. He stood straight as Nikola circled him, reaching out to touch Gage's broad back, sweeping his hand down, and stroking his firm ass. Nikola then stepped up behind him and pressed his fully clothed body against Gage. It was a power play on Nikola's part, and Gage knew it as well. He took a deep breath when Nikola circled his arms around his waist.

Nikola rested his chin on Gage's shoulder, his mouth next to Gage's ear. "Have you ever let anyone fuck you before?" Gage didn't answer as he stiffened in Nikola's arms. Nikola knew the answer since Gage already told him, but he wanted to hear the whole story. "Gage, answer the question," Nikola prodded when he took too long to respond.

"Yes." The word was a barely there whisper.

"How long has it been? How long since someone sank into this hot, tight ass?" Nikola's breath skated across his neck and Gage shivered in response.

"A long time—not since college—only my first boyfriend and only a couple of times."

Nikola was rubbing Gage's hips in slow circles, but when he admitted that he was almost a virgin, Nikola's breath hitched, and he pulled Gage back against his denim-clad erection. "Why has it been so long? Didn't you like it?" Nikola asked. Gage relaxed back into him just enough for

Nikola to know he wasn't going to run or fight so Nikola gave him time to answer the question but figured Gage would either avoid it or flat-out lie.

"I haven't been with anyone who wanted to fuck me," he said, skirting the question.

"That's not exactly what I asked, now is it?" Nikola pushed.

"I don't know how to answer the question."

"Okay, let me rephrase the question into one that you can understand. Did you like getting fucked, Gage?"

"Not so much. Nikola, do we really—"

"What about it didn't you like? Did he hurt you?"

"No, he didn't hurt me anymore than I expected having a cock up my ass would hurt. There's always that element of pain. I didn't trust him. I couldn't relax enough to enjoy it. There was always the fear that if I let my guard down he could hurt me."

Nikola understood. Hadn't he just told Gage the same thing earlier? "Gage, you know that I'd never hurt you, right?" He moved his hands to rest his palms on Gage's chest, his left resting right over Gage's heart, which was beating quickly. It was important to know Gage trusted that he wouldn't do anything to hurt him.

"I don't think that you would intentionally hurt me, Niky."

"So what would it take for me to convince you that I wouldn't hurt you even unintentionally? How did you get your boyfriends to trust that you wouldn't hurt them?"

"I guess some people don't have trust issues like I do, but I do trust you—as much as I'm able to, at least." Gage rocked his hips back into Nikola and put his hands on top of the ones on his chest. "Is it a deal breaker if I can't let you fuck me?"

That wasn't a deal breaker, but if he couldn't trust Nikola, it would eventually be. It was too early for him to expect complete and utter trust from Gage, so he decided not to push the issue. "It's not a deal breaker, and I promise I won't fuck you unless you ask me to, but Gage..." He paused to grind his prick against Gage's ass. Gage pulled Nikola's hands from his chest to his groin. He caressed Gage's cock lightly with one hand. It was only semi erect, but twitched at the touch. "The next time I have you bent over and you beg me to fuck that fine ass of yours, I'm going to, and you're going to love it," Nikola said, finishing his thought.

Gage shuddered at Nikola's proclamation.

Abruptly releasing Gage, Nikola turned him so they were face-to-face. Gage nervously licked his lips, and Nikola took that as an invitation. With just the touch of Nikola's tongue, Gage opened for him, and Nikola took full advantage of the open, willing mouth. Gage put his arms around Nikola's shoulders and rubbed his naked body against Nikola's fully clothed one, the friction reminding Nikola that his dick was trapped behind his zipper as Gage humped against him. He gripped Gage's hips to help grind their pelvises together, making Gage gasp as Nikola first kneaded and then spread his ass cheeks roughly.

Gage pulled away from the kiss, his eyes glazed over with lust. "Tell me what to do Niky. What do you want?"

"I just want to feel you against me. I need to be naked with you." Nikola would be content just to hold Gage if that's all he wanted, but Gage's actions told a different story. He clutched Nikola's shirt roughly, dragging it up and over his head. Nikola pulled him into another kiss as Gage divested him of his pants and underwear, and Nikola kicked them to the side before Gage backed him to the bed.

He pushed Nikola back and away from him and their gazes met and held. Nikola recognized the lust in his gaze, but he could also see something more. Gage opened his mouth to say something, but suddenly stopped. Looking down to break the eye contact, he said, "Get on the bed, Niky."

Nikola sat and then lay back on the mattress, and Gage followed, laying himself out on top of Nikola, who spread his legs so Gage could fit between them. Gage stilled, the only movement was his back as it slowly rose and fell with his breath. His face was pressed into the side of Nikola's neck, making their bodies a perfect fit against each other. The quiet stillness unnerved Nikola enough that he had to ask, "Gage, baby, are you all right?" Gage nodded his head slightly, but he didn't speak, so Nikola rubbed his back, giving him time to work through whatever it was he was feeling at that moment.

Chapter Nineteen

GAGE DIDN'T KNOW what he wanted. Just lying there on top of Nikola, he felt like he was where he belonged, like he'd finally found what he was looking for all his life. How did he explain that to Nikola without making himself sound insane? He wanted Nikola to know how he was feeling but didn't have the words to express something that had grown so suddenly out of control. Nikola was patient, rubbing his back, soothing with his touch.

After what must have seemed like forever to Nikola as Gage lay there crushing him, he came to a decision. There was only one thing Gage could give to Nikola to show him how he felt, something he knew Nikola wanted. With no warning, Gage rolled to the side, pulling Nikola on top of him. When their positions were reversed, Nikola pulled back to study Gage's face. He didn't know what Nikola was looking for, but he must have seen something, and whatever it was, it spurred him into action. Nikola growled before crushing Gage's lips beneath his and taking total control of Gage's mouth, his lips and tongue demanding surrender. Gage surrendered but still wondered at how having someone else take control in bed could be such a turn-on.

Nikola pulled back after he'd kissed Gage breathless. "Put your hands above your head and grab onto the slats in the headboard." He waited while Gage did as he was told. "Don't let go until I tell you that you can." Gage nodded. Nikola kissed him again, this time slow and languid before sitting up to straddle Gage's thighs and letting his gaze rake over Gage's body. "You're so beautiful. Your body's amazing, and when I look at you, all I can think about is all of the things I want to do to you." Leaning forward, he ran his hands from Gage's wrists to his biceps. Gage flexed the muscles there without even thinking about it, and Nikola smirked at the unconscious preening. "I know you're strong, Gage. You don't have to prove it to me."

Nikola continued his slow caress down to Gage's chest and ran a finger around each of his nipples until they pebbled. "You have the broadest chest of any man I've ever known, but your nipples are so small and sensitive," he murmured. As if to prove his point, he pinched each tiny bud, making Gage hiss out in pain and pleasure. "I'm going to use clips on them one day and watch you squirm. Would you like that?" he asked, and when Gage nodded, he released them. He let his fingers trace the ridges of Gage's abdomen. "How much do you work out to keep this six-pack?"

"A couple of hours, a few times a week," Gage answered in a tremulous voice. What Nikola was doing to him amounted to slow torture, but Gage was loving every minute of it.

He hummed his approval as his hands moved to Gage's hips. "When I first saw how wide your hips were, I imagined how wide I'd be spread if I straddled you. Do you know how hot that got me? When I'm around you, I'm like a walking hard-on. I have trouble thinking because most of my blood is pooled between my legs. I've never wanted a man as much as I want you, Gage," Nikola confessed. He looked up from Gage's hips to meet his eyes, the longing plain to see.

"I want you too, Nikola, ever since the airport. I think about you all the time." Gage admitted to his own obsession.

Nikola looked back down at Gage's body splayed beneath him before continuing his downward journey. He bypassed Gage's groin to rub his hands down his thighs. "Do you, Gage?" Nikola paused to lick his lips, and then his eyes met Gage's again. A frown crinkled his brow. "I wonder, you see, my cousin told me that you were spending quite a bit of time with that Austrian tart. Were you thinking of me while you were with him?"

Gage tensed at his words. That was so not where he'd guessed the conversation was going. "He's just a friend. He knows..." *that I'm falling in love with you*, Gage couldn't give voice to the end of that sentence. It was too soon, and Gage didn't think Nikola would believe him if he said how he felt. He couldn't risk having the first man he'd ever said "I love you" to reject him on the grounds that it was too soon.

"He knows what, Gage?" Nikola was working his way back up Gage's body while he waited for an answer, and when he hadn't gotten one by the time he was once again straddling Gage's thighs, he leaned forward, crossed his hands on Gage's chest, and rested his chin on them. He looked up at Gage expectantly. "Tell me what he knows, Gage."

"He knows that..." Gage stumbled before he could say the words. He took a few deep breaths as Nikola lay there patiently waiting for his answer. "He knows how I feel about you." That was something—an answer—at least Gage hoped it was one that would satisfy him for the time being.

Nikola quirked his head to one side and studied Gage for a moment before asking the inevitable question. "How *do* you feel about me, Gage?" The question came out of his mouth on a breathy whisper, and it was then he realized Nikola was just as scared of what he was feeling as Gage was.

Gage held Nikola's gaze as he steeled his resolve but then closed his eyes and took the plunge. "I'm pretty sure that I may feel something like love, or at least a feeling along those lines, anyway." Gage held his breath as he waited for the inevitable rebuke from Nikola. When Nikola's weight shifted as he lifted himself off Gage's chest, he expected Nikola to leave the bed but, instead, his hands came down on the pillow next to Gage's head. Gage squeezed his eyes shut tighter but finally started to take in air again.

Nikola's breath ghosted across his face. "Open your eyes, Gage. Don't hide from me." Gage slowly opened his eyes to find Nikola's face only inches from his own. "I told you that I didn't want you to hide from me, and that means never shutting me out, no matter how hard you think it is to face me." Gage nodded his understanding and maintained eye contact with Nikola. "Now, let go of the bed, and wrap your arms around me."

Gage hadn't even realized he was still holding on to the headboard, that, in fact, he had a death grip on it. Letting go, he did as Nikola told him and clutched Nikola to his chest, releasing a ragged sigh in relief. Nikola hadn't rejected him. He hadn't reciprocated either, but that was okay. Gage knew he was jumping the gun telling Nikola how he was feeling. Nikola pulled back and just gazed into his eyes for a few seconds before he kissed him thoroughly. When Gage was breathless, and his cock was paying attention to the goings-on again, Nikola pulled away. When Gage chased his lips for more contact, he was denied.

Shaking his head, Nikola smiled that sweet smile Gage always associated with Hana, but this time he realized it was for him. "Gage, that was probably the most wishy-washy declaration of love I've ever heard," he said. When Gage tried to protest, Nikola brought a finger up to his lips to shush him. "But, at this point, I'll take whatever I can get. I know that you'll be able to tell me you love me someday and look in my eyes while you do it. I'm willing to wait for that day because, although I know it's crazy early for either of us to even think the word, I can tell you that I think I may have fallen in love with you the minute I saw you."

Gage couldn't hold back the chuckle that rumbled out of his chest. "You are even more unbalanced than I am. At least it took me a couple of days to go gaga over you, and the fact that you have the cutest, sweetest little person I've ever met gives you an advantage I don't have," he said.

"I'm not sure that I like you calling my dick cute. Sweet's not so bad, but when someone calls something cute, I always think small and—"

Gage kissed him to shut him up and to stop the unmanly giggles bubbling up inside of him. When he felt like he had himself under control he said, "Get your mind out of the gutter. I wasn't talking about your dick. Though if I was going to describe it..." Gage stopped to think, but he didn't get a chance to come up with anything because Nikola started doing things to his neck that made it hard to concentrate on witty banter.

He moaned as Nikola worked his way, nibbling and sucking, to his ear. *Oh my god, the things that man can do with his tongue.* Nikola made a full-out assault on the shell of his ear. Gage reached down to palm each of Nikola's ass cheeks to pull his hips down so their cocks lined up as he pushed up, creating friction between them. Nikola let off the ear he'd been mauling and started sucking up a mark on the sensitive skin behind it. Gage drew in a harsh breath at the pain, and Nikola stopped sucking and kissed the pain away.

"Gage, I want you," he murmured into Gage's neck. "Please..."

"I want you too. Nikola, I want to try it with you," Gage said softly and wondered if Nikola heard him when he didn't move.

Pulling back, Nikola searched Gage's face. "You don't have to do this, Gage. I know you're not ready for that, and I'm okay with it. I can wait." Gage could see the want in his eyes. Nikola's need to possess was stronger than he could control or hide.

"I trust you. I'm ready, just go slow, okay? And stop if I ask you to?" Gage asked even though he knew Nikola would anyway.

Nikola rolled off him and started digging in his nightstand before Gage could blink. When Nikola had what he wanted, he crawled back toward Gage with a predatory look on his face, and for a brief moment, Gage had doubts about his decision. Though he knew Nikola could be gentle, the look in his eyes made Gage nervous as he wasn't sure Nikola could hold back his baser desires now that he was going to get what he wanted. Gage's original fears rushed back at the realization of what he'd agreed to.

Nikola's expression changed into one of understanding at the emotion Gage wasn't able to hide. He put his supplies on the bed next to Gage's hip and lay next to him, gently taking Gage's face in his hands to kiss him tenderly. "We don't have to do this. I don't need you to prove anything to me. If you want to try it, we will, and if you want to stop at any time, you just have to say the word, and we're done," he said reassuringly. "But Gage, I need to be able to trust that you'll tell me if you want me to stop. This is a two-way street, and I can't read your mind. Can you do that for me?"

The tight knot of fear that settled in Gage's belly loosened at the tenderness in Nikola's voice. He could trust Nikola. The fact that Nikola knew he would go through with it, even if it hurt, said a lot about how much the man got him. Being stoic and not telling his first boyfriend to stop had only lead to resentment and their eventual breakup, not to mention Gage's total aversion to bottoming for anyone else for all those years. It was time to claim that part of himself back.

"I trust you, Niky. I'll tell you if I need to stop."

"I promise to make it good, Gage." With a cocky smirk, Nikola pecked Gage on the lips and said, "Now, assume the position." He wasn't sure what Nikola wanted, so he started to roll over onto his stomach before Nikola stopped him. "No, on your back. Grab your knees and spread for me." The commanding tone in his voice, combined with the setting, went straight to Gage's cock.

Gage felt foolish lying there while Nikola looked him over, and he couldn't help remembering the last time he'd been in that position with Nikola. The flush of desire rose through his body, but Nikola took his time, just looking, before he settled between Gage's spread thighs. He started like he did last time, long slow licks all the way along Gage's crease. When Nikola concentrated his efforts on the tightly puckered hole, Gage lost all coherency. The need was so great to have something fill him, he begged shamelessly for Nikola to ease the emptiness. Why had no other man ever made him feel that way?

"Please, Niky, fuck me now. I need…" A slick finger entered Gage, and there was no pain, just an odd feeling of intrusion and a sharp spike in his pleasure. Nikola's tongue laved around the buried digit as he pumped slowly in and out. "More, more—I need more, please," Gage begged like a wanton whore, but he couldn't stop the words. Instead of more, Nikola pulled out, but just as Gage was about to protest, he entered again with two thick fingers, and this time there was a stab of pain. Nikola crooked his fingers inside Gage, and all thoughts of anything ever hurting again were banished from his mind. Nikola took Gage's cock into his mouth as he rubbed the tiny bundle of nerves he'd found. In no time, Gage felt the pressure building.

"NO!" Gage shouted. It was over too soon. Fireworks exploded behind his eyelids. Nikola pulled off and Gage spurted onto his own chest while Nikola milked his prostate.

When Gage opened his eyes, Nikola was staring down at him in awe. "That was the single, hottest thing I've ever seen." He gently resumed pumping his fingers in and out of Gage's ass. "Are you too sensitive to finish this?"

Taking a second as his mind came back down from the stratosphere, Gage assessed how he was feeling. But before his mind was even on board, his body was answering for him. He'd unconsciously been rocking his hips into Nikola's hand to get more of his fingers into him as he stroked his own flagging cock.

"I guess that's as good an answer as any." Nikola's face took on a look of concentration as he worked to open Gage for the next step. Gage knew when Nikola's fingers went from probing to stretching, concentrating less on pleasure and more on preparing Gage for him. After some time, and at least three fingers, Nikola finally leaned down to kiss Gage as he pulled his hand free.

"Roll over. It will be easier for you that way," Nikola said as he patted Gage's hip. Rolling onto his stomach, Gage then started to get onto his hands and knees when Nikola put a hand on his back. "Just lay like that." The unmistakable sound of a condom wrapper being ripped open, made Gage turn to look over his shoulder to watch Nikola roll it down his length and lube it up. He pushed Gage's thighs apart, placing one of his legs out to the side and bent at the knee.

"Nikola?"

Nikola lay out on top of him, nestling his lubed cock between Gage's equally lubed ass cheeks. "Trust me, in this position, I can make you fly," Nikola whispered in Gage's ear before nuzzling into his neck. He kissed and nipped at Gage's neck and shoulders, and bit down on the tender flesh where the neck meets the shoulder. Gage hissed, but Nikola didn't release him as the head of his cock pushed at Gage's prepared hole. Gage pushed back into Nikola, hoping to help ease his way.

He let out a whimper when Nikola finally breached him. Nikola stilled, releasing the flesh clamped between his teeth. "You okay?" The question was asked through clenched teeth, telling Gage just how hard it was for Nikola to hold back. Something about being treated like a fragile virgin made him push his ass up into Nikola forcing more of his cock in, but Nikola grabbed Gage's hips to stop him from moving again. He groaned, and Gage gritted his teeth through the initial pain. "Fuck you, Gage. I'm not going to let you top me from the bottom," Nikola growled. The whole situation struck Gage as funny, and he barked out a laugh before he could stop himself. Nikola groaned as he thrust his hips until he was fully seated. Gage's breath caught—cutting off his laughter at the last pinch of pain—as the thick base of Nikola's cock stretched him one final time.

"I can see that I'll have to restrain you if I want you to behave. I need to teach you I'm the one in control when we're in bed. I'm going to add to your next punishment, so you'll learn your lesson for this." Nikola rocked his hips as if to put a fine point on it. "Now, let me show you what you've been missing all these years." *Cocky bastard.*

Nikola shifted on top of Gage and started fucking him slowly with measured strokes. When Gage pushed back to get more, faster, harder, Nikola changed his angle and hit that magic spot. "Oh fuck," Gage moaned. Nikola kept up the same rhythm, hitting Gage's prostate with every other thrust. Gage was writhing beneath him, begging him to do something more, but his pleas fell on deaf ears as Nikola took his pleasure the way he wanted.

After a couple of dozen of those smooth thrusts, Gage couldn't take it anymore. He pushed up, trying to get his knees under him so he could wrestle some control from Nikola. Pulling back, Nikola helped Gage position himself the way he wanted, and this time, when Nikola slid into him, he pushed back and got what he wanted. "Fuck, Gage, you're going to make me come if you keep that up," Nikola ground out as Gage did it again.

"That's the point, Niky." Gage gasped when Nikola thrust into him fast and deep. "Fuck me harder," Gage demanded. Nikola slapped Gage's ass before gripping his hips and slamming into him, giving Gage what he'd asked for. Gage moaned and pushed back for more, and Nikola took up a punishing pace, fucking into Gage with reckless abandon. Gage grabbed his cock and, after a few strokes, felt his orgasm building. "Gonna come, Niky." Gage warned him only seconds before he let go.

Nikola shuddered when he came buried as deep as he could get inside Gage's ass. "*Hvala bogu, volim te*, Gage," Nikola said as he collapsed, making Gage fall into his own mess on the sheets. Gage couldn't bring himself to care—in his blissed out state nothing mattered.

Chapter Twenty

THEY LAY THERE in a heap until Gage's moan reminded Nikola he was on top of him, probably making it hard for him to breathe. As he rolled to the side, the noise Gage made as their bodies separated sounded suspiciously like a sob, and he hoped Gage didn't regret what they'd just done. When he pulled Gage to him and wrapped him in his arms, Gage hid his face in Nikola's shoulder and shuddered.

"Hey, babe, what's wrong?" Gage shook his head instead of answering. "Did I hurt you?" Nikola was worried. He'd promised not to hurt Gage, and if he had, he'd never forgive himself. Nikola remembered how hard he'd been fucking Gage at the end and wanted to kick himself as Gage shook his head again. "Please, Gage, would you look at me, at least?"

Gage shook his head almost violently, but at the same time, he wrapped his arms around Nikola. The strength with which Gage clung to him took Nikola's breath away. Smoothing Gage's sweaty hair back from his forehead, Nikola tried to force Gage's face from his chest, but he shook him off. "Can we just sleep?" Gage asked in a small voice muffled by Nikola's chest.

"If you tell me what's wrong, we can sleep."

Gage sighed, his warm breath making Nikola break out in goose bumps in the chill of the room. "Nothing's wrong, absolutely nothing."

Nikola decided to let it go. It was obvious he wasn't going to get anything out of Gage at that moment. He reached between them to strip off the condom, which he dropped into the trash can by the bed before feeling around and picking up the first piece of clothing he could find from the floor. He tried to clean them the best he could with the dry cloth, but they were going to end up sleeping sticky. He would have preferred to take Gage into the shower and clean the two of them, but it would have to wait until morning. He grabbed the blankets that were pushed to his side of the bed and covered them, and Gage snuggled in until they were pressed together at every point their bodies could possibly touch. He made a contented sound that made Nikola think he may have misread Gage's refusal to talk. Maybe he was fine after all.

Nikola kissed the top of Gage's head. "Good night and sweet dreams." Gage sighed again, his body relaxing in Nikola's arms, and within minutes, he was sleeping. As Nikola lay there listening to the calming sound of Gage's steady breathing, loving how good it felt to be there in the arms of the man he was almost certain he was destined to be with. The fact that Gage had almost admitted to feeling as strongly for him as he did for Gage after such a short time must be some kind of sign telling them this was right. Nikola drifted off, thinking of new beginnings in new places surrounded by new people.

NIKOLA WOKE UP to giggling, and it took him a few seconds to remember why he was pressed into the back of a large, warm body in his own bed. He wiggled his hips getting a little friction for his morning wood when the giggling erupted again. Holy hell! Hana! Nikola's brain engaged and immediately his hard-on deflated.

"Your dad is still really tired because he bet me that he could do more jumping jacks than I could, so I made him do jumping jacks for over an hour last night to prove it." Hana giggled again. "So we should let him sleep. Maybe you could go get the stuff for coffee out, and I'll come and make it for us. What do you think, B? Sound like a plan?" he asked in a hushed voice.

"I could make the coffee," Hana offered.

"No, you remember your dad said you weren't allowed to use the stove."

"But if you say I can, then he can't get mad," she countered.

"No way, B. That would just get us both in trouble, and your dad gives spankings when we're bad." Nikola wanted to laugh but tried to hold it in. When Gage felt him shaking with the effort behind his back, he reached back and patted Nikola on the hip.

"He doesn't spank me. If you got a spankin', then you really did something bad."

"Go get the stuff out and wait. I'll be there in a second. Maybe I can convince your dad to get his lazy butt up too."

"Okay, Uncle Gage, I'll go, but if you take too long kissing Babo I'm going to come back," Hana said before she left. He finally released the laughter he'd been stifling, when Gage turned to him. The look of disbelief on his face was just too funny.

"That kid is just freaky. You should have her checked out."

"Yeah, she's got ESP or something, I think. Sorry she woke you up."

"Nah, that's okay, I'm just glad we were both covered when she came in. Could have scarred the poor girl for life, and paying for a psychiatrist would put a big dent in our budget." Gage looked seriously concerned for Hana's mental health.

Nikola's heart pumped fast at the way Gage casually lumped them together by using the word "our." The idea that they'd have anything that was theirs together made Nikola grin like the village idiot and then pull Gage down for a kiss. "So how are you this morning?"

"I'm good, so quit asking."

"Gage, we really should talk about last night."

"Why? Why do we have to talk about anything? We were both there. We both know what happened, and that's all there is to it." Gage flopped back against the pillows.

"But—"

"Nikola, I'm not good at the whole talking about my feelings thing, okay? You got more from me last night than Lucas got out of me in five years. Just give it some time, and let me get a grip on all of this before you make me analyze it to death."

Nikola gathered that Gage didn't like to talk about his feelings, but he figured that was probably part of his problem. Gage kept everything bottled up, and most likely, he didn't know how to express himself. If Hana hadn't been waiting for them in the kitchen, Nikola would have pressed the issue, but he'd let it go for the moment. He leaned over Gage and kissed him again.

"Okay, fine, you process, and then we'll talk."

Gage scowled as he sat up and got out of the bed. "You're a giant pain in the ass, you know that?" Hunting for his clothes in the pile they'd left on the floor, he found his pants and yanked them on. "And I don't mean in the good way, either." He pulled his shirt over his head and left Nikola on the bed, chuckling to himself.

"Are you and my babo in love?" Hana asked Gage as Nikola walked into the kitchen. Gage looked relieved, when he saw Nikola before he needed to answer.

"Morning, baby girl, how was your sleepover?" Nikola asked, hoping to distract her until they'd at least each had a cup of coffee.

"It was good. Uma got scared, and Nana called her mommy, but then she was fine. We watched *Beauty and the Beast*."

"Why did they leave so early?"

Gage coughed and looked pointedly at his watch. "It's almost noon."

"Babo?"

"What, baby?" Nikola checked the pot to see if the water was boiling so he could make their coffee.

"Are you and Uncle Gage in love?"

Oh boy, apparently she wanted an answer to that question, and there was no distracting her from it. He looked at Gage who was smiling down at Hana. He loved the way Gage looked at her—like she was important to him.

"Well—" Nikola started to answer her.

"Yeah, I think we might be," Gage interrupted.

Hana's face brightened and her smile lit up the room. "Can I tell Nana?"

"NO!" they both said in unison. They exchanged a knowing look, but it was up to Nikola to convince Hana to keep it quiet.

"Hana, I'm not sure it's a good time to tell Nana. Can we keep it a secret just between us—me and you and Gage—for right now?"

Hana's face screwed up as she thought about it. "I guess so, but I think Nana already knows."

Nikola looked at Gage, who shrugged probably because it wasn't his problem. His mom was not going to take the news of Nikola having a boyfriend very well, and he considered just packing their bags and leaving before he told her. Maybe give her a call when there was an ocean between them. Yeah, that should be far enough away to survive the fallout.

Nikola finished making coffee, and when he handed Gage his cup, he leaned in and kissed him. Hana giggled and Nikola blushed, but Gage looked relaxed in a way Nikola had never seen him. Gage turned and winked at Hana, who gave him a thumbs-up. Nikola's original suspicion of the two of them being trouble when they were together resurfaced, and he shook his head at them.

THEY SPENT THE rest of the day just bumming around the house, watching movies, playing board games and laughing as Gage tried to make them dinner. It felt good just to be with his two favorite people in the world; snuggled on the couch with Hana sprawled on top of the two of them was Nikola's new favorite place to be.

As Hana's second movie of the night came to an end, Nikola roused her, but Gage stopped him. He stood up and took her in his arms, and when Nikola got up too, Gage stopped him again. "I'll put her down. Stay there."

She wrapped herself around him as he carried her to her room. Nikola got up to get her a glass of water, knowing she'd wait until Gage was leaving her room to ask for one, but he stopped short when he heard them talking.

"If we come to live with you, will I get my own room?"

"Well, when you come to visit, you'll stay in the guest room, but I'll make it up just for you, and it'll be your room for as long as you want it," Gage said. Nikola was glad Gage wasn't telling her they were going to go there to live. He didn't want her to start thinking that until they'd had some time to work out what was going to happen. He would need to visit and check out the schools and look for a job. Nikola stopped his train of thought—he was getting ahead of himself, and he needed to rein himself in.

"But if you and my babo love each other, you have to get married, and we have to live with you so you can be my daddy," she said, pulling Nikola from his musings.

Gage laughed softly. "Hold on there, girl. Slow down. Your dad and I still have a few things to work out before we start planning the wedding. I haven't even asked him to marry me yet."

"You should," she whispered. "I think he'd say yes."

"I'm not so sure about that, but even if we don't get married, we can still be together, and I hope you both will come visit me soon."

There was silence for a moment, before Hana broke it. "Okay, I want to see your cows and the bull too if we come."

"I'll be sure to take you to see all the animals. You can meet them and my family too. Now, you need to go to sleep. It's getting late." Nikola stepped into the doorway to watch as Gage leaned down and kissed her on the forehead before she kissed his cheek.

Getting up to leave, Gage smiled when he saw Nikola standing by the door. "Uncle Gage?" Hana's voice stopped him, and he turned around to look at her. "I love you."

He took a couple steps back to her bed and bent to take her in his arms. "I love you too, B." Nikola's heart about leapt out of his chest. Hearing Gage say that to his baby sounded better than hearing Gage "almost say" it to him. He kissed her again before standing. "Good night, B. Sleep tight and don't let the bed bugs bite. See you in the morning."

"Night," she said, and Nikola watched as she mouthed *Daddy* at Gage's back.

Gage rubbed Nikola's arm as he passed him to go into the hall. Nikola took the glass of water in to Hana and said his good nights after she'd had her drink.

Gage was lounging on the couch when Nikola went to find him. He smiled that great smile again, and Nikola started thinking he could get used to this new Gage.

"Boy, she's a pushy one," Gage said as Nikola got them each a beer from the fridge.

Nikola smiled to himself because people always said she was just like her father. "Yeah, she can be. You know you didn't have to say it back to her, right?"

Gage gave him a sideways look as he took his beer. "It wasn't a problem. Even if I didn't love her, which I do, I'd have said it and meant it. I really love all kids."

"All kids?"

"Yeah, I mean, why wouldn't you? They're just kids. All of them deserved to be loved, and I guess I got a soft spot for little people," Gage said.

That was probably one of the nicest sentiments Nikola ever heard, and he was starting to realize under that big, muscled chest beat a big, soft heart. "I bet you love all animals too." Nikola lifted his beer bottle to his mouth and took a drink.

"Nah, I hate penguins. Oh, but they're technically a bird, right? And you know I hate pigeons, so anyway, birds don't count, right?"

Nikola snorted and choked on the beer he'd just taken a drink of. Who hated penguins? He didn't even want to ask. Leaning back on the couch, he pulled Gage into him, so he was lying on his chest. Gage grunted, settled in, and took a drink of his beer. Nikola stroked him as they sat there in companionable silence, watching some show on the Discovery channel. Before long, Gage's empty beer bottle fell out of his hand, and Nikola realized he was sleeping. He woke Gage gently and took him to bed.

NIKOLA WAS FINALLY back to work, shuttling Gage from meeting to meeting, keeping them both busy, but Gage's nights belonged to Nikola. Gage only went back to the hotel for appearances, but he moved most of his things to Nikola's, and for the remaining two weeks of Gage's stay, they were a family. Nikola tried to get Gage to talk to him about their future, but he was often distracted with work, and when he wasn't, he was dragging Nikola to bed. Finally, when there was only one day left before he'd get on a plane and end up halfway around the world from Nikola, he made Gage sit down and listen to him.

"Gage, we really need to talk. You can't avoid the fact that you're leaving tomorrow." Nikola knew Gage didn't want to think about it—that it was ending. They'd be separated for at least a couple of months until Gage returned for another round of meetings.

Gage's shoulders slumped, and the look on his face damn near broke Nikola's heart. "Niky, I really don't know what to say. I know that you've wanted to talk about this for a while now, but I just didn't want to ruin the time we have left."

"You know you're talking about it as if one of us were dying. It's not like we'll never see each other again, right?" Gage was scaring him, and he hoped Gage wasn't thinking he'd just forget about them when he left.

"I know, but it just seems wrong."

"What seems wrong?" Nikola was afraid of the answer even as he voiced the question.

"Leaving you, leaving Hana. God, Niky, you have no idea." Nikola raised an eyebrow, because hell, he knew what it felt like to leave an entire life behind. "No that's not what I mean," Gage said like he could read Nikola's mind already. "I've never wanted to spend every minute of every day with anyone before. Do you know what I was thinking as Lucas was breaking up with me? I was thinking that I'd wished he'd never moved in with me, that he'd stayed almost a four-hour drive away. That it was so much better when I could just see him when I wanted to and to not have to put up with him when I didn't want to. I'm a selfish prick."

"Maybe you were a selfish prick, but it could have been because you knew it wasn't right," Nikola reasoned.

"And I'm supposed to know that this is right? You're telling me that after only what—a month?—that I should know when I couldn't even figure it out after five years?" The plaintive tone of his voice made Nikola ache for him. It was like he was lost and needed someone to find him and take him home and love him.

Straddling his legs so they were face-to-face, Nikola pressed in to get as close as he could. "Gage, you need to let it go. Relationships break up for a lot of reasons. If you think about it, if you couldn't tell that man you loved him after five years, what makes you think you were ever going to?" Nikola asked. When Gage opened his mouth to answer, Nikola put his finger on Gage's lips to shush him. "You told me you loved me after knowing me for fifteen days, and ten of those were spent with you hating me. You've said it every night since the first time." Nikola paused to take in the shocked look on Gage's face. "Yeah, I heard you whisper it when you thought I was sleeping. You know this is right." Nikola put his hand on Gage's chest above his heart. "In here."

Gage's eyes shone as he pulled Nikola in for a kiss. "Just for the record, I never hated you," he said when they broke apart.

Nikola got up and took Gage to his bed. They made love that night. It may have been sex all the times before, but not that night. That night Nikola showed Gage with his body how much he needed him, would take care of him, and loved him.

When they finished, Gage surprised Nikola by looking him in the eye and saying, "I love you, Niky."

Nikola settled into Gage's arms. "I know, and I love you too, Gage."

Chapter Twenty-One

JJ AND HIS wife, Vicky, were waiting for Gage at baggage claim when he got off the plane. Gage smiled, shook JJ's hand, and hugged Vicky as they waited for his bags. Being back among familiar faces and hearing a language he understood being spoken all around him made Gage's experience in Sarajevo seem surreal. Kissing Nikola goodbye before they left his house for the airport seemed like it was a dream, and now Gage awakened to the harsh reality that this was his life without Nikola and Hana. They were so far away, so unreachable.

"Does it feel good to be home again?" JJ asked as he grabbed one of the bags before it started the journey back around the conveyor belt.

"Yeah, it's always good to be home." Gage wasn't really feeling it. The relief he usually got at being back on his home turf refused to ease the tension in his shoulders. Gage got ahold of his other bag, and the three of them headed toward the door for the parking lot.

"Well, it's good to have you back. Your mom was upset that you were gone for your birthday. Lordy, that woman can go on. After hearing her tell about how big your head was, I never want to hear another birth story." Vicky slapped Gage's shoulder.

JJ put out a hand to stop Gage before they exited the airport. "You might wanna put on your jacket. It's almost twenty below out there."

"Oh yeah. Crap, where's my head? Of course, it would be colder than a witch's tit on the night I get home." Gage put his bags down and pulled on his heavy coat and gloves.

"Um, we brought your truck for you," JJ said. He and Vicky exchanged a glance that seemed to hold some sort of meaning but went over Gage's head. "We have somewhere to be, so...sorry, but you gotta drive yourself home."

"Okay, I guess it won't kill me to drive home. Want to tell me what's up?" JJ was acting a little cagey. There was something they weren't telling him.

"Nothing's up. Me and Vicky just have somewhere to be, like I said." JJ didn't meet Gage's eyes as they walked out into the frozen night.

Gage almost slipped on the hard-packed ice, and for the hundredth time, he wished he was still in the more temperate climate of Sarajevo. Of course, the weather was only a small part of the reason he wished he'd never left. Gage suddenly couldn't wait to get home, so he could call Nikola and Hana.

"Fine, I won't ask any more questions," Gage said as they loaded the bags in his truck. He was too tired to play guessing games with them, and if he hurried home, he might be able to talk to Nikola before it got too late.

"Okay, so see you at Pop's for Sunday dinner, right?" JJ asked.

"Yeah, I'll be there. Hopefully my jet lag will be under control by then." One day of rest until he would face the entire family was nowhere near enough, but it would be easier to go than to argue. They said their goodbyes, and Gage drove to his condo.

There was a light on inside when Gage pulled up in front and when the garage door opened, JJ's sudden departure from their normal pickup procedure made a lot more sense when he saw Lucas's little compact was parked in one side of the garage. His hands tightened on the steering wheel. This was the last thing he'd expected to have to deal with. After pulling into the garage, he sat in his truck, trying to get up the nerve to go in to face Lucas.

When he finally got out, he grabbed his laptop bag and carry-on, took a deep breath, and opened the door. The smell of roast beef hit him in the face as he stepped into the kitchen to see Lucas bent over taking the roaster out of the oven. He set it on the stovetop and turned to Gage with a huge, welcoming smile on his face.

"Gage, you're home!" Lucas practically flew across the kitchen bumping into Gage's chest before standing on tiptoe and wrapping his arms around Gage's neck. "I missed you so much. I'm sorry I acted like such a brat before you left. Can you forgive me?" He batted his long eyelashes at Gage as he made puppy-dog eyes, knowing Gage could never resist him like that.

It was a familiar scene, and the sense of déjà vu hit Gage hard, making his stomach roll. He made no move to hug Lucas back, but it still took Lucas a few seconds to get that it was a one-sided embrace, and he finally dropped his arms and took a step back.

"I thought you'd moved out," Gage said, careful not to put any emotion behind the words. He moved into the living room and set his bags down, and Lucas trailed behind him.

"Well, you know me—all drama queen all the time." Lucas waved his hand as if brushing off the melodramatic exit that left Gage questioning everything was just that easy. "I just needed a little space to see that you need more time. I've waited this long, so what's it going to hurt to wait a little bit longer, right?"

Gage wasn't sure what to say, because he felt nothing when he looked at Lucas. No, that wasn't true. He was fond of Lucas, but now that he knew what love was, he was sure he'd never loved Lucas at all. He had a lot of great memories of them together, but his feelings for Lucas were more along the lines of friendship—nothing like how he felt for Nikola. Just the idea of Nikola waiting for Gage to call him gave him the courage to tell Lucas what he needed to say.

"Lucas, I've met someone." There was no easy way to break that kind of news. Lucas stared at Gage wide-eyed and mouth agape. "In Sarajevo."

"What the fuck, Gage!" Lucas's voice hit a pitch that was only one step away from only being audible to canines. "You met someone? What about me? What about us?" Lucas was angry more than anything.

"*You* broke up with me," Gage said calmly. "*You* left me. *You* said it was over, *you* said that *you* didn't want to wait for me to be ready for what *you* wanted."

"Yeah, Gage, I did because I've been waiting for five fucking years for you to be ready," he screamed. "You're going to throw that away for a fucking fling you had on a business trip?"

"Lucas, calm down." Gage wasn't equipped to handle this. After all those years, Gage should have gotten used to Lucas's theatrics, but this time it was different. This time it was Gage's decision to end it, and this time, it was final.

"Calm down? Are you kidding me?" Lucas sneered, hand on his cocked hip.

"Yes, calm down so we can have a rational conversation. There's no reason to scream or to fight about this."

"Oh really, so there's no reason to fight for what we have? I'm just supposed to do what, Gage? Congratulate you and walk away?" Lucas's eyes were bright, and Gage knew he was about to start crying.

"Lucas, I'm really sorry, but I'm not going to change my mind, and that's why there's no reason to fight. I don't want this to be harder than it has to be." He hated to see Lucas cry, but Gage knew he needed to hear the truth.

Lucas's shoulders hunched, his breath hitched, and the tears flowed. He looked so pathetic that Gage had no choice but to pull him into his arms. He melted into the embrace, and Gage felt so bad for hurting him—that had never been his intention. He realized then he'd been really shitty to Lucas, and he deserved better than someone like Gage.

"Why, Gage?"

"I don't know. I'm so sorry. I never meant for this to happen."

"For what to happen?" he asked. When Gage didn't answer, Lucas pulled back so he could glare up at him. "What happened, Gage?"

Gage sighed. How did he tell him? Lucas would find out soon enough since one of Gage's best friends worked with him, and there was no way Payne could keep this a secret when Gage eventually told him and Matt. It would be better if Lucas heard it directly from him.

"I fell in love," Gage admitted.

Lucas pushed out of Gage's arms. The look of incredulity on his face replaced the sadness that had been there a moment before. "You fell in love? You? 'Mister never says I love you even after five fucking years'? You fell in love in a month? Do you really expect me to believe that?" He let loose a maniacal laugh.

"Lucas, come on, please," Gage said, trying to stem his hysteria.

"Oh, no, this is just too rich. I wish I had this on video because it surely needs to be preserved for posterity. How many times have you told me that you don't do love? At least, that was your excuse for never telling me you loved me." Lucas's angry glare was sharper than a knife to Gage's chest.

"I'm sorry, Lucas." Gage was getting sick of saying he was sorry. "But this is as much on you as it is me. You should have realized that if I couldn't say I loved you after all that time, then obviously I was never going to." Gage wished he could take those words back the minute they left his lips, knowing, no matter how true they were, it was the wrong thing to say.

Lucas gasped, and his hand flew to cover his mouth to stifle it. He turned and walked to the kitchen. "Your supper is on the stove. I'll text you when I can come and pick up my stuff. I'd appreciate it if you could plan to be gone when I do." Lucas pulled his coat on and reached for his keys.

Gage followed him and grabbed his hand before he could get them. "Lucas, please don't be this way. You were right when you said that you needed to leave me. You should have done it a long time ago. I'm a bastard, and you should have someone who can love you as much as you deserve to be loved. You're a great guy."

Pulling his hand out of Gage's, Lucas snatched up his keys. His lip trembled as he looked Gage in the eye and asked, "If I'm so great, then why couldn't you love me?"

"I'm so sorry, Luke. I really wish things were different." But did he really? One thought of Nikola and Gage knew he'd lied.

"Yeah well, you know what they say, 'wish in one hand and shit in the other and see which one fills up faster.'" Lucas pulled his ridiculous multicolored hat over his head and jerked the door open.

"Lucas, please, can't we at least be civil? I really don't want it to end this way." At that moment, he realized that he didn't want Lucas completely out of his life but knew it was selfish of him to ask him if they could remain friends.

"I need some time to digest this, Gage. Please respect that. I'll text you," he said before walking out.

He listened to the garage door open and close, and then Lucas was gone. Gage sagged against the wall and let out a ragged breath. The only thing he wanted at that moment was Nikola's arms around him. He went to the living room and grabbed his laptop, set it up, and pushed the Skype icon, making the call to Nikola, knowing it was way too early in the morning to be calling him but not being able to help himself. Nikola expected him to call when he got home. Gage waited as the computer did its thing.

Nikola's face filled his screen and an overwhelming peace took over. "Hey there, I was starting to think that you just stumbled to bed and forgot about me."

"No, I could never forget about you." It was the truest thing Gage ever said.

"What's wrong?" Nikola's expression changed from a welcoming smile to concerned in a nanosecond.

Gage tried to smile to cover up his emotions but knew it was a lost cause when his lip trembled slightly. "Nothing. Everything's fine. I'm just tired, and I miss you guys already."

Nikola cocked his head. "Gage, you can't lie to me. Just because I'm thousands of miles away doesn't mean I can't keep track and make you pay when we're together again. Tell me what has all those frown lines popping out."

Gage told him the whole story. How could he not? Nikola listened intently without interrupting. "So that was not my finest moment, to be sure," Gage concluded.

"I'm sorry you had to deal with that when you got home. I wish I had been there for you." Nikola rubbed his stubbled chin as he stared into the camera. He could see how much Nikola meant what he'd said, and Gage wished it too.

Gage nodded, but all of a sudden, he was just so tired. "Hey, I'm sorry, but I really need to get some sleep. Can I call sometime tomorrow to see Hana?"

Nikola's soft smile told Gage he appreciated his need to connect with Hana. "Sure, you can call anytime. You know her schedule. Go to bed and get some rest."

"Okay, I will." Gage waited a second and then added, "I miss you guys so much already."

"I know. We miss you too. Okay, you need to go. I love you, Gage. Good night."

"Love you too, Niky. Give Hana hugs and kisses from me when she wakes up." Gage hesitated to end the call, but thankfully, Nikola had the fortitude to do it on his end, otherwise Gage would have sat there looking at him instead of taking the nap he needed. He dragged his ass to the shower and then to bed so he could pass out.

"SO YOU MET some kind of hustler, and even though Lucas was willing to give you another chance, you blew it because of him?" JJ asked, the disbelief clear in his voice.

"He's not a hustler, and Lucas and I were never going to work out," Gage said.

His entire family was gathered in the front parlor of his uncle's house. They'd just finished dinner, and the conversation, as always, revolved around business, for the most part, up until they sat down for after-dinner drinks. JJ innocently asking Gage where Lucas was brought on the current conversation.

"What do you mean? You and Lucas were so good together," Gage's mom said.

Gage tried to stay calm. *There's no reason to get defensive.* They'd all liked Lucas, and Gage knew it wouldn't be easy for them to accept the end of his relationship or to accept Nikola as the new man in his life so soon after.

"We weren't working out. I love Nikola and Hana," Gage said, thinking, *There, it's out.* He'd said he loved Nikola to his family, so it was official. Of course, that wasn't what they focused on, and Gage hadn't realized he had not yet mentioned Hana until the confused murmurs were voiced.

"Who the hell is Hana?" Gage's father was the one who directly voiced the question on everyone else's minds.

Gage couldn't help but smile when thinking about Hana, who he'd already come to think of as his little girl too. "Hana is Nikola's daughter. She's the most beautiful, charming, special little girl I've ever met," Gage said in all honesty. Then he remembered there were other little girls playing in the adjacent room and quickly amended his statement. "Well, you know, present company not included."

There were just too many reactions to take in all at once, so Gage focused on his parents. His mom's hand fluttered to her chest as she was clearly trying not to get overwhelmed with excitement at Gage's new revelation and what it meant for her. His dad was a bit slack jawed as he stared at Gage.

"What the hell?" JJ exclaimed. Vicky put her hand on his arm to calm him down. Gage had no idea why JJ was so upset. He pulled away from his wife and got in Gage's face. "So what's his angle? Does he need a work visa so he can come here? If that's what he needs, he doesn't have to fuck you to get it."

The hairs on the back of Gage's neck stood up. Putting his drink on the table, Gage stood toe to toe with his cousin. "No, he's got his American citizenship already, but apparently, there's got to be something he wants from me, right? I'm just a means to an end because nobody could possibly want me for any other reason, right?" He turned on his heel and left them all in stunned silence. He wasn't going to let anyone else tell him how he was only being used as a meal ticket. He was back—the old, unlovable Gage at his finest. He knew that's how they all saw him.

Gage sat in his cold truck, fuming. He didn't know what he'd expected from them when he told them. He was so happy that he assumed it would spread to everyone, and they'd just accept the fact that Nikola and Hana were the reason for his happiness, and they'd all be happy for him too. He started the engine and drove away. He would deal with the fallout of his tantrum later. He needed to get home before it was too late to call Nikola. Gage desperately needed to talk to him. He had to figure out how he was going to convince Nikola he needed him and Hana there with him, and the sooner the better.

GAGE ROLLED OVER and blindly groped for his phone. After having taken a couple of pills to help him sleep, he'd been dead to the world when it started ringing, and by the time he got it in hand, the call had gone to voicemail. He briefly considered ignoring it and letting the pills pull him back into dreamland, but then he saw that it was three a.m. and the missed call was from Nikola. Sitting up, he rubbed his hand over his eyes, trying to focus his vision as he returned the call. He was surprised when it wasn't Nikola's voice that greeted him but Hana's. Something had to be wrong for Nikola to let Hana call him in the dead of night.

"What's wrong? Has something happened?" Gage asked, sleep clouding his judgment and making him quick to jump to conclusions instead of remaining calm. He should have taken it slowly with the child who he soon realized was sobbing on the other end of the line.

"It's Babo," she choked out between her sobs.

Fear made Gage's gut clench into a knot, but he took a deep breath to center himself to deal with Hana without upsetting her more with his own emotions.

"Okay, sweetheart, slow down and tell me what's happening." Though his words were said in a soft, soothing tone, he was fully awake and out of bed, pacing the room, already thinking of how quickly he could get to Hana. His brain thinking ahead to check for the next flight out of Fargo to somewhere that would have a connection to one of the few cities in Europe that had flights to Sarajevo.

"Babo was sick and Nana made him go to the hospital. I think he's dead," Hana wailed.

"Hana, baby, calm down. Are you at home?"

"No."

"Where are you?"

"At the hospital."

"Okay, so where's your Nana?" Gage listened to Hana's sobs as he opened his laptop and punched in the website he used to buy his airline tickets.

"She's here, but I want you."

"I'm working on it." Growling when he realized the soonest he could be in Sarajevo was what would be the day after tomorrow for Hana, which was an eternity when he thought of how badly he needed to see what was going on and hold Hana to comfort her.

"I'm scared." Hana's cries broke Gage's heart, and he cursed the distance between them. He was sure Nikola wasn't dead, but there was obviously something going on and he should have been there to help Nikola and look after Hana.

"Coming to you, just have to find the right tickets—dammit!" Gage pulled up another site to check availability. His outburst making Hana cry harder. "It's okay, sweetie, I'm just mad at the computer, not at you."

"Hello? Who is this?" A male voice in Gage's ear surprised him, but it was a familiar one, and Gage's anxiety lessened a bit just knowing Nedim was there with Hana and Nikola.

Leaning back in his chair, Gage sighed. "Nedim, it's Gage Hoffman."

"Ah, Gage, I should have known Hana would try to call you."

"Tell me what's going on. She's really upset and told me she thought Nikola was dead." Gage wondered why nobody would tell the little girl everything was fine...unless maybe it wasn't?

"Nikola is in surgery. He has *upala slijepog crijeva*...I don't know the word in English for it, but it is common, and he's going to be fine," Nedim said, leaving Gage in the dark, still having no idea what was wrong with Nikola.

"Can you spell that for me?" Gage asked as he pulled up Google translate on his laptop. Nedim spelled the words out slowly and when Gage hit translate he sighed in relief. "Appendicitis, okay, I can deal with that. Did you tell Hana he's going to be fine?" The band of steel that gripped Gage's chest loosened with the news. People had appendectomies every day and survived. He still wished he'd been there but knew at least Nikola had gotten help in time and was going to be fine.

"I have assured her and so has Alma, but you know how children are—they do not understand and are easy to upset. She keeps asking for you, but you are not able to be here."

"I want to be there for her, but I can't get a flight out of Fargo to anywhere that will get me to Europe until this afternoon and if I drive to the cities it's the same damn thing since there aren't any European flights that will get me where I need to go without taking three more. I'd spend more time in airports than I would in the air."

"And by the time you got here, the crisis would have passed, and then we would all feel stupid," Nedim said with a chuckle.

"Tell me he's going to be all right."

"He's going to be fine. Alma was able to use Hana to get him to the hospital before anything worse could happen. The doctor said it was a routine procedure and he should be out soon."

"Okay, can I speak with Hana again?"

"Sure, and I will keep you updated as to Nikola's situation."

"Thank you, Nedim. I really appreciate that."

"It is no problem. Here is Hana."

"Hana, sweet pea, I just talked to Nedim and he said your babo is going to be fine," Gage said in a soothing voice. Though she wasn't sobbing any longer, he could still hear the aftermath of her crying jag in the way she took hiccupping breaths.

"Are you sure?" Hana asked.

"I'm absolutely certain," Gage said, hoping it was the truth but feeling confident he could give her that without having to face the consequences of it blowing up in his face.

"Okay." Her voice was tiny as it traveled so many miles to reach him, and once again, Gage was reminded of just how much distance separated him from the ones he loved.

"If you want, I'll stay on the phone with you until you can see him."

"Really?" Hana's voice brightened, and so did Gage's mood.

"Of course I will. I want to be there for you. I'm sorry I couldn't be there when you really needed me to be."

"It's okay, Uncle Gage. At least I can talk to you on the phone."

"I'm glad too and I'm happy you called me, B." But Gage didn't want to be just a voice on the phone. He wanted to be the guy who was there holding Hana's hand when things got rough. He wanted to be the guy who was there when the man who'd stolen his heart woke up in recovery and searched for a familiar face to put him at ease.

"Nana said I shouldn't call and wake you up, but I did anyway, and I'm sorry if you were sleeping."

"Don't ever apologize for waking me up when you need me."

"Never?" Hana asked, and Gage heard a hint of mischief in her voice.

"Never." Gage didn't care if he'd just doomed himself to years of Hana waking him in the middle of the night for whatever reason, because it was true—he'd never get angry at her for needing him. Hana's soft giggle made him smile. "So, tell me what you've been up to."

Gage listened to her babble away as he sat at the computer, first googling and reading everything he could on appendectomies and then moving on to looking at real estate for sale in the area. He had ideas that just wouldn't leave him alone.

Chapter Twenty-Two

"THIS WILL BE your room when you come to visit." Gage's voice came through loud and clear, even though he was swinging his laptop around to show Hana his condo.

"It doesn't look like a girl's room," Hana said as she stared raptly at the screen. The room was as plain as they came, white walls, beige carpet, and a bed that had nothing but a quilt covering it.

"Well, we'll just have to go out and get stuff to make it a girl's room, then, won't we?" Gage's face filled the screen once again. They'd been talking for over an hour, and it seemed like there was no end to the things they had to say to each other. As always, it started with Hana once again assuring Gage that her babo was fine and all recovered from his surgery, which made Nikola roll his eyes, but secretly he loved that Gage was so concerned about him.

Gage had been gone for a month, but he'd called that morning to say he was coming back for a week to sign more papers to get the permits so construction on their new building could start as soon as the deed was transferred. It never failed to amaze Nikola how fast the government could move with the right incentive, but he also wondered how much his little stint in the hospital had to do with how quickly Gage was making a return trip.

"Babo, it's your turn." Hana's voice broke into Nikola's rumination. "I'm going to go to Nana's. She said I could help her make pita today." She said goodbye to Gage one more time, blowing him kisses, before she hopped off her chair and ran to her bedroom.

"Hey there," Nikola said as he sat down. He studied Gage's face. Once Hana was out of the picture, Gage let down his guard, and Nikola could see how ragged he looked. "Have you been sleeping at all?"

Gage made an effort to smile, but it failed miserably. "Yeah, I sleep. Just been really busy at work lately. You look good. Are you doing okay? No complications?" He tried to change the subject to redirect from him, but he couldn't fool Nikola. Nikola could read him like a book.

His question only served to remind Nikola of how weak he'd been and how helpless he'd felt when he'd fallen ill in the middle of the night. How much he'd wanted to make the call to Gage before he let Nedim drive him to the hospital. It had taken all the restraint he'd had not to do it, only to have Hana call while he was in surgery. He'd just wanted Gage there with him but knew there was no way that could happen so calling would have been a mistake. All it would have done was make Gage crazy with worry, knowing he couldn't do anything to help.

"Uh huh, I don't believe that work is the only thing on your mind, and how many times do I have to tell you I'm fine? You've seen the incision, which is almost healed already and barely noticeable. Now that I've told you that for the twentieth time, can we get back to you and what's eating you?"

Gage sighed and shook his head. Though Nikola could read him, he had much less success when it came to getting Gage to open up to him. Since Nikola didn't have a way to physically get Gage in a position where he felt safe enough to say what was on his mind, they'd been at a standstill on the relationship front.

"It's just the whole thing with Lucas," Gage finally admitted.

"I don't see why that's such a problem." Lucas decided not to move back to the cities, much to Gage's chagrin. After what Gage told Nikola, he knew it came as a surprise that his ex hadn't hightailed it back to where he'd come from.

"It's a problem because we have the same friends, and anytime we're within ten feet of each other, he gives me the cold shoulder, and I feel like everyone else thinks I'm an asshole for what I've done to him."

Nikola couldn't help but smile. It was funny how Gage cared so much about what other people thought of how he decided to live his life. His family was also a huge sticking point for him lately, and Nikola felt bad that he was part of the mess without being there to help Gage deal with it.

"Babe, you'll know who your real friends are when they start splitting into camps. The ones that shun you were never really your friends to begin with. I'm on team Gage if it helps any," Nikola said, hoping to inject some humor into their conversation.

It did make Gage grin. "Yeah, I know you are, but even fucking JJ is on my ass about this. I have no idea why. It's not like him and Lucas were close or anything. Payne and Matt are staying neutral, which is nice, and Spence is...well, Spence, so I guess my closest friends are still there for me." His grin faded when he asked, "Have you thought about what I asked?"

"I'm still not sure, but I want to," Nikola said, which got the first real smile out of Gage, and he made up his mind then and there. Gage asked if Nikola and Hana wanted to go back with him for a visit when he returned from his trip in March. Nikola would have to pull Hana out of school for a few days, but it was looking like it would be worth it if it made Gage look like he did right then. Plus, maybe they could talk about the idea Nikola had about making the move to the states. He'd even found a way that wouldn't trap Gage into feeling like he was stuck having to ask Nikola to live with him. He'd been looking at jobs in the area and was confident he could find one that would pay enough to support him and Hana in a small apartment of their own. Maybe a trip over there to see how Gage handled them being in his space would help Nikola make the decision to take the leap and ask what Gage thought about it.

Gage's phone started ringing from somewhere in the background and his face fell. "I have to go. I talked to Hana too long again."

Nikola loved that about him. Gage had been so engrossed in talking to Hana he'd forgotten he only had a limited amount of time for his call due to an appointment or some other engagement. It meant Nikola got less face time with him, but he couldn't explain how much it meant to him that they got along so well. He'd never complain, even if he felt cheated out of talking to Gage for longer.

"It's okay, you can call me later, and we'll see a lot more of each other." Nikola's leer making it obvious as to what he was referring to.

"I won't be back until about two a.m. your time."

"Don't care. Call me," Nikola commanded.

"Yes, sir. Love you, Niky," he said, laughter in his voice, which Nikola loved to hear.

"Love you too, babe." Nikola hung up, knowing if he didn't do it, Gage would just sit there looking at him for as long as Nikola let him, and then he'd be late for whatever it was he was supposed to be doing.

Nikola closed down the computer and went up to see what Hana and his mom were doing. He found them in the kitchen on the floor. There was a sheet spread out, and Hana was watching his mother stretch the dough into a large circle. It was so thin you could see the pattern of the sheet through it. Nikola loved watching his mom make pita and wished she would have taught him, but of course, it was unmanly to want to learn to cook, so she never let Nikola participate like she did Hana.

He decided to tell them both at the same time that he and Hana would be taking a trip soon. Nikola cleared his throat and caught their attention. They looked up at him from their positions on the floor, and he noticed the resemblance around their eyes and wondered how two people who looked so alike could be so different in personality.

"So, Hana and I are going to take a trip next month. Gage has invited us, and I decided to accept." Hana squealed in delight as she jumped up and into his arms.

"I can't wait! Can we go to the mall?" she asked excitedly.

"I don't know. It's going to be a short visit. You can't miss too much school," Nikola told her, but he was watching his mom's reaction to the news. The disapproval was clear in the set of her jaw. Nikola put Hana back on her feet. "Can you go downstairs for a little bit? I need to talk to Nana alone."

She looked from him to her nana and bit her lip. "Yes, Babo, but please don't fight with Nana."

Nikola crouched down to look her in the eye. "I'll try not to, baby, but we have something to discuss, and I'd rather you not hear some of it."

"Adult talk," she said, and Nikola nodded. She kissed his cheek and then hugged his mom and left without another word.

He waited as his mom finished rolling the piece of dough around the cheese she'd put in as filling and then placing it in the pan that was sitting on the floor next to her.

"So, Mom, do you have something you need to say?" Nikola finally asked because he knew she wouldn't start talking unless he prodded her.

She stood up and faced Nikola. "This is wrong, Nikola, and you know it."

He remained calm. Hollering at her would do him no good, no matter how much he wanted to rant. "It's not wrong, Mom. I want to be with Gage, and he wants me. How can love be wrong?"

She snorted. "God says it's wrong and you know it. Two men together is a sin, and two men together shouldn't be raising a child. I didn't raise you—"

Nikola cut her off there. "I know you didn't raise me. You weren't there. I mean, you were there, but mentally and emotionally you checked out by the time I was nine." It was the truth, but it hurt him to say it and to see the hurt it caused her. He knew the situation that brought on her emotional collapse was in no way her fault, but he'd watched other people who went through the same thing cope a whole lot better than she did. It made Nikola angry that in her eyes he wasn't enough to live for.

"I know there were things I could have done better, and I blame myself, but you have a choice. Sabina is a nice girl, and she would be good for you and Hana."

"I don't want Sabina, and she doesn't want me either. I'm not attracted to women, Mom, and that's not going to change. I want Gage, and he wants both me and Hana, and there's nothing you can say that will change my mind." Nikola got his stubbornness from her, so this was going to end with neither of them feeling like they'd won.

"You were attracted enough to a woman to make Hana. It's a choice, and if you choose to live like that, then I'll do everything I can to make sure that Hana doesn't have to live with your sin," she spat.

Oh, now Nikola was mad. How dare she threaten to take Hana from him? "Hana's an American citizen, and they have laws there that protect my rights. There's nothing you can do," Nikola raised his voice just a little to get his point across. He turned to walk out but then remembered one more thing he wanted to say to her that he'd never said directly. "*Ja sam* gay, Mama, *to nije izbor rođen sam tako.*" Telling her he was born gay wouldn't change her view but it felt good to finally make the declaration to her face.

The tears finally fell from her eyes as she shook her head sadly. "What would your father say?"

"He'd tell me he loved me and that no matter what, I was his son and he was proud of me," Nikola said, not knowing if it was true or not but wanting to believe his father would have loved him no matter what. He walked out, thinking his mom would have to change her mind on some things, or they'd never be able to heal the rift in their relationship.

"PLEASE, NIKY PLEASE." Gage panted as Nikola swung the paddle once again and landed it on the tops of his thighs.

"Please what, Gage? Tell me what you need." Nikola landed another blow. Gage's ass was bright red, the skin almost glowing from the punishment it was taking. His hips swayed invitingly with every blow, and Nikola knew Gage was almost at his limit.

"You, just whatever...you, Niky." Gage let out low grunt as the paddle landed for the last time.

Nikola put the paddle on the nightstand and stepped up behind him. He rubbed the raw-looking skin on his buttocks, making Gage hiss at the contact. It was very warm, with all the blood that had come to the surface, and Nikola couldn't stop himself from bending and kissing the heated flesh. Gage pushed back into his face, showing Nikola what he wanted.

He got to his knees and spread Gage's ass cheeks, before nosing his way from the top of Gage's crease to his balls. Stopping to suck one into his mouth, Nikola listened as Gage's breathing sped up even more as he suckled him. He was a begging, pleading mess, and Nikola loved him even more when Gage let him make him that way.

When Nikola brought him home from the airport, Gage had a small run-in with Nikola's mother, which Nikola knew hurt him more than he was letting on. Gage was keeping it all to himself again. He'd buried himself in work and Nikola, instead of talking about it. After a week of watching the pressure build up to the point where he could no longer ignore it, Nikola decided it was time to break Gage down.

He let go of Gage's balls and laved his tight little pucker until he was pushing for more. When Nikola entered him with a finger, and then his tongue, Gage gasped. He was so sensitive that it made this act one of Nikola's favorites, his own dick throbbing in his jeans, but he ignored his own wants to focus on what Gage needed.

Reaching around, he stroked Gage's thick cock while he rimmed his ass. Gage jerked his hips to push into Nikola's hand but whimpered at the loss of Nikola's tongue when he didn't follow. He was being mean, but he loved Gage's frustrated whimpers and satisfied moan when he pushed back to get more of Nikola's tongue again. Nikola could listen to Gage all night.

"Please, Niky, I need more. Fuck me, please." Gage was shameless in his need, and it was almost too much for Nikola when he allowed himself to give in to his inner slut. Nikola wanted to give Gage anything he asked for, but he had his own rules to follow. Gage was always so vulnerable when Nikola had him like that, and Nikola tried to not overstep Gage's boundaries, doing things he worried Gage would regret when his sense returned. This was still too new for them, and Nikola knew he was being overly cautious but better that than fuck things up.

He let go of Gage's cock and pulled his face away from Gage's ass, ignoring his feeble protests. Turning Gage around to kiss him hard. "I want you inside me," Nikola said when he let Gage go.

"No, Nicky, please, I need you." Gage trembled with his desire.

Nikola shook his head as he got the lube and a condom from the drawer and then unbuttoned his pants and kicked out of them. "No, baby, not tonight. It's my turn." Nikola opened the foil package with his teeth, and Gage let him roll it on, patiently waiting while Nikola lubed it up. He got on the bed and beckoned for Gage to come to him.

Gage crawled up Nikola's body until he was nestled in the V of his thighs. He kissed Nikola's neck and asked, "Prep?" Nikola shook his head, and Gage shuddered. Nikola didn't want to wait, and besides, he liked the burn and stretch as Gage entered him. Nikola also loved how slowly Gage took him when he didn't let the other man stretch him to get him ready for his cock.

Gage got on his knees only long enough to get the head of his cock lined up with Nikola's entrance, and then he covered Nikola with his big body. Gage made eye contact as he pushed forward, and the first burst of pain as the head breached him made Nikola cry out, but Gage knew him well enough by now not to stop or to ask if he was okay. Gage pressed in a bit more and then pulled out and pushed back in, repeating the process slowly, inch by inch, until he was completely buried in Nikola—only stopping when his balls were pressed firmly against Nikola's ass, so he could let him adjust to the fullness.

Nikola was breathing hard and fighting to maintain the eye contact Gage wanted. When the burn subsided, he rocked his hips to let Gage know he was ready. It was like Nikola fired the starting pistol because Gage leaned in to take his mouth and then began to fuck Nikola in earnest.

He used his powerful hips to drive into Nikola, and even without pulling back off to get the leverage an average man would need, his thrusts were bone-jarring. Gage devoured Nikola's mouth as he moved, but when Nikola bit his lip hard enough to draw a little blood, Gage reared back with a growl. He put his arms under Nikola's legs and folded his body in half as he pounded into him at a new angle. Nikola's hard cock bounced between them, slapping wetly on his own stomach and streaking Gage's with precome on the upswing. There were times when Nikola feared Gage would break his back with his forcefulness, but the way he started nailing Nikola's gland with every well-aimed thrust made him think it may be worth it if Gage just...kept...hitting...that...spot.

Nikola fisted his own cock, which started him on his way to a mind-blowing orgasm as Gage hit his stride. Nikola knew when he was past the point of no return, and so did Gage. Just before Nikola started to come, Gage dropped his legs and pulled him up to straddle Gage's thighs so he could shoot into the warmth of their pressed-together bodies. Gage held Nikola tightly as he continued to fuck up into him, kissing and biting Nikola's neck and shoulders. Nikola wanted to fall in a boneless heap, but instead, he used his quivering thigh muscles to help Gage drive into him faster and deeper until Nikola felt him let go. He swallowed Gage's cry of ecstasy and continued to kiss him until he fell forward, landing on Nikola with all his weight, quivering from the strength of his own release.

Gage nuzzled into Nikola's neck as he slowly rocked his hips, wringing every last bit of pleasure from his orgasm as Nikola clung to him. He stopped after a bit, and Nikola just lay there enjoying the afterglow and the heavy weight of Gage's body on his. Sex with Gage was something unlike anything Nikola ever experienced. He'd had boyfriends with whom he was the top and some with whom he was mostly the bottom, but never one where they were equally versatile. Nikola always believed those relationships were a myth started by guys who were waffling on which way they wanted to go. Of course, if Gage hadn't trusted Nikola, he'd have been Gage's bottom bitch until the lack of trust eventually broke them up. *Ah well, no use dwelling on something that never happened.*

Nikola sighed, and Gage finally stirred enough to prop himself up on his elbows to look down at him. "What was that for?"

"Nothing. Just thinking about how much I like it when you beg me," Nikola teased.

Gage didn't blush or get angry—his normal response when Nikola pointed out his wanton ways during sex. Instead, he drew his eyebrows together. "I've been meaning to ask you why it is that you always do the opposite of what I want."

"What do you mean?" Nikola asked, a little baffled by the question.

"Anytime I'm begging for it, you don't do it, but when I'm begging to fuck you, you turn it around and fuck me. Why the hell do you do that?" Gage looked genuinely confused.

Nikola laughed at how his brow was furrowed, and Gage tensed like he was preparing to roll off Nikola, but he held Gage tightly so he couldn't. "I guess you would see it that way, wouldn't you?" Nikola asked but didn't wait for the answer. "The only time you beg me to fuck you is after I've spanked your ass, and I can never tell if you're in the right frame of mind to be asking for it. I like to know that you're capable of forming a coherent thought when I fuck you."

Gage looked pensive, and Nikola prepared for an argument that didn't come. "I am always able to form a coherent thought." Gage got up to take care of the condom as Nikola chewed over his last statement. He threw a wet rag on Nikola's chest when he came back, and Nikola wiped himself down before grabbing the lotion that he used to rub into Gage's ass. Gage lay on his stomach and was quiet as Nikola began to lightly smooth the cream into his red cheeks.

"It's not that I don't think you know what you need, but I just don't want you to be upset that I took advantage of you when you're like that. We haven't discussed any of this in detail. Now that I know you actually want some of the things I want to do to you, we need to talk it out and set boundaries we're both comfortable with."

Gage brought the paddle Nikola just used with him, giving Nikola a shy look as he pulled the surprise from his suitcase. Nikola's breath hitched at the sight of it, and he knew Gage had given it some thought while they'd been apart. He wanted to let Gage set the pace and decide how far he wanted to take their bedroom play. It wasn't as though Nikola wanted to have a hardcore BDSM relationship with Gage—that wasn't his scene. Nikola couldn't be a full time dominant, but he did get off on spanking Gage, and Gage letting him take charge, when he wanted to, floated Nikola's boat more than Gage probably knew.

Nikola continued to massage the lotion into Gage's skin, using a firmer hand once he had gotten used to the touch. Gage was nice and relaxed when he said, "I just really like that you don't see my size and think that I don't need to be taken care of too."

The shock Nikola felt at those words caused his massaging hands to still for a moment. "Of course, you need someone to take care of you. Where would you ever get the idea that you don't?"

Gage didn't answer, but Nikola was sure he could figure it out. Gage exuded manliness and most other guys would see him as a caregiver, a provider, and a protector—not as someone who needed to be taken care of. Nikola suddenly had a whole new perspective on what made Gage the way he was. He promised himself he would make sure Gage knew he would always take care of his needs.

Nikola lay next to him on the bed and gathered Gage close. He rested his head on Nikola's chest and let him run his fingers through his hair. One more night and they'd be at Gage's place, and then Nikola would have to figure out how to impress Gage's family so they would stop giving him shit about their relationship. He could feel in his bones how much Gage needed him, and Nikola wasn't going to stand by and let anyone make Gage feel like he didn't deserve to be taken care of, loved, and happy.

"Love you," he murmured as he snuggled in closely to go to sleep.

"Love you, too." Never had those words meant so much to Nikola.

Chapter Twenty-Three

HANA WAS SLEEPING with her head in Gage's lap when the fasten seat belt announcement flashed overhead. It was almost nine thirty, and the lights of the city were bright as the plane approached the airport. Gage gently nudged her into a sitting position and made sure her seat belt was clasped around her waist. Hana was awesome on the three flights they'd taken to get them to their destination, and Gage proudly accepted the praise heaped on them as they deplaned in Minneapolis after a seven-and-a-half-hour flight. All the passengers around them commented on what a great little traveler Hana was.

Brushing her hair back from her face, Gage leaned down to kiss her forehead because he couldn't resist that angelic, sleeping face of hers. Nikola chuckled next to Gage, making him turn to him. "What?"

Nikola's chuckle turned into laughter as he shook his head. "She's got you so wrapped around her finger it's actually so past the point of being funny that it's funny again."

Gage put his hand over Nikola's on the armrest between them and smiled back at him. The corners of Nikola's eyes crinkled in the most gorgeous way when he laughed, and like always, it made Gage want to kiss him. "She's not the only one who has me tied in knots."

Nikola leaned in close to whisper in Gage's ear, "Tied in knots? Sounds interesting."

Gage squeezed his hand as the warmth spread through his chest. Nikola was so inappropriate sometimes, but God, did he turn Gage on. "Stop that. This is no place to talk dirty to me. Add that to the fact that we've been awake forever, and your chances of me doing anything but falling into bed after a quick shower is zero to none."

Nikola just grinned his evil, sexy grin and nodded in supposed agreement.

Hana wouldn't wake up fully, so Gage ended up carrying her while Nikola wrangled the carry-ons. They weren't in any hurry since it had been warm enough when Gage left that he parked his truck in long-term parking. JJ was still being an ass so Gage had forgone his out-of-the-blue offer of a ride when he'd left. Nobody was waiting to pick them up, so they could take their time.

They hit the escalators that would take them down to the baggage claim. Gage was laughing at Nikola's first impression of the small airport when his gaze fell on familiar faces waiting at the bottom of their ride. Nikola must have felt Gage tense. "Is there a problem, Gage?" Nikola's eyes followed Gage's line of sight, and he shifted bags to one hand so he could put one hand on the small of Gage's back.

"My parents," Gage said as they stepped off. He hugged Hana tighter to his body in a protective gesture, even though Gage knew she was in no danger from his elderly parents.

"Gage." His mom waved an arm while making her way over to them.

Gage watched as she first took in Nikola, who was standing at attention to his right, and then her eyes landed on the sleeping child in Gage's arms. Her face melted in the way only someone her age looking at something precious could.

"Mom, Dad, this is Nikola." Gage introduced them to the man now clutching at the back of his shirt.

Stepping up beside his mom, Gage's dad stuck his hand out to Nikola. Nikola hurriedly took his hand off Gage and tried to switch the bags around so he could shake the offered hand. "Nice to meet you, Mr. Hoffman," Nikola said, once he was able to shake.

"And you, young man. We've heard a lot about you and are looking forward to getting to know you better," Gage's dad said in return, with a smile, no less.

Gage's jaw almost hit the floor when it dropped open. *Since when?* When he'd left, they'd still been in the "Gage is being used" school of thought.

"Gage, honey, is that Hana?" his mom asked. Gage fought the urge to tell her no, it wasn't, and that he'd just picked up some random little girl because he's crazy that way. Instead, he nodded and turned so she could see Hana's face. "Oh, poor dear, she looks totally whipped. We were hoping we could visit a little before you all went home and turned in for the night." There was real disappointment in her voice, which shocked Gage.

"You could come to the house," Gage offered. They were making an effort, so he figured he should too.

Gage's dad and Nikola wandered off toward the baggage conveyor, so she had no one to confer with. She nodded and then hugged Gage the best she could around Hana. Hana let out a snore louder than any six-year-old should be capable of, startling both of them. They laughed together, and it felt good to see something other than disappointment in his mom's eyes again.

"Let's go get the bags and get out of here. I've had enough of airports in the last day to last me for a good bit," Gage said.

His mom nodded happily and, after a brief conference with his father, decided that instead of going to Gage's place they'd wait until Sunday dinner to give them time to get settled in. They then gave hugs and kisses and handshakes before getting in their car and driving off.

"DO I HAVE to wear this dress? Can't I wear the purple one instead?" Hana looked down at the frilly, yellow thing Nikola picked out for her to wear to meet Gage's parents.

Nikola blew a breath out between his pursed lips as Gage smiled and said, "Sure, whatever you want, sweetie, but you have to hurry to change. Everyone will be waiting for us. You don't want to miss out on the egg hunt do you?"

She squealed and ran off to her room as Nikola shook his head at Gage's permissiveness when it came to Hana. Nikola looked stunning in a pair of tan slacks and a dark green V-neck sweater that fit him like a glove—very European looking and sexy as hell on him. His stubble was still present. No amount of pleading could get him to do more than trim it back from a full-on beard, but truth be told, Gage just pretended to try to get him to shave because the stubble only enhanced his dark good looks.

"You know I forgot this weekend was Easter. With the packing and traveling, it totally slipped my mind. How many people are going to be at your parents' house for this?"

"Oh, I don't know, somewhere between fifty and a hundred. It varies every year. But most of them leave after lunch, which is just people standing around eating on the lawn, and then the egg hunt. It's just family for dinner." Gage tried not to flinch when Nikola cringed at the news. He wrapped Nikola in his arms. "Sorry, I wish there would have been time for you to meet my family, without the circus, but at least you'll get it all out of the way in one shot. Plus, Payne, Matt, and Spence will be there too, so you'll get to meet my friends." Gage was trying to reassure him, but going by the look on Nikola's face he wasn't doing a very good job of it.

"Gage, are you sure this is a good idea?"

Gage was hoping it would turn out all right. His parents had been busy with setting up their annual Easter get-together. The entire family, a bunch of family friends, and most of the company's office staff would be there. Though it was nice having the whole day Saturday to just settle in and rest by themselves, it meant that even his parents only had the initial contact with Nikola and Hana at the airport. Though it had gone well with his parents unexpectedly welcoming Nikola, Gage knew there was still a faction of his family—led by JJ—who didn't approve of his relationship. He was hoping they would get to know Nikola during the party, smoothing the way before they would have to face the family alone without an audience.

"I'm sure." Gage kissed Nikola long enough for his breath to come a little faster and for Hana to shriek in delight when she caught them.

"I'm ready," she pronounced after giggling at them.

"The princess is ready," Gage said as he pulled away from Nikola. "Better get her royal highness her coat so she doesn't freeze her royal behind off."

Hana giggled some more, and Nikola snorted as he held out her coat for her. "Does it ever get warm enough to go without a coat here? It's the last week in March, and I think I could still see my breath last night," he grumbled. He slipped into a lightweight jacket himself.

Gage wasn't going to wear his coat and most likely the other guests would be wearing only sweaters or suit coats, because after a couple of months of twenty below zero temperatures, fifty felt like heaven.

NIKOLA WAS TENSE as they drove to Gage's parents' house a couple of miles out of town. His eyes took in the surroundings, and Gage wanted to know what he thought about the place that he was going to ask Nikola to make his home. Hana chattered happily away in her booster seat in the back. Her running commentary on everything from the big cars, to questions about where the mountains were, kept Gage's nerves from getting the best of him.

Nikola's response to Gage's parents' house was worth taking note of. His eyes widened, and he let out a soft breath. "You like it?" Gage asked.

"It's beautiful."

Gage looked at the house, trying to see it for the first time through a stranger's eyes. It was a huge, old farmhouse that had been updated through the years. Gage could still remember when the lawn around it had been patchy from the chickens the previous owners kept, and it took years for it to fill in.

"Were you raised here?"

"Yep, moved here when I was three. That's when my dad and uncle's company started to make some money. Maybe I'll show you my old room later."

Nikola gave him a fond smile, but Gage could see he wanted to roll his eyes at the obvious meaning behind that promise. Parking at the back of a long line of cars, Gage got out and helped Hana climb down from the big vehicle. She walked between them, holding their hands and swinging off her feet every few steps. As they approached the house, they could hear voices coming from around back and the occasional loud shouts of the assembled children.

They took the path that lead to the patio, and Nikola's steps faltered just enough for Gage to notice as he took in the scene before him. Giving him an encouraging smile, Gage swung Hana up into his arms and stepped close enough to grab Nikola's hand. "It'll be fine," Gage said with confidence he wasn't feeling.

Gage's dad spotted them first. He and Gage's mom were standing near the buffet table greeting people who just arrived.

"Happy Easter, Mom, Dad." Gage gave his mom a one-armed hug. "This is Hana. Hana, this is my mom and dad. They're really excited to meet you." Hana held out a hand but clutched at Gage's neck to let him know that she didn't want to be put down.

"Oh my goodness, that is a pretty dress, Hana. Is purple your favorite color?" Gage's mom asked her as she took her little hand.

"Yes, but I like pink and yellow too," Hana said.

"Well it's good to finally meet the sleepyhead," his dad said as he got a handshake too. Hana giggled but didn't act shy, which made Gage proud, though he didn't know why. He guessed he wanted them to see what a great kid she was, and her outgoing personality would for sure win her points with them. Before they could get past more than the introductions, they were interrupted by Payne and Matt. Gage let out a sigh of relief. Once Nikola met his two best friends, he'd at least have them as allies.

"Gage, it's about time you got here." Payne's lilting voice carried over the noise of the crowd. He hugged Gage's side, opposite Hana, and then let out a squeal at Hana. "Oh my god, look at that beautiful creature! Give her over right now, mister," he demanded.

Gage looked at Hana, who was taking in Payne with a bemused look on her face. Payne was a slight, short man, who looked like he was a teenager, even though he just turned thirty. He was wearing a pair of yellow skinny jeans and a pastel-pink shirt, in keeping with the holiday. He'd also dyed his usually pale, strawberry-blond hair with chunky streaks of pastels. Payne was a character, and how he ended up with a stick-in-the-mud cop like Matt was a whole other story. Payne stomped his foot and held out his arms. Hana shrugged and went willingly to the odd little man who wanted to hold her. Matt gave Gage and Nikola an apologetic look over Payne's head but did nothing to stop his husband from taking Hana into his arms.

"Look, Matty. Isn't she just the most adorable little thing you've ever seen?" Payne asked as he squished Hana to him.

"Yes, dear, she is certainly adorable. Don't squeeze the life out of her now," Matt said in his whatever-you-say-dear, long-suffering husband tone. "Hi there. I'm Matt. You must be Nikola." Matt introduced himself since it looked like no one else would dare to interrupt Payne's cooing over his newest obsession. Nikola shook Matt's hand. "And this strange little imp is my husband, Payne. Sorry he's abducted your daughter. He has absolutely no manners." Payne turned to stick his tongue out at Matt, which made Hana giggle and Payne look at her with adoring eyes once again.

"Watch out, mister. My babo gives spankings for that. Right, Uncle Gage?" Hana asked innocently. Gage nearly choked on his tongue, and he was sure his face was beet red, but Nikola burst into laughter, drawing the attention of the entire crowd to their little group.

Gage's dad patted his shoulder. "I'm going to go see if the Easter Bunny is done hiding those eggs. We'll talk later." He walked away with Gage's mother while trying to hide his amusement.

Payne was eyeing Gage, and Matt was unsuccessfully trying not to laugh. "Well, well, well, sounds like your daddy knows how to keep his man in line." Payne winked at Gage and blew him a little kiss when Gage growled at him. He put a wiggling Hana on her feet, and she looked up expectantly at Gage.

"Go, find the kids and have fun," Gage said.

"Bye," Hana called over her shoulder as she ran away from them. She'd probably had enough weirdness for the day.

"So…" Payne said.

"No, you just shut your trap, Payne," Gage warned him.

"I was just going to ask if your man was always this quiet or if he was just afraid of little old me." Payne fluttered his eyelashes.

"I'm sorry. I'm just a bit overwhelmed by all the new people I'm supposed to meet and impress," Nikola said.

Payne fanned himself dramatically. "Color me impressed." He turned to Matt, "Did you hear that accent? Oh my god, one word from this one, and I'd drop my pants and bend over."

Nikola's eyebrows shot up, and he looked to Matt and Gage for help. They both shook their heads because Payne was…well, he was Payne, so you just had to take him as he was. Payne put his hand on Nikola's forearm. "Don't worry, sweetie. I'm totally devoted to my other half, my knight in shining armor." He sighed and gave Matt a soft, loving look. "But he doesn't mind if I look, and honey, I just found me some new eye candy, so get used to it."

Nikola surprised them all by putting his arm around Payne's shoulders and pulling him into his side. "I think I just found my new best friend. I'm sure if I keep you next to me, people will think twice about getting mixed up in a conversation with us."

Payne made a pouty face as he looked up at Nikola. "I'm not sure that was a compliment, but if I get to snuggle with you all day, then I guess I don't care if it was or not." He snaked an arm around Nikola's waist and smiled in triumph at Gage.

"Just don't get too comfortable there, and make sure you return him in the condition you found him in," Gage said. With a wink and a shimmy, Payne walked off with Gage's man. Nikola threw Gage a look, but he waved them off. Nikola was right about having Payne with him. Nobody railroaded that man, so Nikola was safe from anyone who would try to start anything with him.

"You sure that was a good idea?" Matt asked when their other halves were out of earshot.

"What's the worst that could happen? Where's Spence?" Gage asked. Matt averted his eyes and fidgeted. "Is he spending the holiday with Lucas?" It was Gage's best guess, when Matt looked like he did—like he was hiding something.

"No, no he's actually trying to talk Lucas out of a really bad idea," Matt said, still avoiding eye contact with Gage.

"What bad idea?" Matt was saved from having to tell him, when Gage's ex-boyfriend and Spence came around the corner, deep in conversation. Spence looked around and caught Gage's eye, and Gage could see Spence was sorry that he was the one caught with Lucas. "You've got to be fucking kidding me, right?"

"He said your cousin invited him. That he was almost adamant that he be here," Matt explained the reason behind Lucas's sudden appearance.

"Fucking JJ. I'm going to kill that bastard." Gage was so angry his hands shook. He looked for Nikola as Lucas and Spence approached him and Matt. Nikola was all the way across the lawn, Payne still next to him, talking to Hana and JJ's daughter.

"Spence went to try to talk him out of coming, but I guess that didn't work. I'm sorry, Gage," Matt said.

JJ, his asshole cousin, came out of nowhere and intercepted Lucas before he could get to Gage, and Spence took the opportunity JJ's interference offered him to leave Lucas in someone else's hands. Gage wondered what the two of them were up to. Couldn't be anything good, that was for sure.

"Hey, Gage, long time no see," Spence said, stepping in for a quick hug. "I'm sorry. I tried my best, but you know what a stubborn prick he can be."

"Yeah, I know better than most," Gage said. "How have you been? How're the businesses doing?"

"Good. Everything's been going pretty good. Nothing on the romance front, of course, but that's nothing new," Spence said with a crooked grin.

"You have to give them more than one night to get the romance, you know?" Gage teased.

"Ah, who needs romance when there's so many boys out there who need some lovin'." Spence eyed the crowd as if he might find one of those lost boys milling around the holiday party.

"So what's the plan?" Matt asked after Spence and Gage were done with their greeting.

"For what?" Spence asked.

"What are we going to do about Lucas?" Matt asked.

"Nothing. I'm going to pretend he's not here, and I'm going to enjoy the holiday with my family, friends, and the man I love." Gage calmed down a fair bit and decided getting angry over Lucas being where he shouldn't be was not going to do anyone any good. It was probably what JJ had been hoping to accomplish, and Gage wasn't going to give him the satisfaction.

Spence laughed and clapped Gage on the back. "Dude, you just said the man you love. That is a phrase I never thought I'd hear out of you. Let's go see if they'll let me join in the egg hunt this year." Both Gage and Matt groaned because it was something he tried every year, but the age limit was never lifted for him.

Nikola and Payne were talking to Gage's mom, aunt, and JJ's wife, Vicky, when they finally found them. Hana and Madison, Vicky and JJ's daughter, were running around their legs playing what looked like a game of tag. Nikola was talking and occasionally looking at Hana with a smile that melted Gage's heart.

Coming up beside Nikola, Gage put his arm around his waist. "You girls aren't filling him full of lies about me are you?"

Nikola turned his smiling face to Gage, and without thinking, Gage gave him a quick kiss. "No. Vicky was just telling me about the schools around here," Nikola said when he recovered from Gage's unexpected show of affection. Gage turned his attention to the women. The way Vicky was looking at them made Gage think she probably wasn't aware of her husband's behind-the-scenes manipulation of his life.

"Hana's just adorable, Gage. You should send her over for a day. She and Maddie are getting on like a house on fire." Vicky turned to Nikola. "And you are even better than Gage made you out to be. You need to have a talk with him about how he presents you to others."

Gage was shocked, but Nikola took it in stride. "Well, we all know Gage is not the best at communicating his feelings, but I'll be sure that in the future he only gives you glowing reviews about me."

The group of women tittered. Gage had never been with Nikola out in public where he could understand his interactions with others, so he was a little surprised at how people, in general, responded to Nikola. He was obviously charismatic, and he held everyone's attention—be it through his exotic good looks or his personality—Gage couldn't be sure.

"Oh, you'll be good for our Gage, that's for sure," Gage's aunt said. "We're all glad he's found someone who will make him happy."

Huh? That was news to Gage. He hadn't heard any ringing endorsements of his new relationship from any member of his family until just then. Maybe he wouldn't need to worry so much about Lucas being there since at least the core female members of his family seemed so taken with the new man in his life.

"Uncle Gage, is that your friend?" Hana asked. She was tugging on Gage's sleeve and pointing at Lucas.

Nikola tensed against Gage, and Payne puffed up at his side, ready to defend him. "That little asshole. I can't believe he had the nerve to show up here. I'ma gonna kick his scrawny little ass," Payne snarled. Thankfully, Matt showed up in time to wrangle his husband into submission before things got ugly.

"TIME FOR THE EGG HUNT TO BEGIN!" Gage's father announced in his booming voice. The kids all swarmed the area where the baskets were waiting for them to fill.

The commotion provided Gage with enough time to pull Nikola close, so he could whisper to him. "JJ invited him. I have no idea why, and Lucas probably doesn't either. Though I'm pissed he came here knowing he shouldn't, I'm not looking to cause a scene with him. I don't know what's going on, but please let me handle Lucas."

Nikola met Gage's eyes, and though Gage could see a little bit of hurt in those deep-brown depths, he nodded. "Whatever you think is best. I'm here if you need me."

He kissed Nikola softly again for his own reassurance and then turned and squared his shoulders, ready to meet his ex head on.

Chapter Twenty-Four

NIKOLA WATCHED AS the man he'd replaced walked toward Gage. The look on Lucas's face was somewhere between anger and sadness, like each was battling for dominance. But even with the storm of emotion warring on his face, he was a beautiful man, and the pictures on Gage's phone had done him little justice. Nikola wondered again how Gage could be attracted to him after having a man who looked like Lucas.

"Gage," Lucas said as he stopped only a couple of feet from them.

"Lucas, what are you doing here?" There wasn't anger in Gage's voice. If anything, he sounded weary of the whole mess.

Lucas looked around him at the people who were obviously eavesdropping, hanging on every word. His eyes landed on Nikola, a scowl marring his prettiness. "Can we go somewhere to talk?"

"No, because we have nothing else to talk about. I think you know that too."

"Gage, please, I just need a few minutes." The look Lucas was using on Gage was a well-practiced one Nikola knew would normally get him what he wanted from the man. It had probably worked hundreds of times in the past, but he knew Gage could resist it with Nikola there to support him.

"No, Lucas, and that's my final word. I didn't ask you to come here. I didn't know you'd be here, and if you really think about it, you know that it was wrong for you to come." Gage squared his shoulders, making him seem even bigger. Lucas's face crumpled.

Nikola made note of the reactions of the people who were paying the most attention to the scene being played out. One man in particular looked more invested in the outcome of this little drama than everyone else, making no attempt to hide his interest. Nikola stepped back and asked Matt, "Who's that?"

"That's JJ, Gage's cousin," he whispered. Matt had a tense look on his face that made Nikola wonder what would have to happen for him to step in between Gage and Lucas. Nikola was glad he wasn't the only one who would get into the mix if things got physical.

He turned back to watch JJ, and as soon as Lucas got the message that Gage wasn't going to give in and started walking away, JJ followed. He was curious as to why Gage's love life was such a concern to his cousin, but Gage's arms around his waist pulled Nikola away from analyzing it further.

"Hey, babe, I'm so sorry about that. Hopefully he got the message this time," Gage said over Nikola's shoulder.

"It's fine. I'm fine. We're fine," Nikola assured him. It hadn't been pleasant, but it hadn't changed anything.

"Wanna go see if Hana found any eggs yet?" he asked. "Or are you hungry?"

"I could eat, but will you show me where the bathroom is first?" Giving him one final squeeze before releasing him, Gage took Nikola's hand to lead him into the house. He walked slowly, letting Nikola take in the house as they went. Gage led him up the stairs, prompting Nikola to ask, "There's not a bathroom on the first floor?"

"I thought maybe since Hana is occupied...I could show you my room after you use the bathroom."

"You're seriously thinking about sex after that little debacle?" Nikola wasn't that surprised, actually, since it was typical of Gage to bury his emotions and sex was one of his favorite ways to accomplish that. There'd be time later for Nikola to probe into Gage's feelings, but for the moment, it wouldn't hurt to get him off so he could relax for the rest of the day.

Gage winked as he opened a door and pushed Nikola into the bathroom. "Hurry up, or I might change my mind."

Nikola didn't waste any time, and when he came back out, Gage led him down the hall a bit farther and pushed open another door. Gage pulled Nikola into his arms as he backed into the room and started kissing his neck, but what Nikola saw over Gage's shoulder stopped him cold.

"Um, Gage."

"Babe, don't worry. No one comes up here," Gage said, misunderstanding Nikola's hesitation. Grabbing Gage's shoulders, Nikola turned him around in time for him to watch JJ pull up his pants and Lucas get up from his knees.

The four men stood there in a frozen tableau for what felt like a long time but, in reality, was maybe fifteen seconds. The trembling in Gage's shoulders reverberated through Nikola's arms, but Nikola wasn't sure what he should do. What did one do when confronted with your lover's ex blowing your lover's married and supposedly straight cousin?

"Gage listen—" JJ was the first to find his voice, but it triggered something in Gage and he cut him off.

"How long?" Gage asked in a voice dripping with menace. The trembling stopped, the muscles in his shoulders now tense and ready to strike. "How long have you two been fucking around behind my back?" He raised his voice when neither of them answered his first question. There was nothing Nikola could do without potentially making things worse, so he just rubbed Gage's shoulders to let him know he was there for him.

"We didn't," Lucas said in a small voice. Tears ran down his face as he sniveled uncontrollably.

"What do mean you didn't? You obviously were just doing it." Gage took a step toward his cousin. "If you wanted him so badly, why were you trying to get us back together?"

JJ's mouth worked, but no words came out.

"Nothing happened between us until after you left for Sarajevo. I swear." Lucas's eyes shifted to Nikola but were drawn quickly back to Gage. "He was trying to comfort me, and it just happened, but it's just sex, Gage. I don't love him. I still love you. Please—"

"Don't," Gage growled when Lucas tried to reach for him. He stabbed a finger at Lucas. "Don't you fucking touch me." He turned to JJ, who was standing there looking lost. "What the fuck are you doing, JJ? You have a wife and kids. Are you willing to throw that away for *him*?" The him came out on an ugly sneer that made Gage's feelings for Lucas very clear.

"Gage, maybe we should just leave them," Nikola suggested. A cooldown period, so everyone could clear their heads, couldn't hurt before any more discussion.

"Nikola, this has nothing to do with you," Gage said. That hurt, and maybe it had nothing to do with Nikola directly, but whatever affected Gage surely would have an impact on him too.

"Yeah, Nikola, butt out—"

Gage's rage was released, and it ended in JJ on the floor with blood gushing between his fingers from his most likely broken nose. "Fuck you, JJ, you fucking bastard!" Gage hollered while standing over the fallen man, his fist poised to strike again.

It only took moments for the footsteps to start pounding up the stairs after that and Gage dropped his hand, but he was still seething when his dad and another man entered the room. There were others in the hallway, but the sight of a fallen man and blood kept them at bay.

"What the hell is going on in here?" the other man asked, going to JJ to help him off the floor. He looked at Mr. Hoffman. "You need to get your son under control, Geoffrey. Are you all right, JJ?" He looked JJ over before turning angry eyes back to Gage.

"Son, what's going on here?" Mr. Hoffman asked Gage. Gage couldn't answer him. Nikola could see he was still gripped by his rage and it had struck him mute. It was just too much for him to handle. Nikola went to Gage and pulled him into the shelter of his arms. He stood stiffly against Nikola but made no move to push him away.

"I think Gage needs some time to calm down. It may be best if we just leave, and you can call later to get his side of the story," Nikola said.

"Bullshit. He's not going anywhere until I know why he hit my son," the belligerent man demanded.

"Jack, calm down. We need level heads right now. There're enough hotheads in here without you adding to it." Gage's dad seemed calm in the face of all the emotions in the room.

"What's going on?" Vicky asked from the doorway. When she saw her husband bleeding, she rushed in and looked at the assembled men. She knew or suspected what was going on between her husband and Lucas. Nikola could tell by the way she wasn't instantly mad at Gage and also by the way she looked between JJ and Lucas. It made Nikola wonder how long their affair had been going on.

Gage went almost limp in Nikola's arms at the appearance of Vicky and was clinging to him with his face buried in Nikola's neck. "Tell her I'm sorry, so sorry. Can we get Hana and go home, please?" he murmured, lips moving against Nikola's skin.

"Vicky, Gage says to tell you he's sorry. We're going to collect our daughter and leave. Sorry. Have a happy Easter," Nikola said preparing to lead Gage away.

"You can't just leave."

Nikola ignored Lucas's shrill voice because, yes, they could leave, and they were going to do just that. The crowd parted for them, and Nikola tried to silently communicate his apologies as they passed Gage's mom and aunt. They took in the sight of Gage clutching at Nikola from the side and had the good grace to leave them be.

They found Hana wide-eyed and clinging to Payne in the kitchen. Payne took one look at Gage and Nikola and followed without a word. By the time they made it to Gage's truck, all three of his friends were following behind. Nikola put Gage in the backseat next to Hana. Hana held her arms out for Gage, and with a sad smile, he laid his head in her small lap and let her pet his hair as she talked softly to him.

Nikola hated to do it, but he had to ask for someone to drive them back to the condo. Matt volunteered, and the other two rode in Matt's car, following them to Gage's. Nikola didn't have the heart to tell them to leave when they filed in the door, so he made a pot of coffee as everyone sat in the living room.

Hana wouldn't leave Gage's side. She was cuddled in his lap, and every so often she'd reach up and rub his cheek. "I love you," she told him softly when she touched him. Gage looked shell-shocked, but he told her he loved her back every time.

Nikola handed out coffee and put out cream and sugar. He was at a loss as to what to say to the men he barely knew so he sat next to Gage and waited.

"Did you guys know?" Gage finally asked after a long, uncomfortable silence.

They all shook their heads. "No. He always talked about working things out with you. Even when I tried to get him to see that you'd moved on. He believed that you'd come around and take him back," Payne said.

Payne told Nikola that he and Lucas worked at the same hair salon, so he probably knew Lucas the best, after Gage. Nikola didn't think Payne was lying to Gage—the three of them really didn't know about Lucas and JJ before now. Gage relaxed a little against Nikola at the reassurance that his friends hadn't known and kept it from him.

They stayed and chatted for another hour. Nikola learned some things about the city and about how they'd become friends. They were so obviously trying to keep the conversation light and away from the scene at Gage's parents' house, which was something Nikola was thankful for. They were all nice guys, and Nikola could see why Gage liked them. Even Payne brought something to the mix that would have been missed without his presence, and the love between him and Matt was inspiring. Nikola hoped that he and Gage would one day celebrate ten years together too.

Nikola ended up showing them out since Hana was fast asleep in Gage's lap. He cleaned up the little mess and then took Hana from a reluctant Gage and put her to bed in her room. Gage hadn't moved when Nikola got back so he straddled him and cupped Gage's face in his hands.

"So tell me what's bothering you more—that Lucas was with another man or that it was your cousin who was with him?" Nikola asked. Gage looked down, trying to avoid eye contact. Nikola knew Gage didn't want to tell him and, instinctively, knew the answer. "It's okay if you get upset that your ex has started seeing someone. I'm not going to get mad. You spent five years with him, and even if you didn't love him, I'm sure you felt strongly for him."

Gage shook his head but still wouldn't meet Nikola's eyes. "It's not that so much that as it makes me wonder how long. You know? How long were they doing it? Was I such an arrogant idiot that I didn't see it? I guess the idea of him cheating on me never really crossed my mind."

Nikola could see how the thought of being cheated on would be a blow to Gage's pride. "So you don't believe what Lucas said about them not doing anything until after you'd broken up?"

Gage let out a long breath through his nose. "Not sure what I believe. I've been going over and over it in my head, and I guess, looking back, JJ wasn't overly upset when Lucas broke up with me. He didn't seem really all that involved then, not like when I came back. But why would he want us together if he was fucking him? It makes no sense at all, no matter how I turn it around in my mind." Gage finally looked at Nikola, the confusion and hurt easy to see on his face. His cousin's betrayal cut deeply.

Nikola rolled it around in his brain for a bit before he started to lay out his theory for Gage. "You said that Lucas planned to go back home when you broke up, right?" Gage furrowed his brow at the question but nodded an affirmative. "So if they started up after that, and JJ didn't want him to leave...maybe he figured if you two got back together then he could keep his wife and still have Lucas on the side because he'd stay here instead of going back."

"But he's not gay. He's never shown any kind of inclination in that direction, and believe me, when I first figured it out about myself, I looked at everyone with suspicion," Gage argued.

"It was just a theory, but as far as JJ being gay, he's most definitely not one hundred percent straight. Or I guess he's…what do they call it, bicurious? Maybe it was just one of those things where it was thrown in his lap, and he just said 'What the hell?'" Kind of like he and Jasmina—stranger things had happened than someone fucking someone nobody expected them to. "Besides, Lucas is a very pretty man. It would be easy for someone to overlook his manly bits if they were just getting a blow job from him."

A small twitch started at the corner of Gage's lips. "If Lucas ever heard you say that, he'd flip his shit. You have no idea how you just hit on his most vulnerable spot."

Nikola sat back farther on Gage's knees and crossed his arms over his chest. "Oh come on, he uses that to his advantage, and he knows it. If I started sniveling at you with big puppy-dog eyes, you'd slap me and tell me to man up, but when pretty boy does it, everyone wants to give him a hug and make him cookies," Nikola said indignantly.

Gage couldn't contain the smile any longer. "I'd never slap you. I've already heard all about your reputation. I don't want to end up in an unmarked grave somewhere in the middle of Bosnia." He watched Nikola's expression carefully as he asked, "Did you want to give Lucas a hug?"

Nikola snorted. "No, a hug was the last thing I wanted to give him." Nikola leaned in for a kiss. "I'd rather put him in one of those unmarked graves you're so worried about. Besides, when a guy's got a man like you, who needs pretty little boys?"

He kissed Nikola hard then and pulled him in tight, crushing him to his chest. "I was thinking the same thing," he murmured against Nikola's lips before kissing them again.

"Babo, I'm hungry." Hana broke them out of their make-out session. She was standing behind Nikola, rubbing her eyes.

"Let's make a couple of pizzas," Gage offered.

"Not much of an Easter dinner, but it'll do I suppose," Nikola agreed.

Later, just as they started in on their pizzas, Gage's phone rang. He looked at the screen and answered it as he got up to go into the other room.

"Babo, why was Uncle Gage sad?"

Nikola wasn't sure what to tell her. "Well, baby, it's kind of complicated."

She nodded. "Adult stuff again."

"Yeah, stupid adult stuff again. Did you have fun hunting for eggs?" he asked, trying to change the subject.

Her eyes widened. "I forgot my basket."

"Oh, honey, I'm sorry, but you got the one the Easter Bunny left you this morning, so you'll be okay, right?"

She seemed to think about it for a minute. "I guess so. Can I go to Maddie's house? She asked me if I could come and see her room."

Nikola was sure the answer to that was going to have to be no, but there was no way to explain to her why she couldn't go. He hedged a bit. "We'll see if there's time. Gage wants to take you to get some things for your room tomorrow, and then I don't know what else he has planned." She nodded and didn't seem too bothered by Nikola's answer, which he was thankful for.

Gage came back and ate a piece of pizza, ignoring Nikola's questioning look until he finished it. "My mom and dad want us to come out to the house after everyone leaves. They sounded a little upset, so I told them that I didn't think it was a good idea. Maybe it's better to let everything cool down a little before I see anyone from my family."

"Why not go and see what they have to say? Do they know what's going on?"

He looked at Hana, and Nikola got that whatever he wanted to say wasn't something he wanted her to hear. She picked up on it and finished her pizza quickly. "Can I watch a movie?" she asked, effectively taking herself out of the picture so they could talk.

"Sure, go ahead and see if there's anything you want to watch. I have cable, but you'll have to stick to the cartoon channels to be safe." Gage got up and cleaned off the table as Hana settled on the couch with the Disney Channel.

"Gage, maybe you should go to see your parents. Hana and I can stay here if you want." Nikola didn't want Gage to have a problem with his family just when it seemed like they were going to mend the rift he felt he'd caused.

"No, I told them they could come here tomorrow some time. I guess there're some things that they want to tell me about what went on after we left. I'm just not up to dealing with it tonight when everyone is still so emotional." Gage pulled Nikola up from his chair and wrapped him in his arms. "I want to go in there and snuggle with my two favorite people and forget the rest of the world exists. Can I do that?"

God, did he know how to get his way or what? "Of course, we can do that. I just don't want you to lose your family over something that wasn't even your fault."

"Everyone thinks they know why I punched JJ."

Nikola did too. He'd let Lucas suck his dick, and Gage slugged him for it, but he still asked, "Oh, and what did you tell them?"

"I told them that he could let anyone he wanted suck his cock. I didn't punch him because of Lucas."

"What?" Nikola asked. Gage had lost him. "Okay, so then what did you tell them? Why did you punch him?"

"I told them that if anyone talked to you the way he did, I wouldn't hesitate to punch them too. Nobody talks to you like that and gets a chance to do it twice."

The warmth rushed through Nikola's body. Gage punched JJ for him, not due to jealousy over Lucas. He squeezed Gage tighter. Gage was his, and Nikola would do whatever he could to keep him.

Chapter Twenty-Five

THEY WATCHED A movie, Gage leaning back on Nikola's chest, Hana cuddled in his lap. Gage felt like he was the cream in the weirdest Oreo ever made. If only he could keep his mind on the movie, but he just couldn't let it go—JJ and Lucas—it made absolutely no sense. How had that even happened? Oh god, Gage really didn't want to know the details, but his mind kept trying to supply them anyway.

Nikola ran his hand along Gage's arm as he watched the movie, occasionally leaning into Gage and kissing his temple. He knew Nikola wanted him to spill his guts, but there wasn't much to tell. Gage decided he was going to believe Lucas and JJ's affair didn't start until after he'd left for Sarajevo, which meant only JJ's attempts at turning his family against Nikola mattered. Lucas was free to do what he'd pleased, and Gage would be a hypocrite if he judged him for moving on to someone new so soon after their breakup, even if his choice in lover was suspect.

He wanted to know if Nikola's theory was right, and Gage was just collateral damage in JJ's quest to keep his booty call in the same city. It sucked, but JJ was family, and Gage fucked up enough family stuff being a stubborn asshole that he was willing to hear what his cousin had to say to salvage their relationship. It wasn't Gage he was cheating on, after all. Vicky and his kids were the ones who would pay the ultimate price for his betrayal.

After they put Hana to bed, Nikola and Gage went to their room. Nikola made slow, sweet love to Gage. He loved Nikola like that, all soft, sweet and tender. He also liked how rough Nikola could be with him, and vice versa, but there was something to be said for doing it face-to-face with long, slow kisses that left him breathless. Again, Gage's mind insisted that Nikola was it—the one. Gage needed to find a way to make Nikola want to stay there with him forever.

GAGE'S PARENTS KNOCKED on the door while the coffee was still dripping into the pot. He wasn't too surprised by that since he and Nikola slept until almost ten, but the line of people who came in after them was a bit shocking for first thing in the morning. They came bearing gifts for Hana and food for brunch. Gage stood at the door and watched them march in as Mom, Dad, Uncle Jack, Aunt Sue, Vicky, holding Maddie's hand—and finally JJ carrying little Jack—all tromped past him into the living area.

Hana squealed in delight at her new friend's unexpected appearance, and they hugged like it had been years, instead of hours, since they'd last seen each other. The women smiled at their excitement, handing Hana the Easter gifts they'd brought before she dragged Maddie to her room, Gage knew they wouldn't see them again until they were called down to eat which would make the upcoming conversation less uncomfortable.

Nikola hung back in the kitchen area while Gage greeted his family.

Both Gage's parents hugged him, without saying anything, as did his Aunt Sue and Vicky. They then took the food into the kitchen, where Gage could hear Nikola greeting them.

Gage stood with the two remaining men and waited for them to make the first move.

"Gage, I owe you an apology," Uncle Jack said as he put his hand out for Gage to shake. Taking it, Gage accepted his apology. "I didn't know all the facts before I put the blame for yesterday's events on your shoulders. I probably would have punched him myself if I'd walked in on that scene." He gave Gage a curt nod before glaring at JJ. Gage didn't bother to correct him on the reason for punching his cousin, letting him think what he would on that subject.

JJ stepped up next and put out his hand. Gage hesitated a few seconds before he took it. "Gage, we need to talk. I guess I have some explaining to do," JJ said, his eyes flitted to the kitchen, landing on his wife. Gage could see the worry there, and he wondered if this had been more her idea than his.

"The only explanation you owe me is why you got me involved in this mess. The rest is between you, your wife, and Lucas. It doesn't mean anything to me."

JJ appeared to be a bit taken aback by his statement. "What do you mean? You're not pissed about Lucas?"

Gage leaned in close to his cousin, lowering his voice as to not be overheard by the others. "The only thing I'm pissed about is the fact that you bad-mouthed Nikola for the past two months to everyone who would listen, and for what? So you could stick your dick in Lucas? I thought you wanted me to be with him, and that you wanted me to see I was making a mistake when he wanted me back, but it was all just because you were fucking him. Have you always liked dick, or is this a new development?"

JJ pulled back to put some space between himself and Gage. "He gave me a few blow jobs and a couple of hand jobs. I don't like dick. I'm not a f—" he cut himself off, apparently thinking twice about using that word in Gage's house when there were two gay men there who could easily take him in a fight. "Look, everyone knew Lucas was good for you and when he called to ask me to check in on the condo while you were gone, we talked. I sort of mentioned that maybe he should give you a second chance. You're a good guy, Gage, and you deserve to be happy." JJ's eyes went to his own family before he sighed. "He decided to give you more time to think about starting a family, but he asked me not to tell you. He wanted to surprise you when you got home from Sarajevo. He called me, crying after you told him about Nikola, and I met him for a drink. He begged me to talk to you for him, and after a few drinks, I jokingly said I'd do it if he sucked my dick. I didn't think he'd actually do it."

"I'm not sure I follow." None of what JJ was saying was making sense to Gage.

"He gave me a blow job in my car and then I felt like I had to try to help him get back with you. I got a little addicted to having him around, always willing to go down on me. You gotta know with two young kids and a pregnant wife, sex is nonexistent in our house, but it was just sex. My head was fucked up, and now I see that. Vicky and I are going to try to work it out, so if you can get past this, then there's nothing else that needs to be said. I told Lucas it was over. He's out of our lives. He was only hanging around because he hoped you'd eventually take him back, but now that he knows you won't, he's already packed."

That was good news. Lucas finally out of their lives would make it easier for everyone to get past this. Gage wasn't happy about any of the things JJ did to interfere in his life, but he was starting to think JJ might have thought he was doing Gage a favor trying to get Lucas to stay. Gage considered that point before telling JJ what he felt he needed to put the incident behind them. "You have to apologize to Nikola in front of everyone, and if I ever hear you say another thing about him, or if you ever talk to him like you did yesterday, you'll have me to deal with, and next time I won't stop at just one punch." Gage wasn't sure he and JJ could ever be as close as they once were, but hearing him grovel to the man he'd tried to put down to anyone who'd listen would go a long way in Gage's book.

JJ nodded and Gage offered his hand. In their family, your handshake was your word of honor, so if JJ didn't honor it, he'd be in the doghouse with both their old men. "I'm sorry, Gage, really I am," JJ said. Gage patted him on the back. Nothing he could do or say would be as tough for JJ as trying to make things right with Vicky would. Gage would just let it go.

They joined the rest of the family in the kitchen where Nikola and the women were busy trying to pretend not to listen in while setting out the food they'd brought. Nikola went to Gage immediately, putting his arm around his waist. He was probably dying to know what had been said, but he just kissed Gage's cheek and smiled at whoever looked their way. Everyone who didn't already have a plate filled one and found places to sit.

After everyone was seated, JJ stood up. "I'd like to say something since everyone is here." He coughed and looked embarrassed before going on. "I know I've said and done some things recently that have been...out of character for me. I'd just like to say I'm sorry. First, to my beautiful wife, I love you so much, and I never meant to hurt you. Secondly, to Gage, I should have stayed out of your business. And lastly, to Nikola, I'm sorry I didn't listen to Gage or wait to get to know you in person before I made up my mind about you. I made a judgment about you that was unfair and also colored by my own desires. I've wronged you all, and for that I'm sorry, and I hope that in keeping with the holiday, we can all enjoy a new beginning."

Gage watched Nikola's face while he listened to JJ make his speech. Nikola's eyes narrowed, and his lips puckered like he'd just sucked a lemon. Gage didn't think Nikola put a lot of weight on JJ's apology; the man would need more than words to satisfy Nikola's sense of justice. Still, Gage had to give it to his cousin. He was eloquent even when the situation was humiliating. He was going to make a great CEO someday.

Everyone seemed satisfied that this little episode could come to an end now that apologies were given and expected to be accepted. Gage looked to Vicky, and though her eyes were red-rimmed, she was smiling at Maddie and Hana. She seemed to be willing to give her husband another chance. Gage saw that Nikola was also taking in the reactions of the group, and he seemed to relax at Gage's side. After finishing their lunch, everyone said their goodbyes.

Gage shut the door once the last of them departed. Nikola was standing, with his arms folded across his chest, and Gage couldn't tell what he was thinking or feeling, but he hoped he wasn't upset that Gage accepted JJ's apology. "Nikola—"

"I'm happy for you, Gage," Nikola said cutting him off. "You made the right decision. Family's important, and losing what you have with them isn't worth it. I'm glad you're not going to hold a grudge." Gage studied Nikola's face to see if he was just trying to placate him, but he didn't see any signs of anger. Maybe they'd be able to put this behind them and get on with their lives.

IT WAS THEIR last night together, and Hana was at Gage's parents' house with Maddie for the evening to give Nikola and Gage a little alone time. They were getting ready to eat the supper Nikola tried to help Gage prepare. He was hopeless in the kitchen, but that was okay because Gage let him know it wasn't his cooking skills he'd fallen in love with. Nikola smirked at what Gage was alluding to and stopped to kiss him as he set the table.

After seating themselves, Gage poured two glasses of wine. His chest aching as he looked into Nikola's eyes, he got to feel the way Nikola must have felt the last two times they'd separated. He didn't like the feeling at all, and it strengthened his resolve to finally ask Nikola the question that had been on the tip of his tongue but steadfastly stuck behind his lips for the past week.

Nikola grabbed Gage's hand and smiled almost shyly at him. "What is it, Gage?"

The question must have been evident in Gage's eyes as he took a deep, shuddering breath. "Nikola, you know I love both you and Hana. I've been so happy this past week, having both of you here with me. My family thinks you two are the best thing that's ever happened to me, and I agree with them. I can't really see my life here without you two in it." Gage rushed the words out but then paused to gauge Nikola's reaction to them. Nikola's head was cocked to the side, as he absorbed Gage's words, and a small smile played at the corner of his lips, encouraging Gage to go on.

"I know it would be asking a lot of you, and maybe you'll think it's too much too soon, but I'd really like it if you'd consider coming back here." Gage swallowed his fear of rejection and blurted out the last bit, "To live with me."

Nikola stood and Gage braced for the rejection he was sure was coming. Maybe Nikola thought he'd jumped the gun, and would be mad at him for putting him in a position where he assumed it was all or nothing. But instead, Nikola pulled Gage roughly out of his chair and gripped the sides of his head. The pain of his own teeth smashing into his lips made Gage gasp when Nikola's lips smashed into his.

Nikola took advantage of the small opening and shoved his tongue roughly into Gage's mouth. He put his hands on Nikola's chest to push him back. This was not the reaction he'd been expecting. Nikola didn't let Gage move him, and it was the first time Gage hated the fact that they were so evenly matched in strength. He managed to gain a little ground when Nikola's hands left his face to grip his shirt, but the sound of buttons popping and fabric ripping caught Gage off guard.

Nikola's deft fingers moved to dispatch Gage's belt and the button on his slacks in swift motions. Gage was still reeling from Nikola's punishing kisses when he pushed Gage's pants downward until their own weight took them to his feet. When his fingers found Gage's nipples, he twisted cruelly, as his mouth left Gage's to bite on the soft flesh where Gage's neck met his shoulder, and Gage's knees went weak. He had no idea what was going on with Nikola, but each time Gage tried to push him off or make him slow the assault on his body, Nikola just redoubled his efforts.

"Nikola, please..." Gage was at the point where he wasn't sure if he was asking Nikola to stop or to give him more.

Nikola turned him roughly, pushing Gage downward, so his chest was on the table, his face hovering just inches from their plates of untouched food. He heard Nikola's zipper, and a moment of panic seized Gage's chest at the thought of Nikola taking him dry. Nikola couldn't be so crazed that he'd intentionally hurt Gage, but then again, his actions from the time he'd asked his question until now were not those of a sane man. Gage clenched his ass and braced for whatever Nikola was hell-bent on doing.

Nikola's hard cock pressed against his ass as Nikola reached over him and grabbed half a stick of butter from the dish. The tightness in Gage's chest loosened a bit, but there was still the matter of...slick, talented fingers—two—entered Gage, and he tried to relax. Nikola wasn't going to hurt him. Gage should have known that, no matter how out of his mind he was, Nikola would take care of him.

Nikola pressed against his prostate, making Gage shout out at the sensation. Nikola loved making him come that way and took an almost sadistic pleasure in it. Gage's hips bucked as Nikola fucked him harder with those fingers, slipping in a third as he twisted and nailed Gage's gland repeatedly. Gage's cock leaked beneath him, and just when he was sure he was going to come, his ass was suddenly empty.

Nikola was still there, and even though Gage couldn't feel him, Nikola's ragged breathing gave him away, and Gage didn't dare move. Nikola entered him faster and rougher than ever before, but Gage cleared his mind and relaxed. Nikola bottomed out and lay across Gage's back, pinning him to the table top.

"I'm going to make you remember this, Gage," Nikola growled into his ear. "This will be a night you never forget. I want you to remember the night that changed your life forever." His words rocketed around Gage's brain. He wanted to know if that meant his answer was yes, but Nikola rocked his hips, and Gage moaned. Nikola had Gage's number, knowing just how far he could push.

"Please, Niky, fuck me. Make me come." Gage wasn't above begging Nikola. This was not exactly how Gage planned for the night to go, but he wasn't going to deny himself the satisfaction getting fucked by Nikola gave him just because Nikola had apparently gone batshit crazy on him.

Nikola stood behind him, his legs nudging Gage's into a wider stance. As Nikola's hands gripped his hips in a painful grasp, his length slid out before ramming back in. The table legs screeched as they slid across the tiled floor, and the wine glasses and bottle toppled over, causing Gage to lift his head an inch as the wine made its way under his hair. Nikola still didn't stop, hammering into Gage brutally, following the table across the room with each thrust until it came to a stop against the far wall. Dishes rattled as Nikola took what he needed from Gage, and the sound that rose from Nikola's chest was a primal scream by the time it left his mouth.

When Gage's orgasm was ripped from his body moments later, it left him too weak to do anything but lie there as Nikola pumped a few final times until he achieved his own release. Nikola's warmth filled Gage and his body landed with no finesse on Gage's back, only the sturdy table keeping them from hitting the ground hard. It took Gage a few seconds to realize it wasn't ragged breathing coming from the man on top of him, but sobs.

Gage pried his fingers from their death grip on the edge of the tabletop and reached back to touch Nikola's head. He did his best to run his fingers through Nikola's tangled sweaty hair, but the angle was wrong, and his boneless shuddering body made it impossible for Gage to even shift a tiny bit.

"Niky, please tell me what's wrong." Gage asked, struggling to get his next breath under Nikola's weight. He hoped Nikola wasn't upset that he'd asked him to come there to live with him. Maybe this was Nikola's way of saying no and showing Gage what he'd miss for the rest of his life. Gage was sure he'd remember that night and whatever was said just like Nikola intended.

Nikola's breath hitched, and his words were so soft that Gage had to strain to make them out. "What took you so long to ask me?"

Fuck, the anguish in that one little question broke Gage's heart. He'd been so stupid, and he'd almost let Nikola leave without asking. What had Nikola been thinking? That Gage didn't want him and Hana there with him? That Gage would put them on the plane in the morning and be able to go on like his heart wasn't in that plane with them? That Gage could live any sort of a life without them by his side? God how stupid could two men be?

Gage shifted his hips enough that Nikola's spent member slipped from his body. Gage ignored the sticky mess between his thighs as he pushed up off the table. Nikola let Gage rise while still managing to stay draped over his back, his arms tightening around Gage's neck until Gage turned in Nikola's arms so he could wrap his arms around Nikola too.

"I'm sorry. I'm an idiot. I've wanted to ask you since the first time I talked to you after my first trip. I just didn't know how, and I didn't want to pressure you because it's a big change, and it's so soon—"

Nikola shut Gage up with a soft kiss that made the earlier scene seem like some dystopian nightmare. He pulled back and looked Gage in the eyes. "Did I hurt you?"

"No, baby, you didn't hurt me. But are you going to give me an answer, or am I supposed to guess?" Gage asked.

"Oh," he said, a mildly surprised look crossing his face. "I was sure I said yes somewhere in there. Yes, Gage, Hana and I would love to come here to live with you."

Gage's heart pounded in his chest because this was it. The rest of his life was about to get underway, and Nikola and Hana would be there with him making it a life worth living.

Chapter Twenty-Six

"ARE YOU SURE this is the best option for you and Hana, *sine*?" Nedim asked Nikola the same question for the third time that night. "You barely know the man. What if it doesn't work out? What will you do then after having cut all your ties here?"

"Are you telling me there's no coming back if I choose to go?" Nikola asked since this was the first time Nedim had elaborated on the "are you sure" question. He couldn't see Nedim chucking him out because Nikola wanted to be with the man he loved; his uncle wasn't like his mother.

"No, *sine*, of course not, but people will talk, and it will be much harder for you to hide your past next time you need to come home."

"He won't need to come back here, Nedim. He's found the man of his dreams. It was fate, and they're meant to be. They're going to grow old and die together," Sabina butted in. She'd had a few drinks and was freely giving her opinion to anyone who would listen. "I have half a mind to pack my things and go with him."

Nedim looked at her fondly, but his words were a little bit harsh. "If you had half a mind, then you'd stop drinking before you accidentally say something you'll regret, my dear girl."

Sabina wrapped her arm around Nikola's waist. "I need to drown my sorrows. Haven't you heard? I'm about to be cast aside for some *vlahnje* who cast her spell on our poor misguided Nikola." She smiled up at Nikola, and he couldn't help but chuckle at what people had been saying to her.

Nikola had heard it all, and now she was being thrown into the role of the poor spinster who couldn't hold on to her man. He felt badly for leaving Sabina in the lurch, but she assured him she could hold her own and was happy for him.

Nikola's aunt snorted. "Yes, it is the end of a great love story. If only people knew the whole truth, it would be a scandal. You're lucky that you'll be so far away. You won't have to deal with the fall out of your little secret. Not like your family will," she said.

"It won't be that bad," Nedim assured his wife. Too bad she didn't drink. She looked like she could use one. Nikola did have to say that he gave her credit, though, she was taking it much better than some people were.

Nikola's own mother refused to accept his decision to move back to the states with "that man" as she insisted on calling Gage. She'd refused to talk to Nikola for the past months, only communicating need-to-know information about Hana and her disdain of Gage. She was nowhere to be found on this the night of Nikola's going-away party.

"Well, we'll all miss you, and I, for one, hope you'll be happy. You deserve some happiness, Nikola. Don't let anyone tell you otherwise," Sabina said before kissing his cheek and wandering off in search of more alcohol.

"You know we'll always be here for you, *sine*, but I do hope we can come and visit you to see what kind of life you make for yourself and your daughter." Nedim clinked his glass with a knife to get the room's attention before making a toast to Nikola's safe journey and a healthy and happy future in "the land of dreams."

HANA WAS UPSTAIRS at Nikola's mom's place as he finished packing their carry-ons for the trip in the morning. The excitement in the pit of his stomach made him nauseous. He hadn't seen Gage on anything other than a computer screen for over three months, and Nikola ached for him.

He walked through the house, making sure nothing had been forgotten. He'd ended up shipping most of their personal things ahead, and Gage confirmed that everything already arrived. They only had one suitcase and a backpack for each of them to take on the plane. The furniture was staying, since the house was Nikola's, and when he wanted to come for a visit, they'd always have a place to stay. Nikola also planned to let Gage use it while there on business, if he wanted.

Nikola couldn't say he was too sad to be leaving. Sarajevo had never really been his home though he did have some fond memories. It was a place of refuge when he'd needed it most, but he still felt like a stranger to the city. He would be happy to come back and visit when he got the chance, but he knew he'd never be back to stay.

Nikola looked up when Hana opened the door, her tear-streaked face making his heart hurt for her. She would miss the only home she'd ever known. They'd talked about it extensively, and she'd insisted that she wanted to go and live with Gage, whom she'd started to call Daddy, with his permission.

"Hey there, baby. Did you and Nana have a good visit?" Though Hana knew his mother wasn't talking to him, she didn't know all the specifics. Nikola didn't bad-mouth his mom in front of Hana. It wasn't fair to make her feel as if she had to choose between them.

"Babo, why can't Nana come with us?"

Nikola sighed. "Because she doesn't want to, baby. This is her home, and she likes it here. I told you that you can come here and spend time with her whenever you like in the summer. She's also welcome to come to visit you if she wants." Nikola would never withhold his daughter from her, but he had a feeling it would be a moot point. His mom hated to travel, and she hated America even more.

Hana nodded her acceptance, and Nikola clamped his lips shut. He wasn't going to ask her again if she was sure about the move. He knew it was ultimately his decision, but if she suddenly had a change of heart, Nikola wasn't sure if he could go through with it if it meant hurting her. He wanted to think he was doing what was best for her, but sometimes he felt like tearing her away from her home and family was the most selfish thing he'd ever done. It kept him awake at night.

"Okay, Babo. I'm kinda tired. Can I go to bed?"

"You need a bath first. Let's go. I'll get the water started." Nikola took her hand to lead her to the bathroom.

After bathing her, he helped her into her nightgown and tucked her into her bed. "I know you're a little sad about leaving Nana and your friends, but just remember that they'll still be here. You can Skype with them, and we'll come to visit next summer, for sure. I promise," Nikola assured her.

"I know, Babo. I miss Daddy. I'm glad we're going home to him tomorrow." She yawned and held her arms out for a hug. Nikola leaned over her and squeezed her tight. "Love you, Babo."

"I love you too, baby." Nikola shut the light off and left her.

It took Nikola forever to fall asleep, and the five o'clock wakeup call came way too early for his liking, but he got up and ready before getting Hana out of bed. She had way more energy than he did. Amel showed up to take them to the airport, and they loaded the bags into the back. Just as they were getting in, Nikola's mom came down the stairs.

"Nikola," she called to get his attention.

As Nikola looked up, he could see she'd been crying. "Mom, we have to leave for the airport now." It was too late for her to do anything more than tell Hana goodbye.

She gave Hana a huge hug and told her she'd miss her and loved her. She had tears streaking down her face as she turned to Nikola. He expected to see something other than the sadness in her eyes. She put her arms around his waist and gave him a quick hug.

"I don't understand your decision, but you are my son, and though I don't like what you are, I can't let that get in the way of seeing Hana grow up. Please make sure she stays in contact with me. That is all I ask."

"I will. Goodbye, Mom. I love you." Nikola hugged her back, but she stiffened and pulled away.

"Goodbye, Nikola, *sreten put.*" Nikola hadn't expected for her to tell him she loved him, so he shouldn't have been so disappointed, but he was.

She stood in front of the house and waved as they drove away.

THE DELAY IN Chicago made Hana antsy. She was overly tired and just ready to be somewhere that wasn't a plane or an airport. When the fasten seat belt sign lit up, and they announced they were descending, Nikola's heart leapt into his throat.

"Babo, we're almost there." Hana gazed out the window at the lights of the city below.

"Yeah, baby, we're almost home." It felt weird to say, but good to know. The man he loved would be waiting impatiently for them at the airport. Nikola heard the frustration in Gage's voice when he'd called him to let him know they were going to be over an hour later than expected.

The landing went smoothly, and it took almost no time to get off the plane since it was, at most, half full. Nikola grabbed Hana's hand to keep her from running down the jetway, but she's the one who slowed Nikola when he saw Gage. There was no way her short legs could keep up with how fast Nikola's body wanted to run to be in Gage's arms.

Nikola let go of Hana's hand, dropped the carry-on bags, and flung himself at Gage. Gage's arms crushed him to his chest so hard Nikola couldn't breathe, but who needed to breathe anyway? Gage gave him a quick kiss, mindful that they were in public.

"Hey, you," Gage said.

"God, I missed the hell out of you." Gage clung to Nikola for a few more seconds before he let him go so he could pick up Hana. She'd been getting hugs and kisses from her new grandparents.

Gage's parents had been unflinchingly accepting of the whole situation after the Easter disaster, and it was nice to have people who didn't judge them at every turn. Nikola got a firm handshake from Gage's dad and a tight hug from his mom. "It's so good to have you two back where you belong," she said as she released him. The smile on her face was genuine, and no matter how tired Nikola was, he couldn't help but return it.

"It's good to be back. I bet he was a bear to live with the last couple of months," Nikola said, looking back at Gage.

"Oh, you have no idea. I haven't wanted to put him over my knee this badly since he was five." Boy, did Nikola know the feeling only too well, but he didn't share that thought with her.

Nikola looked at Gage, who tried to look contrite but failed because he couldn't wipe the happy smile off his face for even a second. "Let's go get your bags and go home," he said.

Nikola held Gage's hand as they walked down the stairs. Hana finally crashed and was sleeping on Gage's shoulder. They waited for the bags and then loaded everything in Gage's parents' SUV. Nikola, Hana, and Gage rode in Gage's truck. One of the first things they'd have to do is go car shopping. No way could Nikola drive this monster around.

Nikola noticed they weren't heading to Gage's condo. "Where are we going?"

"It's a surprise, so just sit back and relax." Gage's eyes flicked to him but went back to the road ahead.

Nikola just wanted to get home and into bed with Gage, but the happy look on Gage's face kept Nikola from expressing that opinion. The drive didn't take long, even though it took them past the city limits and into the next state. Nikola sat at attention when they pulled into a long, tree-lined drive.

The driveway was at least a quarter of a mile long, and at the end, was what had probably been an old two-story farmhouse at one time but had obviously been updated recently. The landscape lighting lit the exterior, and the soft glow of the lights in the windows made an invitingly cozy first impression.

"Um...Gage, what's this?" Nikola had his suspicions but wanted it confirmed before he got too excited by the possibility.

Gage parked the truck in the circular drive behind his parents' vehicle and opened his door. "Just get out, and I'll tell you." Nikola climbed out of the truck as Gage opened the back door to lift Hana out before walking around the front of the truck with Hana once again held safely against his chest. "Gage?" Nikola inquired as Gage grabbed his hand and started walking to the porch steps.

"Just come on." Gage tugged Nikola's hand and pulled him along behind. He put the key in the lock and stepped through the door. Nikola recognized Gage's furniture right away, and he knew what Gage had done. He stood in the middle of the living room, holding Hana and waiting.

Nikola went to Gage and hugged him, with Hana smooshed between them. He kissed Gage like he'd wanted to at the airport. Gage bought them a house so they could make a home. If Nikola had any doubts about him before, Gage effectively laid them to rest with this grand gesture. Hana and Nikola were home. They didn't need the big house—nice as it was—all they really needed was Gage.

"Welcome home, Niky," Gage whispered.

Epilogue

NIKOLA WAITED PATIENTLY. He sat at his desk in the sunroom that doubled as his home office and watched the wind blow the leaves off the trees at the edge of the property for almost half an hour. Everyone told him the pleasantly cool weather would soon turn into bone-chilling cold, and if Nikola survived the first winter, he could officially call himself a Minnesotan. With the sun coming in the windows and making it a little too warm, his thoughts were miles away from frigid. Nikola checked the clock once more, the fourth time in less than ten minutes. Gage should have been home by now.

He shut down the file he'd been working on and silently thanked God once again for the job he'd found. He got to work from home, just going into the office for team meetings twice a week. Nikola loved being home taking care of the house, and he'd even learned to cook some in the past couple of months. The smell of supper—roast chicken and potatoes in the oven—could attest to that fact. They still ate out too often, and some of the things Nikola cooked came out of boxed mixes, but they were finding their way. Gage cooked on the weekends, and Nikola paid close attention because cooking was one of Gage's many talents.

The sound of tires crushing gravel made Nikola perk up. It was a Pavlovian response—that sound meant what Nikola had been waiting for was finally home. But he didn't get up to meet Gage at the door. Nikola wanted Gage to come to him. He listened as Gage came in from the attached garage. He could hear him and knew, from the subtle noises he was making, exactly what he was doing: hanging up his coat in the hall closet, taking off his shoes, throwing keys on the counter, sifting through the mail, and finally, putting his travel mug in the sink. Then standing in the kitchen wondering where Hana was, since she always greeted him at the door. Footsteps coming down the hall and...

"Hey, babe, where's the munchkin?" Gage leaned on the doorjamb, his posture and tone, broadcasting the stress he always brought home from work with him, was especially heavy.

Nikola couldn't help the smile that overtook his face at the sight of Gage. His reaction to Gage was spontaneous, and the warm feeling never got old. Nikola stood up to kiss him. It had been ten hours and twenty-three minutes since he'd kissed him last, and that was just too long. Gage wrapped his arms around him and sighed as Nikola leaned in for his kiss. Gage opened his mouth for him, knowing just what he needed. Nikola kissed him possessively, like he owned him, and Gage's shoulders relaxed as some of the tension left him. Nikola loved that he could soothe Gage with just a kiss.

Nikola pulled back so he could look Gage in the eyes. "Hana's spending the night with Madison. JJ and Vicky are taking the girls to look at Halloween costumes and then out to supper. She won't be home until at least noon tomorrow," Nikola said, hoping Gage would see where he was going with that news.

Gage's brow furrowed and he bit his lip. "I wanted to buy Hana's costume with her."

"I know. That's why I told her she could just look and get ideas. Vicky knows not to buy her anything. Come on, I have supper in the oven. Let's eat before it dries out, and you can tell me what has you looking like somebody killed your dog." Nikola grabbed Gage's hand and pulled him toward the kitchen.

Gage sat on one of the stools by the kitchen island, where they often ate when it was just the two of them. The guarded expression on Gage's face was one Nikola had come to know and dislike since it usually meant Gage had something to tell him but was trying to find a way to say whatever it was he wanted to say without upsetting Nikola. Gage was so careful with him, sometimes, that it drove him mad.

They'd had very few fights in their months together, and none of them were serious so it always made him wonder why Gage still felt he needed to weigh his words so carefully before saying what he needed to say.

"Gage, love, just tell me," Nikola said as he set the roaster on top of the stove. He pulled the cover off and tried to get the chicken on the platter without it falling apart, and he managed to get it all out and set on the table before Gage said anything. When Gage heaved a heavy sigh as Nikola dished food onto their plates and poured a glass of wine for each of them, Nikola stopped and looked at him, waiting for him to spill.

"I have to leave for Sarajevo on Tuesday, week after next." Gage's gaze left Nikola's face and went to his food. "This looks good. Did you use the lemon pepper?"

"Gage." He knew they were dealing with more than the usual stress of Gage's job. The last time Gage left a boyfriend behind for a business trip he'd been dumped. "Look at me, please." Nikola waited for Gage to make eye contact before he continued. "I'm not going anywhere. I know you have to travel for your job. It's how we met, for Christsake. Hana and I will still be here when you get back. We're not going anywhere." Nikola hoped his words were reassuring because what else could he do but tell Gage the truth?

Gage's fears were still there for Nikola to see in the lines on Gage's face. Nikola didn't want him to stress over something that would never happen, so he stood up and grabbed Gage's arm, pulling him from his stool. Without either of them saying a word, Nikola dragged Gage up the stairs and into the master bedroom where he released his hold on Gage's arm.

"Strip."

"Nikola, the food's going to get cold, and you can't solve everything with sex you know." Gage was stalling, and the way his eyes darted around the room told Nikola he knew it.

"Gage, do you remember your safe word?" If he didn't use the safe word, Nikola wasn't going to stop. Gage needed this, needed to know who he belonged to and that this wasn't something that was going to end just because he had to spend a couple of weeks away.

Gage's hand went to the knot of his tie to pull it loose and then over his head. Nikola watched as he unbuttoned his shirt, with trembling hands, took it off, and hung it over the back of the armchair. His undershirt, pants, and briefs followed quickly. His eyes never left the floor as he removed every last piece until he was standing before Nikola in all his naked glory.

He didn't watch to see what Nikola pulled out of the chest at the foot of the bed. Gage knew better than to be nosy or to offer an opinion. He'd suffered punishments for trying to exert his will, and he'd learned his lessons fairly well. Nikola's man hated when he was denied orgasms. It was Nikola's most effective tool against Gage's need for control. Nikola used it sparingly, so it still packed a punch when he employed it.

Nikola took off his own shirt when he'd selected his tools for this particular session and stood before Gage in only his well-worn jeans. He loved how vulnerable Gage looked standing before him with his cock hard and leaking in anticipation, Nikola's own arousal uncomfortably trapped in its denim prison.

Nikola touched Gage's chest, using feather-light fingertip touches to trace his nipples until they puckered and stood at attention. He removed the clips from his pocket, the chain that linked them jangling as they emerged. The hiss that escaped Gage provided Nikola with more evidence of his need. Nikola clamped first one and then the other of his small pink nubs between the jaws of the clips. Gage didn't make a sound until Nikola gave the chain a little yank, his moan at the mix of pain and pleasure going straight to Nikola's dick.

"I think we need to make that appointment we talked about before you leave. I'd like knowing that every time your nipples rubbed against your shirt, you'd be thinking of me." Nikola gave the chain another sharp yank, making Gage whimper. Nikola could see the idea of him making Gage get his nipples pierced turned him on. "I can call them tomorrow," Nikola said, dropping the chain to let the weight do its job.

He circled behind Gage, trailing a hand across his muscled abs, feeling them twitch as he clenched, until his hand rested on Gage's hip. He liked to watch Gage sweat, waiting for whatever he chose to do next. There were times when Nikola made him wait while he just looked for over half an hour, but he didn't have the patience for that tonight. He also had the feeling Gage was going to make him take the control from him at some point—one of those nights where Gage fought to submit.

"I've been watching you this past week. You knew this was coming before today," Nikola said. He'd seen the change in Gage's demeanor over the past few days. He'd started hovering, never far from Hana or Nikola, the same things he'd done when he'd left them in Sarajevo the last time. "How long have you known?"

Gage didn't answer right away. Nikola knew him and all his stalling techniques, and they never worked, but he always tried. Nikola didn't know why he still tried using them, and it was a bad habit they'd been working on breaking. He pressed in against Gage's back and reached around for his balls. Nikola squeezed, not hard enough to hurt, but enough to make Gage shudder.

"A-a week. There's been talk for the last week or so." Nikola eased off the pressure, and Gage let out a rush of air in relief.

He needed to figure out what Gage wasn't telling him. Gage was hiding something, and he hated that this was the only way he could make Gage feel safe enough to say whatever it was he needed to say. They'd been struggling a bit. Gage simply refused to discuss things unless Nikola forced the issue. Gage was not a submissive man, not at work, not in any other aspect of their relationship—not even in bed for the most part. Nikola had to wrest control away from him because Gage needed him to. Once Gage submitted, he did so beautifully, but it was the war he fought in his own head that caused the power struggles.

"In position," Nikola commanded.

"Niky, I—"

"Now, Gage, no discussion. You had your chance to talk, and you chose not to. Now it's my turn to choose," Nikola said. The words were harsh but sometimes Gage needed that.

Gage turned and took two steps so he was next to the bed. He bent over, planting his hands firmly on the mattress and spread his legs, presenting his ass to Nikola for whatever he wanted to use it for. The sight took Nikola's breath away just like always, and he had to control the urge to just dive in.

Nikola rubbed Gage's ass, loving the feel of the smooth skin and light dusting of hair. When Nikola's hand left Gage's body, his breath hitched in anticipation of what was coming. He landed a blow across Gage's left cheek, then his right. His hand prints stood out, a glaring red against Gage's creamy flesh, and Gage gave his first whimper of the night. Nikola stopped himself from rubbing away the sting for Gage, instead choosing to give him four more, his ass cheeks tightening with each blow.

"Tell me what it is you've been mulling over in that thick head of yours." Nikola landed blows seven and eight. "Tell me, Gage. You know you can tell me anything. Nothing you can say is going to make me stop loving you."

Gage was quiet for a few beats after Nikola landed nine and ten, but then a sob escaped from his mouth, and he said, "More."

Nikola took a calming breath and went to the chest to grab the hard, leather paddle. Whatever it was Gage needed to say was going to be big. Nikola tried to steady himself. He couldn't show Gage how he affected him when he was the one who was supposed to be in control, and Gage needed that so he could fall apart.

"NIKY, PLEASE," GAGE begged. Nikola wanted him to talk, but what Gage wanted to ask him was so big it wouldn't come out. Nikola was digging in the chest, and Gage knew what he was looking for. He'd asked for more, and Nikola would do what he asked because he knew what Gage needed. Nikola was behind him where he couldn't see what he was doing, but Gage resisted the urge to turn his head to see. He did his best to follow Nikola's rules, but sometimes it was difficult. This thing that had started out as a game between them evolved into something essential, something they both needed—Gage needed it to prove to himself he could trust Nikola, and Nikola needed it to know he had Gage's complete trust.

"Gage, you're going to count them off." Nikola knew Gage hated counting them for him, but resistance was futile.

Clenching his jaw as Nikola landed the first blow with the paddle, "One," he said through gritted teeth. The humiliation he always felt at being made to count made his ears burn. The whistling of the paddle through the air signaled the second blow. "Two." The third made Gage sway. "Three." Finally, his mind started to drift, and the pain was less, even though the strength of the blows had steadily increased. "Four." Gage pushed back to meet the paddle. "Five." He was moaning, and he had no idea why. "Six." Then it was just sweet oblivion, nothing but the *thwack* of the paddle and Gage counting. "Seven. Eight. Nine. Ten. Eleven. Please..."

The paddle stopped. "Please what, Gage?" Nikola asked. He was slightly winded, and Gage didn't know if it was from the exertion or from his arousal.

"Please...Niky, I need you. Fuck me, please." Gage begged for it, shameless in his need.

"No."

"Please, please, just this once, please. I need you to." Begging never worked before, but Gage had to try.

"You know that I won't." Nikola was immovable in his position. Nikola's movements behind him told Gage nothing of what was coming. Nikola's hands roughly spread Gage's ass and made the stinging red flesh reach out for a soothing touch that never came.

Gage shuddered with the first touch of Nikola's tongue to his pucker. God, Nikola could drive him nuts with that tongue. Gage was already begging to be fucked. What more did Nikola want from him? He pressed back into the touch, and Nikola swatted his already throbbing cheek in admonition. Gage groaned out his frustration, but like always, Nikola did as he pleased.

When his hand snaked between Gage's legs, he hoped Nikola would finally give him some relief, but instead, he grabbed the chain that hung from Gage's chest and pulled. The steady pressure weighing down on his nipples as Nikola used a spit-slicked finger to enter him almost knocked Gage off his feet, his legs trembling as he tried to keep his knees from buckling.

"Oh god, please, please... I need you to fuck me. Goddamnit, Niky," Gage pleaded, but he knew the last was pushing it. Nikola released the chain but added another finger to the one already probing Gage's entrance. Gage pushed back, just like Nikola knew he would, and again, a stinging slap to his ass made him still his movements.

"You're being bad tonight, Gage. You know the rules," Nikola said as he stood up so he could run his free hand down Gage's back. Nikola's thick fingers pumped into him steadily, slowly driving Gage insane.

"No, I won't, I can't, not like this," Gage said firmly. Nikola had no idea what he was asking Gage to do, and this was not the way he wanted to remember asking Nikola the question he needed to ask.

"Then we should stop." Nikola's fingers stilled, and Gage wiggled his ass to get Nikola to resume the fingering. Nikola harrumphed at Gage's attempts to get him to continue. "I don't think that you've had enough of the paddle. You're still too much in your head."

"No, please." Gage didn't think he could handle more. He really just needed Nikola to fuck him.

The bastard chuckled at Gage's plaintive wail as he pulled his fingers from Gage's body. Gage shuddered and resorted to whimpering at his loss. Nikola was evil when he didn't get his way. He walked away from Gage, back to the chest and pulled out... No, no, no, that meant he definitely wasn't going to get fucked.

Nikola walked toward Gage while lubing up the anal beads he'd retrieved from his chest of toys. The string was one of the biggest they owned, with the smallest tip the size of a marble and getting gradually bigger until the last was the size of a golf ball. Gage moaned in expectation.

"Spread 'em for me," Nikola commanded.

Gage took his hands off the bed and reached back to grab his own ass cheeks and spread them, presenting Nikola with his hole. Gage hated feeling so exposed, but it was part of Nikola's strategy to make him accept that he had no control here. The tip entered slowly, and Gage felt each bead as Nikola fed the string into him.

He patted Gage's ass when he was done. "There, that should help you keep from begging for my dick for a while. Hands back on the bed."

Gage put his hands back on the bed and braced as he saw Nikola reach for the paddle he'd discarded earlier on the floor. Closing his eyes, he waited for Nikola to begin. He wasn't instructed to count this time, and the blows came hard and fast. Each one jostled the beads, and one of them rubbed Gage prostate in just the right way so that sparks flew behind his eyelids.

Gage wanted so badly to touch himself but knew Nikola wouldn't allow it, but he couldn't hold on to the thought long enough for it to matter anyway. He had no idea how many blows Nikola dealt before his cock started spurting as he came all over the bedspread. Gage's knees gave out as his orgasm rushed through him. If not for Nikola's strong arms around his waist, he'd have fallen to the floor.

Nikola heaved him onto the bed and rolled him over. Gage lay there panting and floating. There was no way to describe the feeling he got when Nikola took him to the edge, let him fall, and caught him as he landed. Nikola was straddling him and how that happened he couldn't say. Gage hadn't seen him strip or lube himself before Nikola was sitting on him with Gage's cock up to the hilt deep inside.

Gage managed to move his arms enough to grip Nikola's thighs, urging him to move. As with everything else, Nikola denied Gage's attempts to exert some control. He sat there looking down at Gage, his expression not hard to read. He never tried to hide his emotions from Gage, so Gage could see desire in the dark-brown depths of his eyes, but the love shone through even brighter. It was always the dominant emotion he got from him, no matter what else Nikola may have been feeling.

"Gage"—he said as he rocked his hips just a little—"you have to talk to me. I hate it when you're so stressed out. I'm afraid you're going to give yourself an ulcer or a heart attack."

Gage grunted—God, why did he have to talk? Couldn't Nikola just shut up and fuck, just this one time? He grabbed Nikola's cock and pulled, and watched as Nikola's body reacted before he could stop it, pushing into Gage's fist for more. But he grabbed Gage's hand and pulled it away before grabbing the other and pinning them above Gage's head. He didn't struggle when Nikola shifted, giving Gage enough room to lift his hips and thrust up. The beads inside Gage shifted, making him lose focus, ruining any endeavor Gage made to get his way. Nikola's soft chuckle brought Gage's attention back to him.

"Keep your hands where they are," he said with a wicked grin, and Gage nodded. Nikola took the clamps off Gage's nipples, eliciting a hissing moan at the pain of the restored blood flow to his poor swollen buds. Nikola rolled his hips and pushed back down, squeezing his already tight tunnel, making the pressure on Gage's cock almost unbearable.

"Fuck, you're killing me, Niky," Gage said as he clenched his jaw. Nikola leaned down, claiming his mouth, effectively shutting Gage up. His slow, undulating movements made Gage's cock ache for wanting more. He needed Nikola to move harder and faster, but he just continued his slow torturous rhythm as he kissed Gage senseless.

Gage was lost to the sensations, and let Nikola do as he wanted until the change in Nikola's breathing signaled the beginning of the end. He pulled back, and using the muscles in his legs, rode Gage for all he was worth. Pulling up and slamming back down with such force that the bed frame creaked in protest with every plunge. Nikola's hand found his own cock, and he frantically stroked.

"Gonna come soon, Gage," he told Gage needlessly. Gage could already tell he was on the edge. He couldn't move his arms, so he did the best he could to add his thrusts to Nikola's movements.

A low growl started deep in Nikola's chest as he painted Gage's stomach with his come, and that combined with the spastic dance of the muscles clamped around his cock as Nikola came had Gage shooting his load inside Nikola before he even realized Nikola reached back and grabbed the end of the beads. The orgasm rocketing through Gage intensified as each of the beads grazed his prostate on their way out.

Nikola collapsed on top of him, and Gage welcomed his familiar weight tethering him to the moment like nothing else could, though it only lasted a few seconds, until Nikola rolled to the side and gathered Gage into his arms. He buried his face in Nikola's chest, knowing Nikola expected him to talk soon, but Gage wanted to revel in this moment of bliss a while longer.

As the minutes passed, Nikola held him, letting Gage cling as he rubbed his back and whispered sweet words Gage couldn't comprehend. When his head stopped floating, and he could form a coherent thought, Gage realized Nikola was speaking in his native language and he had no idea what he was saying.

After some time passed Gage's stomach growled, protesting its lack of food. Nikola nudged him. "Come on. Let's shower and then get some food into you."

"Umm-hm." Gage murmured in agreement. Nikola untangled their limbs and got up, holding his hand out to Gage. After leading him to the adjoining bathroom, Gage stood quietly as Nikola got the water going and then followed him into the stall. He let Nikola wash him since he knew Nikola liked taking care of him on nights when they did these things. After Gage was clean and rinsed, Nikola quickly washed himself. He toweled Gage off when they stepped out and then made Gage bend over the sink so he could apply some aloe vera gel to Gage's still throbbing ass.

They put on robes to protect them against the chill of the house before heading to the kitchen where Gage let Nikola serve the reheated chicken and potatoes. Gage was ravenous, so there was no conversation as he stuffed food into his mouth. Nikola let him finish his meal, but he could see the question on Nikola's face that was still waiting to be answered the whole time he ate. The way Nikola picked at his own meal betrayed the nervousness he tried to hide.

Gage got up, put his plate in the sink, and washed his hands. Nikola would know he was stalling, but he needed the time to get his thoughts in order. Gage was going to do this, and Nikola's answer could go either way. The food he'd just eaten rolled viciously in his stomach.

This time, Gage was the one who took Nikola's hand and led him into the living room. Gage sat gingerly on the couch and pulled Nikola down next to him. "Nikola, I wanted to ask you something," he started.

Nikola's posture was tense, and Gage could see him gearing up for a fight. "Okay, you know that you can ask me anything." His was voice as tense as his shoulders.

"This isn't exactly how I'd planned this, but I know you know there's been something on my mind. I can't hide anything from you, and to be honest I don't want to, but I'm kind of afraid to ask this, and please, before you answer... I mean if you need time to think about it before you can give me an answer, then you shouldn't feel like you have to tell me right now—"

"Gage," Nikola's sharp tone cut Gage off, "Just ask."

"Okay." Gage took a deep breath and closed his eyes. Gage remembered when he'd first told Nikola that he was in love with him, and he'd made Gage look at him. Gage opened his eyes and looked into the eyes of the man he loved as he asked, "Nikola, will you marry me?"

Nikola's slack-jawed expression wasn't the one of happiness Gage hoped for, but at least he didn't laugh or look disgusted. "Can we... Is that even possible?" Nikola asked.

Okay, not what Gage expected. "Yes, it's legal. I want to marry you and adopt Hana if you'll let me," Gage said, breaking eye contact to look at his hands, twisting in his lap.

"Y-you want to marry me?" Nikola asked. "And Hana, she'd... You'd take her too?"

"Well, we'd share her I suppose, but yes, I want both of you. I want to make it legal so that nothing could—" Nikola's lips stopped Gage midsentence. He was in Gage's lap and kissing him like he'd never get the chance again. When Nikola finally let Gage up for air, Gage asked hesitantly, "Is that a yes?"

Nikola smiled that smile that always tugged at Gage's heartstrings. "Yes, that is most definitely a yes."

About the Author

CL Mustafic is a born and bred American Midwesterner who mysteriously ended up living in one of those countries nobody can ever find on the map of Europe. Left with too much time on her hands—let's be honest here—it was the lack of television channels in her native language and too many voices in her head trying to fill the silence that led her to decide to give her lifelong dream of writing a novel a shot. So now, between shuttling kids back and forth from various activities and risking her life on the insanely narrow, busy streets of her new hometown, she loses herself in her own made-up world where love always wins.

Facebook: http://www.facebook.com/100010673946675

Twitter: https://twitter.com/CL_Mustafic

Website: http://www.clmustafic.com

Email: clmustaficwrites@gmail.com

Also by CL Mustafic

Satin Secrets - A story in the Beneath the Layers Anthology

Falling for Him

Also Available from NineStar Press

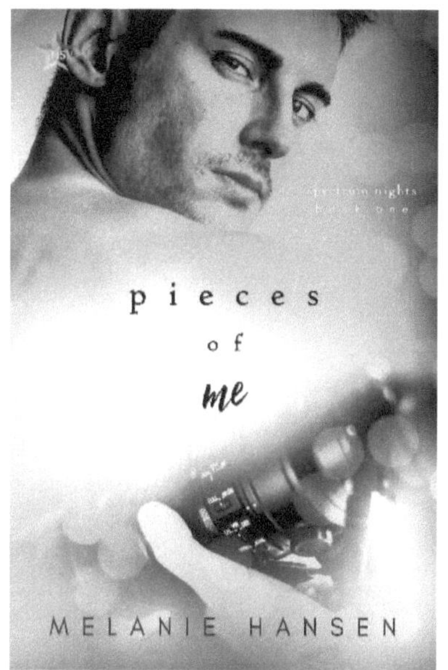

Connect with NineStar Press

www.ninestarpress.com

www.facebook.com/ninestarpress

www.facebook.com/groups/NineStarNiche

www.twitter.com/ninestarpress.com

www.tumblr.com/blog/ninestarpress